Lucy Blue

and the Daughters of Light

Books by Dana Redfield

Ezekiel's Chariot

Lucy Blue
and the Daughters of Light

a novel

Dana Redfield

HAMPTON ROADS
PUBLISHING COMPANY, INC.

Cover design by Marjoram Productions
Cover photo by Jonathan Friedman

For information write:
Hampton Roads Publishing Company, Inc.
134 Burgess Lane
Charlottesville, VA 22902

Or call: 804-296-2772
FAX: 804-296-5096

e-mail: hrpc@hrpub.com
www.hrpub.com

If you are unable to order this book from your local
bookseller, you may order directly from the publisher.
Quantity discounts for organizations are available.
Call 1-800-766-8009, toll-free.

Library of Congress Catalog Number: 98-71588

ISBN 1-57174-107-0

10 9 8 7 6 5 4 3 2 1

Printed on acid-free paper in the United States

Dedication

For My Daughter, Michelle

Table of Contents

Prologue
Secret Sight

Billy

Your old men shall dream dreams,
Your young men shall see visions

Joel 2:28, *The Holy Bible*

When the vision takes him over, Billy Sang Hightower is up on a ladder in the dining room, about to replace a teardrop bulb in the chandelier. Without warning, the lights behind his eyes snap out. He gropes in darkness. He drops the bulb; it clatters across the table and hits the floor.

If he could scream, curse, move, do anything to stop the vision, Billy surely would. What he views is never good. Death is usually the theme, and today is no exception.

11

Somewhere behind his eyes, Billy sees a small aircraft plunge to the earth and explode. God, no! The boss! A pillar of fire shoots into the air. Billy hears a roar, feels heat, smells a stench of fiery metal and flesh.

The cook, Leona, comes into the room and gasps when she sees Billy on the ladder in a frozen posture. His eyes are wide open. He looks horrified, as if viewing something hideous inside the china cabinet.

"Billy?"

The sound of her voice breaks the vision. He grips the ladder, trembles, sucks in air.

Leona creeps closer. "You okay?"

"Must be coming down with the flu," he mumbles, then begins to descend the ladder.

The cook bites her tongue. She has always known there was something strange about Billy, but if he wanted her to know his secrets, he would tell her.

Moments later in his room, Billy lies down on the bed, curls his body like a child and cries for the third time in his life.

Chapter One

The Lord Giveth a Fan Dancer

Shandie

From childhood's hour I have not
been
As others were — I have not seen
As others saw.

> *Alone*
> Edgar Allan Poe
> (1809–1849)

People do strange things upon hearing that someone they love has died. For instance, my behavior the morning of April 12, 1990, when my mother called to inform that my sugar daddy was dead.

Inform is the correct word. You would have thought Mom was calling to tell me she'd misplaced her recipe box for all the emotion in her voice. Looking back, I think she might have been gloating; but subtleties are lost under the scream of shocking news.

She said Carson Blue crashed his Piper Seneca the day before at the Cannon International Airport in Reno, Nevada.

The first thing I did after hearing the news wasn't so strange. I picked up my purse and went to the ladies room to repair my makeup. I was employed as a Realtor at Sweet Realty, in Denver, Colorado. Pat, the secretary, followed me and asked what was wrong. I told the skinny bitch.

"The Lord giveth and the Lord taketh away," she said in a pious tone.

"A pox on the Lord," I snapped.

Pat bumped her skinny nose on the door frame on her way out of the room.

If her Lord was the Supreme Taker, He was no friend of mine. Seven years ago I lost my father to heart failure, I lost my daughter —she didn't die, I just lost her—and now my lover and best friend was dead.

"A pox and a toboggan ride through hell," I said through my teeth as I brushed rouge on my cheeks to cover the tracks my tears had made.

The first strange thing I did was to drive home and put on some sexy clothes. I had gone to the office dressed in the usual business garb, but suddenly I had an urge to dress the way Carson liked me to dress; as if his ghost were lurking around, interested in what people were wearing.

Facing the full-length mirror in my bedroom, I slipped on a short, tight black dress with plunging neckline, a red sequin-spangled jacket and black pumps with stiletto heels.

Halfway through the transition from Realtor to Carson's girl, a snatch of memory rose in my mind like a kite on a windy day. I recalled a game I used to play as a child, a variation of "dress-up."

I did more than dress-up when I played the game. I pretended for days to be someone else, usually "Shanadera." Such power I felt in having this secret name with more letters than Regina, my sister's name. Shanadera was a queen who resided in a castle in medieval Ireland. Queen Shanadera often ordered her knights to chop off the heads of the maids (my mother and sister).

Another character that evolved in my young imagination was "Sondra," a grown woman who owned an art gallery in Paris, France. And there was "Shayla," who did all the exciting things forbidden to a girl of twelve. She cussed, smoked, drank whiskey, beat up all of the boys in school, and slept with all of the handsome men in town.

When I was seriously engaged in one of my imaginary roles, my mother would have to repeat my real name a dangerous number of times before I would respond. Sometimes her patience would end with a slap before I would relent, which would jar me painfully back to myself.

I hated my first and middle names. Shandie Olva. My father named me Shandie, after his Irish grandmother, whose maiden name was something like McAwful. Dad would laugh and say, "Oh, you're a Shandie, through and through." It meant rambunctious, he said.

Olva was Mom's middle name and the kids at school found it fair game for teasing, the boys twisting their faces as they gobbled out the word like turkeys. I remembered telling a substitute teacher once that I was Irish and my name was Shandie O'Lorrain. "Oh?" She laughed. Lorrain was French, she knew.

As I topped my outfit with dark glasses and a black fedora hat, I wondered how much of who I was today was influenced by Shanadera, Sondra, and Shayla. Was this Shayla decking out in black and red sequins, all smirk and dry-eyed, so soon after hearing that my lover was dead? I still played the game, easing in and out of nameless characters throughout a given day, as gracefully as ballet dancers wearing identical costumes move across a stage to tell a story. But I was no "multiple personality," as you hear about on talk shows. I had never experienced "lost time," had had no gruesome sexual encounters as a young child—which is cause for a person to split into different personalities which inhabit the same body. I was still, and had always been, Shandie Olva Lorrain, with an imagination as unruly and unpredictable as a baby monkey. And considering my attitude toward marriage, I'd probably be Shandie Olva Lorrain until I died.

On my way out to my car, I saw Ed, the maintenance man employed by the townhome association. He was lugging a window screen. He stopped a few feet away and cocked his head.

"Shandie ...?"

"You must have me confused with someone else," I said with an accent as close to Parisian as I could muster. I climbed into my car, leaving the poor man standing there, mouth agape.

I drove a Cadillac Seville the color of blackberries; lush with tinted windows and fake tiger skins over the bucket seats. I loved that baby, all the pretty lights and electronic gadgetry, most of which I had not a clue how to operate. The Cad was mine, all mine, save for one detail: I leased it from Richardson Cadillac.

My destination was my mother's house in Doubletree. At the end of her informing of Carson's death, I had said, "I'll drive down."

"Shandie ..." (big sigh), "it's going to be very confusing around here today."

"So what do you think I should do, Mother? Go home and cry my brains out? Get drunk? Maybe I'd like to be around some family in my hour of need."

"So come."

"Thank you for inviting me."

My last visit home had been six months prior, to help Grandma Nickersson celebrate her seventy-fifth birthday. It was Grandma I wanted to see; unfortunately, she lived with Mom (her daughter).

Created about forty years ago as a kind of company town, Doubletree was no town at all. It featured one mini-mart with a gas pump called Archie's, and a park with a pavilion and two huge brown plaster dinosaurs that provided, along with the jungle gyms, something for the children (and the occasional drunken adult) to climb on. And, of course, there were homes, a scattering of about one hundred, most of them pricey.

Carson Blue's French provincial mansion was the largest in Doubletree and the most expensive. It sat on twenty acres and had an airstrip. Blue Acres, everyone called it. At the time of Carson's death, a staff of four lived in the house. Five if you counted Sid Winkowski, the airplane mechanic, who stayed the nights before Carson's frequent morning flights. The regulars were Billy Sang Hightower, manager; Leona Hanks, cook; Olson Early, a kind of houseman; and whoever was the current housekeeper. The gardeners lived in Elizabeth, the nearest real town.

A lot of people to provide for in a will was the way I thought about this crew. No doubt in my mind that Carson had left everyone he cared about a chunk of his estate. No doubt he had remembered me. Maybe he left me an oil well? After my father died, Carson promised that if anything ever happened to him, I would be "taken care of."

I did something else strange that morning. On the way to Doubletree, I stopped at the South West Plaza shopping mall and went into a children's clothing store. On rare occasions I had browsed in the children's sections of department stores, but never before had I gone into a shop exclusively for tots.

I almost purchased a frilly dress. Size five. The size my daughter might have been wearing that very moment. But the sales clerk lost the sale for being so nosy. She kept trying to find out who I was buying the dress for. What the hell was it to her? Maybe I collected toddler dresses. Maybe I had a box stuffed with little dresses under my bed. Was that a crime?

I left the shop feeling shaken for having almost purchased something for a child I hadn't seen since the day of her birth. On the other hand, maybe it wasn't so strange. Carson talked me into giving up Briana for adoption, so maybe there was a connection. Maybe news of his death had stirred in me an unconscious hope that I would see my daughter again. As if, with Carson out of the picture, I could tinker with the hands of time and undo the adoption. This is in retrospect. I can honestly say the thought of seeing Briana again had never crossed my mind. Carson and my mother had convinced me that giving her up was the best thing I could do for the child, and I believed them. I was hardly a motherly type. A socket wrench had stronger mothering instincts.

The strangest thing about that day was my lack of emotion following the initial shock. Less than two hours ago I learned that the most important person in my life was dead. Why wasn't I racked with grief? Instead I felt almost high, as if I were on my way to do a market analysis on a home I hoped to list. I even cut up a little, pretending to talk to someone on my cellular phone as I whisked down the highway. Halfway to Castle Rock, I removed my hat, lowered the windows and let the wind wreck my shoulder-length hair as the Cad sailed over the road like a greased glider.

Traffic was light; the weather, cool and sunny. Clouds were piling up over the mountains to the west like meringue on top of a pie. A promise of rain later in the day. I could almost smell the wet dirt, sniff the fragrance that drenched trees and grasses give off. I slipped a cassette into the player and the heavenly music of Yanni filled the car and sent vibrations out to the hills and byways.

I could have driven the distance with my eyes closed. South to Castle Rock, east about twenty miles through Franktown to Elizabeth, then north about eight miles on County Road #21 to Doubletree.

Country for kings and queens and the word was getting around. No longer could you drive the distance from Castle Rock to Elizabeth and see mostly trees, meadows, and outcroppings of jagged rock. Luxurious homes, many of them horse properties, were springing up all over the place, increasing the traffic and stinking up the air. I wondered how long it would be before the sprawl pushed against Doubletree's boundaries. I wondered how long the birds would stick around. Beyond Elizabeth was a burg called Kiowa. Lots of open prairie and stands of pine trees out that way, a good place for birds; and people who liked to drive a long way to the nearest shopping mall.

Closer to Doubletree, it became more difficult to suppress thoughts of Carson. I would like to say I had to choke down tears thinking about him. There were reasons for my callousness, you will see.

My attraction for the man defied all logic, his money notwithstanding. He was old enough to be my father and no one called him handsome, though he did have remarkable bluish-green eyes.

Our affair started when he took me in his Lincoln Continental when I was seventeen ... ten years ago. People would have been shocked to know that I was a virgin then. Everyone thought I was a sleaze-ball. Carson was shocked. But he didn't back off one bit. That man hounded me.

At the start of our relationship, I fantasized that he would marry me eventually and move me into his glorious mansion. That was before I understood how serious he was about the business of marriage. To him, marriage went with business like sausage went with eggs. If you had known his ex-wife, you'd believe it. Rosalyn Blue was as homely as a suppository, but the woman knew how to run an elite household and properly entertain business people, especially the "old money" ones. Carson convinced me that I was in the better position. We could live it up and not be bothered by his boring old business. We lived it up until Roz caught wind of our affair and demanded a divorce. (She was already unhappy, and discovery of our affair tipped her over the edge.)

Soon the entire community heard the news, including my parents. Dad took it in stride; after all, Carson was his employer and Duke Lorrain was known to cat around himself. Mom freaked. She featured herself a kind of community noblewoman and was "ashamed to show her face" when the smut hit the grapevine. I'm sure the ladies of Doubletree missed a couple of days of television soaps during the flap. Mom tried to shame me into ending the relationship. As if I had cast a spell over some innocent man who would jump free of my clutches the moment I said the word. I was the one under the spell.

No one understood (least of all, me) that apart from Carson, I had no life of my own. I wasn't one of those people who knows in the tenth grade what she wants to be when she grows up. I was ripe for plucking, I was plucked, and that was that.

Under Carson's spell, I was (not unhappily) doomed to eternal adolescence. I missed all the gateways to maturity, every one. Months after Carson died, I was shown a tarot card that symbolized my state of being at the time of his death: the eight of swords. A woman is bound to a pole and blindfolded. Eight swords stick in the ground around her. The character on the card is a prisoner of self, bound by materialism, and blind and deaf to the callings of spirit. This was me all the way. I had my reasons.

I called Blue my sugar daddy for lack of a better term. But I was more than a plaything to Carson Blue. To some degree he realized the stifling effect our affair had on me, and honestly tried to steer me in directions of independence and self-improvement. Wasn't his fault I had little inclination for either. I was better at the self-improvement gig. He'd bring me books to read so we'd have something interesting to talk about. Over time I found my way into bookstores and surprised him by selecting titles he thought were beyond my capacity. But my effort was more to enhance our relationship than it was to embrace anything like genuine self-improvement.

As for independence, all I can say is, I tried. It was difficult, if not impossible, to get serious about work when Carson continually pumped cash into my bank account. "Career, career, career," he'd say three times in a row as if to program my subconscious mind. He wanted me to go into something lucrative that would leave me free to play when he wanted me. Three years ago I gave in to his whim and got a Realtor's license.

Not that we "played" that often during the last few years he was alive. I wasn't threatened by his diminished interest in sex. Christ, the man was in his fifties! He adored me, he took care of me; that's what had me hooked.

The lucrative part failed because about the time I got my license, home sales began to slump. This occurred because of the decline in the oil business, which hurt Blue Oil & Gas severely. Which is why Carson began to explore other options; the reason he began taking so many trips, mostly to Reno. He wasn't one to expound on the nature of his business ventures. Once he muttered something about developing pilot biomass refineries—nothing I was dying to learn more about. So what if the oil business was in trouble? The man was rich, rich, rich.

As I drove the remaining tree-bordered miles, I fantasized in blissful morbidity about the funeral to come. I was sure it would be held in the largest church in Denver. Carson wasn't a bit religious so it mattered not whether it was in a cathedral or a synagogue, so long as it was large enough to accommodate the hundreds—maybe thousands of people who knew the man. He was the only living Blue (he and Roz were childless), so the front pews would be occupied by his best friends. I would be front and center, facing the casket, which probably would be constructed of pure gold and inlaid with diamonds.

Engrossed in the fantasy, I almost missed the turnoff at Archie's store. Three cars parked in front; one, a gold-toned Mercedes Benz.

There were a greater number of homes in Doubletree than an uninformed someone driving through might imagine. Most of the residences were hidden behind stands of pine trees. I ducked my head out the window to drink in the intoxicating smells as I drove past the park, veering northeast toward Blue Acres. I passed two cars and one pickup, recognized no one.

The gray brick mansion perched on a rise. A black wrought-iron fence encircled the property, along with Russian olive trees. I gave Blue's house a kind of salute as I drove past it. My mother's house, a tri-level A-frame, was located about a half mile from Blue Acres. My father, Duke Lorrain, built the house in 1966, about a year after Carson hired him to run his drilling operation. Before that, Duke was a roughneck, working on oil and gas wells in Texas, Oklahoma, Kansas, Nebraska, and Colorado. I was four years old when my family moved to Doubletree, so remembered little of what my mother and sister referred to as "our gypsy days."

After Dad died, Mom converted the ground level of the house into an antique store. She called it Kate's Attic. Big "CLOSED" sign in the window today. Seemed to me the shop was closed more than it was open. Mom and my sister, Regina, weren't in it for the profits, Carson had explained. The business was a tax write-off and, as Regina had put it, "something fun to do."

I parked the Cad next to my sister's silver BMW, switched off the key, climbed out.

Billy drove around the curve in his Jeep. He threw on the brakes, which almost slammed the squat vehicle on its nose. I got the impression he wasn't all that happy to see me. Then again, maybe he saw four cars jammed into the tiny area reserved for the antique shop and threw on his brakes because he saw no place to park. Being a resourceful man, Billy slipped the Jeep to the other side of the cottonwood tree that shaded the dog run on the south side of the house. Mom's dog, Clyde, a white standard poodle, was going crazy; barking, begging a pet. Billy ignored him. I set my hat on my head, slipped off my dark glasses, and leaned against the Cad as Billy walked toward me. The weight of his grief was evident in the way he moved.

Billy Sang Hightower. Half Cherokee, part Chinese with a dash of English or Irish. He was thirty-five, about five-foot, eleven inches tall and built for love. He wore his black hair pulled back in a ponytail, about the only thing he did that hinted there might be something reckless beneath his stoic exterior. As usual, he was dressed in a crisp, white, long-sleeved shirt, pressed jeans, and polished cowboy boots. A mystery how he kept them looking so shiny. It was as if those boots repelled dirt.

I couldn't recall seeing Billy dressed any other way, but Leona had said he was known to slip on a sports coat when the occasion called for dressy. Sometimes Carson had summoned Billy to business meetings and sometimes to parties. Billy detested both. And there were times, Leona said, when he left the house "all spiffy" to rendezvous with a woman who required ostentation. Rare occasions. Billy seldom suffered a woman with uppity notions. Word was, he seldom suffered women, period.

"Got his heart under an ice-pack," Leona claimed. "Still grieving for his little wife." How the cook knew to describe Billy's deceased wife as "little" is up for grabs. Doubtful that Billy told her that. He was so close-mouthed it was a wonder he managed to eat.

Carson met Billy fourteen years ago, immediately after an auto accident that killed Billy's young wife. Carson was a witness, called an ambulance, then stayed at the scene until medical help and the police arrived. Carson was so impressed with Billy, he visited him frequently at Swedish Memorial Hospital in Denver where Billy recovered from broken ribs and a mean gash in his forehead. Right in the hospital Carson offered him a job as a gardener. And he insisted that Billy's mother, Ling Sang, move to Blue Acres, too. Ling died of a stroke one year before my father suffered heart failure.

From day one, Billy was Carson's most devoted employee. In less than a year he was promoted to the position of manager. Leona said Billy's devotion was due to some twist on the old Chinese tradition about serving the person who rescues you, for life.

As he came nearer he shifted his dark, exotic eyes away from mine. Even in a foul mood, Billy was gorgeous. A fantasy to think he was walking toward me. Six feet away he turned and headed for the cedar stairs that rose to the main level of the house.

"Hey—"

He stopped, turned and seared me with a look of red hot pain. The devastation I saw in that look almost moved me to tears, but my own pain was locked down with ball and chain. It would be a while before I could tear through the walls and touch the place where I'd once loved Carson Blue.

I could also see in that look what Billy thought about the way I was dressed. As if he were watching a whore about to enter a chapel. He went up the stairs without a word.

At the stairway I removed my stiletto heels, now regretting the change of clothes. What the hell was the matter with me? Coming to my mother's house dressed like this for any occasion was asking for trouble. Carson would have laughed. He thought I was funny. But Carson was dead.

The thought sliced through me fast and cold. I swooned against the railing, dropped a shoe; it tumbled off the stairs. I threw the other one as hard as I could. It sailed into the elm tree, disturbed the birds, hit the ground. I went up the stairs and opened the door.

My mother was sitting beside Billy on the sofa in the living room. She jumped when I came inside, narrowed her eyes, dismissed me with a sideways glance, whispered something to Billy; then they both rose and walked stiffly upstairs. Probably to her sewing room. The room that used to be mine.

I dropped hat and purse on the Queen Ann chair and padded past the dining room table toward the low buzz of female voices in the family room. Four women shut their mouths when I came into view.

Only two of Mom's friends, Felicia Perry and Beverly DeWitt, were present, a surprise. I expected the room to be full of weepy women. Carson's death was the biggest event ever to hit Doubletree, and Mother's house was a kind of gathering place during times of crisis. Even minor disturbances would bring the ladies of Doubletree running like gazelles; then they'd sit around all day, suck up coffee or booze, and savor the disgusting, terrible, or alarming news.

"Phone's off the hook," I said, pointing to the side table next to Beverly DeWitt.

"For a reason," my sister said.

Regina was sitting on the sofa, ramrod straight. Grandma was slumped behind her on a dining room chair. At the opposite end of the sofa sat bleached-blond Felicia Perry, and mousy Beverly was in an armchair in front of the snack bar, which served as a boundary between kitchen and family room. The decor was straight out of an L.L. Bean catalog. Lots of wood and brass, dried flowers, and wooden geese painted blue and pink with cute polka dot bows at their necks.

"Hi there, Shandie," Grandma said with a grin.

It tickled me to see Grandma Maddie Nickersson puffing away on her cherrywood pipe. Maddie liked to light up when Mom had company, to show off. It was one of life's mysteries how an old hell-raiser like Maddie could have a daughter like my mother. Grandma looked her age. She was totally wrinkled. Rims of light around her grayish-blue eyes. She reminded me of photos I'd seen of Mark Twain. When I grew old I wanted to be exactly like her: a gnarled old brat.

I smiled and waved at Grandma, then padded into the kitchen and got a Diet Coke out of the refrigerator. The verbal buzzing began again, then stopped abruptly as I went over and sat in the wing chair that was angled at the edge of the triangulated window that filled the A-configuration.

"How's by you, Regina?" I said and took a sip of Coke.

"Not so well under the circumstances," she said frostily.

Tall and willowy with clear blue eyes and long smooth hair the color of copper, Regina favored the Nickerssons, Mom's side of the family. An impeccable dresser, she had on dark slacks, a beige blouse and one of those colorful scarves you drape this way and that, over the shoulder, tucking into the waistband, and so forth. Far too complicated a piece of attire for me to ever consider messing with. At thirty-three, Regina was six years my senior. She had done everything right. Especially in marrying Drew Hillborne, an attorney, and giving birth to Zachary, a perfect grandchild.

"I'm not feeling exactly jazzed myself," I said.

Grandma Maddie laughed, but the other women continued to stare at me. I felt like a glob of bird doo that had just dropped from the sky onto their crepe suzettes.

I looked over the array of untouched cold cuts on the coffee table. Seeing no reason to starve just because Carson died on us, I reached for an olive, popped it in my mouth. Grandma chuckled. I was about to collect bread, pastrami and cheese, when the front door slammed shut.

Mom came into the room. Kate Lorrain had fine Nordic features and lustrous blond hair, even if it was beginning to fade. But she did nothing to play it up, pulling her hair back in a bun, and dressing in pastel blouses and nondescript skirts; Rockport walking shoes completed the package. She reminded me of one of those women who do commercials for laxatives. Her face was etched with a look of perpetual concern.

For better or worse, I favored my father's side of the family. My eyes were a darker blue, my hair the color of ashes. While Mom and Regina were tall and angular, I was a mere five-foot-five and my face was heart-shaped. But I was curvier. For better or worse.

All eyes were fixed on my mother as she sat down in the armchair next to Beverly DeWitt. "Billy brought some interesting news," she confided.

We all leaned forward.

"The funeral will be held in Reno."

Beverly gasped.

"Carson will be cremated. We'll have only a memorial service out here."

"Reno?" Felicia Perry said. "Why Reno?"

Following a delicious pause, Mom said, "Because he had a wife there."

A cold wind swept up from my feet and chilled my face.

"He was married," she added, as if addressing a bunch of idiots who failed to grasp what it meant for a man to have a wife.

"I don't believe this," Beverly said, patting her chest.

Regina's mouth was open and Grandma was pumping smoke into the air as if to send an urgent message to a neighboring tribe.

I shivered against the icy wind enveloping me.

"Her name is ..." Mom's hand came to her cheek. "Let me get this right. Lucinda ... Desserita ... Xavier." She nodded. "Lucinda Desserita Xavier Blue."

"Lucinda Desserita Xavier Blue," the ladies said in unison as if reciting the chorus of some archaic poem.

"SOUNDS LIKE A FAN DANCER," Grandma said loudly.

"Her brother is flying her out for the memorial service," Mom said. "And then ..." She shook her head. "She says she's going to move here. Billy is understandably upset. What kind of woman would decide to move the day after her husband dies?"

No one offered an answer.

"LOTS OF FAN DANCIN' OUT THERE IN NEVADA," Grandma almost shouted, her pipe raised in the air.

"She asked Billy to organize the memorial service. That's why he came over. To solicit our help." Mom looked at Regina. "He tried to call, but the line was busy."

"You make it sound like we're the outsiders," Felicia said.

Mom shrugged. "According to Billy, Carson married this woman over six years ago."

I froze into a block of ice.

Grandma pointed her pipe at the back of Felicia's head. "FAN DANCIN', GAMBLIN', AND WHORIN'; YOU BETTER BE-LIEVE IT."

Chapter Two

A Slow Fix in Fairy Land

With fiery thoughts like mine, one cannot remain a block of ice for long. I torched my mother with a look. This Lucinda Desserita person had to be Carson's out-of-town mistress.

"There's more," she said. "Carson's wife ... doesn't that sound funny?" No one laughed. "Uh, this woman Carson married is fairly well known on the west coast. She's a tranced channeler." She looked at me. "Is that the way you say it?"

"I wouldn't know a tranced channeler from a fan dancer," I muttered.

Grandma laughed.

"It's trance channeler," Beverly said. "Remember 'Out on a Limb,' that Shirley MacLaine movie on T.V.? She had her own trance channeler. That cute young guy in the white suit and the white hat? He took off his hat when he channeled, of course. And remember, Felicia, when we went to see that channeler in Taos who claimed to speak for an ancient spirit from Atlan—"

"We knew it was a scam, Beverly."

"Oh, yes," Beverly said. "We knew it was a scam."

"Bet she's Basque," Grandma said. No one asked to whom she referred.

"What makes you think so?" Mother said.

"Lots of Basque in Nevada. And that name."

"Xavier sounds Spanish," Regina said.

"The Basque live between Spain and France," Grandma said. "They herd sheep and whatnot. Up in the Pyrenees mountains. Oldest race in Europe." She flashed an impish smile. "And the meanest."

Mom scowled at her, then said to Regina, "Billy wants you to call him this afternoon."

Before marrying Drew Hillborne, Regina worked as a convention organizer for the Sheraton Hotel in Denver, so she was the logical one to help organize the service. But it rankled me. Why didn't Billy ask me to help? He knew I was Carson's girl.

News of this trance-channeling, fan-dancing shepherdess having lifted the ladies' spirits, they now hovered over the cold cuts like chickens over corn. As they nibbled on sandwiches, clucking at a merrier pitch, I made for the front door.

"Where do you think you're going?" my mother said.

Earlier she had tried to dissuade me from coming home; now she wanted to know where I was going. Impossible to please her.

"To see Joe," I said over my shoulder.

Hippie Joe Inglehart, first person to pop in my mind. The so-called minister of the so-called community church in Doubletree. He held services in his home on Sundays. A big joke. Hardly anyone ever went.

"I have a phone."

"I know you have a phone, Mother, but I want to see Joe."

She knew something was up; she always did. I picked up my hat and purse in the living room. But Regina caught me before I escaped.

"Wait ..."

"Mother hates me."

"She doesn't hate you, Shandie. You just embarrass her sometimes."

"I've been an embarrassment ever since I was born."

Regina's expression made it clear she considered my complaint absurd.

"Sold any homes lately?"

I opened the door and nodded downward.

When she spotted the Seville she said, "Wow. You must be selling a lot of expensive homes."

"I do all right."

I felt sick to my stomach. No sales in the past five months, no listings, no prospects, and less than five-hundred dollars in the bank. The lease payment on the Cad was a cool four-hundred, the mortgage on the townhome, eight. Twelve-hundred dollars a month just to get out of bed in the morning. And there were other standard expenses: food, gas, utilities, clothes, housekeeper ... Another wave of sickness ripped through my guts.

"You okay?"

"Great shape. See you around." I stepped outside, shut the door, and hurried down the stairs, clutching my gut.

Mom was right. I had no intention of calling on that goofy Joe Inglehart. It was Billy I wanted to see. For six years that poor excuse of a Cherokee-Chinaman had sat on this secret about Carson having a wife! (As had Carson, but I wasn't ready to look that point square in the eye.)

Carson claiming a loss of interest in sex for the past six years. Because he was banging his so-called wife. But his so-called loss of interest had not been total. During those six years he had tumbled Shandie O. Lorrain more than a few times. Engaging me in adultery without my knowledge!

I found my shoes, slipped them on, got in the Cad and slammed the door. A wife! The car shot over the gravel.

I drove like a maniac, probably uprooting a couple of trees on the way to Blue Acres. The wrought-iron gates at the entrance stood open, as always. I shot past them and came to a screeching halt at the end of the driveway in front of the hedges.

Up the flagstone path I walked, past the crocuses, tulips, lilac bushes, and daffodils. Nervy flowers, I thought, flaunting their blooms when the king was dead.

The stairs up to the porch reminded me of tiers on half a wedding cake, an irony there. I banged one of the brass knockers against the door; eight foot double doors, constructed of dark, rough wood with diamond-shaped peepholes of thick beveled glass. You could see shapes and colors through the glass, but it drove you dizzy to try to identify anything. I banged the knocker again.

Finally Olson Early opened the door on the right a crack. His eyes were swollen and pink from crying. Olson was short and spare with blond hair that curled around his neck. Sweet blue eyes behind rimless glasses.

"Is Billy in?"

A nod from Olson. He continued to stare as he white-knuckled the edge of the door.

"Could I see him?"

"I'll check," he said softly. "You're—"

"Shandie. Shandie Lorrain?" The man knew damn well who I was.

The door closed. I heaved a sigh, turned to the southwest and gazed at Pikes Peak. A wall of mountains towered northward for miles. Border for the smog that hung like a giant golden-brown rag over Denver. The clouds over the mountains were beginning to look sinister. Light breezes carried a faint, spicy scent of dampened earth.

My gaze wandered, coming to rest on the spired top of the pavilion in the park and the heads of the dinosaurs; one, a Tyrannosaurs rex, the other, a Brontosaurus. The park belonged to the Blue estate and was groomed regularly by Carson's personal gardeners.

Carson's father, Royal Guthrie Blue, an oil baron from Oklahoma, moved to this span of prairie in the early fifties on a bet that the region would one day become an energy metropolis. His speculations fell short; still he made a ton of money. He was one of the first to drill a number of successful wildcat wells in the Denver Basin, where rich oil and gas deposits were discovered in an area called the Gurley Pool, which stretches from eastern Colorado into Nebraska.

I was reminded of how Doubletree got its name. The spot where Carson's father built the mansion was up against a ridge between two dry creeks called Running and Hay Gulch. Plenty of trees atop the crest, most of them, ponderosa pines. West of the ridge was another story. Oldtimers said R.G. stood with his back to the ridge, looked out over the prairie toward Pikes Peak and saw two trees. Probably bent and gnarled scrub oak. While eyeballing those two pathetic trees, R.G. was struck with the notion of calling the place Two Tree.

As employees of Blue Oil & Gas began buying lots from R.G. and building their own homes, they planted gobs of blue spruce, birch, cottonwood, poplar, juniper, maple, aspen, and more ponderosa pines. By and by the prairie blossomed and the uppity residents decided that Doubletree sounded more sophisticated than Two Tree.

Sole heir to the Blue fortune (his parents died in the sixties), Carson made a ton of money himself during the seventies, the energy boom years. But boom years are the exception, he taught me. During the eighties, crude oil prices began to slide. Now, practically speaking, Blue O&G was an accounting firm, the employees, primarily money tenders.

As I tapped my foot on the brick porch and examined my fingernails, I wondered what now? You could hardly expect a fan-dancing, tranced channeler from the Pyrenees Mountains to run an oil and gas operation. The company would probably shut its doors. People would be bailing out of Doubletree like …

I jerked up my head. Like a splash of cold water in the face, it dawned that Doubletree was on the verge of becoming a Realtors' paradise. I'd heard about deals like that, entire subdivisions going up for sale. And it wasn't as if there were some problem like bentonite in the soil, something that no one wanted to touch; this was no panic situation.

The change would be gradual—say, a half dozen homes going up for sale a month. Unloading them would be easier than selling homes in Denver proper because so many people ached to move to the country. The high-ritz country; none of that cow and chicken shit, not the real country. People wanted a country area with class. A place like Doubletree.

I envisioned Sweet Realty FOR SALE signs scattered around Doubletree like daisies in a field. My name and phone number in bold black letters on the metal flaps that hung beneath the signs. I flashed on back-to-back closings, and fat commissions. My bank account would swell like a pregnant sow. And if I listed a home and found a buyer, that would be a double-whammy. Most would sell through the Multi-List Service; I'd hardly have to lift a finger.

Lost in the fantasy, I was slow to react when Billy opened the door. But it wasn't Billy. It was Olson again.

"He's resting, Miss Lorrain."

"Resting."

"Yes. Good day."

He shut the door.

I felt like taking an ax to that fancy, high-dollar door. I felt like nuking those special shuttered windows. I marched down the wedding-cake stairs, stooped and gathered fistfuls of gravel.

I was about to bombard the house when I remembered Leona. I dropped the gravel, slid my hands over my skirt. Leona liked me. She'd sympathize. She wasn't afraid of Billy; she'd make him ask me to help with the service. Billy might be manager (a glorified handyman, really), but Leona had been with Carson the longest and wielded a lot of power.

I slipped off my high heels, threw them near the Cad and headed over the grass toward the back of the house.

Halfway there it occurred to me that Leona must have known from the start about Carson's so-called marriage. I smelled a conspiracy. Imagined Carson swearing everyone to secrecy for the sole purpose of keeping me in the dark. But even with my ego, the idea was a hard-sell. So maybe he got married as part of some business scheme? And kept it secret because if word leaked out, it would tip off competitors, which would hurt Blue Oil & Gas stocks. Business was full of all that cloak and dagger stuff. Carson probably didn't want to burden me with the complexities ...

So who the hell did this bogus wife think she was, planning to move to Blue Acres? Poor Carson, thinking he'd married someone he could trust. The bitch would probably challenge the will and try to claim the entire estate for herself. Well, she could forget that! Carson had a league of attorneys and accountants who would make sure the people most important to him got what was coming to us.

Billy's Jeep, Olson's van with the frilly curtains, and Leona's blue Tercel were parked near the back door entrance on a stretch of gravel. Except during the winter months, no one bothered using the five-stall garage. No one but Carson. His Buick Riviera and Land Rover would be inside the garage now. Orphans.

The airstrip to the north was not visible from the mansion, but if you looked closely you could see the orange windsock through the trees.

A gray cat shot out from behind a bush and streaked toward the guest cabins beyond the garage. Billy's mother used to live in one of the cabins.

Trees, bushes, and flowers congregated around the cabins and the mansion, and there were trees galore to the south. Carson used to talk about chopping some of them down out there, with the intent of constructing a golf course. He never got around to it. Too busy with his shenanigans in Reno. Too busy with all his women. Maybe he left a slew of secret wives. Maybe he left a goddamned harem.

Inside the mud room, clothes were piled on top of the washing machine, bags of fertilizer and yard implements were stacked against the south wall below the windows. A yellow slicker, jean jacket, and various hats hung from hooks on the wall. I walked past buckets, baskets, rubber boots.

The silence in the mud room was cool and uninviting. Usually you could hear Leona banging around in the kitchen, singing offkey to country music on the radio. I tiptoed toward the door and peered through the window.

She was seated at the round oak table. Hunched over, smoking, her free arm curled around a cup of coffee. Her face looked like a rose that has withered following an early freeze. Carson adored Leona, calling her "the best and skinniest cook west of the

Mississippi." She loved telling the story of how he hired her. She was working at Wyatt's Cafeteria in Denver when Carson came down the line and asked if she had prepared the fried okra. No, she said, she just served it up. Then he asked if she could cook okra that way. Of course! She was from Oklahoma where folks knew how to fry up okra, and hominy and grits, and chicken and gravy that would put to shame Colonel Sanders'. Partial to Oklahomans (he was born in Tulsa), Carson asked her then and there if she wanted a job cooking for a gentleman who lived in the country.

I tapped on the window. She looked up, smiled at me faintly and beckoned me inside.

It was a room that put its arms around you and eased your worries and pains, even on a day like this. Pans with shiny copper bottoms hung over a center island, and the red-brick wall on the west was covered with fifty kinds of utensils. Baskets of produce hung at various levels around the room. Interspersed with dark wood cabinets, spots of wall were adorned with antique implements, calendars, placards, and chilies—some fresh, others shriveled. The predominant colors were red, brown, yellow, copper, and silver shine. Huge rack of spices next to the yellow refrigerator. The air smelled of cigarette smoke, coffee, and grief.

Leona insisted I share a cup. She was dressed in baggy jeans; her scarecrow arms dangled out of a plaid sleeveless shirt. Hazel eyes, and short, curly gray hair in a style that never changed. She was older than Carson, maybe sixty.

"Well, don't you look pretty," she said, her chair scraping across the linoleum as she rose to pour coffee. "You must have been about to go on a lunch date when you got the news."

"Yeah." I sat down at the table and stared at the pile of butts in the ashtray. One pack of Newports open, another wadded up. A green Bic lighter.

As she came with the cups, we heard someone climbing the stairs in the hallway. Easing into her chair, Leona glanced in that direction.

"Hope that's Billy going up for a nap. Don't think he slept a wink last night. Then he was on the phone all morning, acting like we had to get everything done today. But that's Billy, always ten steps ahead of everyone else."

"He came over to Mother's."

"I know, I know." She shook her head. "I thought that was pretty strange, considering you have to hogtie that man to get him to go see anyone. Nerves, that's all it is. He was trying all morning to get hold of Regina to see if she could help with the memorial service. No answer at her house, and he kept getting a busy signal at your Mother's. Then he just kind of lost it and went tearing out of here like his pants were on fire."

She laughed at her joke, then scowled, as if remembering this was not a day to clown around. She lit another cigarette, inhaled deeply, blew a stream of smoke at the ceiling. "Maybe I shouldn't have come ..."

She reached over, patted my arm. "I'm glad you did." She laid the cigarette in the ashtray, pulled a tissue out of her pocket and blew her nose. "About had my fill of being on the pity pot. Carson wouldn't want us weeping around like this. He'd want us to be brave and strong. Like you."

I jerked my head, a "who-me?" reaction to her remark.

"I felt strong until I heard about his wife," I blurted.

She smiled, nodded and picked up her cigarette as I took a sip of coffee. It tasted like liquid leather.

"Oh, yeah, I bet that hit you kind of hard."

She stared into her cup for a moment, as if to glean from the grounds at the bottom how much to tell me.

"The thing was, Shandie, Carson didn't want anyone to know about Lucy." She scowled, tapped the lighter on the table. "I don't know what it was for sure. Maybe it was just that so many people knew so much about his personal business. I think he liked having this one big secret." She smiled sadly. "And you know how he liked being a little eccentric."

But why didn't he tell me? I wanted to scream. A thought so charged with emotion, Leona picked it up.

"I expect he didn't tell you because he was afraid you'd call it quits."

I thought of how seldom he stayed overnight at my townhome the past few years. He always treated me to dinner when he was in town, but he couldn't stay over because he had a pile of work to do at home, he was tired, or wasn't feeling quite up to snuff.

"There wasn't much to call quits," I said, trying for a casual tone. "We were just friends."

Leona nodded.

"Does she know about me?"

"Who?"

"Lucy. Lucinda." I refused to call the bitch Carson's wife.

"Oh, no! I'd say to Car, 'Car, you better clean this up or it'll blow up in your face.'" She ground out the cigarette.

"And what would he say?"

"He'd say, 'Don't you worry. Lucy is very broad-minded.'"

"So he wasn't worried about what I would think."

"Now, Shandie, you know Carson cared about you deeply. He always thought of you like his daughter."

From her expression it was evident she realized how stupid that sounded.

"I mean, after you got older and got a life of your own."

A life of my own. There was nothing in my life that had not been molded and manipulated by Carson Blue. Even when I dated other men, it was at his suggestion and approval. I wore the clothes he liked, the furniture I bought was the kind he told me to purchase.

The one thing that had been solely my own, my baby, he urged me to give up. Even there he couldn't keep his hands out of my life. In fact, Briana's father was a man Carson suggested I go out with. For my own good, I should date other men. Eventually I should settle down and get married, which failed to square with the fact that the man Carson suggested I go out with, the one who got me pregnant, was married already. But I couldn't blame Car for the pregnancy. That was my own stupidity. I'd never had to worry about birth control because Carson couldn't have kids, so I was careless.

"Nice of him to think of me."

"Hey, I agree, Shandie, his thinking on this was kind of crooked. He had himself convinced no one was going to get hurt. See, this marriage to Lucy was supposed to be a kind of business investment. He helped her finance this 'calling' thing she thinks she has. After she married him, she quit the restaurant business—she and her brother used to own a restaurant—then she started traveling all over the place, speaking to groups of New Agers, that sort of thing. She made pretty good money doing it and Car shared in the profits."

"And now she's moving here."

"Well, I don't know about that. Lucy's got a good head on her shoulders. Good chance she'll change her mind. Ain't too many New Agers out here."

Having heard all I wanted to hear, I told Leona I needed to go back to Mom's. (My original intent, to ask her to suggest to Billy that I help with the service, had completely slipped my mind.)

As I opened the back door, she said, "Sure do look pretty. Hope your date wasn't sore about you standing him up. 'Course he'll understand when you tell him why."

"Oh, yeah, he'll understand. See you later, Leona."

"I'll be here, girl. Don't be a stranger."

Before I got around the corner, the tears came in an angry flood. I stumbled, half-blind, toward the Cad. I was in no shape to go to Mother's house, no shape to see anyone.

I drove west to the nearest county road, then swung north. My mind was like a blender, grinding piles of rocks. I passed acres of farmlands, turned onto dirt roads, drove in a cloud of dust for miles, until my anger was ground into a fine powder. I circled southward on Cemetery Road, drove past Ponderosa Park Estates, Pawnee Hills, and Elizabeth High School, my alma mater.

As I cut through Elizabeth, then north again toward Doubletree, I began to think in terms of survival. It had to be faced: Carson had left me high and dry. He got married for business, for love, it didn't matter which, and his wife would probably inherit the works. Which meant I was going to have to get to work myself. What a fool I'd been to depend solely on Carson! For years I'd let the bills stack up, secure in the knowledge he would take care of them next time he was in town. Now there'd be no more next times.

My career as a Realtor was a fairy tale. The only houses I'd sold were as a result of the referrals Carson had sent my way. Not once had I chased down a sale myself. And even when I had scored a sale, Roger Sweet, the broker, had done most of the work. But that didn't mean I wasn't capable of taking the job on. I'd passed the Realtor test, hadn't I? They didn't give out licenses to just anyone.

I was glad to see the cars were gone in the parking area in front of Kate's Attic. The garage door was open; Mom's Honda Accord was gone, too. Good. I could use her telephone without having to explain myself. Without having to explain why I was without shoes (I'd left them at Blue Acres), why my nylons were streaked with runs.

Grandma woke from a nap on the sofa in the family room when I came inside. Groggily she said Kate had gone with the "girls" over to see Ivy Chumbly. I told Maddie to go back to sleep, I needed to make some phone calls. She tottered down the hall and I sat down in the armchair in front of the snack bar and dialed Sweet Realty.

My boss was with a client, Pat reported but said he was about to wind up his conversation. While I waited for Sweet to come on the line, I indulged in a fantasy fraught with fur coats, diamonds, trips abroad, and handsome foreign princes. All this and more would be mine after I sold half the homes in Doubletree. Once people heard about this Lucinda dame and her New Age weirdness, they'd beg for Realtors. I knew I was right. All I needed was for Sweet to give me an advance so I could get going on some heavy-duty advertising. Maybe I'd do a T.V. commercial! You had to spend money to make money, Carson always said. Roger's voice broke the spell of my muse.

"Good news!" I said.

"You got a listing."

"Not yet, but listen to this. The deal is, Carson had this secret wife stashed in Reno, and people around here are in an absolute uproar. She's moving to Doubletree, Roger. She's some sort of New Age freak, knows nothing about oil and gas, and the word is, Blue

O&G is on the skids. People are on the move, practically the entire community going up for sale—"

"Uh, Shandie ..."

"What."

"I got a notice from the Board of Realtors today. Your annual fee is delinquent."

My stomach pitched, rolled, heaved. The fee was two hundred dollars, and if you failed to pay it you couldn't hang your license with a broker who had access to the Multi-List; and sans access to the Multi-List, you couldn't sell a dog house. All these stupid rules! Sometimes it seemed to me that I lived in a communistic country.

"Well, can't you spot me?"

"Shandie, I've carried you all I can afford ..."

"Sweet, listen! I just told you about the hottest deal in Colorado! Didn't you hear? Blue is dead, the company is on the skids, people are panicking!"

The silence on the other end of the line was beyond my comprehension. Just my luck to hook up with a broker with zero vision.

"Listen, Sweet," I tried again in a calmer tone. "I'll have the fee before the end of the month, no sweat." Today was the twelfth, plenty of time to scrape up a measly two hundred. The contents of my stomach dipped, heaved, sloshed.

"You have some closings scheduled I know nothing about?"

"I have sources of income other than real estate, Roger, I told you that."

"Yes, you did. But he died."

Red stars danced in front of my eyes. "What are you saying?"

"That if you can't pull your own weight, you're out. Just like anyone else."

"Firing me the day after my best friend dies! What an asshole!"

"I didn't—"

I slammed down the phone. Mom's Persian, Emil, sauntered by, an arrogant look on his face. I kicked at him. He stood his ground, swishing his tail just beyond my kick range. "Scat, you foul little beast."

A bird's touch on my shoulder. Grandma.

"What's the matter, Shandie?"

"I just got fired and I don't even have enough money to pay the mortgage this month, much less that stupid old Realtor fee."

"You young women these days," she said, stepping away to wander the room. "Don't know why you can't find a nice boy and settle down. If you got married, maybe you could afford some shoes." She stroked each piece of furniture as she padded around the room, nose in the air, as if scenting the approaching storm. She was wearing a flowery dress she'd probably purchased during World War II.

"Maybe I can help," she said.

I sat up straighter.

"How much you need?" She was staring out the floor-to-ceiling window. "Twenty?"

I cocked my head. "Twenty hundred?" An odd way of saying two thousand, the fix I had in mind.

She laughed. "Don't I wish! Twenty dollars, Shandie. What do you youngsters do with your money these days?"

I almost burst into tears. The old bird had no idea what it took to survive. Like Mom, she'd been no more than a mother all her life. Never had a real job, and now lived in some fairy land when it came to real life issues. How could you talk to a person who was so out of touch with reality? But I had to make the effort. Now that Carson was dead, who the hell could I turn to for help?

"Grandma ... I need two thousand."

"Oh, my." She sat down abruptly on the sofa. Wagged her head. "I wish I could help, Shandie, but the social security I get don't amount to a hill of beans. I spend it as I go; on what, I can't rightly say."

You give it to Mother, who doesn't need it like I do, I thought with an emotion that bordered on rage. I stood up, grabbed my purse. This was stupid, humiliating, crawling on my belly before my grandmother, as if I were some welfare case.

"Don't worry about it, okay?" I swung my purse over my shoulder, bent down and pecked her wrinkled cheek. She smelled like an old hairbrush. "I'll just sell some stock or something."

I had no stock, but I couldn't let Grandma see me as a complete failure. I was just a person who got her finances tangled up once in a while and needed a little help. Same as everyone. "Bye, Love—" As I traipsed into the living room, I waved and blew a kiss.

The front door snapped open. Mom was home. Mom and Regina.

"SHANDIE NEEDS SOME MONEY," Grandma yelled.

"Oh, Grandma. I said I'd take care of it myself."

"What's the problem?" Regina asked.

I looked at my sister. I'd never considered Regina as a source of financial help. When Carson Blue was your source there was no need to consider anyone else. "I just got hit with a temporary snag," I said.

With grim expression, Mother went up the stairs. *Up yours*, I almost said to her.

I turned back to Regina. "The place where I hang my license? They have to reduce forces. Can you believe it? On the day I hear Carson died? Is that a cruel twist of fate or what?" She nodded, sympathetic. "So I'll have to find another broker, hopefully someone with his feet on the ground. But the problem is, this happened at a bad time. I'm between closings and this major Realtor fee came due, so I need a couple of thou to tide me over. Nothing I couldn't fix if I sold some stock ..."

She gave a regal wave. "I can help." Said as easily as if she'd been asked to loan a cup of sugar.

I was suddenly saturated with feelings of love for my sister. Regina had a heart of gold! Everything was going to be fine! I'd pay the lousy fee, pay the mortgage, the car payment ... hell, maybe I'd buy a new frock to wear to the memorial service.

She walked over to the desk near the fireplace, sat down and opened her Gucci. Removed her checkbook. "Two thousand is more than I can handle ..."

My stomach dropped to my knees.

"How much is that Realtor fee you mentioned?"

"Five hundred," I snapped.

She looked up. "I'm sorry, Shandie. I should have been more clear. I can't lend you two thousand, and I'm afraid five is more than I can swing. When I said I could help, I ..."

"Forget it." I went for the door.

"Wait! Would two hundred help? You could offer to pay half the fee. People are usually good about waiting if they see you're making an effort."

The frustration I felt was almost unbearable. My sister was offering to give me the exact amount of the fee, but it was way too slow to fix what ailed me.

"I'll pay it back as soon as I can."

"I know you will."

I barely had the check tucked in my purse when Mom stormed down the stairs. She had on a white chenille bathrobe and her hair was flying around her face. It was obvious she'd done some major crying. She came like a hot wind across the room and pointed at me.

"Someone died today!"

"I know someone died today, Mother. God."

"No emotions! Just like when your father died! What is the matter with you?!"

If she would have looked closely at my eyes and damaged makeup she would have seen I'd cried earlier.

"You're not human!"

Regina turned away at that and Grandma said, "Now, Kate ..."

"All you care about is your own material well-being! People mean nothing! And look at the way you're dressed—like a tramp!"

Regina walked over, put her arms around Mom's shoulders and coaxed her back upstairs.

"What's the matter with her?" I said to Grandma as soon as they were out of sight.

Maddie was digging in her pocket for her pipe. "Maybe she's reliving your father dying. Might have some unfinished business there."

"So why doesn't she go see a psychiatrist or something?"

Chapter Three

A Hot Pink Dress

Later that night in my den, with only a bottle of Mateus for company, I sifted through my bills. Symbols of the trust I had placed in a man whom I had thought would live forever. A man who promised to take care of me, if ever he died.

There were late notices from Visa, Mastercard, AT&T, three department stores, one boutique and a snotty little note from the townhome association, demanding payment of the quarterly maintenance fee. The mortgage payment for April was overdue, as was the lease payment on the Cad. All these fussy people demanding their little payments and fees! Couldn't they understand that sometimes there were circumstances beyond a person's control?

My mother's accusation that I cared only for my own material well-being still festered. As if she cared nothing for money. Her in that big paid-for A-frame that housed a lucrative antique business.

In all fairness, should I suffer the brunt of the blame? Had not Carson created in me a false sense of security? Thinking these thoughts, a wife abandoned for a younger woman could not have felt more scorned. And in a way, had I not been left for another woman?

As I lounged in the lamp glow, the unpaid bills heaped in my lap, it came clear that this Lucinda character *was* the other woman. A woman who had cheated me out of my rightful chunk of the Blue estate. Had he not been tranced (trance channeler!) into an illicit marriage, Carson would've kept his promise. Would he conceal a legitimate marriage from his best friend?

Which meant Lucinda Desserita Xavier had come into Carson's wealth deceitfully. And because I was perhaps the only person aware of the deceit, the responsibility fell to me to throw down the gauntlet. I pictured myself confronting the witch. Saying something like, "Either pay up or face the legal consequences."

Three glasses of wine later emerged a better plan: cultivate a friendship with the woman! Said friendship established, she'd sympathize and help me out of the financial pit. (How long would this take?) As for making her acquaintance, after I introduced myself she would take my hand and say, "The pleasure is mine, Shandie. Carson spoke with such fondness ..."

Six glasses of wine later, the vision expanded to include an invitation to move into the mansion. Then I could lease the townhome, which might be a smart tax move ...

At the thought of taxes, I began to perspire and shake. Four days until April fifteenth. I owed the IRS thousands of dollars. And I was already in trouble over last year's return ...

I stumbled out of the chair, clutching my stomach. The bills scattered as I ran to the bathroom, where I upchucked a mixture of wine and chocolate cake.

The next morning, fortified with coffee, I realized the solution had been revealed in a kind of vision the day before: half the people in Doubletree were going to pull up stakes after they understood that with a tranced channeler at the helm, Blue O&G was doomed to failure. I knew I was right. Knew I had been granted this special knowledge from Whomever or Whatever grants wisdom to innocent people in trouble. But special insight is only valuable if one acts on it. I had to get moving. Set some appointments.

I snapped my fingers. At the memorial service! When my prospects would be gathered in one place. I would be discreet.

Gently remind everyone that I was a Realtor. Not any old Realtor but one who had grown up in Doubletree, an insider. Carson's girl, for years.

Friday, dressed in my best suit, I mailed a check to the Board of Realtors to cover their important little fee, then I set out for the office.

Roger hadn't really fired me, I reasoned. His complaint about "carrying me" was totally unfounded. It wasn't as if I received a regular paycheck. Realtors worked on a commission basis and the costs of providing desks and telephones were minimal. Piddling expenses Roger Sweet could well afford. After all, when a home sold he got the largest cut. He was just in a foul mood when I called him. People always bitched about money when they were feeling grumpy.

My plan was to pick up a couple of hundred brochures and staple my business cards to them. These I would distribute at the memorial service, which, according to Grandma, was scheduled for next Tuesday.

As I drove north on Wadsworth Boulevard toward the office, I daydreamed about meeting Lucinda Blue. She was probably pushing fifty. Probably hefty. Short and hefty. Regular hair, no particular style. Gray. Definitely gray hair. She wore thick glasses—at her age, bifocals. Mrs. Blue dressed like my mother. Conservative. No splash.

What did Carson see in the woman?

I was relieved to see no sign of Roger's car in front of Sweet Realty. I could breeze in, leave a message, breeze out.

Pat greeted me like she might a pornography salesman. Obviously still upset at my remark about her Lord. She was a tall, bony woman. Glasses with black frames. Her hair brought to mind an upended bowl of oatmeal.

"Roger in?"

"No, but he left you a message."

I glanced at the mail boxes.

"Not a written message." She smiled as if this pleased her. "He said to find out when you were going to clean out your desk."

I returned the smile. "Tell him I changed my mind. Tell him I was a bit overwrought about my best friend dying, but I'm back on track now. Tell him I'm working on some very substantial leads."

Pat shrugged and turned back to her typewriter. The phone rang, she picked it up and I walked into the main room, a bull pen.

Twenty desks were available for use, but all but six of the most serious Realtors had quit since home sales had taken the plunge. I was serious. I seriously liked telling people I was a Realtor. I seriously liked driving a Cadillac with a cellular phone and deducting the expense from my taxes. I loved coming in whenever I liked and doing whatever I wanted: lining up luncheon dates, reading magazines, flirting with the cute mortgage lenders who came by with flyers that detailed the latest rise or fall in interest rates.

Besides me, the only other Realtors in the office today were Jake Abbey, a man I'd dated a couple of times last year, and Diedre Cummings, Sweet's top salesperson.

Diedre was as plain as a clapboard house in Kansas. Beyond my comprehension how someone like her could be a top salesperson. Scratch sleeping with the boss. Roger's wife resembled Mary Hart on "Entertainment Tonight," so Diedre had some other secret. Maybe had connections with some powerful people. She was haggling with someone on the phone. She flashed me a plastic smile, fluttered her fingers.

Jake was at the computer. I saw him shoot a quick glance my way that pretended not to see me. Like he was so absorbed in his work a buffalo in a leotard dancing across the room would escape his attention. He'd behaved like this before, as had others. I'd told myself it was because they were all a bunch of stick-in-the-muds who were jealous of anyone who preferred to kick up her heels and have a little fun rather than acting serious all the time. But today, my invisibility in Jake's glance touched a deep fear inside me. Maybe people avoided me because they found me shallow. It was a feeling that came over me sometimes, like finding half a worm in the apple you're eating. A vague, sick feeling that the whole world is dancing to some tune you can't hear, laughing at you behind their glassy-eyed stares; because, not only are you deaf to the tune, you aren't really dancing. Instead, you're running in place—thinking you're hot stuff doing it.

I was reminded of a time when I was a teenager and visited a church with a friend. Down the aisle was a woman singing loudly, off-key. Evident by her big smile as she belted out the sour notes, she was oblivious to her tone-deafness. Everyone nearby was giving her sidelong glances, their blank expressions masking urges to explode in giggles. I was like that woman, I feared, in everything I did. Tone-deaf and out of step. It would explain why I'd never been able to form intimate relationships (except with Carson). Even women with whom I tried to form friendships acted remote after one or two shared social events. I tallied their faults and wrote them off. I didn't need them. I didn't need anyone. I had Carson.

I rummaged around in my desk and found the brochures and cards I needed. I thought about leaving Roger a note but decided against it. He wanted proof I could earn my way, I would bring him proof in a stack of signed listing agreements. Leaving the office, I imagined a look of stunned joy on his face when I dropped the stack of agreements on his desk.

Saturday I shopped for something to wear to the memorial service. Considering my elaborate plans, it was essential that I dress in something that would strike a response in the sleepyheads in Doubletree who had not a clue of the trouble Mrs. Blue was about to wreak on the community.

In a dozen or so boutiques, I tried on an array of garments, finally settling on a full-skirted, hot-pink dress. It had big rhinestone buttons, encased in black, that marched down the bodice to disappear beneath a wide, black cinch-belt. The dress cost two hundred. I found a pair of spike-heeled black patent leather shoes on sale for a hundred and spent another seventy-five on a black straw hat with a pink rose pinned on its side.

"Charge it," I told the clerk with a wave of my hand. "Charge it all."

Chapter Four

Sleeping Quarters

Billy

She moves a goddess, and she looks
a queen

Translation of *The Iliad*
Book 3, line 1
Alexander Pope
(1688–1744)

While Shandie is in
the boutique, Billy Sang
Hightower is standing on
the tarmac near the hangar,
next to Sid Winkowski.
Both men are squinting
into the glare as they watch
an aircraft circle the property. The pilot is treating
the passengers to a bird's
eye view of Blue Acres. Sid
says the man only recently
got his private pilot's license, and it shows in the
way he handles the craft,
like some cowboy riding
the airwaves on a bucking

49

bronco. Billy's stomach rises and falls with each dip and sharp turn, as if he were up there with them, about to lose his lunch. He imagines Leona and Olson peering out the windows of the mansion, hands smashed against their ears to shut out the rumble and roar.

The silky orange windsock on top of the hangar bobs listlessly and the sky is the color of pale blue satin, interrupted here and there by puffball clouds. Serene conditions getting raped by the hotdog who is tearing up the sky. Sid says the aircraft is a Cherokee Malibu Mirage, a rich man's toy that costs about three hundred thousand smackers.

At last the pilot is done showing off. As he brings the gleaming machine around and lines it up for a downwind approach, Sid fiddles with his elaborate mustache and remarks that he has heard that the turbocharged Mirage has a tendency to dart for the ditch on impact.

Billy wishes Sid would shut up and leave him to his own reflections, however disquieting their content. Impossible for him to watch with dispassion the approach of the airplane that carries Carson's widow, so soon after the boss was killed.

After the vision it was gruesomely difficult for Billy to maintain composure. He had to act as if nothing was wrong for long, grueling hours before Carson's wife called with the news. Only then could he release some of the pent-up shock and grief. But his reactions were tainted by foreknowledge. Leona saying over and over again how strong he was. Counterfeit strength. She did not see him in his bedroom after the vision, crying like a small child who has lost his father.

To counter the pain he threw himself into preparing the house for guests. At one point thinking crazily it would be better to mess it up, make it less attractive, so as to dissuade Lucy from following through with her decision to move to Doubletree.

Lucy's brother lands the plane sloppily, no doubt jarring the passengers, as the left wheel slams into the tarmac well before the right wheel makes purchase. Sid hunches his shoulder and grimaces. But the aircraft does not dart for the ditch. Engine roaring like the howl of a dragon, the craft judders toward the two men.

When the airplane is positioned at an angle facing the hangar, the engine speeds up, then whaps to a stop. Splitting the sudden silence, a blackbird in a tree nearby caws a complaint. The pilot pops open a window and pries off his headset.

All Billy can see of the man is that he is tall, broad-shouldered, dark-haired and wears aviator glasses. He dislikes Steffen Xavier on sight.

As Sid hurries toward the airplane to talk with Xavier, Billy strides toward the passengers. He has spoken with Lucinda Blue numerous times on the telephone, but today is the first time he has met her face-to-face. His instincts say she is a woman of substance who can be trusted. But he is repulsed by her cheerfulness. As he helps the smiling woman out of the airplane, he wants to yell, "Your husband died only five days ago!" Show a little respect.

He helps Xavier's fiance, Marilee Conners, to the ground, and the children are next. They grab hold of him eagerly, as if he is a favorite uncle. Handsome children, who, despite their olive complexions and dark hair, resemble Carson. Eye color, and something in the way their faces are structured.

As soon as Billy lets go of the children, they run over to Xavier and Sid, full of exuberance. He can forgive them their gaiety so soon after their father has died. They are children, and he knows that Carson was less than a fully engaged father.

These are Lucy's children. Her payoff in a marriage that served to grease the wheels of a lucrative mining venture with a group of Basque businessmen. The children weren't the only payoff. The money Carson made on the deal freed Lucy to sell her restaurant and pursue her special interests. Extravagant times before things went haywire.

Popular opinion thinks Carson Blue died a wealthy man, but several bad business decisions over the past few years whittled away a significant chunk of the estate. There are a score of creditors to satisfy; Blue Oil and Gas is mired in debt and the house and grounds are mortgaged. Insurance money would have helped, but Carson allowed the policy to lapse. Billy recalls Blue saying only a year ago, "If a man can't afford insurance, he should not fly." Amen, Blue, amen, dammit.

The National Transportation Safety Board will conduct a routine investigation that Sid said will take a good six months. Billy and Sid can only speculate as to what caused the crash. It happened just after takeoff. Fierce and erratic winds could have played a part, but it is doubtful; Carson was used to takeoffs and landings in almost hurricane gales. More likely the cause was mechanical. The Piper was fifteen years old. It needed a new mag needle, new fuel tank bladders, and the fuel tank itself was suspect. Sid reminded Carson numerous times that the parts needed replacing, but the boss was squeezing his pennies. Breaking his own principles.

"Should have knocked him upside the head and insisted he get that new mag needle," Sid lamented, after the crash. "Should have forged his signature on a check for the insurance," Billy said. After a litany of "should haves," Leona told both men she was going to send them to bed without any dinner if they didn't shut up. Maybe they'd never know exactly what caused the crash, but one thing for sure, Carson wouldn't want them wallowing in self-recriminations. Leona putting them in their places with her homespun logic.

After a few moments of awkward—and, to his mind, inappropriate—conversation, Billy ushers the women and children over to Carson's white Buick Riviera. Piles in the luggage. He is designated chauffeur while Sid helps Xavier cancel the flight plan and tie down the aircraft.

During the short drive from the airstrip to the mansion, Billy shuts his mind to the babble about the beautiful grounds, and the grand house that comes into view as they pass the guest cabins.

He parks in front of the hedges. The sprinklers are on full force. As he helps the women and children out of the Buick, a strong breeze sweeps a cool mist over them all. The children shiver and laugh. Billy hastens toward the back of the house with the intention of turning the water off, but Lucinda orders him to stop.

"It's wonderful!" she says and raises her hands to the sky. Billy wonders if his instincts are wrong.

"Refreshing!" she exudes. "Let it be!"

The children dance in the spray momentarily, then run up the path to join Xavier's fiancé on the porch. The woman is haughty-looking, just the sort Billy would pair with Xavier. He begins unloading luggage from the trunk of the car.

Hands on her hips, Carson's widow gives the house a long, meditative look. She turns slowly to take in the rest of the property, the stands of trees to the south, the tree-laden ridge above and behind the house, the five-stall garage and the seven cabins.

"Billy ... ?"

He sets the luggage down on the porch and turns around. Only then does he permit himself to observe keenly Lucinda Desserita Xavier Blue. Carson never produced a photo of her, and Billy never asked about the woman's appearance, or anything else of a personal nature. Not in his most impetuous imagination would he have pictured the boss coupled with such a woman, the business arrangement notwithstanding. She is Earth Mother, the ancient crone, the wicked witch of the East, the Statue of Liberty, beckoning the masses. He wants to run, hide, capture her, lock her in a dungeon, place her on a pedestal, bow down before her. He turns away in fear and disgust. How could Carson do this to him?

" Billy?"

He shifts his eyes in her direction.

"How many people do you think the place can sleep comfortably?"

"How many people ..." The question unnerves him. "There are six bedrooms," he says, annoyed that he is forced to raise his voice to be heard. Can't she come a little closer?

"Utilizing those six, plus any other available space, such as down in the basement, and counting those ..." She points at the seven log cabins, "how many would you say, maximum? Fifty?"

Billy tries to envision fifty people bedding down on the premises. The idea is abhorrent. Maybe he will have to leave. An equally abhorrent idea. He is barely reconciled to the fact that Carson did not leave him the house, as promised.

"Maybe thirty," he says.

"Okay, thirty." She nods. "Good." She walks briskly toward the porch. She is wearing rose-red pants that billow around her legs and taper at the ankles. On top, a loose-fitting rose-red blouse. What appears to be sparkling pink and purple sand is glued down all over pants and blouse, in a haphazard design. Billy adds a turban, a shawl and sees her holding aloft a crystal ball the size of a grapefruit. Eight rings on her fingers.

She stops at the base of the stairs and smiles. "Counting us ..." she gestures to indicate Marliee and the children, "and you and Olson and Sid, you think thirty others could live here comfortably?"

Billy narrows his eyes. "You forgot Leona," he snaps. "The cook. And the housekeeper and the gardeners." Not all of them live at Blue Acres, but they'd always had the option.

She smiles. "Yes, I'm aware that Carson was generous and a collector of people." She turns to the children. "Shall we acquaint ourselves with our new home?"

Billy picks up the luggage, nudges open the door with the toe of his boot, and walks into the house that he has called home for the past fourteen years.

"Oh, Billy ..."

His jaw tightens; he stops but does not turn around.

"Life goes on. Carson would have it no other way."

That said, the woman with the raven-black hair that hangs to the middle of her back walks past him, her children in tow, as if she owns the place. Which she does, now.

Shandie

The heart has its reasons which
reason knows nothing of.

Pensees
Number 277
Blaise Pascal
(1623–1662)

Chapter Five

A Fifty-Eight Thousand Dollar Shock

It was raining the morning I set out for the memorial service in Doubletree. As my mind took sail above the clouds, the Cad was a fine yacht gliding through silken waves.

I imagined Carson encouraging me from the other side. First he apologized, explaining that he'd kept the marriage a secret because of his fear of losing me. Leona was right, the marriage was a business arrangement, and Carson's ghost was terribly upset by the rumor that his business partner planned on moving to Blue Acres. He was doing what he could on the other side to discourage her from making the move. If she refused to listen, all of the help would quit. Maybe Carson would whisper the command in their dreams. Not that he'd have to urge them. Leona, Billy, and the others were loyal to him and him alone. Blue Acres would go on the market (I would get the listing) and the profits would be split among Carson's best friends.

He whispered encouragements as I weaved in and out of traffic, the windshield wipers providing background music for the drama playing on the stage of my mind. Yes ... he whispered ... it is wise that you take steps today to insure your future. Then he told me he had made a will leaving me a substantial part of the estate. But Lucinda had found and destroyed it. Unfortunately, no one would ever know the truth.

Unfortunately, I was on my own.

In Doubletree, the wind was slamming sheets of rain into the trees, bending them low. No one else had arrived at the park yet, so I drove around to the north of Blue Acres where the airstrip was visible from the road.

An aircraft with a single engine was parked near the hangar. Mrs. Blue's brother's air machine.

Flying terrified me. Carson used to try and persuade me to fly to exotic places with him. He offered to fly me to Reno for dinner once. (Where his secret wife lived!) Would things have been different if I had sucked up my guts and gone flying with him?

I drove back to the park and slipped the Cad next to the curb on the west side. Not a soul in sight. The two brown plaster dinosaurs seemed to stare at the black metal creature crouched at the curb with macabre satisfaction at the prospect of a ruined party. Lightning flashed, thunder roared, and the rain came down harder. What if the memorial service had been canceled? Unthinkable. This was my day! Hadn't Carson's ghost said as much?

I used the time to think through my sales approach. Some might be offended at the idea of a Realtor doing business at such an occasion. This I would soften with a strong hint of insider information that could not wait. "Mrs. Johnson," I would say, "please forgive the intrusion, but I want you to know I'm here if the situation in Doubletree takes a turn for the worse in the near future." Something like that, emphasized with a discreet nod at Lucinda. People would sense something wrong with this secret wife business and would feel grateful that someone else, someone with a solution, shared their concern. "The future does look a little dark," Mrs. Johnson might say. "Don't worry, I'm here," I would say and slip her one of my brochures. I imagined a look of relief on her face. "Call me anytime. And Mrs. Johnson? Those who list their homes first will have a definite advantage ..."

Around noon the clouds began to part like velvet drapes in a theater. The sun appeared and vegetation glistened, as if splashed with a coat of liquid diamonds.

At last people began to arrive; first, Sid Winkowski, driving his Dodge pickup, which was loaded with folding chairs. Olson Early came in his van, then my mother and sister drove up in Regina's BMW. Hippie Joe Inglehart came in his Bronco. I watched others, including Leona, get out of their vehicles and walk up to the pavilion. There they huddled, talking, pointing, waving arms. More pickups filled with folding chairs arrived. Several men began unloading the chairs. Others crawled into the back of Olson's van and lifted out several large sheets of plywood. These were hauled near the pavilion and placed flat on the ground in front of it. Olson lugged a portable podium with a built-in microphone and speakers that would plug into the wall of the pavilion, while a man dressed in coveralls began to lay out smaller pieces of wood, obviously meant to form a makeshift platform. Folding chairs were placed on top of the rectangles of plywood, and Olson set the podium at the center.

My first steps across the grass explained the reason for the plywood path and platform. The heels of my new patent leather shoes sunk into mud. And the wind was cold. I was without a jacket because I didn't own one that matched my hot-pink dress. The women up on the pavilion were dressed in woolen pants, sweaters, scarves, and sensible shoes.

Several men were hauling tables up to the pavilion. I spotted a van with Buffalo Bill's Catering Service painted on the side panels. No one had mentioned a catered picnic. I stopped. Tried to picture myself up on the pavilion with the ladies, helping them arrange the food. I turned, slogged back to the Seville, drove to Mom's house and helped myself to a pair of her flat black shoes. I offered Grandma a ride to the park, but she was waiting for Harold Waters to escort her.

When I returned, the park was crawling with people. And kids everywhere, all over the dinosaurs, the play equipment, as if this were a holiday. Why the hell weren't the little demons in school? The smallest in day care centers? Then I remembered Carson raving about how much he adored children. So people probably figured his ghost would enjoy seeing the brats at his service. Carson was a kind of Santa Claus to the children of Doubletree, distributing bags of toys and candy at Halloween, Christmas, and Easter festivities.

"Sorry, kids, no toys today," I muttered as I scuffed across the grass in my mothers shoes. Folding chairs were now arranged in curved rows that faced the pavilion. Tables up on the pavilion were loaded with covered dishes. White tablecloths flapped in the chill breeze.

I saw people I knew and spoke with many of them, pressing Sweet Realty brochures into their palms, which, to my surprise, turned out to be quite the conversation stopper. I got the message. People were in no mood to contemplate selling their homes on a day when death was the main subject. The reality of Carson leaving a wife totally incapable of running an oil and gas company would hit them later. The panic would hit and they would remember me and call it a strange coincidence.

Several people were talking excitedly and pointing at something. The arrival of Carson's white Buick Riviera. I cupped my hand at my forehead to shield my eyes from the sun. Billy was chauffeur. Dressed in jeans, white shirt, tie, and a black sports coat, he looked as slick as a baby dolphin.

He walked around and opened the passenger door for a woman who could not be Lucinda Desserita. But as soon as the thought chomped into my brain, I knew it could only be her. She was wearing a magnificent white hat. I lifted my own hat slowly, positioned it on my head.

Out of the back of the Riviera emerged a tall, well-built man and a pretty woman. Then two children clambered out of the Buick, both dressed in their Sunday best.

Okay, so the man was Lucinda's brother, the woman was his wife, and the kids belonged to them.

Billy led the entourage, as if preceding royalty. I wanted to run over and slap him for that. The crowd parted to allow the group to move along the plywood path toward the pavilion, where they were met by a small welcoming committee that included Mom, Regina, Felicia Perry, Beverly DeWitt, Ivy Chumbly, and several people I failed to recognize.

As the introductions began, I stepped closer. The woman in the white hat was Lucinda, all right, and the man was her brother, Steffen Xavier. Woman hanging on his arm was Marilee Something-or-Other, his fiancé. And the brats were ...

Impossible to lose one's footing while wearing flat shoes and standing on solid ground, nonetheless I felt myself sliding, as if down an embankment slick with mud. I grabbed at the man next to me. He scowled and jerked away. I tried to apologize, but all that came out of my mouth was a moan that sounded like gravel scraping across glass.

Ivy Chumbly introduced the children as belonging to "Lucy" and Carson. Carson's "special family." I felt my mouth open wide of its own accord, as if about to chomp into a Big Mac.

Carson had secret children? Impossible. He had a low sperm count. I remembered him saying that was the reason his ex, Roz, could never get pregnant. They tried everything. They both went to doctors. An extremely low sperm count ...

I stared at the brats. Jennifer and Alex Blue. Ages six and three. I removed my hat and fanned my face. Okay, they were adopted. Must have been a challenge for the adoption agency to find children with eyes the same peculiar bluish-green color as Carson's. It was a bitch, but they managed. Lucinda's eyes were dark, so if the kids were hers for real, their eyes would be dark, too. Wasn't that an irrefutable genetic law?

Lucinda—Lucy Blue failed to fit my image even vaguely. She was large-boned, shapely, tall, maybe five-foot-nine. She had on a navy-blue sweater dress that hung to mid-calf, a slit on the left side, up to her knee. On her feet, white high-heeled pumps, explaining the reason for the plywood path. The queen must not sully her shoes. Her thick, glossy hair tumbled over her shoulders and down her back like a black waterfall. As she spoke she touched it frequently, as if her tresses were an integral part of the conversation. People were gathering around her, pressing close, mesmerized.

Her brother looked like a snob. Silver streaks in his dark hair. The woman hanging onto his arm had on a simple but elegant black dress. Long, wavy brown hair.

The children were dark-haired. Beautiful children and not one bit shy. They were darting about as if they had lived here since birth.

Billy and Olson were up and down the stairs of the pavilion, delivering Styrofoam cups of coffee to Lucinda and company. I wobbled over and sat down next to Grandma and her beau, Harold Waters, who were engaged in conversation. Harold was a wisp of a man with hardly any hair. Nothing matched; coat, tie, shirt, trousers.

"You left your purse at the house, Shandie," Grandma said. "I was going to bring it, but whenever Harold comes around, I'm lucky if I remember my name."

The geezer blushed.

I sat like a stone. That Carson was really dead was beginning to sink fangs into my gut. He was gone for good and had left a special, secret family. A detail his ghost forgot to tell me.

When I spotted Regina's husband, Drew Hillborne, and my nephew, Zachary, I slouched down. But golden-haired Zach saw me and yelled, "Aunt Shandie!" He tore across the grass.

"Hi!"

The boy was dressed in a double-breasted blue suit with red bow tie. He looked dashing. I snarled at him to go play in traffic.

Maddie stretched out her arms, but Zach ran away, not before I saw the tears in his blue eyes. "So I'm a bitch," I said. Grandma said nothing.

I felt lower than low. The only thing that could save me now was if people fell on their knees and begged me to sell their homes. Probably the wildest fantasy of all. The residents of Doubletree were swarming around the Queen Bee. There was no panic in the air. Life in Doubletree would go on, even prosper.

Billy was at the podium testing the microphone. As Lucinda and party stepped across the plywood platform and sat down in the special row of chairs, people hurried to claim seats. Besides Carson's special family, his "friends" (he always called his servants friends) were seated up front, along with a number of men and women scheduled to speak. Joe Inglehart began to tune his guitar. He wore a suit that looked as though it might have fit when he was in high school. As for religious representation, there was none, unless you counted Hippie Joe.

Billy was the key spokesman. Looking as gorgeous and untouchable as ever, he began the service with a moment of silence, then Joe, accompanying himself on the guitar, sang a ballad Billy said was one of Carson's favorites. A song I'd never heard. Then the eulogies began.

Under the sun's hot-fisted blaze, I dozed.

"Wasn't that nice?" Grandma said when Joe finished singing a second ballad. That jarred me awake. I sat up straighter. As I straightened, a gust of wind lifted my black straw hat with the pink rose off my head and tumbled it over the people in the front row, onto the grass directly in front of three-year-old Alex. The boy jumped down from his chair, seized the hat and smashed it down on his head. The crowd tittered; the brat swished his hips. Lucinda did nothing. If anything, her expression telegraphed approval. Her brother did zip to discourage the boy and his fiancé acted as if nothing weird was happening. Six-year-old Jennifer looked disgusted but made no move to correct her brother's behavior.

Like the head baton twirler in a band, the urchin began to strut back and forth, my hat sliding down his nose. The children in the audience pointed and laughed, as did a number of adults. At the podium, John Houseman, one of Blue O&G's vice presidents, gave up trying to complete his eulogy. He smiled, embarrassed, as the brat continued to strut. People were laughing openly now, and still Mrs. Blue and her brother did nothing to stop the boy.

I sprang from my chair. Another gust of wind caught the brochures in my lap and whirled them into the air, out over the dinosaurs, where they fluttered about like a flock of deranged birds. I scuffed across the grass and snatched the hat off the boy's head. More clapping and laughter. I set the hat on my head and scuffed back to my seat. Another round of applause.

John Houseman finished his speech, Hippie Joe played one more tune, and the service was over.

Grandma and Harold stood up. "Aren't you coming?" Maddie said. She gestured at the pavilion where people were forming a line.

"Can't. I've got a sales appointment in Castle Rock." A lie, but I wasn't about to stick around and watch people drool over Lucinda and crew. Maybe I'd get stinking drunk at Tucker's Lounge. Maybe I'd ask Tuck for a job as a cocktail waitress. Maybe I would beg him for a job.

I set out over the grass toward the Cad. Halfway there I heard a woman yell my name. I turned around, and saw to my astonishment, Lucinda Desserita Xavier Blue coming toward me, the heels of her white shoes sinking into the soft earth as she came. She was no longer wearing her hat and the breeze swirled her hair like a lustrous black cape. One of my brochures was clenched in her hand. She walked up, offered her other hand, and we shook.

"I know who you are." She held up the brochure, as if presenting proof.

"Well, I know who you are, too," I said, nonplussed. I pulled on my hand but the woman would not give. Her dark eyes bore into me like lasers. I was certain she about to say something like, "You're Carson's little slut."

What she said was: "You're the woman who owes my estate fifty-eight thousand and whatever dollars and cents."

For a moment I was too shocked to say anything. "You're crazy!" I blurted, and jerked my hand.

"I am not crazy. The record shows that my husband loaned you fifty-eight thousand, and whatever dollars and cents. And I want to know when and how you plan to repay us."

"Well, shit," I mumbled and tried to free my hand. The witch had the grip of a gorilla.

People began edging toward us.

"And if you think I'm letting you off the hook, you're crazy."

I thought I detected a flash of amusement in her eyes. Sadistic amusement. She knew I was Carson's girl, had to know, and she knew of his generosity. Rather than confront me head-on about it, she was out to humiliate me.

"So sue me!" I cried. At last she released my hand. I rubbed it, stared at the woman, too befuddled to move.

She cocked her head. "Perhaps I will." Again the flash of sick amusement. "You have some nice assets to reconcile your debt? A nice car, silverware ... " She flicked her hand at my ears. "Diamonds?"

"Car gave me that money!"

"I doubt that." A small crowd was forming around us. "And I expect every cent to be repaid."

The woman's brother stepped forward. "What's the problem, Lucy?"

She pointed. "This is the woman who owes the estate fifty-eight thousand and whatever dollars and cents."

Xavier smiled at me, then said quietly to his sister. "Is this the time to bring it up?"

"I brought it up, didn't I? Must be the time."

People were whispering, pointing, frowning. I spotted Grandma and Harold Waters at the edge of the crowd.

I backed up, but the witch grabbed my arm.

"How do you intend to repay what you owe?"

"I don't owe anything!"

Billy was standing a few feet away, thumbs hooked in the pockets of his jeans. He looked sad. Probably thinking, *Poor*

Carson, tangled up with a whacko girlfriend who ripped him off. That's what they all were thinking. Before Carson died, no one in Doubletree had even heard of Lucinda Blue, now she had their sympathy. Even Leona looked disturbed. I ached to scream out the truth. "Carson loved me!"

"I have canceled checks as proof," the witch said, her hand still clamped on my arm.

Mom and Regina popped out of the crowd like bagels in a toaster. Mom pointed at my feet. "Aren't those my shoes?"

"Good Christ!" I yanked my arm free. "Would everyone just leave me alone?"

Lucinda looked at my mother. "Does she always behave like this?"

"Well, I ... "

Alex Blue ran over and grabbed my leg. "Gimme that hat!" he cried. Several people laughed.

"It's not your hat, Alex!" His sister tried to pull him away but the little devil clamped onto my leg like a vice. "It belongs to the lady who owes us fifty-eight thousand dollars."

"Not, not!" I cried insensibly and smacked the boy with my hat. He screamed, fell back on the grass.

"Shandie—is that true?" Mom said. She looked hurt. No one seemed a bit disturbed that Carson's widow was attacking me at his service. Had these people no sense of decorum whatsoever?

"Is what true?"

"You owe these people ..."

"I don't owe anybody a damn thing!"

"Oh, but she does," Lucinda said, crossing her arms over her chest. "And we will sue."

I stumbled out of my mother's shoes and tore across the grass toward the Seville. Yanked open the door, slid in, fired up the engine, and sped away.

Chapter Six

An Exquisitely Fair-Minded Curse

I hobbled out of Tucker's Lounge five hours later, my feet shackled with ugly gray shoelike contraptions called "soft orthotics." I got them from a fellow drinker, a podiatrist who took a shine to me. Conveniently, he'd had the contraptions in his car, so Tuck couldn't throw me out for being barefoot.

I stumbled into the blackness of night, squinting to find the Seville. I needed to call the office, talk to Roger. The foot doctor, who had a brother in commercial real estate, got me all fired up about what a raw deal I had at Sweet's, and I was determined to set the matter straight now.

I found the Cad, then had difficulty getting inside. I was convinced someone had taken a screwdriver and reversed the handles on the doors while I was inside Tucker's downing a few beers. Eventually I got the damn thing open, then had trouble seeing the numbers on the cellular phone. The pole lamp nearby wasn't bright enough to sufficiently light up the interior. I stabbed around until I pushed the right buttons.

Sweet was in the office, as was often the case on Saturday nights. His mood was surly because earlier that evening one of his deals fell apart. Something told me it wasn't a good time to confront the man, but it was a vague, fuzzy something, so I pressed on with beery determination, explaining that a broker's main responsibility was to provide his agents with leads. And if he continued his policy of favoritism—showering leads on Diedre Cummings, who, God knew, needed help least of anyone—I was going to switch to commercial sales.

"That's a peach of an idea," he said.

I thought the peachy idea was that he saw my reasoning and would give me some leads.

"You haven't sold a home in months, you haven't got any listings, and you've done zip to get any listings. So go bother some poor sucker in commercial sales; that's a terrific idea. When can you clean out your desk?"

I slammed down the phone.

I was cursed! Witch Blue hadn't said pointblank, "I hereby curse your existence from this moment henceforth," but her threat to sue for fifty-eight grand was certainly the equivalent.

"From start to finish, those were loans," I could hear her assert in court as clearly as I could see the stack of canceled checks marked "Exhibit B" up on the judge's bench. Exhibit A might be a videotape shot by a detective at a restaurant where Carson and I had innocently dined. And me with no money to hire an attorney to plead my case! Which was no case, considering those canceled checks. Physical evidence!

I wanted to go back inside Tucker's and drink myself stupid. But that damned podiatrist was in there. Let him buy me more drinks and he'd think I owed him a night in a motel room. I snatched up the phone, dialed my mother's number. Regina answered.

"You live there now?" I said.

"Drew took Zach to Denver this evening to a high school basketball tournament. They've had it planned for weeks."

"I left my purse there."

"It's on the sideboard."

"Can you bring it to Tucker's in Castle Rock?"

"No, I cannot bring it to Tucker's in Castle Rock! Shandie, why don't you come over here? We have tons of food left over from the service and I've been telling Grandma the most interesting things about Lucy. After you left? She said you were destined to become—get this: a Daughter of Light. Isn't that wild? She also said you were a funny little person and she would forgive you the debt if you worked for her, for a year. She'll provide room and boa—"

"Daughter of huh? Work for her? Doing what?"

"I haven't the faintest."

"That woman is crazy!"

"She's different, I'll grant you that."

"I want my damn purse."

"So come and get it."

So I did. Without going back into Tucker's to thank the foot doctor for the beers, the shoe contraptions, or the lousy advice that got me fired. But I wasn't seriously worried about that. Roger was just having a bad day. He'd change his mind.

Work for a witch who danced with fans? For a whole year? Work for zero salary, she meant. In which case, how the hell was I supposed to keep up the payments on my townhome, the car and all? That woman had a severe mental problem if she thought Shandie O. Lorrain was going to work her butt off for a year to repay some debt I didn't even owe!

And what was this crap about me becoming a "daughter of light?" Maybe she was a female Jim Jones who lured innocent young women to her pad, worked them to the bone and filled their heads with New Age tripe. Maybe she was skilled at separating gullible people from their cash, like one of those so-called gurus who trick you into "donating" your material goods, with the promise you will be saved if you go to a certain hill in Ohio next month during the full moon when a space ship from Uranus will pick you up just before the Chinese set off the Big Bomb.

Why the hell did Carson give checks instead of cash? I could have killed him for that.

As I turned onto the dirt road that snaked to my mother's house, anemic looking clouds were scuttling around the moon. The sky was the color of tar. A witch sky. Black denizens shaped like trees chased me up the road. Believing it, my heart bonged against my chest as I parked the Seville next to my sister's BMW.

I hobbled up the stairs in the orthotic wonders on my feet, opened the door a crack, and listened for sounds of my mother's voice. With any luck, I could grab my purse and split without encountering another fit-thrown scene. I tiptoed into the living room. Curled on the sofa, Emil hissed and bared his claws.

"One of these days you're going to get hit by a car, Emil, and when you do, know what we'll call you? Flat cat."

"Is that you, Shandie?" Grandma said.

I scuffed into the dining room. Spotted my purse and high heels on top of the sideboard.

"What're those cute things on your feet?" Maddie was chewing on a turkey leg. "You have more trouble with footwear than anyone I ever saw."

I wanted to hug the old woman. Her mundane remarks could turn the most aggravating circumstances into something to chuckle about. Too bad she wasn't around during my childhood. I might have been an entirely different person.

"They're the latest rage, Grandma. I'd like them even better if they weren't both made for the right foot."

I scuffed into the kitchen, got a Diet Coke out of the refrigerator, then sat down next to Grandma, across from my sister. Regina was still dressed in sweater and slacks. Her hair was pulled to one side and tied with a blue ribbon. Maddie was wearing an ancient ruffled housecoat.

"Where's Mom?"

"In her bedroom," Regina said. "She's really tired."

I then heard the soft mutter of the TV upstairs. Safe for the moment, I looked over the ravaged food. Piles of leftover turkey, probably crawling with Salmonella, pale, withered carrot and celery sticks, loaf of bread, plate of toxic lunch meats. And part of a chocolate cake. I sliced into the cake, slid a wedge onto a paper plate and picked up a fork.

"So tell me about this trance-channeling dame from Nevada."

"She was never really in a trance when she channeled," Regina said. "She says she has too much ego to allow another spirit to overwhelm her. She's more a mystic."

"What the hell's a mystic?"

"The way she explained it, her higher self gets in touch with your higher self ... "

"What a bunch of shit." I rubbed my forehead. "We need every damn light on in the house?"

My sister arched a brow. "Bright lights bother people who drink too much. Smells to me like you fell in a keg of beer."

"I was just a little rattled after being accused of owing all that money to an Amazon shepherdess, Regina."

"Really, Shandie. Lucy is a very attractive woman. I think she's beautiful."

"Twice as big as Carson."

"Now girls," Grandma said.

"The point I was about to make," Regina said, "is that Lucy stopped channeling altogether. She got so popular it began to interfere with her family life. She's really big on family. That's one of her main themes. You guessed right, Grandma, she is Basque. And the Basque are a very family-oriented people."

I finished the cake, got up, rummaged in the refrigerator, found some Swiss cheese, sat down and munched on that as Regina continued to blather.

Something about the witch and her brother co-owning a sheep ranch near Ely, Nevada. Some cousins and uncles had been running the place but now wanted to go into something else. They were buying a motel, Regina thought. So the ranch was up for sale when Carson died. Carson had planned to put his and Lucy's home in Reno on the market once the ranch sold and move his special family to Blue Acres.

"Now, of course, Lucy won't have to wait for the ranch to sell before she moves here. Steffen can handle the sale of both the ranch and the house."

Boiled down to, the witch was rich. So what the hell did she need fifty-eight grand for? Bitter grapes, that's what. In that stack

of canceled checks, Mrs. Blue had discovered her husband's fondness for Shandie O. Lorrain. So she wanted to grind me down, ruin
me, make me suffer.

"Well, forget it, you big cow."

"Shandie's talking to herself again," Grandma said.

"It's the beer. She must've drank the whole keg. Look at her eyes."

"It's an old Irish custom for a person to get drunk when her best
friend dies, Regina."

She shook her head. "Oh, Shandie ..."

"He was my best friend."

"Could've destroyed those checks."

"Grandma ... he didn't plan on dying."

Regina sighed, leaned back, untied the ribbon in her hair. "Lucy
said Carson was so excited about finally connecting the two parts
of his life. So she didn't make the decision to move after he died,
as we assumed. It's so sad the way it happened. But she says it's
probably best this way because Carson would have flipped when
he found out what she had planned for Blue Acres."

Lucy thought Carson died so she could do what she wanted
without him flipping out? What kind of dame was this? Before I
could channel my thoughts to my mouth, Grandma spoke.

"What does she have planned?"

"I told you," Regina said. "A retreat for women."

Maddie made a face.

"I can't believe Car married such a weirdo," I said.

"Well, you know how eccentric he was." Regina giggled behind
her hand. "I asked Lucy why she did nothing when her son paraded
around in your hat? She said it was the high point of the service.
She said people are too solemn about death. In her opinion, death
is like a graduation to something better."

"So why don't we all just kill ourselves?" I said.

Grandma laughed, nodded, said, "So how's she going to run a
retreat and Blue Oil at the same time?"

"She's selling her interest in the company ... oops." Regina
grimaced. "Billy told me, and said not to say anything to anyone.
So please don't repeat it."

"Bet she turns Blue Acres into one of those hippie communes," Grandma said. She pointed a turkey bone at me. "Why don't you go work for her? A year isn't much."

"Grandma ..."

"That way we'd have a spy on the inside. Someone to keep an eye on that woman and her strange doin's."

"Oh, great. Sell me down the river so you can keep tabs on a crazy woman. Thanks a lot."

"Do you owe her that money?"

"You calling me a liar?"

"No, but the best of us can get confused sometimes. Especially when it comes to money. I remember once when your grandpa loaned Duke some money to buy some new-fangled piece of sports equipment. Your father felt like you do, that Albert gave him that money. That's why I say write things down. But Albert was from the old school." She scratched her chin and squinted. "Well, hell, he was old ..." She shrugged. "Anyway, he thought a handshake was good enough. Duke was probably half-tanked when they made the deal. I'm sure your father meant no harm, but he was good at turning things around in his head."

"I didn't turn anything around in my head. Never once did Car say I'd have to pay back one red cent. How many times do I have to say it? It wasn't—was not—a loan. And what he gave me was nothing near fifty-eight thou."

Before Grandma could respond, Mom came down the stairs. I tensed. Again she was dressed in her white chenille robe and her hair was down around her shoulders. She appeared to be calm, which meant nothing. She walked over to Regina, stood behind her, resting her hand on the back of the chair.

"I've been thinking about Lucy's offer to let you work off the debt, Shandie."

"Debt! I wish everyone would stop ... "

Mom held up her hand. "Maybe Carson told Lucy he loaned you the money. Maybe she discovered the canceled checks after he died. Either way, the record shows a substantial amount of money went from him to you. And I can't blame Lucy for wanting to recoup her losses."

Lucy! Lucy! As if they'd known her for years!

"You make it sound like I was taking food out of her kids' mouths! I didn't even know she existed until last week. Nobody did. Can I help it if Car threw his money around? He always acted like he was as rich as the King of Siam."

Mom sat down next to Regina and folded her hands on top of the table.

"A gift, a loan, it doesn't matter, Shandie. The fact is, fifty-eight thousand went from Carson to you and his wife perceives it to be a loan. She's certain enough to take you to court. And quite possibly a judge would decide that everything you own was purchased with Carson's money. In which case, he might order you to sell everything and give the proceeds to the widow."

"Maybe you haven't noticed, Mother, but I am a working woman. Carson wasn't totally supporting me."

She smirked. "Oh, come now. We all know the sales you did manage were as a result of the referrals he gave you."

I turned to Grandma. "You think I'm lying about owing that money?"

"Sounds like Carson gave it to you then told his wife it was a loan." She scowled. "The old peckerhead."

Regina leaned toward me with a concerned-sister expression. "We all know that home sales have been tough for everyone the past few years, Shandie. Maybe it's time to consider another career. I know Lucy's offer sounds wild, but maybe while you're out there you'll get in touch with something you really want to do."

Lucy! Lucy! Regina's old pal, Lucy!

"I can't believe this! You all want me to throw my career down the drain! Grandma ..." I gave her a desperate look.

"Oh, go give it a try, Shandie. You're young; a year ain't much, then you won't have this loan thing hanging over your head. And anyway, we need a spy on the inside."

Mom shot her a look.

"Well, thanks a lot!" I said. "My own family, selling me down the river!"

Mom slammed her fist on the table. We all jumped.

"Cut the dramatics, Shandie! You make me sick. You destroyed Carson's first marriage; you continued to chase him all through his second marriage; you hounded him for money and now you're insulted that his wife wants to help you!" She glared at me with bloodshot eyes. Grandma and Regina were both staring into their laps.

She wasn't done.

"If you would have left the man alone he could have moved to Reno years ago, or moved his wife and children here, but no, no, you had to squeeze him dry like a leech. Maybe you belong in jail. Maybe in jail you would learn something about responsibility. It amazes me that you have managed to sidestep every life challenge put in your path. Even motherhood. You just stepped over your own child like she was a blob of garbage on the sidewalk."

Someone under this kind of attack for the first time might have jumped up and ran out of the house. It was old hat to me. I was skilled at hardening my emotions, like a suit of armor. Would it do any good to remind her that she insisted I give up Briana? Waste of breath. She would say she insisted because poor little Briana deserved a decent mother. Try to explain that my agreement to go along with her and Carson wasn't exactly like stepping over your child like she was garbage and she would say that if I'd kept Briana I would have treated her like garbage.

"You done now, Mom?" She glared at me but said nothing. I bent down, slipped off the shoelike contraptions. They had lost their cuteness.

"Grandma? Regina?" I nodded at them both, got my purse and high heels off the sideboard and walked out of the house.

Monday morning I dressed in my most powerful suit and rehearsed what I would say to Roger. First I would apologize for calling him Saturday night and railing at him, when he was feeling down about his lost deal. Then I would outline my plan of action. Tell him I was now willing to knock on doors, do anything to drum up business. He would see the change in me, and apologize for his rudeness.

But when I got to the office, Roger was gone. Pat said he'd already sent my license back to the Real Estate Commission. Her pleasure was evident. The contents of my desk were in a box in the corner and there was a striking red-haired woman sitting in my chair, using my telephone. Nothing atop the desk but the telephone and a vase full of red roses.

I carried the box out to the Seville and shoved it in the trunk.

At home, in the room I used for an office, the red light on my recorder was blinking. I spun the tape back, hit "play."

"Pretty fancy-wancy having your own telephone answering machine."

The voice was unmistakable.

"What else you got over there that you bought with my husband's money? Your sister says you are aware of my offer, which I think is exquisitely fair-minded, and if I don't hear an enthusiastic 'Yes, thank you, Lucy,' by Friday, I'm gonna' file those papers. You understand? Of course you do. We talk the same language, don't we?"

Then she laughed and broke the connection.

I parked my hands on my hips, leaned over and said to the recorder, "Lucy, Baby, you can take your exquisite offer, mix it with cow paddies, and eat it!"

Chapter Seven

The Slave Option

Five weeks later I was sitting on the carpet at home, sipping cold, two-day-old coffee. The power was off. Save for my bed upstairs, the townhome was devoid of furniture. "The," not "my" townhome. A week ago I discovered it wasn't mine. It belonged to the Blue estate. This hit me harder than losing the Cadillac. I had thought I had some equity in the townhome. Now all I owned were clothes, a CD player, a portable Sony TV, my bed, and that damn Green Bomb.

Maybe you're wondering how a person of my talent and intelligence could end up in such a mess. It didn't happen for lack of me trying to get a job and working the best deals I could with the snooty people who held my fate in their hands. I even tried to collect unemployment. The people who run that outfit just laughed. I didn't know you weren't eligible for unemployment benefits if you got paid commissions and your employer didn't contribute to a "state unemployment fund." I didn't know such an animal existed. Things people fail to tell you when they woo you to come to work for them. I thought about suing Sweet for breach of something, but what little money I had wasn't enough to make ends meet, much less cover the legal fees such a suit would require.

The day Lucy left her first message on my recorder, I drove to the nearest money machine and tried to draw cash on my VISA card. The machine spat out a slip of paper, nothing more. This had happened before when I was late with payments. A problem Carson had always fixed. I stared at that machine for five minutes. You can't talk to a machine. You can, but it's stupid; it won't respond. Not even with a whir. I leaned my head out the car window and said, "How the hell do you expect a person to catch up if you refuse her cash?" I honestly could not understand this. Was it any wonder there were so many homeless people? If I had owned a typewriter, I would have sent letters that day to our senators and congressmen in Washington D.C. to alert them to this quirk in the financial system.

The uncooperative money machine was only the first problem I encountered. I tried to sell back my six Ladro figurines to Sydney's Jewelers in Tamarac Square. Ladro's appreciate in value, so I expected to get at least a thousand for them, but the woman who promised to buy them back if ever I wanted to sell, no longer worked at Sydney's, and the pompous bluenose I had to deal with would give me no more than fifty apiece for them, since they looked "slightly used." He went on and on about a minuscule chip in the base of one and he said they all looked "rather yellowed."

"Thieves!" I yelled on the way out of the store.

Then, like a woman possessed, I walked into Chocolate Soup, a children's store. I had no explanation for the fact that I was always calmed when I touched clothes for children. A mystery since I had no love for kids.

I flipped through a rack of sundresses. One particular dress caught my eye, a darling white frock with Minnie Mouse appliques on the straps. Something came over me: I had to have that dress. No one was looking; the clerk was busy with other customers. I yanked the dress off the plastic hanger and stuffed it in my purse.

I'd never shoplifted before, so wasn't sure what to do next. Run! But that would call attention. I moved to a rack of frilly dresses and began thumbing through those, my heart lodged in my throat. The clerk spotted me. I smiled. After a moment I walked out, my legs rubber hoses as I hurried out of the mall. I fully expected a security guard to run up and bonk me on the head with his night stick before I reached the car.

Safe at home, my heart back in my chest, I removed the dress with the Minnie Mouse straps from my purse, smoothed the prize out on my lap and looked it over thoroughly. I removed the tags, cut them into tiny pieces, and flushed them down the toilet. To destroy evidence in case the cops came with a search warrant. Then I placed the dress in my special velvet-lined box.

Lucy left a message on my machine the following Friday, saying she would extend her exquisite offer another week. She could extend until the stars fell from the sky! I was not, not going to go be that woman's slave! I'd sell my body first. Sell body, mind, soul. It had a familiar ring.

Over the next two weeks I did everything possible to get a job. I responded to ads for cocktail waitress, restaurant hostess, various sales positions, and I even applied for some clerical jobs. I'd taken a typing class in high school; how hard could it be? But the snots all stressed they required "on-the-job" experience. I studied ads for other positions, such as department store clerk, but even these piddling jobs required experienced personnel.

Lucy left more messages on my machine. Her persistence more than annoyed me. Would she file suit? Was Mom right? Would I end up in jail?

The second week of May was almost shot, and nasty notices were flying into my mailbox like swarms of angry bees. I had resolved not to call any of my friends until I was financially stable again, but the gong of desperation was sounding. Maybe someone could float me a loan?

"What friends?" I said after the tenth call. I kept calling. An old drinking pal, Trixie, suggested I file bankruptcy. Wipe the slate clean. Go on welfare. Start over.

"Shoot myself."

"Oh, Shandie. Get a grant and go to school! Find another rich boyfriend. Move back in with your mother for awhile. That's what I'm doing. There are hundreds of options."

I called Grandma. She wanted to know why I hadn't returned any of her calls. She'd called Sweet Realty and the gal said I didn't work there anymore.

"We missed hearing from you on Mother's Day. I reckon you were still sore at Kate for being so hard on you the last time you were here. She got that tongue from Albert's side of the family. He had a sister who every time she opened her mouth, she drooled acid. You find a new job?"

"No."

"So maybe you should come work for Lucy. I've been over there, Shandie, and I think she's okay. Maybe a little forward, but that shouldn't bother you."

She said Lucy had gone back to Reno recently, packed her things, returned, and now the mansion was full of her furniture and "whatnot."

"On top of Carson's stuff?"

"She sold all that. I mean she let your mother sell it. For a week or so this place was busier than a fly festival at an outhouse. Sold every cotton-pickin' thing. I think people would have bought Carson's boxer shorts if Lucy would've sent 'em over."

"He wore Jocks."

"Huh?"

I sighed. "Never mind."

"Some of the rooms at the mansion are stark empty now, Leona says. Rooms where Lucy's going to entertain her New Age friends. Might be kind of interesting to work for her."

"Never once has she said what she wants me to do."

"Maybe you'll be a kind of assistant. Olson quit and Lucy laid off that good-for-nothing housekeeper."

"Then she probably needs another housekeeper." I tried to picture myself down on my knees scrubbing floors, slopping out toilets, washing, ironing, dusting, polishing the silverware.

"Never thought I end up slaving for a New Age freak," I said morosely.

"Well, I'm sure you have other options."

"Yeah. Hundreds."

The next day I drove to King Soopers to buy some essentials. I was out of everything important: Diet Coke, toilet paper, mascara, coffee, deodorant, popcorn.

When I came out of the store, my car was gone. The way things had been going, I felt like I was in the middle of a Stephen King novel. A bag of groceries clutched in each arm, I stared for a good five minutes at the spot where I'd parked the Cad.

My townhome was at least two miles from the grocery store. I started walking. For weeks I had been careful to lock the Seville in the garage so the Richardson Cadillac people couldn't swipe it when I wasn't looking. But the sneaky, slimy bastards had followed me like I was a common criminal.

I was glad I was wearing my Ray-Bans. Losing the Cad was something to cry about. Which reminded me I was yet to cry about losing Carson—the man, not his money—which made huge tears swell in my eyes and leak down my cheeks. I wasn't crying about him yet; these were tears of self-pity, tears for a twenty-seven year old woman who had wasted ten years of her life stepping over and around everything important, to the extent that she was now broke, unemployable, and had, it seemed, but one option in life: to go be a slave for the woman who had cheated me out of my share of Carson's fortune.

I had to stop, set down the groceries, and blow my nose. Some jerk in a orange Pinto slowed, maybe to inquire about my problem. I gave Orange Pinto the bird, picked up the bags, and kept walking. Luckily, I wasn't wearing high heels. Unfortunately, the strap of my skimpy sandals rubbed a bloody sore on my left foot.

About a block from the townhome. I saw, parked in the driveway of a two-story house, an ugly green Ford Fairlaine with a FOR SALE sign in the window. I would rather have gone permanently cross-eyed than to be seen driving an old clunker like that, but I was desperate.

I memorized the telephone number and called the owner when I got home. Todd Hansen said he could let the Ford, a '69, go for four hundred. I told the young man I'd think about it, hung up the phone, and cried until my eyes looked like two sick fish. I could have killed Carson for leaving me in this mess.

I called Hansen that evening. He came down twenty-five dollars, so the Green Bomb (his pet name for the beast) was mine for three hundred, seventy-five. Which left me with less than four hundred dollars to my name.

I pawned my jewelry. Gifts from Carson: a diamond necklace, diamond earrings, an emerald and pearl brooch, ruby ring, gold bracelet. Then I had enough money to pay an attorney to help me file bankruptcy. I saw no other way. I called several lawyers and chose the one who charged the least.

Halfway through the process I was hit with the biggest shock of all: Carson had been the mortgagee on the townhome, not me. The attorney couldn't believe I wasn't aware of this fact. How could I explain the way Carson had handled everything in my life? I remembered signing a bunch of papers, remembered the closing, but not the details. Details were Carson's department.

So the townhome now belonged to the Blue estate. Which I was reminded of when Lucy called again. I was to vacate by June 1st so she could put it up for sale. The profit would cover not only the late mortgage payments and association fees, it would be used as well to square up the unpaid balances on all of my charge accounts. Which weren't mine either. Carson got me the cards, and because they were in my name, ignorantly I had thought they were mine.

But the damn furniture belonged to me! And fine furniture it was. I thought it was fine, but the only buyer I could locate who would pay cash in a hurry was the owner of an antique-junk store who offered me five hundred dollars for the lot.

It then made perfect sense that the IRS would choose this time to bear down. Lucy must have put the word out, must have worked some voodoo, spread the curse around. Those Internal Revenuers would put me in jail or worse, so I had to pay enough to back them off.

After registering the Green Bomb, the five hundred I had left shrunk to almost three. Enough to catch up the power company bill, but I was afraid to relinquish any more cash until I could figure a way out of the pit. May 22nd, the lights went out. I bought candles. Cheap ones.

Strange how something you thought was yours takes on a different quality when you find it never belonged to you. A ratty motel room would have been more friendly than was the town-home the last two days and nights I spent there. At least motel rooms, even the rattiest, had furniture.

No one called. No one came. I had long conversations with Carson's ghost. Trying to understand why he had left me in such dire straits. I ranted at him, begged him to explain, collapsed on the floor, sobbed, pounded my fists. Did the man ever really love me? Did I love him?

Thursday, May 24th, I sat cross-legged on the carpet in Lucy's townhome, sipped foul coffee and weighed my options, one more time. I'd narrowed them down to three. One, I could turn myself into one of those shelters for women down on their luck. But I'd done that before, the one time I tried to break with Carson, and the experience was ghastly. I'd rather paint myself purple and sit naked atop a flagpole in January than to go that route again. Two, I could sell my body. Become a hooker. But, believe it or not, I was fussy about the men I slept with. I met an honest-to-God prostitute when I was in that shelter for women, and she said you had to sleep with whomever your pimp sent you. Fat, ugly, old men and some of them were mean. She didn't have to tell me. I watched television; I knew what went on in this scary world.

I tried to convince myself I had a fourth option. Get a job, any job, rent a small apartment, save some money, take some college classes, make something of myself. I just wanted to be a regular person—was that too much to ask? Apparently. I'd already tried getting a job. I even applied at MacDonalds and K-Mart. One said I was over-qualified and the other said I lacked necessary experience. I think the interviewers just didn't like me. They sensed I wasn't regular.

That left me option three. The slave option. I felt like breaking all the windows in the townhome. I wanted to tear the kitchen cabinets off the walls, set them afire. Fill the tub, flood the place. Who the hell did this trance-channeling Basque Amazon think she was, ordering me to work off a fictitious debt? I jerked my arm; the coffee flew and splashed the wall. An ugly brown stain. There.

I felt like throwing up. Wished I could, right there on the carpet. I wasn't sick, I was terrified. Like the time I tried to get a guy named Matt to marry me, thinking if I got married I could keep my baby. Then ending up in a shelter full of women who had kept their babies and wished the hell they hadn't. Such pitiful children! I then realized Carson and Mom were right. It would be morally wrong to keep my child, considering the kind of life she'd have with me. So, Carson and Mom didn't decide for me; simply, they saw the truth before I did.

That time in the shelter was bad, but this was worse. I was at the end of something. Like I was at the end of myself. Like to commit suicide would be redundant.

I don't know how long I brooded before my one saving grace kicked in. Some people talk about imagination like it's some sort of brain disease. In my case, it saved me over and over again. I began to toy with Grandma's remark about Lucy needing an assistant. I imagined running errands in Carson's Riviera. My own room in the mansion. A room with a view of the mountains. Down the hall from Billy. He was an old grouch, but nice to look at ...

I reached for the telephone, stopped. Think! I would call Lucinda Desserita, ask her what she wanted me to do. It seemed a humiliation to give her even that.

I picked up the receiver, pressed it against my ear. The damn thing was dead. So I hiked a block to the 7-Eleven.

Cars were zipping in and out of parking spaces. Men who needed shaves buying coffee, pastries, newspapers; brats on bicycles feeding on soft drinks and junk foods, their dogs sitting by patiently. I located the phone around the corner on the store's south-facing brick wall. Plunked in a quarter.

Billy answered. I disguised my voice. "Is Lucy there?"

"Yes, Shandie, but she's outdoors with the kids. I'll have her call you back."

"I'm at a pay phone. Do you know what she wants me to do?"

"She'd probably prefer you hold on while I go get her."

I sighed. "Good idea."

I watched a couple of brattish boys argue over how to split a pile of candy as I waited for the witch to come on the line. When she did, I had trouble finding my voice.

"Hello, Shandie. Shandie ...?"

"Yeah."

"I assume you're calling to accept my offer." Her voice had a musical quality. To my ear, musical gloating.

"I'm a lousy housekeeper. Terrible. Ask my mother."

"I don't need a housekeeper. I have something else in mind. Something that suits you perfectly."

All these weeks torturing myself with visions of slopping toilets and the woman really did need an assistant? Someone to set appointments, run errands, do the paperwork? Handle the money. I could have jumped for joy. Until I heard what she said.

"I want you to take care of my children."

Chapter Eight

More Than a House

The brick wall I leaned against suddenly felt as unsubstantial as a balloon that was going down, me with it.

She wanted me to watch her brats? Like be a babysitter? It was so absurd, I laughed.

"You obviously don't know me. I can't stand kids."

"You obviously don't know yourself," came the musical response.

The woman sees me once and knows me better than I know myself. Maybe I could go on welfare? Collect food stamps. Wheel my belongings around in a shopping cart.

"I'm telling the truth," I said. "I hate kids." I flashed on the boy strutting in my hat, his sister parroting her mother, saying I owed them fifty-eight big ones.

"I'm confident they can handle it, but if doesn't appeal to you, I can always turn on that lawsuit again."

"Hey—" I stabbed a finger at the receiver, "let's get one thing straight. I'm not considering doing this because I owe you any money. It's just that real estate sales have been lousy and I need some time to figure out what career I'm going to pursue next. And about my wages—"

"Wages! You are one funny girl! Room and board. Which I should tack on to what you owe me, but stones and turnips and all that, I realize you might be strapped for cash."

I couldn't believe I was still on the phone taking this crap.

"When can you start?"

When elephants waltz! I wanted to yell.

To salt my wounds, Billy was coming tomorrow to help me move. I told Lucy I could handle it myself, but she insisted on sending him. Years ago I would have thrilled at the prospect of spending a few hours alone with Billy Sang Hightower. Before I learned what a tight-ass he was. I could picture him helping me move the dregs of my existence, snickering with a big told-you-so expression. Not a realistic picture; he wouldn't be that blatant. But I knew he would be thinking told-you-so.

I had a crush on Billy long before I became Carson's girl. All the young girls in Doubletree fantasized about him, as if he were a rock singer or a movie star. But I wasn't content with a mere fantasy. I built castles in my mind and tried to live in them.

I recalled a time when I tried to make one of my fantasies about Billy come true. It happened shortly after Carson divorced Roz, and we had fought. He left town. So I put on my tightest jeans and skimpiest halter top, a red one, and drove to Blue Acres to set my fantasy in action.

Leona said the man of my dreams was out in the woods, chopping firewood. Crazy man, it was August. He chopped wood for relaxation, Leona said. Then I knew he was crazy. But Billy was so handsome you could forgive him a range of idiosyncrasies.

I set out toward the stands of trees in the direction Leona had pointed. There was a kind of path through the trees, though it was doubtful Royal Guthrie Blue had planted with any particular design in mind. I passed blue spruce, birch, maple, juniper, scrub oak, and cottonwoods. Most of the path was shaded, but the sun managed to stick long fingers through the branches, scorching my head and shoulders as I stepped over fragrant beds of leaves, avoiding the occasional rock that jutted out of the ground. Above the cacophony of birds and insects, I heard the chop of an ax against wood and made my way toward the sound.

I first saw his white shirt hanging on the branch of a juniper tree. I was surprised the shirt wasn't on a hanger. Billy was ridiculously neat.

He was working in a cluster of scrub oak. Piles of wood cut in uniform lengths rested on the ground near the fat oak stump he was using for a chopping block. He straightened, held the ax crosswise as I came into view. His black hair, chest and face glistened with sweat. Lovely tawny skin. He looked concerned that I was a messenger with bad news.

"Those environmentalists catch you chopping down trees for fun, they'll string you up, Billy."

"It's firewood." He leaned the ax against a boulder near the piles of wood, removed the blue paisley band from his head and wiped his face and armpits. Save for the slant of his exotic brown eyes, he looked full-blooded Cherokee.

As were Carson and Leona, Billy was born in Oklahoma. His birthplace was Tahlequah, a town close to Tulsa. Billy had never met his father, and Carson said Billy didn't care if he ever did. His mother raised him. His father worked for the Bureau of Indian Affairs when Ling Sang married him, but he took to drinking and walked out before Billy was born, never to return. Ling eventually moved, first to San Francisco, later to Denver. She never got a divorce. She worked as a professional housekeeper until arthritis rendered her unemployable; then Billy quit high school and went to work as a gardener to provide for them both. He married young, then lost his bride in the accident that brought him and Carson together.

Carson offered to send him to school, but Billy declined. That old Chinese tradition of serving the person who saves you, for life, according to Leona. But Carson said that wasn't it. Billy was only about one-fourth Chinese and his mother was totally American-ized. He just preferred the simple life and had no use for a college degree. He was as bright as a whip without it, Carson said.

At first I tried some small talk, but Billy wasn't much for idle chatter. I knew he was taken with me by the way his eyes traveled my body. He always looked at me with a kind of hunger.

I told him something was wrong with my stereo. (True. The damn turntable had ceased to rotate. Likewise true, I could've taken the machine to Waxman's, where Carson had bought it.) Would he, Billy, be willing to come to my apartment and take a look at it?

"I'll fix us a small dinner," I added as enticement.

My plan was to buy some Chinese take-out, Billy would mess around with the stereo, we'd eat, the sun would sink behind the mountains, I would suggest we listen to some music on the radio, we'd start making out, moan and groan for awhile about how we shouldn't do this to Carson, then we'd hit the sack.

He narrowed his eyes, said nothing for a few moments. Working it out in his mind, I thought.

"Shandie ..." he finally said. "You're young, smart, and attractive. You're wasting your life."

An odd way of saying I should ditch Carson for him, I thought. "Maybe ..." I said coyly to encourage him to get specific.

"Have you ever thought of leaving Colorado?"

It took me a moment to switch channels. "What does that have to do with fixing my turntable?"

"You need more fixed than your turntable." He picked up the ax, threw it over his shoulder and smacked the log. Chainsaw up at the house, but macho man had to use an ax, to show off his muscle power.

I waited for him to say something else. What he'd said sounded like an insult, so I knew there had to be more. I walked around to face him.

"So you can't come?"

He seemed surprised I was still there.

"I work for Carson," he said grouchily.

"So? He dates other women." Which was the cause of our fight. I'd heard that Carson had spent a weekend in Vail with a runner-up in the Miss Colorado contest. When I confronted him, he said he was doing business with the young woman's father and had spent time with the entire family. Regina, who had ratted on him, was in Vail that weekend and saw him with Miss Beauty Queen at one of the nightclubs. She said they were "very cozy," danced, then left together, no family around. It was one of her life purposes to get me to break up with Carson. If Billy would show some interest, maybe I would.

"You must have other plans for tonight," I said to give him an out. Maybe he was free tomorrow night, or the next. Carson would be gone for five days.

"Yeah. I need to get this wood chopped."

"It's August, Billy."

"You're almost twenty-one, Shandie."

I was flattered he remembered that my birthday was two weeks away. "So?"

"You're old enough to become a woman."

What the hell did he think he was looking at? "I have to be twenty-one to be a woman officially?"

"You have to start caring about yourself."

"What's that supposed to mean?"

I was sincerely thrown by the remark. My mother was always telling me I cared only about myself.

He chopped off another branch, cut it into three precise pieces, stacked it. He seemed to be struggling with how to respond to my question, as if what he'd said was perfectly clear. Man pops out with a puzzler, then refuses to explain. Billy was handsome, but if I succeeded in luring him into my dream castle, he might very well drive me nuts.

Finally he stopped messing with the wood. "If you cared about yourself, you'd get on with your life. Quit chasing after a man who is never going to ..." He paled, turned, resumed chopping.

Me quit chasing him!

"Carson takes damn good care of me, Billy. He never promised me more. It's not like I'm waiting around for him to marry me. I don't care about getting married anyway, I'm too independent. I'm sorry if I insulted you by asking you to come look at my stereo. Like it would be disloyal for you to do that."

"Bring it out," he said. "I'll give it a look."

"Fine, I will."

I took it to Waxman's. And that was the last time I flirted with Billy Sang Hightower. The big self-righteous snob.

And now he was coming to help me pick up the pieces of the life I'd squandered, in his eyes.

He did not come alone. He brought "Mr." Floy. (Floy was his first name, but unreasonably, Lucy called him Mr. Floy.) Lucy's uncle did nothing to help. He just stood around with a dazed expression. Geezer looked as strong as an ox, but he was old, white-haired, and a slob, one suspender hanging around his hip. A stark contrast to Mr. Neat, Billy in his starched white shirt, those polished boots and jeans with well-defined creases.

Acting as if he was in a big hurry, Billy swept into the townhouse and asked me to show him everything that needed to go. He had an attitude about my clothes. He must have walked from one bedroom to the other forty times, shaking his head as he peered into the closets. He spread his arms and looked at the ceiling with an expression that said, "Who can understand women?"

He said he didn't think there'd be enough room in our vehicles to carry all of my clothes and shoes in one trip. An exaggeration, I thought, because he'd come in Sid Winkowski's pickup, which had a camper shell on the back. He was almost right. Both vehicles were filled to capacity. We worked swiftly, got the job done with little strain and almost no conversation. All went smoothly until he picked up my special velvet-lined box. I don't know why I didn't let him take it out to my car; he wasn't snoopy, he wouldn't remove the ribbons, open it, peek inside. But I yelled, "Don't touch that!" and ran over and rescued it as if it were a live thing that would die on the spot if touched by another person.

He shoved the box at me. I mumbled that there were some delicate things inside.

Then we had a disagreement when he insisted we clean up the joint before we left.

"It's not that dirty," I protested.

"All those papers, that stuff in the kitchen."

Bunch of half-full boxes of cereal and other garbage; nothing I wanted.

"Someone's going to come and clean before the place goes on the market," I said. "They can dump this stuff then. It's what they get paid for."

He walked past me into the kitchen and began stuffing debris into a green plastic bag.

"You could show a little respect," he said.

"For garbage?"

He gave me one of his sad looks.

I was glad I didn't have to ride in the truck with him and that weird Mr. Floy. Show a little respect for garbage!

As we cut across the city, I tried to convince myself I was embarking on a grand pilgrimage that would change me in significant ways. Maybe in a year I would look in the mirror and be unable to recognize myself for all the maturity in my face. Maybe I'd sprout crow's feet at the corners of my eyes, like an older woman who laughs often and easily. I'd be so different I'd have to change my name. Maybe I'd be a Constance or a Melody.

By the time we turned onto the Interstate, I had come down to Earth. Screw a whole year, it would be a miracle if I lasted two months. I'd be over the shock of Carson dying in another month and would then be in a better position to land a job of substance, a real job. In the meantime it was okay with me if Lucy provided room and board; she owed me at least that much.

If the real estate market was still in low gear in a couple of months, I'd find another sales job. I liked sales. You could set your own hours and the earning potential was higher than the moon. I'd find a company that paid me a draw on commissions, say, a thousand a month. A company that offered a big fat advance to start.

As for my so-called job at Blue Acres, brats the ages of Jennifer and Alex took long naps, didn't they? I could read them a story or two, take them to the park now and then (sunbathe in my bikini, turn a bronzy brown), and the rest of the time they'd play with their toys. Two months would zip by in nothing flat.

The sun was high and bright in a cloudless sky when we drove in tandem through the wrought-iron gates at Blue Acres. The grounds were a luscious green, the trees had filled out and a variety of flowers were in bloom. I was so busy scanning the scenery I almost missed the fact that Billy drove past the mansion. He was parking in front of the guest cabins! I slammed my hand on the horn, gunned the engine and raced the Ford over the gravel.

Not far from the mansion, surrounded by mature oak and maple trees, the seven log cabins were arranged in cockeyed fashion. Each cabin had a tiny porch. Marigolds and petunias graced the walkways, and bird feeders hung from the lower limbs of several trees. Finches, sparrows, blackbirds, having a party. The beauty of the setting was totally lost on me. I jumped out of the Bomb before the engine stopped its sputtering and coughing.

"Hey!" I yelled. "Aren't I staying in the house?"

Billy was already out of the pickup; he shut the door. "Count your blessings. She's turning it into a kind of hospice. Place is going to be infested with women."

So. He still didn't see me as a full-fledged woman.

He went around and unlatched the back of the truck as Mr. Floy stumbled off in the direction of the mansion, suspenders dangling around his hips. I wondered if Lucy was going to move all of her weird relatives to Blue Acres. Grandma said she had a huge family.

"Hospital? Who's sick?"

"Hospice. It's similar to a boardinghouse." He began unloading boxes, setting them on the grass. "Not really a boardinghouse. I don't know what you would call it. Women will be coming and going. I moved into one of the cabins myself."

"You're not thinking of quitting ..."

He looked surprised. Shook his head. "I promised Carson I would help take care of his family."

"You knew he was dying?"

"We knew he would die someday. We talked about it."

That Billy had moved into one of the cabins raised my spirits a little.

As we continued to unpack both vehicles, I asked him about the retreat Lucy was staging. Grandma had said it was going to be a big production. But then, Grandma thought going to the grocery store in Elizabeth was a big production. So why, I asked Billy, had Lucy fired half the staff? Seemed to me she'd need more workers, not less. Some of the participants would work in lieu of payment, Billy said. He frowned, shook his head, mumbled, "Bunch of women running the place."

"Some are paying to come to her retreat?"

For the moment, Billy was the only one moving boxes; I was following him around, trying to get to the bottom of this mystery.

"She has to do something to generate income. She's forty-two and got those two kids to raise."

"Yeah, but she's loaded."

"Oh? You have some inside information?" He climbed into the back of the truck; I waited until he emerged, lugging a box of books.

"Come on, Billy. Airplane insurance. Carson's oil and gas wells. Her property in Nevada. This ..." I waved my hand to take in the whole of Blue Acres. "And all that Blue Oil and Gas stock."

"Carson's lifestyle cost a lot of money, Shandie. Supporting two homes, the travel, and he wasn't exactly frugal. You can't judge a person's financial status by appearances."

"Well, the insurance ..."

"He didn't have any."

We heard a door slam. Sid came out of the mansion, followed by the two urchins and a black sheep dog. Billy said the dog belonged to Alex and Jennifer. Sid waved at us, then the crew disappeared into the garage through a side door. One of the stall doors rose with a whine and out slid a lemon-colored Fleetwood Cadillac.

"Sid get a new car?"

"Belongs to Lucy."

"Please." I parked my hands on my hips. "You don't have enough vehicles around here, what with your Jeep, Sid's pickup, and Carson's Land Rover and Riviera."

"He sold the Rover years ago." Billy went over to the cabin nearest the mansion and opened the door. Boxes were stacked all over the place, ready to move inside. I watched the Fleetwood until it disappeared from sight, then went inside my new home, such as it was.

One large room, a bathroom with no tub—just a shower—and a kitchenette. Scant and boring furniture, double bed, brown easy chair, small table with two ancient wooden chairs in need of paint, a dresser, and shelves for books, I guessed—four wooden planks set on cinder blocks. Teensy closet. Place smelled of Pine-sol and I saw no dust. Someone had worked the place over recently.

In the seventies Carson often entertained guests from out of town, and they stayed in these cabins. He used to throw parties, two, three times a month, and take his visitors to Vail or Aspen to ski. Sometimes people in Doubletree stayed overnight in the cabins, when they were too drunk to drive home. After the oil business hit the skids in the eighties, there wasn't much to celebrate on the weekends; but someone had kept the cabins in good repair, probably Carson, hoping the hog wild days of entertaining would return.

"Lucy said you might need two cabins," Billy said.

"One for a bedroom and one for a living room, right?"

"One for a closet, looks like to me."

I spent the entire day unpacking. Sid and Billy moved my bed, plus the one in the spare cabin, down to a storage room in the basement of the mansion; then Sid erected a metal bar that stretched the length of the second cabin, so I'd have a place to hang my clothes. When Sid started work on the metal bar, Billy disappeared.

Late afternoon I saw Lucy come out of the house. She was wearing a suit and carrying a purse. Not so much as a glance at my cabin. She drove away in her fancy Fleetwood. I had been glancing over my shoulder all day, expecting her to come do a big Welcome to Blue Acres! number on me, but I was spared.

Sid had said Leona would have dinner ready by six, but I decided to skip that scene. Lucy was home by then. Still raw with feelings of defeat for having given into her, I wanted to postpone, for as long as I could, seeing her gloat.

Around nine o'clock my stomach began to feed on itself, so I went up to the house and sneaked into the kitchen. I could hear voices nearby; light spilled in from the hallway. I eased open the refrigerator door, grabbed some cheese and bologna, hurried outdoors and gobbled it down.

As I began the trek back, I heard some faint, mournful guitar music. There was a light on in the cabin farthest from mine. Had to be Billy's cabin. Earlier I'd seen the geezer, Mr. Floy, go inside the cabin I assumed was his.

I walked toward the light. Billy was sitting on a lawn chair on his small porch. When he saw me, he stopped strumming and looked embarrassed.

"I didn't know you played guitar."

He plunked a few strings. "Some say I don't."

I sat down cross-legged on a patch of grass in front of him. He fooled around, strummed a few idle chords, then leaned the guitar against the log wall, picked up his beer, asked me if I wanted one.

While he was inside, I realized I was feeling better than I had in weeks. Maybe the stay here wouldn't be half bad. There'd be many evenings like this one, listening to Billy strum his guitar under a velvet sky studded with diamonds. Sooner or later a man and a woman alone under the stars would do more than fiddle around with a guitar, I couldn't help thinking.

As we sipped bottled Coors, I tried to pump him about what I could expect, living here. He gave vague answers but seemed a lot friendlier than he had earlier. Maybe he was lonely. The loss of Carson leaving a hole in his gut almost as big as the one in my life.

"You okay talking about Carson now?"

He squirmed in his chair. "Yeah, I'm okay."

"I'm still not feeling it," I lied. "I think I'm still in shock over the mess he left me in."

"He wasn't very tidy about the way he left things."

The longest sentence he'd uttered since I'd sat down on the grass. I was afraid to speak again, worried I would break whatever spell had loosened his tongue. The moment I let pass was threaded with insect noises and wafts of cool air. The ground beneath me was cool and damp. For the chance to talk with Billy, I would have sat on a block of ice.

"I was really shocked he didn't have a will. He promised me he'd take care of me, and he didn't even leave me the town-home."

"Don't feel like the Lone Ranger."

The curtains drawn over the window behind him obscured the light, so I couldn't see his face clearly, but I had the impression he instantly regretted saying that. I jumped on it.

"Screwed you, too, huh?"

He was peeling bits of label off the Coors bottle. Sticking the pieces into his shirt pocket. Mustn't leave a mess on the porch.

"I don't know screwed. He said he would leave me the house."

"Oh, wow! How can you work for Lucy when he broke a promise like that?"

He shrugged. "She needs the help. If he had kept his word, I'd be in hot water. It would have taken all of my savings—more, to keep the place up. What would I do with a house that big anyway."

"You could have sold it, Billy. It's worth a million, easy."

"I don't need a million."

I believed him. Billy had never been one to get excited about material goods. Something told me he'd wanted the house for the house itself, whether it was worth a million or two cents. But the thought went by too fast to process, like when you think you hear a jet and look up and see empty sky.

Later I would understand that the pain of loss for Billy was tied to neither the house nor its monetary value. That house stood as a symbol for Carson's honor and integrity. Carson cheated us out of more than money and property, you will see.

Because I was yet to understand, I said: "You just want to stay here for the rest of your life, live in that dinky cabin, and be Lucy's houseboy?"

He got up so fast he banged his guitar against the post, grabbed it before it fell. Said he was tired. Then he went inside and closed the door, leaving me there on the grass. "Thanks for the chat," I said to the porch. "It really made me feel welcome."

Chapter Nine

A Prince of a Guy

I was so hungry when I woke up Saturday morning, if I'd had any Tabasco sauce I would have eaten one of my shoes. I did have coffee and fixed some, but it only made the problem worse. The Green Bomb was parked just outside the cabin. I threw on sweats and drove to Archie's store and bought donuts, potato chips, popcorn, Hostess Twinkies, a package of Colby cheese, and Diet Cokes. I saw no one when I left the grounds, not a soul when I returned, but I knew wherever they were, they were patting their stomachs after a big breakfast of eggs, bacon, toast, and potatoes. Food isn't everything. I felt a kind of superiority in putting off going up to the house. Let them all know I valued privacy and could take care of myself just fine.

I'd already arranged everything in the two cabins the best way possible; but to kill time I switched things around, only to return them to their original positions. There was nothing I could do to make the place look like anything but what it was: temporary quarters. Most of my goods were still in boxes in the spare cabin.

Nothing but cartoons and bad movies on TV, so I leafed through some of the books displayed on the makeshift shelves next to the bed. Displayed is the right word. I had historical books, books about politics and business, and several trendy biographies. Books I'd bought to impress Carson. I'd glance through them, enough to get the gist, then try to talk to him about them, as if I'd read every page. A waste of breath. Carson was seldom interested in discussing books. He would say, "That's interesting—is that a new dress? Lovely, lovely ..." Remembering this, I felt like crying.

After a long hot shower, I settled on the bed with a paperback novel by Mary Higgins Clark, sacks of junk food surrounding me. Now and then I got up and peered out the windows. Perfect view of the mansion from the window above the sink in the kitchenette. I saw everyone at one time or another, but no one came to welcome me or tell me to go to hell.

Sid arrived around one and lugged some boards into the garage. Soon, Billy joined him. I heard a lot of pounding. When I finally ventured out to the porch to sit in the sunshine, the kid's dog paid me a visit. I gave him some popcorn that was too salty for my taste. He liked it so well I dumped what remained in the sack out on the ground and he snarfed it down.

I stroked his black coat. "What am I doing here?" I asked him and got a sorrowful look. "All I have left are potato chips and I don't think those are good for you."

I could still hear the pounding in the garage. Then someone yelled my name. Leona. She waved. "Leg of lamb for dinner!" she yelled, then disappeared back into the house. The dog took off in a fast trot, as if the cook had announced horse would be on the menu and he was invited.

Around three I began to dress for dinner. I changed clothes six times. Billy would be wearing his uniform of white shirt and jeans; Leona would be dressed like an ad for a second-hand store, and Lucy ... That was the thing. What would she wear? I decided on black slacks and a tailored beige blouse with black trim. Onyx earrings trimmed in gold. I brushed my hair, touched up my makeup, and took three deep breaths before I walked outside.

I entered the mansion through the double doors and heard voices in the kitchen. The rest of the house was quiet. Lucy was probably upstairs counting her tiny stack of gold, poor thing.

Curious about Grandma's reports about the terrible things the mistress of Blue Acres had done to the house, I crept from room to room. Carson's elegant antique furniture, his paintings, and expensive knickknacks were gone. As if Lucy had purposefully stripped the place of anything that reminded her of him. Nothing in the living room save for what appeared to be the same folding chairs used at the memorial service, and an Oriental rug. The chairs were stacked against the walls on either side of the fireplace. Nothing in the den, not even a throw rug on the polished hardwood floor. The sun room seemed the same as I remembered it. A collection of white wicker furniture, jungle of plants.

In place of Carson's antique table and chairs in the dining room were two immense medieval-style tables of dark wood with matching high-backed chairs, seats covered with a wine-colored fabric, tacked down with brass fittings. The tables were so large there was barely enough room to walk around them. The china cabinet and sideboard were still in place; the witch hadn't sold those.

No furniture in the library, though the shelves were still crammed with books. I spotted a telephone and was tempted to call Grandma, but Mom would probably answer and cause my ear to throw up. The smell of hot juicy meat drew me down the hall. Alex appeared at the entrance to the kitchen. Save for my mangled black straw hat and a smear of something purple on his cheeks, the tot was naked. He screamed, grabbed hold of my hat with both hands, and scampered back into the kitchen. I walked in there.

The room was a cluttered mess. Stack of dirty dishes and pans in and around the sink, potatoes boiling atop the range, tray of homemade rolls on the counter, covered with a white towel. The bib apron Leona had on over her jeans and shirt was blotched with dried food.

The naked boy squealed, ran out to the mud room and peered around the corner.

The girl was on a stool next to the butcher-block table, watching Leona chop vegetables. She had on a candy-striped dress with belled sleeves. Long black hair like her mother's, tied at the crown with a red ribbon. I noticed her distinctive bluish-green eyes again. Damn, they looked like Carson's eyes.

She said, "You our new *au pair*?"

"Your what?"

"It's a fancy French word for nanny," Leona explained.

To test my new authority, I ordered the prissy little thing to go outside and play with her brother. She slid off the stool, stuck her nose in the air and marched toward the dining room.

"I'm telling Mama you're a bitch!" she yelled, then cut through the room and ran for the stairs.

"That kid's got the mouth of an oil rigger," Leona said as she moved to the sink. She ran water over a bunch of celery. "So how do you like it so far?"

"Like what?"

She arranged the celery on the chopping block and began slicing it. "Living here. Your cabin. I was tempted to move into one of those dollhouses myself, but I'm up so early and down so late it makes more sense to stay put."

I perched on the stool the brat had vacated. Leona plunked down a bunch of green onions and handed me a knife.

"You want me to cut them up?"

"No, I want you to play me a tune. Of course, I want you cut them up." She threw a handful of celery pieces into a huge stainless steel bowl on the counter behind her, then started slicing carrots.

"I'm not exactly dressed ..."

"Clean aprons in the drawer." She pointed.

"I'll be careful," I muttered. What if Billy came in and saw me in an apron?

"Yuck."

"Find a bug?"

"They're slimy."

"You peel off the slimy part. How old are you? You never touched a slimy green onion? About time you did. You have to get through the slime to get to the good." She laughed. "Listen to me. Trying to make a profound comparison between the peeling of onions and life. That's being around Lucy. I best leave the profundities to her." She laughed again, then looked up sharply. "Hey—what I said sounded kind of like a poem, didn't it? Here—you can chop a little closer to the heads and leave some of the green. It's good for digestion."

"So Lucy's always saying profound things."

"Don't get her started."

"How'd she meet Carson?"

"At her restaurant. She and her brother used to own a place near Reno called Xavier's. They sold it after she married Car."

The dog ambled into the kitchen and whined. Leona left to check his food dish, returning with his water bowl. She filled it, took it out to the mud room. "Will you look at him? He's lapping it up like there was no tomorrow." She came back and inspected the green onions, tossed them in the bowl and handed me a cucumber.

"Leave on the green."

"So what about this retreat business?"

She reached for the pack of cigarettes in the pocket of her shirt, poked one in her mouth, snapped her lighter. "All I know is, she's into New ... metaphysics. Don't say 'New Age' around her. Whatever you call it, it's a bunch of hooey."

"So why did she fire Olson and the housekeeper?" I asked, worried I'd be expected to babysit, cook, clean.

Olson wasn't fired, he quit; moved to California. And losing Ardell was no loss because she ate like a pig and was a lousy housekeeper. Lucy was going to hire "temporaries" to help until the retreat started.

"Seems you'll be needing extra help worse than ever then."

Leona stubbed out her cigarette in the ashtray on the counter. Said Lucy had all that worked out. "Some of the women coming will help. Until then, we can pull together to keep the place afloat."

As she tossed the salad, she said I was expected to eat all of my meals at the mansion, and my job would begin officially on

Monday. I would have one day off a week, Saturday or Sunday, depending on Lucy's schedule.

"And you'll be the one relaying her orders."

"Oh, don't be so serious. We're real casual around here. I'm just passing on what I heard. I'm sure she'll have a talk with you later."

"Can't wait," I mumbled.

When the lamb, mint sauce, rolls, salad, and potatoes were ready, Leona skipped out to the mud room and clanged the dinner bell. She clanged and clanged. I clapped my hands over my ears. She returned looking pleased with herself.

"Lucy says whoever's in charge of the food is plenty powerful ..." she thrust a fist in the air, "and I oughta let'er rip! Say's I'm the high priestess of the kitchen."

"But that New Age stuff is all a bunch of hooey, right?"

She looked puzzled, then laughed. "Oh, yeah! Well, I guess I like some parts of it."

I helped her transfer the food from kitchen to dining room. She told me to sit down, she'd be back in a jiffy. My stomach gurgled at the smells. I was about to stick my finger in the bowl of mashed potatoes when Jennifer ran into the room.

Glaring, she settled in a chair opposite me.

"Mama says you're gonna be a GROWTH experience for me and Alex, so we're just going to have to put up with you."

"Screw you," I said under my breath.

Lucy arrived looking stunning in a faded purple granny dress. The kind of woman, I thought begrudgingly, who would look fabulous in a garment made of flour sacks.

Then came Billy. He had on a fresh white shirt. His hair shone. That ridiculous ponytail. He nodded at me; I returned the nod.

Sid followed. About six feet tall with a barrel chest, Sid had long sideburns, a bald dome, and a flamboyant mustache. Leona had said earlier that he would continue to work for Lucy on a contract basis, fixing and building things, and servicing her brother's airplane when Steffen came to visit. Sid was married and had grown kids. He boarded horses at his ranch near Kiowa and was going to expand the business to absorb the cut in income.

Mr. Floy shuffled in with Alex. Hat was gone, but the boy was still naked. Eight around one table and still room for ten more. The food was passed.

I said, "If I would've come to the table without my clothes on when I was a kid, my parents would've taken a strap to my butt."

Lucy shrugged. "People are different. Pass the butter, Leona."

Jennifer fanned her face with her hand. "Sure is hot in here. Maybe I'll take off my clothes."

Halfway through the meal when Sid was expounding on the history of Elbert County, Jennifer's head disappeared beneath the table. A moment later, up it popped, along with her bare foot. She wiggled her foot. Alex stuck his bare foot up on the table, wiggled it. Both children were giggling so loudly you could barely hear what Sid was saying. Billy caught my eye, winked. Like I was supposed to think the darlings were cute. The little rotters had it in for me was what I saw. I pictured tying them to the back of the Bomb, taking them for a hot, fast ride through Doubletree. This thought made me smile, but I quickly adopted a frown again so that Billy wouldn't think I agreed that this foot-wiggling behavior was innocent fun.

After we devoured the butterscotch pudding, everyone helped clear the table. Then Lucy lit three white candles in a brass candelabrum, and Leona served coffee. The men drank one cup each, then rose to leave, the brats going with them to inspect the dog house Sid and Billy had built for "Bugle," the mutt who liked popcorn.

I rose to join Leona in the kitchen. Washing dishes was one of the last things I wanted to do. The last thing was to stay in this room with Lucy.

"Stay." She pointed a finger.

I eased back down.

Without preface, she said, "My kids live by few rules. They are not allowed to harm the fowl of the air or the beast of the field, and that includes other human beings. I don't allow them to damage things, and they are expected to clean up the messes they make. Other than that, they are free spirits and I expect them to remain free spirits." She took a sip of coffee.

"Okay ..." I waited for the other rules.

She appeared to be deep in thought. "Mind off in the tulies," Grandma would say. I'd seen this same intense expression on Lucy's face before; the day of the memorial service, and during dinner. Like she was on the verge of revealing some universal mystery. Regina had called her beautiful. I supposed she was, for an older woman. Her dark eyes seemed filled with light. A face artists would sell their souls to capture on canvas. They'd have to touch up her neck, I thought smugly.

"This," she said. I jumped, but she seemed unaware. "When my kids make mistakes, I never call them bad. I don't believe in bad or evil. People make mistakes only out of ignorance or inexperience."

I assumed she was telling me I was never to use the "b" word when her snots behaved like demons. Would it be okay to call them ignorant? I did not ask.

The sun was setting. The glow through the windows across the hall in the den dusted the room with a soft grayish-gold shine, but the candles provided a stronger light. Huge chandelier above us, off. I wondered if Mrs. Blue was trying to save on the electric bill. Her with her big financial problems.

I thought I heard the kids in the kitchen.

"Questions?"

I jumped again.

I had questions aplenty. Were Jennifer and Alex adopted?

She combed her fingers through her hair and gazed in the direction of the foyer. Then she nailed me with a look that demanded a response.

"Leona says you hate the term 'New Age.'"

She raised both eyebrows. "What's new about it?"

I stared at her blankly.

"I don't object to the term, I just don't want anyone using it to describe my work. You see the re-emergence of some very old ideas, and it's hot stuff and the wheeler dealers are hot to turn a profit, so they come up with this term, or someone does; and they grab it because they need a catchword, a slogan, something to trigger that lust for something new, something someone else has got that you don't, and as soon as it's clear it's getting popular, you have to have it. Now, in whatever form is being pushed at you, you don't think, you don't investigate, you just hear the term 'new age' and you begin to salivate and you open your pocketbook and you sit down in a chair at a psychic fair and get your palm read so you can say at the office you're into this wonderful outre thing. Soon you hear it's passe. New Age is nothing but cheap thrills. No thinking person would be caught dead wearing a crystal or paying an astrologer for a chart. So you say, oh yes, I dabbled in it, ha ha, but it was only fun. Nothing of substance. You write it off. What happened? You got sucked into the commercialism. You didn't try and find out where these ..." she made quotations marks with her fingers, "'new age' ideas came from; you just opened your mouth like a baby bird and sucked in the plastic worm."

She squinted at me, as if to discern my reaction, then added, "There is a wealth of ancient wisdom behind all the trappings for anyone with enough curiosity and gumption to explore it. It's not new at all. It's old. Very old."

"I never went to any psychic fairs and got my palm read," I said. "or any of that other stuff."

"Of course not. A savvy person like you."

Leona was clanking pans out in the kitchen. Suddenly Alex screamed, then Leona yelled, "You get down from there this instant, Jennifer Blue!"

A normal mother would have gone to see what all the commotion was about, but Lucy seemed oblivious. Such a look on her face. I was afraid she was gearing up to channel some dead spirit.

"Any more questions?" she said dreamily.

That dreamy look annoyed me. Like she was above everything common in life. New Age was even too "outre" for her. High-sounding bitch.

"Are Jennifer and Alex adopted?"

That wiped the dreamy look off her face.

"You don't think they look like me and their father?"

That was the real question: Who was the father?

"Well, the adoption agency could've ..."

"They were not adopted. They were planned. Why do you ask?"

I should've said "just curious," but this secret children business bothered me so much my mouth took on a life of its own. "When he was married before, he said he tried everything to get his wife pregnant. But he had a super low sperm count. He said it would be a miracle if he ever got her pregnant, like it was ninety-nine percent impossible."

Shut up, I commanded myself, but the words were already out there, dancing around, kicking up their heels.

"It only takes one," she said. In response to my puzzled look, she added, "one sperm."

I flashed on Carson insisting on using condoms the past few years — not because he was worried about getting me pregnant, but because of the AIDS scare. But if he got her pregnant (twice!) ...

Was he Briana's father?

Impossible. He wouldn't have encouraged me to give up his own daughter. He would've married me.

Then I remembered he was already married to Lucy when I got pregnant.

But that wasn't the point, dammit. I'd gone over all this a hundred times. It was doubtful I slept with Carson even once during the time I got pregnant. Positively, I slept with Dillinger several times. Dillinger accepted total responsibility, even though he was married. If he'd had doubts, would he have agreed so readily to raise Briana? And his wife went along with it when she probably wanted to scratch my eyes out. Would she take on a baby that wasn't her husband's?

"Is something wrong?"

I shook my head. Felt heat on my face.

"Any more questions? No?" She crossed her arms over her chest, cocked her head. "I have one."

I don't know if she stretched taller or I shrunk. Definitely she was looking down at me.

"I'm still trying to figure out why Carson loaned you all that money."

So. She wasn't going to let it drop. Leona, Billy, someone had told her about Carson and me. She knew, and now she was needling me, trying to trick me into confessing. Then what? Boil me in oil? But if she knew, why did she want me to take care of her snots? Because she was cheap. She saw a way to avoid paying a real *au pair*. Figured I'd do it gratis out of guilt. She forces me out of my townhome, waits until I'm almost dead broke, then offers me the job of a lifetime.

"I told you. He gave it to me."

"Which, if true, makes it all the more mysterious. A loan is one thing. I can understand him wanting to help someone in trouble. But why would he give ..."

"Maybe he liked me," I snapped.

"Fifty-eight thousand is an awfully strong like."

This time when I rose to leave, she said nothing.

My first thought Sunday morning was: get the hell out while the getting is good. But where the hell would I go?

After downing half a pot of coffee, I regained my former perspective. I wouldn't have to stay long. I could check the want ads in the newspapers every week and work in some interviews. The job market was flooded with college students in the summer, so maybe I'd have to stay longer than two months, but the important thing was having a plan.

And screw Leona's edict that I had to eat all of my meals at the house. (Screw making myself available for more of Lucy's harassment.) I drove to Elizabeth and bought enough food to last me a week.

I spent the day reading and watching the tube. Preachers screaming for money, and a couple of old movies. I resisted looking out the windows or going outside to sit on the porch.

When the dinner bell clanged that evening, I was building a cheese and salami sandwich. I glanced out the window over the sink and saw Jennifer and Alex running down the path, Bugle at their heels. A moment later the brats pounded on my door. I yanked it open.

"You're late for dinner!"

"I'm eating here tonight."

"All by yourself?"

"No, I have a little green Martian visiting. He's under the bed."

The boy clapped his hands over his mouth.

"She's just kidding, Alex," his sister said. "You won't get any chocolate cake if you don't come," she said to me.

"I hate chocolate cake. So why don't you kids take a powder?"

"What's a pow—"

I shut the door, ignored their complaints, and soon they gave up the battle. I drew the curtains over the windows and turned on the tube again.

The sun eased behind the mountains. I switched on a lamp. Peered out the curtains. Admitted to myself I was watching for Billy. Under the stars Friday night, it had seemed that he and I could develop at least a friendship. We both had been hung out to dry by the most important man in our lives. A man we both had loved and respected. Billy might be able to resolve the conflict alone, but I needed a friend, someone who could help me understand why Car had left me in such a mess. The man does everything to insure that I will remain "his girl;" he marries behind my back, has two children, leaves me zip in his will. His secret wife discovers he's given me a lot of money, decides it's a loan, and demands I watch her brats for a year to square up the so-called debt.

The most bizarre outcome was that I was here, as if in agreement that she was right. While it was true that I was without viable options, in some strange way I had felt drawn to Blue Acres. Maybe because it seemed impossible to build a new life until I resolved the mystery of why Carson had left me in this bind. I was sure Billy could shed some light on the mystery, if only he would.

My feeling of despondency grew. Imprisoned at the North Pole and forced to chop down a glacier with a teaspoon began to seem more feasible than to stay at Blue Acres for any duration without Billy's friendship.

Around midnight my black thoughts reached critical mass. I tore out into the night and marched over to his cabin, with only the spotlights near the mansion to guide my way.

It was dark inside his cabin; he was probably in bed, possibly asleep, but I was beyond such trivial concerns. I rapped on the door. He answered quickly and asked me to wait until he put something on. I wasn't surprised when he appeared in jeans and white shirt. He stepped out on the porch, pulling the door shut behind him.

"What's up?" He spoke in almost a whisper, as if to show respect for the insects that might be slumbering nearby.

"I need to talk," I said in my regular voice.

I sat down, rested my feet on the porch stairs. After a moment, he joined me, sitting a safe distance away. I stared at the outlines of trees, barely visible in the pale glow cast by the spotlights around the mansion. Not all of the insects were slumbering. Crickets were chirping up a storm. Breezes sighed through the trees. I brushed hair away from my face.

"I'm sorry I called you Lucy's houseboy the other night."

"Hmmm."

My eyes began to swell with tears. He was thinking what a weirdo I was for waking him up when I could have saved the apology for tomorrow. His hands were on his knees, his gaze fixed straight ahead. Probably praying I would leave and put him out of his misery.

"Say something."

"I accept your apology."

"Oh, dammit, Billy, it's more than that. I feel awful! Somehow I was able to keep Carson's death at arms-length all those weeks I was trying to find a job, but now, being here, I feel him gone something fierce. I'm so mad at him for leaving me in this mess, I don't think I'll ever be able to grieve properly."

Unable to contain my tears, I bowed my head to my knees.

"You'll get over it in time, Shandie. We'll all get over it."

I jerked up my head and stared.

"Easy for you to say! You didn't lose everything. Sure, he lied to you about the house, but you didn't even want it."

Though he moved not a muscle, I felt him increase the distance between us.

"Shandie ... I don't want you to tell anyone about him promising me the house. He told me that before he married Lucy. He had good reason to change his mind."

"Yeah, he was a prince of a guy."

"Yes, he was."

Tears streamed my face. Never had I felt so alone, even when I was alone. If there had been an ounce of compassion in Billy's soul he would have taken me in his arms, or at least placed a comforting hand on my shoulder. It was idiocy to think we could ever be friends. Carson lied, he left me in the lurch, but he was always quick to comfort me when I was hurting. This man had ice in his veins.

I jumped up and ran into the darkness.

Chapter Ten

Something in the Air

I tore into my spare cabin, flipped on the light, and fell on my knees, in front of my luggage. Hands on the largest suitcase, I bowed my head and babbled incoherently, as if to invoke an incantation that would transform the bag into a magic carpet. Oh, how I wanted to flee! I visualized throwing what I could into the Bomb and taking off—where? Anywhere but here! I thought hysterically. I collapsed on the floor and sobbed. A woman with guts would leave, whether or not she had a destination.

By the time I crawled into bed, I knew the anger and disappointment I'd felt toward Billy was a mile or ten removed from what really bothered me. The truth cut through my brain like a sword. It wasn't so much the mess Carson had left me in that drove me to seek comfort with Billy, it wasn't Car's failure to provide for me financially that haunted my nights. What had me in shambles was learning about his secret life, his secret children, his lies about why he had used condoms (it only takes one!), his absolute certainty that he was not Briana's father—because we hadn't slept together during the time I got pregnant, he insisted—assuring me that if there'd been even the slightest doubt, he would have jumped at the chance of fatherhood; after all, was there anything he wanted more than children? But not like this; I was so young, so beautiful, I had my whole life ahead of me, it would be a shame to saddle myself with a baby ...

These thoughts left in their wake a kind of cruel peace. I could stop chasing Billy. If he swept me in his arms and declared undying love, it wouldn't heal the wound inside me. Nothing would, nothing could, ever.

I settled down with this cruel peace, certain that by morning, as always, the pain I felt would be gone, forgotten, as would memory of having succumbed to such thoughts. It had happened before, it would happen again, as surely as the sun shines on the good and the evil alike.

Not long after I fell asleep, a loud noise jarred me awake. Someone was at the door. I groaned and burrowed into the covers. But the nervy someone knocked again, harder. A child giggled. So it was them! I flipped back the covers. I would set the little rotters straight right now: I was a late riser. And today was Memorial Day, which Leona had obviously forgotten when she'd said my "job" would begin on Monday. I flung on my robe and jerked open the door.

"Listen, you little ..."

"Good morning, Shandie."

She was dressed in a gray suit with a smart beige blouse. Jennifer clung to one hand, Alex clutched the other.

"I'm not even awake," I said, squinting against the rude glare of morning light.

"I thought Leona told you ..." Mrs. Blue reiterated that my hours were from seven to five, six days a week. At times I would be required to watch the children round the clock; for example, when she flew to Reno on business.

"But this is Memorial Day," I protested.

Why weren't they at the cemetery? Then I remembered there was no grave. As far as I knew, there wasn't even an urn full of

Carson's ashes. So, why weren't they inside the mansion, praying for his soul?

"I consider most holidays irrelevant," she said and checked her watch. She was going to meet with the Blue Oil and Gas board of directors in the main offices in Castle Rock, and expected the "dreary business" would take most of the day to resolve.

She gestured at the bird feeder on the maple tree in front of my cabin. "It's almost empty. Leona can show you where she keeps the bird seed."

"Hey ..." I tapped my chest. "I'm the *au pair*."

She smiled. "You misunderstand. Everyone must pitch in and do whatever needs to be done. If you are ever to become a Daughter of Light you must attend to the details as well as the more glorious functions, such as looking after our tiny friends."

She bent and kissed "our tiny friends," told them to be "fun and amusing children," then walked up the path toward the mansion, swinging her hips. She turned once to wave and blow a kiss.

"I'm not even dressed," I lamented.

"Yes, you are," the girl said. "You have on your pajamas and robe."

Both brats were dressed in bib-overalls and pastel T-shirts. Jennifer's hair was braided. No ribbons.

"I thought you were a fancy dresser."

"Last week I was a lady. This week I'm a tomboy. I alternate."

I looked at Alex. "I haven't heard you say one word. All you do is yell?"

He clenched both fists and let rip with a scream that reddened his face and brought him up on his toes.

"Cut that out!"

"Can if he wants to," his sister said.

He screamed again. I slammed the door. The imps began pounding on it. "Let us in! Let us in!" they yelled, the girl piping, "—by the hair on our chinny-chin-chins!"

"Only if you promise no more screaming!"

"We promise!"

I opened the door, shook my finger at the screamer. "No more, you hear?"

He glanced at his sister; she gave a slight nod.

"Okay, I'm going to close the door again so I can take a shower and fix myself a cup of coffee. So go on, go play ..." I gestured at the lawn, the mountains, Utah.

Jennifer plunked her hand on her hip, jutted her chin. "Mama says you got us from seven to five and you're gonna be a GROWTH experience."

"And we gotta put up with you," Alex said.

I ran my hands over my hair. "Okay, come in and sit on the floor—there—and don't touch a thing. What time do you go down for naps?"

"Naps?" The girl made a face.

"Tell me you take naps. One in the morning, one in the afternoon. Long ones."

"We're not babies. Only babies take naps. Even Alex is too big for that."

"I never get tired," he said. "Even at night."

I went into the bathroom and slammed the door. When I emerged the boy was playing with a small green truck and my coffee maker.

"It's his garage," Jennifer explained.

I kicked the toy truck across the floor, bent down, picked up the coffee maker.

"We're supposed to use our imaginations," she said.

"Not in my cabin, you won't."

Outdoors, my own imagination was fired when I got them interested in a game that involved chasing the cats that lived in and around the garage. Bugle got right into it before hearing the rules. I told the kids to pretend they were African hunters, and the cats were tigers that, upon capture, would bring a thousand dollars a head. My fantasies usually involved money.

Having disposed of the little monsters (for the rest of the morning, I thought), I went up to the house to find Leona. She was unpacking boxes of plain dishes and utensils.

"Had to buy extra for Lucy's retreat guests," she explained. She motioned at the dishwasher. "Feel free to help."

I picked up a bunch of knives and forks, jammed them into the container. "Who are these Daughters of Light I keep hearing about?"

"That's what Lucy calls the women who'll be coming to the retreat."

Each session would last one week, and Lucy hoped to run the program for ten weeks. Twenty-four different women each week and the cost was four hundred dollars, discounts offered for those who wanted or needed to work. I did some quick calculations. If everyone paid full price and there were ten sessions, Lucy stood to rake in almost a hundred thou! I almost respected the woman.

"And we're supposed to participate?"

"Us? You and me?" She laughed, shook her head.

"Well, she called you a high priestess."

"That was a joke, Shandie."

I wasn't in the kitchen ten minutes before the kids ran inside. Leona laughed, apparently at the shocked look on my face.

In my cabin, I tried teaching them gin rummy, but Alex was too young to comprehend the game. He threw his cards up in the air and cried in frustration. So I drove them to Castle Rock and bought an inflatable swimming pool. But Jennifer was quickly bored with that. At my wit's end, I locked myself in my cabin and screamed they could go drown themselves in their mother's toilet. As they ran up the path toward the mansion, crying, I lay down on my bed to take a nap. Within moments, Leona was banging on my door, saying she had a mountain of work to do and I had to keep the kids out of her hair.

"What about my hair?"

"You don't like your job, talk to Lucy."

I told the brats to go get their toys, bring them down to my cabin. Jennifer said Mama didn't want them playing with toys when it was nice outside; she wanted them to "experience life."

"You want experience? Allow me to introduce you to the primary activity of every red-blooded kid in America." I lugged my Sony over to the spare cabin, plugged it in and ordered them to sit down and shut up.

"There's nothing on but soaps," the girl complained.

"Here ..." I switched to channel 20. "Pictionary" was on. "See? There are plenty of game shows." They were staring at my clothes that hung from the metal bar along the east wall of the cabin, and the boxes stacked along the north wall. My luggage was there, as well, but seeing it summoned only a vague memory of last night's emotional storm.

"And don't touch a frigging thing."

I went next door, put on my bikini, gathered up towel, lotion, sunglasses, and a paperback novel by Elmore Leonard, then stretched out on the grass behind my cabin. I heard a screen door slam. Billy came out of the mansion. It appeared he was on his way to his cabin; clearly to avoid me, he cut a wide path around the garage. I had a mind to tell him he needn't worry about me bothering him again. I could get more comfort from a tree.

When I went to check on the brats, I found Jennifer decked in my red sequin-spangled jacket, a pair of my high heels, and a red felt hat. Alex was swallowed in a black crepe dress, a white brassiere slung over his chest. They'd dug into my boxes, found some old makeup, smeared red gloss on their lips, and painted harsh black lines around their eyes. They looked like a couple of midget whores from Saturn.

I checked the laugh in my throat. Laugh and they'd think they could rout through my belongings whenever they pleased. I raised my hand to smack the girl; she cringed. I lowered my hand. Lucy's bit about not harming the fowl of the air or the beast of the field probably applied here. So how the hell did you discipline them?

"GET MY CLOTHES OFF, YOU LITTLE CREEPS!" I yelled. "You're bad!"

"Nobody's bad," Jennifer said.

"I know—just ignorant."

"We're all evolving," she said with a jut of her chin.

"Yeah? You could've fooled me."

Watching kids turned out to be radically different from any-thing I'd imagined. "Watching" suggested something passive — a word no one experienced with kids like these would ever use. By the end of the first week, I understood my role. Forget supervision, forget I was an adult, forget the high-paying sales job I would find when I found the time to look. To these kids, I was an oversized playmate who had been assigned to entertain them while their mother did whatever she did, which interested them not at all. The arrangement was old hat to them. Leona said that in Reno, "Aunt Cecelia" had lived in as a nanny, so they were accustomed to spending a great deal of time with an adult other than Mama.

Leona also said that if the children wanted or needed to see Lucy during the day, I was not to prevent them from seeking her out. But Mama must have trained her darlings to leave her alone, because even when they were angry with me, even when I suggested they go see what Mama was doing, they refused to budge. They'd shake their heads and say they would "tell her tonight."

Everyday I saw everyone, but only to nod or say hello, except for Leona. I was resigned to do my time, and that was all. The kids ate lunch up at the mansion daily, but unless I knew Lucy was gone, I'd fix myself sandwiches in my cabin, as I did most evenings. When I did go up and eat dinner with the crew, I never stayed for coffee, to avoid being the target of Lucy's focus again. I seldom talked to Billy, and when I did, I was cordial. He kept his distance in a head-hanging kind of way.

The days were long and hot, the nights, lonely. I pretended I was just out of high school, working the summer before college began; I was a child psychologist in training, I was married to an Air Force pilot who was stationed in Germany, and had volunteered to do this *au pair* bit to kill time until he sent for me in September. The truth hurt too much.

The place was a ruckus of activity the second week of June. Lucy hired a half dozen students on summer break to help get the mansion ready for the Big Cosmic Event. Delivery trucks came and went; one from Sears loaded with bunk beds and dressers, which were hauled to rooms in the basement and upstairs where Billy and Olson used to sleep.

Lucy spent a lot of time in a room in the basement she used as an office. The retreat required tons of paperwork, Leona said. Save

117

for Mr. Floy, everyone was busy getting the house ready for guests. Leona said the codger was writing a book, something political. The old man would emerge from his cabin around one o'clock, after listening to Rush Limbaugh on the radio, then spend the rest of the afternoon trying to get someone to discuss with him what he'd heard on the radical program. He tried me once. I told him I didn't even know the difference between a Republican and a Democrat. "Perhaps you're a Civil Libertarian," he said.

I took the kids and dog to the park; I bought them Dove bars at Archie's store; I drove them to Denver to see the movie "Cinderella," and swung by Waldenbooks to buy a stack of discounted kiddie books. We manicured and painted toe- and fingernails, we dressed Bugle in my underwear; we crept around the trees south of the mansion, looking for signs of Big Foot. It amazed me to no end to hear, at dinnertime, the imps talk about all the things they'd done, as if they'd been in the company of a fairy godmother rather than a woman who longed to strangle them.

Thursday afternoon, the second week, I spotted Lucy walking with my mother over to Mom's beige Honda Accord, which was parked in front of the hedges. I ducked inside my cabin and stationed myself at the window above the sink. Thinking this was some new game, the brats followed me.

"What do we do now?" the girl asked.

"Silently count to one hundred. You start."

Watching out the window, I tried to discern from their expressions and body language what the two women were talking about. Had Mom come to divulge my secret past with Carson? Though I still felt frustrated that I had no concrete plan for the future, I had begun to fall into a kind of rhythm here—I almost enjoyed the brats. Was Mom going to blow the whistle and ruin it? Not if I was reading Lucy right; she seemed bored but polite.

"Thirty!" Jennifer said. "Your turn."

The two women said their goodbyes, Mom got in her Accord, and Lucy walked back toward the house.

Just then Billy drove through the gates in his Jeep. Lucy waved for him to stop. Told him something and gestured at the house. He whipped the Jeep around to the parking area next to the mud room, got out, and followed Lucy into the house.

"Game's over."

"But who won?" Alex wanted to know.

"You did."

I'd seen nothing to indicate there was anything to feel threatened about (Lucy and Mom probably had business, something about the consignment of Carson's antiques, and Lucy calling Billy into the house was nothing out of the ordinary); nonetheless, I felt nervous about going up to the house that night. By Friday night my paranoia seemed foolish; and anyway, Leona had fixed fried chicken coated in honey and cornflakes, one of my favorite dishes.

Besides me, the only ones in the dining room that evening were the Blues, Leona, Mr. Floy, and Billy. As usual I paid Billy no special attention. To him, I was just the woman who watched the kids, and despite my apology, I still thought of him as Lucy's houseboy. I wanted to think he was as high-minded as everyone said he was, a man so loyal he would sacrifice independence, freedom, everything to stay on and help his deceased friend's family make a go of it; God knew I needed a hero, but the way he dragged around, head hanging low, rang a sour note in the pure devotion song. I had the feeling he wanted to leave as much as I did, but something other than loyalty was keeping him here. Something that made him feel ashamed. Somewhere in this assessment, I lost a little respect for him. My true hero would say the hell with staying to help the wife of a man who had lied to him. A true hero wouldn't work second fiddle for a woman when he had managed the place almost single-handedly.

I looked up and caught Mr. Floy staring at me.

"My dear, you have the most incredible eyes."

I glanced at Leona, hoping to glean from her expression a clue as to whether or not I had been paid a compliment.

"Thank you," I finally said. No one laughed.

"You're quite welcome."

That this old man, whom I had thought was a dullard, spoke with such eloquence bothered me immensely. It seemed the bane of my existence that rarely did anything prove to fulfil my expectations. Sometimes I wondered if I had originated on another planet. Maybe Mom found me under a rock.

As I rose to help Leona clear the table, Lucy asked me to come upstairs; she had something she wanted to discuss. The alarm I felt obscured an ambient awareness that Billy left the room in a nervous haste, as if he knew exactly what was about to happen.

I was alarmed but not surprised. The past couple of days I had sensed something in the air. Maybe the kids had ratted on me, every night, full of tales about how horribly I'd treated them. I rehearsed in my emotions the humiliation I would feel getting fired from this non-job.

Leona removed the plates from my hands. "Go on, I can handle it."

Lucy was already on the stairs. I hesitated another moment, then followed her with a vow that I would walk out the instant she got lippy. If she wanted to fire me, fine, I'd go, but I'd be damned if I'd let her lay any crap on me.

My palm was clammy with sweat as I slid it along the polished bannister. Lucy was wearing black slacks, a long black tunic top, her hair falling around her shoulders like black water.

She went into the master bedroom. As I stepped inside, I said, "I warned you I hated kids ..."

Chapter Eleven

The Ugly Mother Wound

"This isn't about your job."

With an inner sigh of relief, I took in my surroundings. In contrast to the rest of the house, this room possessed an air of having belonged to Lucy for years. The change in ambiance was such that it was difficult to place Carson here, even in memory. I remembered making love to him in this room. On a king-sized water bed, elevated on a pedestal base. It happened soon after Roz left, as if to punctuate the divorce. He snuck me up here and I was gone before the staff woke up the next morning. Stupidly, I had thought that someday I would call this room my own.

The pedestal base was gone. Lucy's bed was a regular double, draped with a pale pink satin comforter and accentuated with colorful pillows. The north-facing windows framing the bed were dressed in off-white curtains. Squat lamps with pleated shades sat atop the bedside tables. Both windows were up about two inches and a light breeze was stirring the curtains. There was a large painting on the wall facing the bed; it featured a white temple shrouded in misty whites and pinks against a deep blue background.

Lucy sat down on the bed, crossed her legs Indian style, and motioned for me to take the pink armchair between two tall bookshelves filled with books. A brass floor lamp stood to my right. On the floor to my left were a blue spiral notebook and pen next to a pile of books. On top, *The Nature of Personal Reality*, a Seth Book by Jane Roberts.

The black outfit Lucy was wearing was relieved by turquoise jewelry set in silver. A squash-blossom necklace, bracelet, earrings, and a ring with a ruby setting.

I could see why people called her beautiful, but in my opinion her looks weren't the first thing to strike you. She emanated a kind of scary power. Easy to imagine her putting a hex on Carson.

"Before I get to the reason I've set this time aside for us, I want to tell you about myself. How I got to where I am today."

Cozy with relief that I wasn't getting fired, I settled back in the chair. Maybe this was going to be a kind of employee orientation meeting?

"When I was growing up the idea of motherhood never appealed to me."

A spark of fear flared in my mind at this opening remark, but her casual manner softened the threat that she might be gearing up to lecture on the merits of motherhood.

"My brother and I fought like cat and dog and I thought to have children would be like that. It's unusual for the Basque to have small families, but my mother was unable to have any other babies after Steffen was born; so I wasn't raised in the company of children, although we did have a lot of cousins.

"I grew up on a sheep ranch in the fifties when women were expected to stay home and raise children. While all the girls I knew were stuffing hope chests and learning how to cook and sew, I dreamt of moving to the big city—Reno was big compared to Ely—and running a large corporation." She chuckled. "I think Ayn Rand's *Atlas Shrugged* was festering in the back of my mind.

"Besides the ranch, my folks owned a motel in Ely and after I was old enough to work the desk on weekends, I decided I could run a hotel in Reno. By the time I was twenty-five, I was reservations manager for the Sparks-Nugget hotel and casino in Sparks, a suburb of Reno.

"Before I turned twenty-seven, Mom and Dad died and left Steffen and me a lot of money. We kept the ranch and motel, hired relatives to run them, and pooled our funds to buy a restaurant. Steffen handled the economics and I managed the place. Xavier's quickly gained a reputation that drew celebrities and dignitaries from all over the world.

"I was in my glory, until Steffen and I began to butt heads. It was enough for me to own a successful restaurant, but he wanted more. He wanted to add a gambling room. Run a poker game. I fought it tooth and nail because I knew it would draw a rougher crowd. In the end I gave in, because I had begun to see something different for myself.

"I met a woman who introduced me to metaphysics. Dr. Jaffee saw in me a potential I never dreamed was there. I was more than intuitive, she said; I could be a channel if I put into practice certain principles. This was before trance channeling became hot stuff. The way she taught me, you don't open yourself up to unknown energies and spout whatever comes into your brain. She taught me that to be a channel ... never mind, I'm getting off track.

"I began spending more time with Dr. Jaffee and soon came to see that she was right. I won't go into all I did to develop my talents and educate myself about metaphysics. The thing I wanted to bring out is that during this transition, my aims and interests changed dramatically.

"For one thing, I got in touch with the fact that I wanted children. Note I didn't say I wanted husband and children." Her eyes sparkled at this ruse.

"As you know, I did marry. But ours was a non-traditional marriage. Carson had his life, I had mine. The children were simply a point around which we could rally." A heave of her shoulders dismissed the subject of husband, children, marriage.

"I became interested in how a culture forms and develops. Our country was in the midst of great changes—some, not so good. I began to study these changes at the level of family. Ironic that I would be drawn there when I had been so slow to form a family myself. I realized I had been influenced by the feminist movement. I saw that I had been enticed by the promise of personal feminine power. The pendulum had been stuck for too long in the direction of male power; it was only natural that it would begin to swing the other way in time. But I saw that it was a mistake to try and swing it completely the other way, as some feminine leaders would have us believe is best. What we needed was balance. A pendulum that swings not so wide and at a stabilized rhythm."

All this talk about women was making me nervous. When was she going to get to the point?

I heard a door slam, Bugle bark, the kids laugh. I glanced out the window. The evening light was fast losing its luster. Shadows were gathering in the room like clusters of gray ghosts edging closer to hear the great woman expound on all these weighty issues.

"We thought the imbalance would be corrected if we became equals in the job place. It became the norm for both parents to work outside the home. On the surface this seemed like progress, but we began to see the emergence of some problems we are yet to solve. By necessity children were relegated to day care centers and the like. We began hearing about 'quality time.' In truth, we had little time left for our children, and were bone-tired when we tried to put into practice this nebulous standard of quality. Many of our high schools have become dangerous places. Armed guards are required. We see a proliferation of gangs and drugs and teenaged pregnancies. We are grappling with the morality of abortion. Our national education system has deteriorated.

"I'm not on a crusade to get mothers to quit work and return to their nests, though some like to accuse me of it. What we have to do is redefine our wants and needs.

"You think I'm talking bullcrap?"

I felt my face color. Could she see I wasn't savoring every word? "I haven't really thought about it ..."

"Hmmmm. I heard you were interested in what a Daughter of Light is."

Big-mouth Leona.

"A Daughter of Light is a woman who knows who she is and has a grasp on what she's here to accomplish. That's my work. I help women who are so inclined to find out who they are and the nature of the work they need to be doing."

"Like a job counselor?"

She smiled. "In a manner of speaking. But not so cut and dried as pinpointing specific jobs people do to support themselves financially. The work I'm speaking of is foundational. If you have a sense of who you are spiritually, you can more easily identify what kind of job or jobs will suit you, and if you know this, you're more likely to succeed on all fronts, including the material. There is nothing wrong with financial success, nothing unspiritual about it. Unspiritual is forcing yourself into roles that are counter to what you were created to do and be. Which is not to say we are born with blueprints that specify things such as secretary or pianist or elementary school teacher. We are all born with talents that can serve the whole while serving us individually. There are myriad ways we can use these talents, and within the limitations of our given genetic background and environment, and the greater plan for humankind, we are all free to creatively construct our own destinies. The point is, we are all endowed with certain talents and potentials, and we are the happiest and most successful when we recognize and act on these gifts."

Her demeanor and tone had changed. Before, she had appeared to be almost disinterested in her own ramblings. Now she was sitting erect with both feet on the floor. Her gaze was fixed to the right of me, as if to address an audience only she could see.

"Because we are, most of us, caught in a cultural web that discourages us from understanding our roles in this sense, many of us waste long years trying to succeed in ways that fall short of our highest potentialities. My work is to help others discover their true talents and encourage them to begin creating lives that will bring the greatest rewards."

"Carson was into all this stuff?"

She smiled and arched a brow. "In a way. I think he applied his talents to the fullest he could under the circumstances. He certainly helped me, though I'm equally certain he would describe the way he helped in different terms than I do."

Carson thought her interest in metaphysics was a bunch of "dilly-dally," but he didn't have a lot to say in the matter since he was only around part-time; an arrangement he liked. Lucy liked it as well. She had had no intention of moving away from her friends and family. That changed when she had a "vision of sorts" about the retreat. It was "revealed" to her that the location was to be in Colorado, specifically at Blue Acres. She'd put off telling Carson about the revelation because of his attitude in regards to metaphysics. Then it was too late to tell him.

"I thought it was a chicken way of giving me the go-ahead."

I didn't know how to respond to that.

"By dying he was saying 'go ahead.' Everyone decides how and when they die. Not consciously, but conscious knowledge has the least bearing on our major decisions."

I thought her belief bordered on blasphemy, but not being religious, I wasn't alarmed. I just thought it was an outrageous conclusion to draw. Never would I believe that Carson crashed his airplane on purpose. He had a lot of faults, but he wasn't stupid. I could think of few more horrifying ways to die.

"Now about you."

Part of me expected to hear her say she saw in me "certain talents and potentialities" that would set me apart from common women; like seeing I had a knack for management, which I'd always suspected. But all this talk about women and families had me on tenterhooks. I sat up straighter.

"Something told me the first time I saw you that I could help you. I didn't know how I could help—I knew nothing about you—but now I have a stronger sense of why you are here."

I gaped in astonishment. "I'm here because you ..."

She gestured. "Things are not always as they appear. I understand how you might feel you were forced to come here, but think about it, you were not bound and gagged and brought in a cage. What I'm telling you is, I was acting on a strong intuitive urge without knowing the reason why myself. I pursued you, this is true.

The fact that Carson gave you all that money was the wedge I used, but if that had not been presented, I would have used something else. The fact that I needed someone to look after my kids was a convenience. I had a talk with Billy the other day."

I clutched the arms of the chair and leaned forward, poised for flight. Damn Billy! He squealed about Carson and me! (Why this would translate to Lucy as needing her help was a question too complex to enter my mind.)

But I had it all wrong. Billy didn't tell her about Carson and me. He told her something worse. He told her my most sacred secret. Everyone who knew me knew about it. It wasn't a *secret* secret, but they all understood it was forbidden to bring it up, and no one ever did, except Mom at her ugliest—that I couldn't stop anymore than I could stop myself from thinking about it. But thinking about it was different than hearing it out loud; I could censor my thoughts, as if to examine a scar where I had cut my finger. Not only did Lucy bring it up, she throttled me with it; she kicked me in the mouth.

"He said that five years ago you had a bab—"

"NO!" I screamed. My hands flew straight out, as if to break a fall. I shot up from the chair and made a flying leap for the door. I don't know how the witch beat me there; one second she was on the bed, the next, she was in front of me. She seized my arms.

"You are nowhere, young lady, nowhere! Do you understand? Of course not! You've been too busy running away from your life to notice your own absence! You must get Briana back, Shandie. The situation in Colorado Springs has deteriorated. Mr. Dillinger began drinking heavily and lost his business, and now his wife has to work and those children ..."

Her words slammed into me like physical objects. "I can't get her back!" I heard myself shout. "She was adopted!" I began racking with sobs. If not for her grip on my arms I would have collapsed on the floor and dissolved in a puddle of anguish.

"Possibly true on the level of lower courts," she said gently, "but the higher courts say she will be yours again. The adoption will be reversed."

If she thought she was being kind, she was wrong; nothing she could have said could have been more cruel. It was horrible to see in her face a kind of attentive concern completely devoid of understanding. How could she understand? She'd never had to give up a baby she'd held for only twenty minutes; she'd never felt the agony only a mother who has lost a child can feel. She planned her children, she hired nannies, she gave a royal wave of her hand and said with a grand yawn, "Let them be free spirits."

"You're crazy!" I yelled, her face a blur through my tears.

"I am not crazy, but you will be if you continue this war against your own spirit. Ever since you gave up that child, you've been doing your utmost to prove your unworthiness. I understand you now, Shandie, I really do. There's no one home inside you. When you gave up Briana, you gave up yourself."

"You sound like my mother!"

"That's an ugly word, isn't it? Mother. The wound in the earth where you dropped out of existence."

In one sudden movement that surprised us both, I yanked my arms free, whirled and ran for the nearest window. But the witch pounced on me before I could raise it and knock out the screen.

"You would break every bone in your body to avoid hearing the truth, wouldn't you!" With mammoth strength, she wrestled me down on the bed and smashed my face into the comforter. I was already stripped of any semblance of dignity, but this kind of bodily contact was the ultimate humiliation, the kind a helpless animal must feel when manhandled by a calloused game warden. Even though I was wailing and sobbing, I was helpless to shut out the words she spit into my brain through the back of my head.

"We're not going to call the money Carson gave you a debt anymore, because I now understand why he gave it to you. He was trying to assuage his guilt for ..."

"GET OFF ME, YOU BITCH!"

The door snapped open. "What's going on?"

It was Billy.

I jerked my head up. "She's trying to kill me!"

"Yes! I'll bring down the body when I'm done!"

I couldn't believe he shut the door.

"Carson was trying to assuage ..."

"SHUT UP! SHUT UP!"

"Relax. I'm going to let you up now ..." She eased up, then quickly backed away from the bed, as if to sidestep a rabid dog.

I sprang up and ran for the door, knocking the standing lamp flat on the floor in a loud clang of metal and glass. Halfway down the stairs, unbelievably, I heard her yell, "You have tomorrow off, but I'll need you on Sunday!"

Chapter Twelve

A Hot Job of Consoling

Billy

I cannot bear a mother's tears.

Aeneid
Book 9, line 289
Virgil
(Publius Vergilius Maro)
(70-19 B.C.)

Moments after Shandie runs out of the house, Lucy comes downstairs, into the kitchen and pours herself a cup of coffee. Billy and Leona watch as she takes several sips, looking for all the world like a woman who has nothing more important on her mind than the weather. Then she looks straight at Billy. "I blew it," she says.

Leona lights a cigarette. Her eyes dart from Billy to Lucy, but neither seem inclined to divulge the nature of this drama. When Billy

131

came downstairs she asked him what in the tarnation was going on up there, but Billy just shrugged.

Billy starts to get up from the table.

Lucy points at him; he eases back down. "I want you to go down there and help her see the benefit of staying put."

"She's leaving?" Leona says.

"I don't think so," Lucy says. Her gaze is still nailing Billy to his chair. "She's upset, but I'm sure Billy can persuade her to stay."

Billy is simmering inside. You cannot see the anger in his face or in the way he holds his body, but it is there, like smoldering ashes long after the log has disintegrated. He was upstairs fetching a pack of cigarettes for Leona when the confrontation occurred, and he heard most of it. He is angry at himself for opening the door; it wasn't his business, not at all. Now he is angry at Lucy for delegating to him her dirty work.

"It would be a shame to lose her now," Lucy says without a trace of emotion in her voice. A stark contrast to the woman Billy heard upstairs. Whatever her agenda, it backfired; and now she wants him to try and piece together the fabric she has ravaged.

"I'm not good at that sort of thing," he says, feeling the anger surge. Why is he still sitting here? Why doesn't he just say no and be done with it?

Leona grinds out her cigarette. "You want me ...?"

"No. Billy is the only one who can reach her now. Trust me."

Trust me. Exactly what Carson said when he set up the adoption. Trust me—the child will be better off.

"Oh ... I almost forgot." Lucy walks over to the table, fishes a slip of paper out of the pocket in her slacks. "Give this to her."

Billy takes the slip of paper. There's an address on it.

"Remember the Dillingers?" Lucy says to Leona.

Leona scowls. "Never met 'em."

To collect his thoughts, Billy detours south of the mansion to walk among the trees awhile, Bugle tagging along at a respectful distance.

He shoves his hands into his pockets and kicks at dirt clods and twigs on the path. The slip of paper in his pocket feels like a sharp-edged rock pressed against his chest. The Dillingers' address. Nothing else, no instructions, just the address. What is the woman thinking, giving Shandie such potentially volatile information? Does she want Shandie to go down there and demand the Dillingers return the child? The woman has lost her cork. Someone will land in jail, and it won't be Lucy, she'll be sitting atop her throne, safe—but not quite sound.

He should have seen something like this coming; there were clues. Early on, Lucy demanding explanation for the pile of canceled checks Carson had issued to Shandie. He pleaded ignorance. Allowed the woman to form her own conclusions. A mistake. Look what happened! Occasionally Billy has visions, but one would have to be a full-blown psychic to have anticipated Lucy manipulating Shandie into coming to work for her. As a nanny! Beside the point. If Lucy wants to turn her children over to Elvira or Andrew Dice Clay, it is none of his business. He isn't precisely sure why Shandie's presence at Blue Acres is a threat. It just isn't right. It's too close. Things could happen, things could erupt, things could get out of hand.

He should have made an effort to steer Lucy's conclusions. He should have concocted some story. He could have said Shandie worked for Carson part-time as a bookkeeper. A bookkeeper who charged exorbitant fees for her services? Well, something; he should have thought of something, anything, to diminish Lucy's interest. What was Carson thinking, leaving those checks around for anyone to find and question? And those damned invoices.

During the second inquisition, he let slip more information than was wise. But to say less might have incited Lucy's curiosity to degrees he dared not imagine. The pieces she did manage to pry from him left him feeling as if there were parts of his body missing. He feels shorter now, his chest seems on the verge of caving in. A few more sessions like that one, he will be hobbling around like a shrunken old man.

The second inquisition occurred on Thursday. Lucy asked—nay, commanded his presence in the room she called her office.

Weeks ago she had Sid and him move Carson's fine mahogany desk from the library down to the basement, jamming it into a cold room next to a mountain of boxes and miscellaneous items that were meaningful only to Carson. She insisted on placing the computer on top of the desk without even a pad beneath it, like slamming a metal box full of greasy tools down on a marble altar. Big bulletin board with a map of Eastern Colorado leaned precariously against the west wall, on top of a black metal file cabinet. Orange, red, yellow tacks stuck in the map, marking sites where Carson and his father had drilled several wildcat oil and gas wells. Carson still owned interest in some of those wells ... Lucy owned interest in them.

She was settled in Carson's fine leather swivel chair when he came into the room. Pile of papers stacked next to the keyboard. The ceiling light was on, the goose-neck lamp on the desk shone a stark light, but the room seemed murky. Billy sat down in a wooden ladderback chair, close to the desk. Too close.

She shoved some papers at him. "Please explain."

Invoices for services rendered by Arnold Knapp. The woman was a detective herself, finding these old bills. Why had Carson kept them? Same screwy reason he kept the canceled checks, if you could use the word reason. In other matters, the boss was impeccable in concealing his mistakes.

"Knapp's a detective," he answered. "Or was. I don't know if he's still in the business."

"I know he's a detective, Billy. It says so on the top."

He nodded. So it did.

"What's this?" She pointed at the body of the invoice. "Carson was investigating some family in Colorado Springs? Why?"

Before he could form an answer, she added, "And why weren't these bills posted?"

"No reason to post them. It was personal business." A lame reply and she knew it. They kept meticulous records on everything.

She leaned back, cocked her head, waiting for more. She was wearing a red cotton dress that hung to mid-calf. Flat black shoes with straps criss-crossed up the foot, like ballet slippers.

"Go on," she said.

His mind was leaping from wall to wall. If he pretended igno-rance, what would she do? Track down Knapp? Continue her snooping. Better to give her a piece of the truth and hope it satisfied her. Save for Lucy, everyone in Doubletree knew about it anyway.

He said it. "About five years ago, Shandie had a baby."

Her mouth formed a capital O. Here was something juicy she could tear apart with her teeth.

He added relish. "A girl. She had a girl."

She leaned forward. "And ...?"

"The father was one of Carson's business associates." He nodded at the invoice. "Wesley Dillinger. He used to sell drilling equipment. Carson introduced him to Shandie, so he felt somewhat responsible for what happened. Dillinger was married. She was afraid to tell him about the pregnancy. I think at first she wanted to keep the baby, but Carson ..."

The thought derailed. He was saying too much, saying it wrong. Irrelevant to say Shandie wanted the baby; she didn't want it for long. Sweat oozed down his chest. A splotch of dampness behind his belt buckle.

"I'm listening," said the woman in the red dress.

"Carson knew Shandie wouldn't do well as a mother. She could barely take care of herself. We all knew it wouldn't work." Defending the boss; Billy, loyal to the end and beyond. He felt nauseated.

"I think I'm beginning to understand. Carson was the one who insisted she give the baby to Dillinger, right?"

Exactly right but something wrong with the way she said it. Insisted was an awfully strong word.

"It was a big mess. Carson went down there himself and talked to Alice Dillinger."

"Uh-huh. The understanding wife." She narrowed her eyes. Snapped her fingers. "Just like that, everyone agrees. Dillinger gets her pregnant, she wants to keep the baby, but Carson says 'no, Dillinger, you take the child,' and everyone's happy."

"I don't think Shandie ..."

She jabbed her finger at the invoice. "So how does this figure in?"

He told her about Dillinger's business going bad not long after the adoption was final. Rumor was, the man started drinking heavily. So Carson hired Knapp to keep an eye on things. Felt bad about his plans going to hell.

"How did hiring a detective help?"

"He—Carson wanted to keep abreast of the situation. Shandie was an old friend. He encouraged her to give up the baby and wanted to make sure it turned out all right."

Lucy did not look at all happy. As if this were any of her business. She crossed her arms over her chest, scowled. "And Knapp reported that things weren't right."

"So Carson took measures to help the family."

"You mean he threw money at them."

Billy jerked inside but moved not a hair.

"And Dillinger drank it up."

"Carson cut them off then," he said, a snap in his voice. "He realized the money was only exacerbating the problem."

"Then what?"

Then nothing! "He'd go down there once in a while, talk to them."

"Uh-huh. Then what?"

Nothing! "Carson never offered to help Shandie reverse the adoption?"

Reverse the adoption? What was she talking about? "I don't think ... The baby was a part of the family by then. The Dillingers had two boys already. The baby fit right in. And Shandie had accepted it. Everyone had."

"What's her name?"

"Who?"

"The child."

He thought for a moment. "Briana."

He is tempted to toss the slip of paper. Maybe he lost it, maybe he forgot to give it to her. But no good. Lucy will ask about it; definitely she has some unspoken agenda here. With any luck, Shandie will throw it away, lose it, tear it up, ignore it. He shudders to think what might happen if she acts on the information. A crazy thought. What could she do? Go down there, pay the Dillingers a visit? What a mess of hornets that could stir up.

He walks around to the north. The evening light is dark violet scored with splashes of yellow spilling from Shandie's two cabins. The Ford junker is backed up to the main cabin, the trunk lid is up, and all four doors are open. She is throwing in her possessions helter-skelter. Her hair is bushed out, her blue eyes electric with rage. The dog slinks back up the path to safety.

Billy has no idea what he can say to persuade her to stay. Capturing a mountain lion would be easier.

He steps into the light. "What are you doing?"

"What the H does it look like I'm doing?"

"Looks like you're tearing up your life."

She stumbles into the second cabin, emerges with a load of clothes. She is dropping hangers, tripping over the hems of garments. She flings the clothes into the trunk. Such a heap there already, it will be impossible to shut the lid. The backseat of the Ford is crammed high with her belongings. She won't be able to see out the rear window.

"We used a pickup to move all your stuff before."

"So be my guest, keep whatever doesn't fit!"

"Oh, thanks." He isn't doing such a hot job of consoling.

She dashes into the cabin, returns with a chin-high armload of shoe boxes. One topples to the ground, spilling a pair of red high heels. She jams the boxes into the backseat on top of blankets, pillows, dishes, books.

As she runs back, he catches her, spins her around.

"Don't leave, Shandie," is all he says and for reasons beyond his comprehension, she bursts out crying and sobbing. He pulls her into his arms. Instantly regrets it. This is no pathetic young woman who needs consolation; the woman he holds in his arms is sexual dynamite, and his body knows it, and responds like a book of matches pitched into a bonfire. He tries to shift his weight, but she is clinging tightly. Irrationally, he wants to tip her head up, kiss her ...

He pushes her away, places his hands where they are safe on her upper arms. "This can be worked out, Shandie."

"Oh, sure!" she cries. "Work for a woman who hates me!"

"If she hated you, would she ask me to convince you to stay?"

"Yes! She needs someone to pick on! Well, I'm not going to be her whipping girl anymore!"

She breaks away and walks stiff-legged into the main cabin. Billy follows. Inside it looks as though a gang of hoodlums have torn up the place. She rips a tissue out of a box on the table and blows her nose. Sears him with a look.

"Why'd you tell her I had a baby?"

No danger of her noticing his sexual distress; her mind is on his treachery. How can he explain the pressure he is under? He can't; he doesn't fully understand it himself.

"She found some old papers where Carson had written something about it. I only confirmed it." Another lie. He is becoming tied up with lies, ropes of lies binding him, body and soul. Squeezing off air to his integrity.

The note in his pocket feels like a hat pin sticking into his skin. He pulls it out, hands it to her.

"What the hell's this?"

"The Dillingers' address."

Her eyes grow large. She stares at the note, stares at him. "C-Carson promised they were going to move away from the Springs ..."

"I don't know what happened, Shandie."

Lies, lies, lies—but what good could possibly come from telling her the truth? Dillinger was to move somewhere not so close to Denver as to minimize the chances of Shandie encountering the baby. It was in the decree. But Dillinger changed his mind after the fact and Carson said it wasn't important. The baby would soon be a child, and Shandie wouldn't recognize her if she walked up to her and said, "Hi! My name is Briana!" A gross assumption on Carson's part, and not the point. What if she encountered the entire family? Billy had not asked; he knew the answer and so did Carson: she would recognize Wesley and put two and four together. Made no sense for Carson to go to such lengths to set up the whole thing, then wave aside this change of plans—this violation of the decree. As if the point for him was to get the baby out of his sight as soon as possible, screw the pain it might cause Shandie—everyone—if she happened to see the family, at a park, in a store, driving down the street. But it wasn't Billy's business; not then, not now.

She holds the slip of paper with thumb and forefinger, as if it stinks. "So what the hell am I supposed to do with it?"

He shrugs, as if to say, "Who can understand Lucy's motivations?"

She crushes the note in her fist, then pitches it out the door. It sails beyond the closest tree. Billy heaves an inner sigh. Maybe that will be the end of it.

She grabs two German beer steins off the makeshift shelves near the bed and stumbles out of the cabin. Billy toys with the idea of letting her go. Tell Lucy he did everything in his power to stop her. But Lucy is strangely passionate about this baby business. He can't see her dropping it. He walks outdoors.

"Shandie ... why don't you think about it overnight?"

She is stuffing the beer steins into the front seat under a pile of clothes. "Because I'm sure I want the H out of here!"

As she heads back toward the cabin, he takes hold of her again.

"You're forgetting something important."

"What."

"Those kids. They like you a lot. You don't want to let those kids down by running out on them."

"How can they like me when I can't stand them?"

Her response is so unexpected, for a moment all he can do is stare at her. How can she be unaware that the kids like her? The past week he watched with wonder as Jennifer and Alex followed her around as if she were the proverbial pied piper. Even Bugle seemed drawn to her. Probably a temporary situation. The novelty will likely wear off soon, and the children will revert to being the pests they were before she came.

"Kids are funny," he says at last.

"Oh, so you think it would be funny if they really did like me!"

He frowns, looks at the ground, looks at her.

"When you can't stand them, yes, that would be odd ..."

"Well, for your information, I don't hate them in particular. I just can't stand kids." She yanks her arms free, steps back and points a finger. "But that woman! I am not working for a woman who, who ..."

"She's different," he inserts, "but there's something about her ..." He stops short of putting into words what he feels about the woman. She irks him, she's strange, she's pushy, but he senses she can help Shandie. Not that it's any of his concern.

"I don't know, but I think you'll profit by seeing this thing through." What is he saying? Nothing but trouble ahead, yet here he is, smooth-talking.

"She's crazy, Billy. And cruel."

She might be right. Crazy, cruel, strange. "Give it until morning. If you decide to go after thinking it over, I'll help you finish packing." He looks at her shrewdly. "Where were you going?"

Her bottom lip trembles. "I know people." She wipes a palm under her nose. "I have friends. Lots of friends."

He looks down. Shandie used to have Carson. Now, other than her family, and things are not right there, she has no one. Again he feels an urge to gather her in his arms. To soothe her ... or to feel her body pressed against his again? He steps back.

"Just think it over. If you still feel the same tomorrow, I won't fight you on it."

There is nothing more to say, but Billy is finding it difficult to move, leave, go home, depart, scram, forget it. He feels ensnared in a confusion of emotions, like a rabbit caught in the glare of a headlamp. Shandie is a manipulative opportunist. A gold digger. So who is this young woman with swollen blue eyes who trembles before him?

"Stay, Shandie," he says brusquely. Then turns and walks away rapidly, like a man who has just seen out of the corner of his eye the glint of a knife.

Shandie

Out of my own great woe
I make my little songs.

*Aus Meinen Grossen Schmerzen
(Out of my Great Woe)*
Stanza 1
Heinrich Heine
(1797–1856)

Chapter Thirteen
A Dumb Story

I woke up groggy with disappointment. I was still here. Such power I'd felt throwing my things in my car. It would have been an ultimate kind of satisfaction to roar past the mansion with my arm angled out the window, my middle finger stuck in the air.

But where the hell did I think I was going after the splendorous moment? I hated Billy for bringing that up. Why didn't he just come out and say I was a loser? An idiot to have put my whole trust in Carson, so that after he died (crashed on purpose?), I was left with only one option: to work for his cruel and cunning secret wife.

A lie. There were other options; welfare, for instance. But the wretched truth was, my best bet was to stay right here, regardless of Mrs. Blue's impromptu attacks. The witch hitting me where it hurt, saying my daughter's name out loud, trampling on the sacred places inside me. Spewing lies whispered in her ear by "higher courts." (Demons!) Why'd she do it? I thought about her big lead-in. All that talk about women and children and how she was someone who helped people get in touch with who they were—then ZAP! she hits me with the big tragedy of my life. Like she's going to help me. "You must get Briana back," she says. Like it's possible, like this will fix me, the woman who has no one home inside her—what kind of thing is that to say to someone?

Such were my thoughts Saturday morning as I downed cup after cup of strong coffee. I took a shower. Sometimes under pounding water a person receives inspiration. A new plan. Unthought-of options popping out of the spray like goldfish. No such luck this morning.

I almost had a nervous breakdown, trying to decide what to wear. For one thing, my clothes were strewn all over both cabins, in heaps, some in suitcases, some stuffed in boxes. That was the physical situation. The crisis I experienced was what to wear—like who was I today? Most of the time I dressed like everyone else, but I had these other times when it seemed crucial that I put on something that made a statement, even if I had no idea what I was trying to say, or what anyone else would think I was saying.

For two weeks I had worn jeans and knit tops and cotton slacks, shorts on the hotter days, but none of that fit for today. Last night I'd crossed some kind of line. Or I was pushed. Whichever, I knew that from now on everything was going to be different.

The problem was, I didn't know how things were going to be different. I spent an hour changing clothes, trying to find something that would make me feel on the outside like I did on the inside. I can't explain this: I finally settled on bright orange calypso pants and a black shirt covered with pink sequins. I knew the outfit was grotesque, but dammit, it spoke. Of something.

Two elfin faces appeared at the window. I opened the door. "It's my day off," I yelled over the noise the tractors were making. The gardeners choosing this time to tear up the grass and explode the quiet. The cabin was filling with the sweet smell of cut grass, something I usually appreciated.

"We're visiting," the girl shouted.

"Your mother send you?"

"Leona said come see if you were up. We had pancakes for breakfast with fresh maple syrup and ..."

"Fresh from that tree outside the mud room, right?"

"I don't know ..."

"Why's your stuff on the ground?" the boy asked.

I backed up and sat down on the bed. Crossed my arms over my chest. "I just felt like messing up everything."

The urchins came inside and looked around. Alex spotted one of my suitcases. The lid was up. With grave expression, he went down on his knees and peered at my nightgowns and underwear.

"Where you going?" he asked.

"New York City. California. I haven't decided yet."

"You're moving?" Jennifer said.

Alex looked up from the suitcase, tears in his eyes. I couldn't believe these kids. Two measly weeks and they were acting like I was the nanny who had suckled them from day one.

The boy burst out crying, ran over and flung himself at me. "Hey, hey ...!" I said, and did what came natural: I pushed him away. He looked so hurt, I then did what was totally unnatural: I started crying myself. Damn snot-nosed ankle-biters. Both of them pounced on me.

We were wrapped around each other, sobbing as if we'd just lost our favorite grandmother, when Billy walked in.

I pushed both brats away, dove for the bathroom, slammed the door, locked it. Sat on the stool and ripped paper off the roll to stanch my tears and blow my nose. As soon as they left, I'd grab a few essentials, jump in the Bomb, and get the hell away from this loony bin! Didn't matter where I went so long as it was far, far away!

A knock on the door. "Shandie? You okay?"

"Go away!"

"There are a couple of kids out here asking for you."

"Tell the assholes to take a goddamn powder!"

He shook the door. I jumped up, unlocked it, slammed it open. "Goddamn little bleeders!"

He smiled.

How is it that a smile can break your heart? He encircled me with his arms and I cried for what seemed like twenty minutes. He led me like a child over to the bed and sat me down, then sat down beside me.

"Shandie had a bad night, but she's going to be okay," he told the brats.

I glared at them.

"She gonna move?" Alex asked.

"No," Billy said, his eyes on me. "She's not going to move."

"Not yet," I said through my teeth. I pointed at Jennifer. "Tell your mother something."

"What?"

"Tell her to mind her own damned beeswax!"

"She doesn't have any bee's wax," Alex said.

"You kids go on up to the house and wait for me," Billy said. "When I'm done here we'll go over to Hippie Joe's and see his horses."

They whooped and ran out of the cabin. Kids turning the angst off like a faucet. Promise them a horse and the crisis is instantly over. I envied them that.

"So," Billy said and patted my leg.

I wouldn't look at him. I had cried off my makeup. I looked at my hands.

"Lucy wants you to sign this." He slipped something out of his shirt pocket. A W-4 form. "She says she can pay you two-fifty a week plus room and board."

If I'd had false teeth, they would have dropped out of my mouth. (Lucy: "We're not going to call the money Carson gave you a debt anymore ..." Then something about Carson's guilt. Her guilt—for being such a bitch. What a nutty woman.)

I gave the form back to him. "I can't sign that. The IRS is after my butt."

"So cut a deal with them. Pay them a little each month. You can handle that on a thousand a month."

"Gee, I'm rich."

"A lot more than you were making selling houses, I bet."

Everybody had my number.

"And you can't find better working conditions."

"It's the people who bother me."

"Yeah ... we're all a bunch of assholes. That's a problem."

I got up, walked over to the counter and pretended to check the coffee-maker. I didn't want Billy to see even slight bemusement in my face. There was something comical going on. But it was bitterly serious, too.

"I better go get the kids before they have Leona climbing the walls." He got up, walked over to the door, turned and looked at me. "I'm glad you're staying, Shandie ..."

I jumped at the sound of an aircraft overhead. Billy stepped outdoors, cupped his hand at his forehead, and stared at the sky.

"Xavier," he said. "He's flying in with papers for Lucy to sign. They sold the ranch."

Something about that bothered Billy. A cloud over his handsome face.

"Which reminds me. You won't need to watch the kids tomorrow. They'll be spending time with their uncle."

He walked away. Something definitely bothering him about Steffen Xavier coming to visit. Apparent in the taut, swift way he walked up the path. Something he knew but would not tell. Billy and his secrets.

As I restored order to my cabins over the weekend, I popped in and out of depression and anger. The highest mood I could rise to was one of resignation. I kept rehearsing what I would say to Lucy the next time she cornered me. One thing for sure: If ever she so much as breathed my daughter's name in my presence again, I was going to tell the witch to sit down hard on her broomstick.

The money helped. I could save a lot in a year. Then I could move. Somewhere.

I stayed clear of the mansion. Drove to Elizabeth and bought more food. Saw everyone at one time or the other, as they came and went from this or that excursion. From the window over the sink I watched Lucy's brother romp with the kids and Bugle out on the lawn. The man was better looking than I'd thought at the memorial service. Not as handsome as Billy, but he had a certain style.

Billy resumed cutting a path around my cabin. Probably figured convincing me to stay was part of his job. Billy, warm and friendly when his job called for it.

Monday morning the sprinklers were on full-force when the brats ran down to my cabin. Jennifer was a lady again. A frothy blue dress a little girl might wear to a piano recital. I gestured at the water swishing over the grass.

"Guess we'll have to leave home."

"What?" Alex said.

I told the brats to calm down, I knew a secret place in the woods where we could hide out while the sprinklers were on. I gathered up the sale books I'd purchased at Waldenbooks, a blanket, a sack of junk food, then led the way up the hill behind the cabins to a special clearing I'd discovered the day before, where the sun barely invaded the cool sanctuary of leaf and wood. Some of the trees surrounding the clearing were blue spruce that towered as high as sixty feet. Bunches of wild flowers here and there. Strong, spicy smells. Alex squealed and pointed at a squirrel that scampered up a fir tree, and the birds scolded everyone.

The children helped me spread the blanket over a relatively flat piece of ground bounded by two boulders. They sat down quietly, as if sensing the spot was sacred. As I opened the brown sack, the crackle of paper alarmed the birds. I gave the brats each a Diet Coke and two Oreo cookies. Jennifer held her cookies delicately and asked for a napkin. I gave her a tissue I had in the pocket of my jeans. Alex bragged that he needed no sissy napkins.

"Bugle found us!" Jennifer said. The dog trotted over and flopped down on the blanket.

"You know what?" the boy said. "Uncle Steff is gonna move here!"

I wondered if Xavier was seriously engaged to that snooty-looking Marilee, whatever her last name.

"First he's got to sell our house in Reno," Jennifer said.

"How's he going to fly his plane and drive all his cars when he moves?" Alex asked his sister.

All his cars. My kind of man.

"Maybe he'll pull his airplane behind his cars. On a big rope—no, a chain!"

"He can't! His airplane is too big for the road!"

"Don't worry. He'll think of something. Uncle Steff is smart."

"Smarter than Mama?"

"Oh, yes, a lot smarter. What're you smiling at?" the girl asked me.

"Life. It's a big joke."

I picked up a book and began to read. After the second book, the kids wanted more of what was in the sack. Again the crackle of paper set the birds off on another chorus of indignant chirping. I gave the brats Hershey bars, which shut them up while I read one more book.

Alex started fooling with Bugle and Jennifer was fiddling with the bow in her hair and singing softly to herself. Three books and they were totally bored. Was there anything that would occupy them for longer than thirty minutes?

"I guess that's all the books for today." I slammed them into a pile.

"Mama says made-up stories are best," the girl said.

"She makes up stories."

"At night before we go to sleep," the boy said.

Jennifer bounced on her knees. "You tell us a made-up story."

"I don't know any."

She laughed. "If it's made-up, you can't know it before!"

"Okay, I know one." I pulled my knees to my chest and looked off into the trees.

"Once upon a time there was a young woman who gave birth to a baby girl, then gave her away."

"What was the baby girl's name?" Jennifer asked.

"Uh ... Belinda."

"Who'd the mother give her to?"

"The baby's father and his wife. They already had two boys, so the baby girl got brothers in the deal."

"Then what happened?"

"I don't know."

"That's all?"

"Yup."

"That's a dumb story."

"Truly dumb," I said.

"I think it's a good story," Alex said, his eyebrows bunched together. "About the brothers."

Chapter Fourteen

Bananas for a Punk High Priestess

Alex seemed content to let his imagination fill in the blanks. Not so for Miss Priss.

"A shitty story," she said.

"Maybe it was a true story."

"Can't be a story if it's true! Why didn't you call it a true fact?" She was beginning to irritate me.

"And even if it's a true story fact, there has to be more."

Bugle yawned. The dog putting in his complaint.

"Okay, okay!" I pressed my fingers to my temples, closed my eyes.

"Yea!" Jennifer clapped her hands. The *au pair* bending to her will.

"Okay. Belinda turned out to be a princess endowed with mystical talents. She grew up and married a billionaire, then got into politics and became the first female President of the United States. One of her campaign promises was to abolish poverty in the land; so soon after she was in office, Belinda ordered the Republicans to share their wealth with all the poor people. Then she ordered that all the children be given Dove bars everyday."

"I wish she was President right now!" the boy said.

He wanted to know what happened to Belinda's brothers. I told him they owned all of the airline companies in the country and their sister cast a magic spell on the airplanes so that none of them ever crashed again. Which reminded them of their father's death. They burst into tears and I had to drive them to Archie's and buy them Dove bars to shut them up. This made-up story business was not all roses and sunshine.

By mid-week the crisis of a few days ago had lost its claw-hold on my psyche. When thoughts of my daughter rose up out of the muck of memory, I got busy and did something to make them go away. Barring unexpected reminders in the external world, these diseased thoughts would, in time, sink back down to hidden depths of consciousness, where I kept them like Peter, in a pumpkin, very well (and very mute).

Wednesday night I showed up for dinner and ignored Lucy in ways she had to notice, but she acted as if nothing had happened between us. I figured Billy had talked to her; told her if she wanted to keep the *au pair*, she'd better straighten up and fly right.

While I was helping Leona clean up the dinner mess, the phone rang. The cook answered the yellow set on the wall next to the refrigerator. It was Regina, calling for me.

"Go on," Leona said. "Take it in the library."

Before entering the room, I paused to stare at the sign over the door. Stupid thing said: "PAST." In bold black letters. Something to do with the retreat. As were the "PRESENT" and "FUTURE" signs above the den and living room doors.

Save for some folding chairs, the library was devoid of furniture. The built-in shelves were still stuffed with books, many of them bound in gold-tooled leather. I wondered how many of them Carson had read. I sat down cross-legged on the carpet facing the north windows and settled the phone in my lap.

After the banal preliminaries, Regina said, "I'm sure you've heard that Lucy is training me as a retreat advisor ... "

"I didn't hear anything."

"You didn't see my car parked there on several afternoons? I meant to come see you, but you were always busy with the kids. Aren't you excited about the retreat? To think you and I are a part of Lucy's original team!"

"I'm just taking care of her brats, Regina."

"An absolute honor."

"So why don't you take the honor and I'll be a plain ol' unimportant advisor."

"I would have no qualms about taking care of Lucy's children if that were my area of expertise. Lucy knows what she's doing, Shandie. She says you're superbly equipped for your job."

I yanked the receiver away from my ear and stared at it, as if it had sprouted horns. Superbly equipped! What did the woman have in her head in the place of brains?

"Which reminds me. I'm sure you heard that Judy Mansanerez closed her day care center. There are other places I could take Zach, but I haven't had time to check them out. I don't know when I'll have time, there's so much to get done before the retreat is ready, then I'll be helping Lucy and Edith ..."

"Edith?"

"Doctor Edith Jaffee. Lucy's main retreat advisor. Don't tell me you don't know about her. She's flying in from Reno this weekend."

"I get it. It's going to get so exciting you'll need a doctor to check blood pressures every hour or so."

"She's not that kind of doctor. She's a doctor of metaphysics. She got her degree in the Science of Mind church. But she doesn't belong anymore. They were too restrictive. So she went independent. Anyway, I was wondering ..."

"Let me guess. You want me to take care of Zachary."

"I'll pay for it, of course. It won't be every day or all day long, so I thought by the hour would be fair. Two dollars an hour? Lucy said she thought that was fair."

"Nice she consulted me. But what the hell, I'm just the *au pair*. What about the antique business?"

"I'll still do that part-time."

"And Zach won't be here every day, all day long?"

"Well ..."

My brain did a tap dance. An extra eighty dollars a week. Watching a third kid would be intrusive, even if it was Zach, and I was irked about not being forewarned, but eighty bucks was eighty bucks.

"Shandie ...?"

"Yeah ...?"

"Now don't get mad, I know you don't like us saying anything about Briana, but Lucy says ..."

"Good-bye, Regina." I slammed down the phone.

So this was how it was going to be. Lucy sneaking around, talking up my personal business with anyone who would listen, figuring someone—one of her admirers—would succeed where she'd failed in pressuring me to act on what she deemed a situation that had to be rectified. As if I could snap my fingers and disappear the adoption. I'd heard about cases where a mother tries to prove in court that she is now able to care for a child who is living with foster parents. In the process, she gets ripped apart by the social service pukes; her past activities, specifically with men are presented with gusto as evidence that she is unfit to raise any child. What they could say about me—what they would say. I wouldn't have a chance ... even if there was such a thing as an "adoption reversal," which I doubted. Even if I could afford the legal fees. How the hell did Lucy know things were so bad at the Dillingers'? Listening to "higher courts." The nut houses were full of people who heard things in their heads. Heard and believed these wild things.

The door squeaked open. Billy. He wanted the phone. I stood up and gave it to him.

"You okay?" he said.

"Don't I look okay?"

"You look fine."

Any other man say that, the way Billy said it, I would consider it a backdoor compliment. "So do you," I said, and winked, just to be mean. It was too dark to see if he blushed, but he sure moved away from me fast, mumbling that he had to get hold of Sid, something about a wrench he couldn't find.

Doctor Edith Jaffee and her four-year-old granddaughter, Castilla, arrived at Blue Acres on Saturday, Billy serving as chauffeur from Stapleton International Airport in Denver. The household stood on the porch and the half-wedding-cake stairs and watched as the woman and her grandkid climbed out of Lucy's lemon-colored Fleetwood. Leona nudged me and whispered, "Lucy says she's French and African-American. That's what they're calling themselves these days. African-Americans."

"The French are calling themselves African-Americans? That's weird."

She jabbed me with her elbow. "You know what I mean."

Billy seemed glum as he unloaded the woman's baggage from the trunk. Poor Billy, about to be overrun by a gaggle of women. He was probably starved for male companionship. Too bad he was so nervous around women. I was available.

I scrutinized the woman who had brainwashed Lucy. Doctor Edith Jaffee looked as old as Leona, but she was more attractive. Short, crinkly gray hair and she wore huge round glasses. A pretty face. She had on a stylish olive-green outfit with a kind of sweeping jacket. Chunky costume jewelry. Her skin color was darker than her granddaughter's. Castilla's eyes were green and her hair hung in thick brown braids that were tied off in purple ribbons. Jennifer and Alex were giving the kid the evil eye.

The moment I was introduced to the grandmother-daughter duo I knew I'd be expected to take care of the brat.

Naturally Lucy was there on the porch presiding. The day was sunny and warm and the mistress of Blue Acres had on a tangerine sundress. After all the phony hugs and trillings, she said to Doctor Edith, "Shandie is our *au pair*. She charges one hundred dollars a week per child."

"Wait a damn minute," I started to say but was distracted by the sound of an extra hundred dollars a week.

"Sounds like a bargain," said the phony doctor.

"Nothing against your grandkid, but no one said anything about me watching her."

The two women exchanged looks. Lucy said, "Our *au pair* would prefer a distinct vision of the future."

"So we'll have to introduce her to the Future Room," said Doctor Jaffee.

They both laughed.

I walked away.

To promote the retreat, Lucy had sent brochures to prospective Daughters of Light all over the western states. Leona said she'd used a mailing list she'd wangled from a metaphysical bookstore in San Francisco, and the money had been rolling in.

Glossy brochure, caricatures of three women on the front, one with long reddish-blond hair, the one in the center with long black hair, and the third, a black woman who wore big glasses. Anyone with an I.Q. above that of a boat oar could tell who the caricatures portrayed. They wore white gowns trimmed in gold. Arms stretched toward the heavens. "Daughters of Light Retreat," featuring "Lucinda Blue," in calligraphed lettering below the images. On the inside, such come-ons as "Discover the Priestess within. Heal the past. Crystallize the present. Map your future."

I examined the slick brochure while Leona, at the wheel of Carson's Riviera, drove me and the children into Elizabeth and Castle Rock, where she had errands to run. Jennifer, Alex, and Castilla were in the backseat, giggling about something.

"But who are these Daughters of Light?" I asked Leona, not for the first time.

"They aren't Daughters of Light before they come. Lucy puts them through the paces, then they'll get enlightened." She chuckled. "You and I ought to let her do her thing on us. Lord knows I could stand some enlightenment."

I made a rude noise. "I'm not about to coop up with a bunch of women stupid enough to fork over four hundred dollars to sit on folding chairs and listen to Lucy's bullshit."

"Mama doesn't say bullshit!" Jennifer piped from the backseat.

"Yes, she does," Alex said. "I heard her say it this morning."

The next day a "pre-retreat tour" was on the agenda for ten select ladies from Doubletree. Leona and I were invited to tag along while the children played upstairs in Jennifer's room.

The select included Felicia Perry and her daughter, Honey, Dolly Halverson, Beverly DeWitt, Ivy Chumbly, three women I didn't know and didn't want to know, and naturally my mother and Grandma Maddie were present. Decked in the same angelic gowns depicted on the cover of the brochure, Lucy, Doctor Jaffee, and Regina served as tour guides.

Two bedrooms upstairs and two in the basement had been converted to guest sleeping quarters. All four rooms were furnished with bunk-beds and inexpensive bureaus. White gowns, like the ones worn by Lucy and her advisors, hung in the closets. I wrinkled my nose. All of the participants were going to deck out like a bunch of angels?

Honey Perry wanted to know how Lucy knew what sizes to order. Lucy untied the sash around her waist and bloused out the one-size-fits-all gown to show that it would fit even fat Dolly. The retreat wasn't to be a fashion show, she said with a toss of her black mane. The gowns were to help them focus on things spiritual.

"You also ordered wings to stick on your backs, right?" I said. Several women laughed. Lucy smiled. Mom murdered me with a look.

Only four bathrooms in the house to be shared by almost thirty residents, but the select voiced no complaints at the prospect of such hardship. To listen to them, one sensed they'd be willing to bunk in tents in a blizzard just to be able to become Light Ladies. I was disgusted with their hysterical optimism.

We moved into the rooms on the main floor with signs over the doors announcing "PAST, PRESENT, FUTURE." Felicia Perry exclaimed over the "pristine beauty of the minimalist decor." Lucy, however, was not tricked by such mewling compliments. If they wanted to know more, they would have to attend the retreat. I recognized a clever sales maneuver when I saw it. By the end of the tour all ten women had signed up.

I pulled Grandma into the kitchen as the ladies passed into the dining room where Leona was serving coffee and cookies. "You're going to pay four hundred dollars to listen to Lucy's drivel?"

"Two hundred. Since we won't be staying overnight."

"What a deal. You going to smoke your pipe during the services?"

"I just might. Wouldn't that just knock off their drawers?"

I laughed. She waved me over to the window. "Who's that gentleman?"

Mr. Floy was wandering across the grass in his aimless fashion.

"Mr. Floy. Lucy's cousin. Or uncle. Isn't he weird?"

"Why, I think he looks robust," she said with an ironic smile.

"I thought you were sweet on Harold Waters."

"Oh, he's laid up with arthritis." She pronounced it arthur-ritis. "Harold's kind of frail."

"Robust," I mumbled as I went upstairs to get the kids—four of them now that Zach and Castilla had joined ranks.

As we climbed the hill to the secret story place, Bugle ran to and fro, as if herding a flock of sheep. When the kids and dog were settled on the blanket, I began the story I'd worked out in my head during the tour.

"Once upon a time there were three queens. The most beautiful queens you can imagine." I described them down to the rubies on their satin slippers. "Each queen had two children, a boy and a girl. WELL. These queens were so busy drinking wine, and snorting coke, and chasing after the good-looking men in the queendom, they had no time to spend with their children during the day. So you know what they did?"

"What?" Alex yelled.

"They banished the poor children to the forest. They said, 'Go eat dirt and twigs!'"

Zach looked frightened and Castilla let out a small cry. Bugle barked.

"BUT!" I threw my hand in the air.

"They found a treasure chest!" Jennifer shouted.

"Yes! But something else! They met a high priestess ten times more beautiful and kind than their old queen mothers."

"Is that you, Shandie," Jennifer said scornfully.

"Hell, no. This high priestess had blue hair down to her butt."

156

"She was a punk high priestess?" Zach said.

"Yes! A punk high priestess. And you know what she had? A magic wand!"

"Did the kids get whatever they wanted?" Castilla asked shyly.

"Yes! And what might that be?"

"A thousand Barbie dolls!" Jennifer said.

"Nossir," Alex said. "They got jet-cars."

And so it went.

On my day off I helped Leona in the kitchen. After chasing four urchins all week, the cook's chores seemed light duty. As usual she was full of news, saving the juiciest morsels for our coffee and cigarette breaks at the oak table.

She eased into a chair and lit a Newport. Shook out the match. "The wedding's off," she said.

"Wedding?"

"Steffen and Marilee!" She leaned forward, a glint in her eye. "I overheard Lucy talking to him on the phone last night. Marilee broke it off because she caught him with another woman. Lucy says, 'Too bad. Marilee's a nice woman.' Then Steffen tells her he's going to move here anyway."

"You were listening on the extension?"

"I could tell what he was saying by what she said. The gist of it, anyway. She tells him she and the kids would love having him in Colorado, but she doesn't want him living here ..." She stabbed the table with her thumb, as if he planned on taking up residence in her kitchen. "She's running a business and, no, she doesn't need any help. Then she goes on about how there are a gazillion apartments, condos, and townhomes for sale and rent around here. In fact, she has a townhome in Denver he can buy if he's serious about staying."

"My townhome," I said morosely.

"Yeah, the one you moved out of. Anyway, he must've been giving her a hard time because she was getting real emphatic about where he's going to live. 'This ain't ...' Well, she didn't say 'ain't.' She says, 'This is no hotel, Brother, and you can afford to live anywhere you want.' I thought she was about to have a fit deluxe.

Then they start talking about closing up her house in Reno and giving the Realtors power-of-attorney to sell the thing and all that."

"That's very interesting, Leona."

"I thought so." She lit another cigarette. Gave me a sidelong glance. "Can I ask you a personal question?"

Something in the way she said it put me on alert. "Sure ..."

"Taking care of kids ... is it hard, I mean considering what happened with Briana?"

I forced myself to stay seated. "Has Lucy been talking about that?"

"She just said one thing and it got me to thinking."

"What was the one thing?"

She looked surprised. Thought she could pop out my daughter's name with impunity.

"Well, I don't remember exactly."

"Try."

She blew smoke at the ceiling. Woman on the spot, nervous. "Something about you being so good with children and it was a shame about your daughter."

"So you feel sorry for me."

"Well, I ..."

"Do me a favor, Leona." I shoved back my chair. "Don't ever mention my daughter's name again."

I got the hell out of there. Good with children!

The brats were playing outdoors with Bugle. Trying to force a T-shirt over his head. I marched across the lawn. Stopped a few feet away.

"Hi!" the boy said. "Look-it—we're dressing Bugle up!"

"Get one thing straight, you little rotters."

Jennifer snapped her head up. Both brats stared at me, their mouths hanging down to their knees.

"I take care of you for the money, got that? The money."

I stomped to my cabin, went in and slammed the door. Good with children, my butt! I was about to fling myself on the bed and throw a "fit deluxe," when someone knocked on the door. Those damn kids coming for more. Goddamn masochists.

"Shandie?"

Billy. The man showing up at my most unstrung moments. Like he was psychic or something. I took a deep breath and opened the door.

"I'm going to Elizabeth and wondered if you needed anything."

"Tampax," I said, just to see his reaction.

His eyes glazed over. Pink blotches appeared on his cheeks. I could see his wheels turning. He wouldn't know what section of the store to look in. He'd have to ask a clerk. A spinster with blouse buttoned to her chin. Her beady eyes glaring at him over the rims of her glasses. Nasty boy.

"D-do they come in sizes?"

Oh, Billy. "Yeah. Teenage, DINKs, Boomers, and Old Maids. Bring me a box of Boomers."

A wrinkle in his left brow, a tiny suspicion poking through the hairs. I should have stuck with small, medium, large. Boomer-sized!

"You need some money?" I asked.

He walked away without another word. His boots making a kind of statement on the path.

I never did get those Boomer-sized Tampax, but my mood sure improved. What I got was a bunch of green bananas. Left on my doorstep in the middle of the night.

Chapter Fifteen

A Real Mother in a Boxcar

Sunday afternoon, we were invaded by the first batch of prospective Daughters of Light. Fourteen from points beyond Denver, and the ten ladies from Doubletree bringing the total to twenty-four. Most of the out-of-towners arrived in cars. Besides Colorado, I showed the kids license plates from New Mexico, Nevada, Arizona, and California. One woman came on a motorcycle from Cheyenne, Wyoming.

The six women who traveled the airways were transported from Stapleton International Airport by Tony Juarez who owned an old school bus that was decorated from rooftop to wheel frames in a swirling psychedelic design. When the monstrosity shuddered through the gates, rattling and belching black smoke, the children laughed and raced over to get a closer look. After Lucy and Doc Edith ushered the guests into the mansion, the children begged Tony to take them for a ride in his carnival on wheels. He drove them to the park and back, honking the horn all the way.

After this pampering, the brats were unruly and difficult to handle, so I herded them into my spare cabin and let them dress up in some of my old evening dresses, vests, and blouses, which kept the little beasts busy for the rest of the day.

The evening meal was a fiasco; Daughter of Light wanna-bes tripping over each other as they tried to lighten Leona's load in the kitchen, which delayed the process. Small women, large women, old, young, skinny, fat, and moderates, all of them babbling at once. Females shoulder-to-shoulder around the two tables in the dining room, platters of chicken, huge bowls of salad, potatoes, gravy, string beans passed from plate to plate, hands reaching for salt and pepper, butter and rolls. Lucy making the rounds, pals with everyone. Regina with a big smile, so proud to be on Lucy's original team. The only man present was Mr. Floy. He sat next to Grandma, the coots cozy in conversation. Grandma with bright lipstick on, the collar of her pink blouse flipped up. Hair combed, curled, sprayed. The old gal scheming on the duffer.

I set the table in the kitchen for myself, the kids, Leona, and Billy—who never showed. I kept thinking about those bananas. A woman with a dirty mind might think a man leaving a bunch of bananas on her doorstep was hinting at something.

By the time I escaped the bedlam at the mansion, I had myself convinced there was a invitation in those bananas. It was eight o'clock, almost dark, and the lights were on in Billy's cabin. I hurried home. Moments later, I reeked of Paloma Picasso cologne and had on a sexy sundress with spaghetti straps. Bananas in hand, I practically skipped to Mr. Hightower's cabin, tiptoed up the porch stairs, and stood outside the door. I could hear classical music playing softly. I knocked on the door. "Billy?"

I had no particular plan in mind. Present the bananas. He would smile—maybe laugh? Ask me in, show me his world. Maybe he'd bring out a photo album. We'd sit side-by-side on the bed and thumb through it. Then he'd look at me, I'd look at him and ...

I could still hear the music. Crickets were raising hell all around me, moths and other insects were diving into the porch light. Maybe he didn't hear me. I knocked again. "Billy! It's Shandie!" Why the hell didn't he answer? I began to feel ridiculous. The man flat ignoring me. What if I was in some kind of trouble? What if I had important news? (What if the bananas were only a joke?)

I jumped when the door opened a sliver. Hid the bananas behind my back. An edge of his head appeared in the sliver of light. One eye checking me out. I wished the hell I had kept on my jeans and shirt. Left the cologne in the bottle.

"What's up?" A get-lost tone.

"I was just wondering why you didn't show for dinner. You okay?"

"I'm fine."

"Good. Okay." If I turned around, he'd see the bananas. "That's all. I was just wondering."

He nodded.

Shut the damn door, Billy!

He did. After a moment I placed the bananas on the porch, carefully squashed them, then walked home with the gooey pulp squishing between my toes.

"Once upon a time there was a beautiful princess who had a boyfriend prince who wasn't very nice."

The brats were gathered around me on the blanket at the secret story place. It was a hot day gentled by a breeze that tossed and swirled leaves around us. The kids had apples I gave them before we climbed the hill.

"Why wasn't the prince nice?" Castilla asked.

"Because he was a geek. He never took her to any movies, he never brought her any candy or perfume, and he was a terrible grouch. He never even kissed her."

"So why'd she like him?" Jennifer asked.

Alex and Zach had already lost interest. They had set aside their apples and were gathering up pine cones, whispering to each other.

"Because he was the most handsome prince in the kingdom."

The girls nodded.

"Well, the princess ..."

"What's her name?"

"Shanadera."

"Sounds like Shandie."

"My distant cousin, if you must know the truth. Anyway, Shanadera decided she'd had enough of this grouchy old prince. So you know what she did?"

"She told him to blow off?" Castilla said. Jennifer laughed and kicked her feet.

"Yes, and more. She went to the store and bought a ton of rotten bananas—you know after they turn black and get so stinky you can't bear to have them even in your garbage can?"

The boys were beginning to show interest.

"Well. She bought this ton of rotten bananas, hired this man with a dump truck and paid him a thousand dollars to dump those rotten smelly bananas all over the prince's house."

"Gross!" Jennifer said.

The boys smiled.

"Which was the best thing Shanadera ever did because the next day a cuter prince moved to town. He had a white horse named Pegasus—he had wings, and Shanadera got to ride on it with him every day."

Steffen Xavier was due to arrive any day. Steffen Xavier, rich, no longer engaged, flying around on his winged horse. I bet if I knocked on his door late at night, he would open it and invite me in. As would any normal man.

"What happened to the prince that got the bananas dumped on his house?" Alex wanted to know.

"He stank of rotten bananas for the rest of his life, and no woman would come within a hundred yards of him."

Not that he gave a big damn.

To avoid the retreat hoopla, I frequently took the kids to the park and up to the secret story place. Billy continued to keep a low profile, eating meals in his cabin, and escaping to Kiowa in the afternoons, ostensibly to help Sid erect a new barn. He didn't seem to mind the stench of a ton of rotten bananas dumped on his cabin, but that was Billy, ever the cool one.

Friday afternoon after lunch I sent the kids out to run in the sprinklers, then worked in the kitchen while Leona went upstairs to take a short nap. I was wiping down counters when I heard a commotion nearby. I peered into the hallway and saw a group of women in white gowns huddled in the dining room. Someone was being consoled. Mom. Grandma looked up, saw me, and shuffled into the kitchen.

"Your mother didn't get out of the Past Room. You can't go into the other rooms until you free up your past. I wasn't in there two hours. My past wasn't much. Had a few things to clear up with your grandfather and Duke, but it was nothing very serious."

"So why didn't Mom just walk into the other room?"

"She'll have to come back next week," Maddie went on, ignoring my remark. "Might be here for several weeks, but I think she'll get clear by next week. She's all hung up about you, Shandie."

She patted her lips, as to stuff the words back in her mouth. "I shouldn't say anything." She eyed a tray of oatmeal cookies on the table. Reached under the cellophane, snatched one.

"You should hear all the stuff Lucy is telling us. She says those quantum mechanic physicists are about to catch up with the mystics."

I rolled my eyes.

"Those scientific types, they have to try and prove everything physically. But mystics know the truth without all that."

"Sounds real interesting," I lied.

"Those rooms we call 'Past,' 'Present,' and 'Future?'" She scratched her hip, a faraway look in her eyes. "Those signs are just symbolic. Represents how we think about time. But really everything's happening all at once. It's like parallel universes, everything overlapping." She chuckled. "Oh, I don't know what the heck I'm talking about. I'm no mystic." She nibbled the cookie. "Lucy says those UFO visitors might be us visiting ourselves in the past. Ain't that something?"

"What UFO visitors?"

"Guess you'll have to attend the retreat and find out."

"I don't have two hundred dollars to spend on hearing about UFO visitors from the future, Grandma."

"Oh, I'm sure Lucy would let you come for free. She's real big-hearted."

"And who would take care of the kids? Forget it. I'm not going." I could just picture Billy's expression if I decked out in one of those shapeless angel gowns. Not that I cared a banana what he thought.

That evening, the first batch "graduated." Mom was not present. I wondered if she called in sick. Maybe, I thought mean-spiritedly, she was told not to come.

The ceremony consisted of champagne in long-stemmed glasses, and presentations of quartz crystals on chains, and certificates with the graduates' names scrolled in gold ink, declaring them officially Daughters of Light. A lot of clapping and big grins. I was impressed by the trimmings, the white gowns, the crystals, the fancy certificates, the gold ink, the "Past/Present/Future" rooms. What a racket. Bunch of silly housewives with time and money to squander. Bored with going to Reno and Vegas to gamble. A week away from their old men. And now they had certificates they could tout to friends and family back home. Which no doubt would bring Lucy more business. Excellent racket. I would never admit this out loud, but the witch rose a notch in my estimation.

Early the next morning, before I was out of my pajamas and robe, my mother knocked on the door. I saw her out the window and seriously considered pulling a Billy. Let her wait awhile, then open the door a crack, plant a suspicious eye on her, say, "What's up," in a foul tone of voice.

"Shandie? Are you awake?"

"Just a minute ..." I said it musically, like I was delighted it was her but, for the moment, was incapacitated. Maybe I had bad knees and had to locate my cane.

"Are you all right?"

I opened the door. She looked haggard. But as usual, well-groomed. Tan slacks, white blouse, tan purse with white trim, muted orange scarf at her neck. That fine blond hair pulled back in a French twist.

"I need to talk with you for a few moments."

I flashed on Grandma saying Mom was stuck in the Past Room because she was hung up on me. Did she blab to everyone about what a burden I had been?

I opened the door wider, stepped back. Wished everything wasn't so neat and organized. I missed the familiar look of repugnance on her face, as was always the case when she used to come into my room at home. One sweeping glance and she dismissed my living quarters. No antiques here, no brand-name furniture, no expensive knickknacks. One painting on the wall, a Transylvanian farm scene worth probably two dollars. She made a beeline for the only comfortable chair, the old brown chair in the corner between the table and the makeshift bookshelves.

I asked if she'd like a cup of coffee. Yes, that would be nice, so I filled two mugs. I sat down on the bed. She stared into her mug and frowned, as if concerned there might be a dead mosquito stuck on the bottom.

"I need to clear up a few things," she said, her interest shifting to something in the kitchenette. Maybe the way the sunlight was spilling in through the window and saturating the counter.

So my mother was here to "clear up a few things." So she could get her fancy certificate and hang it over the mantel for everyone to see. This was the first time I could remember her coming to me on bended knee, so to speak. I sipped my coffee, calm with power.

She sighed. "I'm having trouble knowing where to start. This is embarrassing. But as they say, 'the truth will set us free.'" She attempted a smile, failed.

"First I want to say I always underestimated what you were capable of. I don't know where I got the idea you were less equipped than Regina to meet life's challenges. I suppose because you were so much younger. Which is unfair and trite.

"I was always hard on you, Shandie, and I'm sure you felt it was because there was something wrong with you. The truth is, after you were born your father started seeing other women, and somehow I got things twisted in my mind and blamed you for it. Yours was a hard birth, and I was a long time recovering my strength. I don't remember thinking consciously that Duke wouldn't have strayed if I had bounced back faster, but now I see it was the conclusion I came to. It was irrational, but as Lucy says, emotions pay no homage to logic, and the best of us can get caught in the web of ego."

She looked at me with a kind of nervous expectancy. I had the feeling she'd been coached. Did she expect me to throw my arms around her and say all was forgiven? Did she expect me to believe her bizarre explanation for all the years of abuse? Woman trying to figure out why she hated her daughter. Having to come up with something so she could graduate the "Past" room. Get her crystal necklace, and the certificate with her name scrolled in gold ink.

"And I'm sorry for the way I behaved when you got pregnant with Briana."

I jerked with such violence, coffee sloshed out of the mug onto the carpet.

"Shit! I wish the hell everyone would shut up about that!" I managed to control the trembling in my hands and set the mug on the bedside table.

"I feel somewhat responsible for your inability to talk about it, Shandie. If I had been less critical ..."

"Oh, you're so powerful."

Her eyes went dead. I knew she ached to tear into me for being sarcastic, but God forbid she flunk angel school.

"I want you to know that I realize I could have been more supportive."

More supportive? I forced myself to remain silent. Keep my mouth shut and she'd get done and get the hell out.

"Lucy tells me she found some disturbing information that indicates that things are not going well for the Dillingers, and she advised you to take some sort of action."

"Yeah. Go down there, knock on the door, say, 'Hi, Alice, I'm Briana's birth mother and I heard Wesley turned into a drunk and lost his business and you had to go to work and the kids are alone during the day. So fuck you, Alice; give me my kid back.'"

She flinched when I used the "F" word. Saint Kate. But dammit, I had to talk tough to keep the tears away. Lucy caught me off-guard that day in her bedroom, but I was ultra-skilled at keeping the shield in place in front of my mother. People who have never felt the kind of pain I felt giving up my daughter thought they could sympathetically reason away the hurt. What they did was, they marched right inside of you and stomped all over the tender places, then called you hysterical when you screamed.

"You're not alone in thinking the idea is absurd," she said. "Lucy is very wise in most matters, but in this case I'm afraid her judgment is slightly askew." The corners of her mouth reported smugness that she had seen in Lucy this flaw. "I suspect she is highly sentimental when it comes to family issues. I would suggest a discreet call to the social services administration. Have them look into the matter and report back to you."

"And if they say Lucy is right—if they say things really are bad?"

"Then let the law do whatever is called for. Perhaps they would engage a sociologist, who would began making routine visits."

I tucked my hands under my thighs to prevent them from attaching themselves, of their own accord, to my mother's neck. "Thanks for the advice," I said, trying to keep my voice level. She set the mug, still full of coffee, on the table. "Surely you don't imagine yourself in a better position now to take on the responsibilities of a mother ..."

The tiniest hope she had come sincerely to clear up the past died a quick, whimpering death.

"Surely not."

"I think it's wonderful you can watch Lucy's children. But taking care of one's own is entirely a different matter. You couldn't send your own up to the house ..." she gestured, "every night or whenever there's a problem."

"I get the picture, Mother."

She nodded, smiled. Picked up her purse, stood, smoothed down her slacks.

"So nice of you to drop by."

She stared out the window. "I hope you can find it in your heart to forgive me, Shandie, for all the years I was so hard on you, and for being critical when you came up pregnant."

"Great, fine. So now you can go into the Present Room. Congratulations."

Without looking at me again, chin in the air, she walked out the door.

I fell on the bed and cried.

Monday, Doubletree was socked in with rain, so I was forced to tell the story inside my spare cabin. Not a story that would wait for the sun to pop through the clouds and dry off the secret story place.

Earlier, Alex and Zach had fought over a pair of Billy's cast-off coveralls, so I had cut them in half. Alex was wearing one leg, Zach, the other, individual straps crossed over chests and looped around necks. Jennifer had on a bejeweled jean jacket that hung to her knees, and Castilla was decked in a black lace nightgown, over her shorts and shirt. Both girls' lips were smeared with bright red gloss and their chests were loaded with gaudy necklaces.

I sat in front of the windows facing the kids, my legs crossed, the rain pinging behind me. The room smelled of damp leaves and old clothes.

"Once upon a time ..." I liked stretching out the phrase to build tension. Inevitably one of the urchins would jump in with a guess. That pause was something they could not abide.

This time it was Alex. "There was a beautiful princess ..."

"Nope. This time a whole family. A mommy, a daddy, three boys and one girl."

"How old?" Jennifer asked.

"Boys were seven, eight, and three, and the girl was six, just like you. She had long red hair she wore in pigtails, like yours, Castilla. But hers were done up in double loops, like a German girl's. Because that's what she was. Name was Gretchen. Her brothers had blond hair and they wore fancy leather shorts with flowers embroidered on the straps. Brother's names were Peter, Hans ... and Beetlenose."

They giggled.

"Don't laugh. Beetlenose was Gretchen's favorite brother. He was three, like Alex and Zach. His nose was so cute! Looked just like a beetle's." Alex laughed and pinched his nose.

169

"Okay. This family was super rich. They lived in a castle with diamonds dripping off the ceiling and red satin walls ..." I expounded on the castle and described the toys the children owned. Not only toys, but each child had a TV set and a VCR.

"And they never had to take baths, unless they felt like it, and then it was so fun because the tub was golden and filled with fish!"

"I'd catch'em with my hands!" Alex said. So would Zach, but Alex would catch more.

I described the love the family members shared, how they were always smooching each other and singing songs and telling goofy stories.

"Then one day this terrible-looking woman with messy red hair comes and knocks on the door. Gretchen answers. 'What do you want?' she says, and the woman with the messy red hair goes, 'Guess what? I'm your real mother.' Well, Gretchen almost threw up! The woman was *so* ugly! She had a black patch over her left eye and big boogers hanging out of her nose."

"Yecch!" Zach said.

"Give her a hanky," Jennifer said.

"Hey—who's telling this story?"

"You, Shandie."

"Okay, but it was just a wadded-up rag with dried snot all over it. She was too poor to own anything as nice as a hanky."

"Was she Gretchen's real mother?" Castilla asked.

"Yes. See, immediately after Gretchen was born, the red-haired lady was captured by the Nazis and thrown into prison. That's why these rich people adopted Gretchen when she was a baby. But they never told her about it.

"You are not my mother!" she screamed, and slammed the door in the woman's face. Gretchen ran and hid under her bed. But this didn't bother the ugly woman one bit. She marched right into that castle and had a long talk with the rich parents. And all of the adults agreed that Gretchen could live with whomever she wanted to.

"So Gretchen had quite a decision to make. She thought about it so hard her brain hurt." I clutched my head, grimaced, then looked up. "Of course, we know what she decided ..."

"Go live with her real mother!"

I glared at Doc Edith's grandkid. "We're talking rich, Castilla. Is she going to walk away from one hundred Barbie dolls and her own TV and VCR? Get real."

"She can take her stuff with her," Jennifer said.

"No way. I forgot to tell you. Her mother lives in a railroad boxcar. If you had any toys the bums would steal them."

"She better stay with her rich mommy and daddy," Alex said. "Right—!"

"No sir, Alex," Jennifer said. "That's her real mother. What if Mama was your real mother and she lived in a boxcar, wouldn't you go live with her anyway?"

The boy brightened. "Maybe she'd let me wear the patch!"

"Never!" I cried. "It covers a hole in her head where worms could crawl out if she took off that patch. You still want to live with her?"

"She can't be that bad, Shandie," Jennifer said. "That's not fair."

"Who said life was fair?"

The girl whipped her arms over her chest, jutted her chin. "Well, I don't care. If she was my real mother, I'd go live with her."

"Oh, bullcrap! Okay, how about this? She only has one leg and has to hobble around on crutches so you'd have to go work—at a vomit factory!"

The younger kids clutched their throats and made gagging sounds.

Jennifer flipped a shank of black hair over her shoulder. "So then she'd need me real bad."

I came to my feet. "You haven't got the good sense God gave you, Jennifer Blue!" I jerked open the door, banged it behind me.

Hunched under the roof overhang, I hugged myself and waited for my heart to calm. The door squeaked open. I heard Alex say in a high throaty whisper, "Look! She's getting rained on!"

I pushed the door open, almost cracking the boy's nose. He fell on his butt; his feet flew in the air.

"IT'S MY DAMN STORY!" I bellowed. "Gretchen did NOT go live with that gross woman in a boxcar, she had more sense than that, she didn't even KNOW the witch, and she LOVED Beetlenose, too much to leave him, never mind the castle and the golden bathtub filled with fish and the TV and the VCR; she wasn't a TOTAL materialist, she was SMART, DAMMIT, SMART! YOU HEAR ME?"

Zachary started crying and the others fixed me smokey stares. I stomped out, slammed the door. Kicked it.

Billy

Chapter Sixteen

A Dead Hairy Something

After the vision, Billy watches Shandie. He observes her lead the kids up to the ridge behind the cabins, packing a blanket and a brown paper sack—stuffed with books? toys? The kids dressed up like gypsies. He sees her pile them into her old car. She drives them to the park, or to Elizabeth, the kids returning with ice cream or chocolate smeared on their faces. He watches her chase them across the grass, playing a game only she and they and the dog understand.

Everything she wears looks sexy on her. Tight jeans, shorts, T-shirts, loose cotton blouses. Her hair is long and clean and shiny. Her eyes, the color of the sky after the sun has slipped behind the mountains. A sensuous woman who seems unaware of it (a dangerous woman). But one who is talented with children. She is also sarcastic and unpredictable. She takes pleasure in causing embarrassment, and shows little respect for a person's privacy. Plenty of reasons for Billy to keep his distance. But he can't ignore her entirely, any more than he can ignore his most recent vision.

He has observed her line up the kids after lunch and march them into the bathroom to wash their hands and faces. If one did not know better, one might think they preferred Shandie to their mothers. No question about it, she is good with children. But hopeless in the kitchen.

One recent Saturday evening, Leona was feeling ill and asked him and Shandie to fix dinner. They decided hamburgers would be the easiest. Shandie offered to fry the meat, then poured half a bottle of liquid Crisco into the pan.

"Why did you do that?" he asked.

"To keep them from sticking."

"Hamburger makes its own grease," he had to tell her.

Then he caught her slicing the onions so thick a horse would have trouble chomping into the finished sandwich. He showed her how to slice them thin. She did know how to pile potato chips into bowls, but that was about all.

"Mom never let me near the stove. Once I tried to make oatmeal cookies, but I thought baking powder was the same as shortening—I don't know why—and those cookies were like little white bricks."

Hopeless in the kitchen, but she delighted the kids by arranging lettuce pieces, olives and pickles to form happy faces on their plates.

A few weeks ago Billy was convinced Shandie had no mothering instincts at all. He was wrong; she might do okay as a mother.

Might, might not. Who is he to judge? More to the point, who is he to intercede? He did not get her pregnant, she is not his woman, never was his woman, and he certainly did nothing to encourage her to sign those adoption papers.

So why this vision?

The mystery drives him to do more than watch from a distance. Compelled to resolve the question, he creeps closer.

Crouched outside her cabin, Billy strains to hear the story about "Gretchen." It is raining, the steady patter serving to conceal unintended noises he might make that will give him away. He is mesmerized by the story, and disturbed. There seems little hope he can ignore the vision now.

When she raises her voice, he ducks and moves across the porch and around to the back of the cabin on swift, noiseless feet. He has studied Chinese and Native American folklore but has decided he is a mutant, and belongs to neither culture. His genes tell another story. He can make himself invisible and slip through a crowd unseen if he wants to. His feet are like feathers when he wants to move without being heard.

He squats behind the cabin in the rain to catch his breath. Hears Shandie slam the door. Kick it.

Billy can count on one hand the number of visions he had before Carson died. A gift, his mother said. A curse, he is sure. What good has ever come of them? His wife Lia might be alive today if he hadn't dismissed the vision foretelling the accident that killed her. She might have gone to art school, might have become a famous artist. She might be here now. The baby she was carrying might have lived.

A gift, his mother insisted. How so, when he was powerless to change the events he saw in his mind? What value was there in seeing Carson plunge to the earth in his airplane the moment it happened?

In the first vision, he saw the accident that killed Lia beforehand but told himself it was a mental aberration. How was he to know the horrible things he saw in his mind foretold the future? When

Lia suggested they stop at his mother's house to see the lilacs on the way to work that day, it never occurred, even subliminally, that this might indicate a route around death. In the vision, he saw a pickup plow into their Volkswagen Bug. He saw the medical technicians peel Lia off the dashboard. Wild imaginings going berserk in his brain, he thought. Some dark force poisoning his mind with visions of his worst fears coming true.

After Lia died, he tore his mind apart trying to recall the details of the vision. Some hidden clue that, if heeded, might have prevented the fatal accident. The thrust of the vision was the pickup crashing into the Bug. But there was also a lilac bush off to the side. In hindsight, a little study might have caused him to question a lilac bush in such a grisly scene. A bit of alertness, a respect for the "gift" might have triggered a response when Lia suggested they drive by to see his mother's lilacs.

He cursed the gift, swore he would never allow it to happen again. Wasn't his mind his own?

A few days after Lia died he saw in another vision his mother slip on a wet floor and break her neck. This time, he reviewed diligently what he had seen. Again there was a clue, a kind of indistinct sub-scene, around the edges, like you might see on an unfinished painting: several log cabins clustered on an expanse of grass. So when Carson Blue offered to hire him as a gardener and he drove to Blue Acres and saw those very cabins, he leaped at the offer, moved his mother into one of the cabins, and forbade her to ever scrub another floor.

There were no more significant visions until Carson died. Then recently he was cursed with another vision. (They seemed to come in twos or threes.) A small aircraft in a turbulent sky over Blue Acres. It did not crash; this was no death vision. The aircraft rocked violently as clouds around it rained down debris, sticks, stones, dirt, mud. The sound of a man laughing in the background. Shandie crying. Off to the side stood a small girl in a swimming suit. She clutched what looked like a dead hairy animal. As before, this sub-scene was indistinct, but he sensed the child's loneliness, and it was deep and bad.

The meaning was clear: A life of turbulence if Shandie hooked up with Lucy's brother. A little girl left behind to suffer. Briana, there was no doubt.

But what the hell was he supposed to do about it? If the vision had shown the airplane crashing, he would have been obligated to warn Shandie—scare her—to stay out of all small aircraft for, maybe, the rest of her life. Even in that case, he would be subjecting himself to undefined and unwanted levels of involvement. She would demand to know why he was issuing such a warning. He could think of no good resulting from telling her he was a freak who had visions.

Maybe this vision was a kind of anomaly. The others were literal, but this one seemed to have symbolic elements. Maybe nothing was required of him. None of his business.

Then the vision reoccurred! The night Shandie came to his cabin and squashed the bananas on his porch. He might have invited her in—might have—if moments earlier he hadn't suffered a rerun of the vision. What in the hell was going on? He'd never had the same vision twice. Was some strange karma operating here? An unpaid debt because he allowed his wife (and unborn child) to die? But if karma worked in such exacting tits for tats, the action he took in response to the vision about his mother dying should have balanced things out.

He remembers clearly what his mother said soon after they moved to Blue Acres. Such a sweet face she had, a reflection of the woman she was. She said, "This all fits into a pattern we cannot see with our eyes. Trust this man, Billy. He was sent to us for reasons beyond simple kindness. Our life will be here and you will serve him for as long as he lives. People will say it is because you are part Chinese and are bound to serve him because he came to your rescue when death was all around you. But it is something else. You will help him in strange ways, and he in return will help you in something equally strange."

At the time, he let the words roll over him like an evening breeze. Ling Sang was always uttering proclamations that seldom proved to be prophetic. Serve the man as long as he lived? Wrong.

He would stay for as long as she lived, and then he would get on with his own life. By the time his mother died he would be over the pain of losing Lia and his unborn child, and would start that landscaping business.

But after she died, he had sunk roots so deep into Blue Acres it would have been like tearing off his legs to leave. So Ling was right to some extent. Her words blowing over the plains of his mind like chinook winds in January.

He never served Carson in "strange ways," not that he was aware. And even if he did so unknowingly, Carson was now dead. Too late for him to return the help in some equally strange way. Unless it had something to do with Shandie ... Nonsense. There was absolutely no reason for this vision about her. Plainly it dramatized the consequences of her ill-conceived choices. Was it his responsibility to try and lessen the suffering caused by her mistakes? By what right could he interfere?

And what right did he have to do something that might shine a bad light on Carson? Carson took him in, took in his mother, provided them both a safe and prosperous life. His mother lived seven more rich years before she succumbed to a stroke.

If he ignores the vision? Shandie will suffer the consequences of her own choices. What is wrong with that? Not that Billy wants to see her suffer, but he isn't the originator of life's karmic patterns. And he certainly isn't obligated to Shandie in any way. He can't imagine warning her about Steffen, much less suggesting she act on Lucy's crazy idea about trying to reverse the adoption. Dangerous to stick his hand in that barrel of snakes. His first responsibility is to Carson. The man who came to his aid after he let his wife and child die.

Muddying the waters, Lucy cornered him recently and issued a disturbing reprimand. It happened down in the basement office, after they worked a while on the new bookkeeping system. Lucy enamored with new software that made it easier for her to check his work. A program she could master, in case he ever left. In case he died. In case she fired him. If ever she did, Billy would consider himself free of further obligation to Carson. But she showed no inclination to want him gone.

Free of obligation, he could start that landscaping business. Or he might become a finish carpenter. Design and build ornate cabinets, splendorous staircases, magnificent doors. Things he had dreamed of doing to the mansion when it became his. Dead dreams.

The new bookkeeping system gave Lucy more control. It was one of the ways she was different from Carson. Carson's interest in the books had stopped at the bottom line. He signed checks without looking at them. Authorized a shift in funds when the operating account got low. The books were Billy's to keep however he saw fit. His domain—except in the arena Carson deemed "personal." The arena where Lucy found the canceled checks issued to Shandie, and those damned invoices.

They had turned off the computer and he was at the door when Lucy said, "You know, Billy, our gifts are a responsibility. Bury them and your spirit shrinks."

He was shocked stiff for a moment. Then he came to his senses and got out of there quickly, before she could say any more.

How did she know? She didn't. She sensed things, Leona said. Maybe she had romantic notions about his Indian blood. People assumed he knew all about sweat lodges and other American Native spiritual practices. Maybe Lucy was like a woman he once dated. Naomi swore she could see in his eyes a "shamanistic quality." A woman he liked but dropped fast. Afterward he caught himself looking in the mirror to see if he could spot that strange quality in his eyes. Damn woman.

The night after Lucy confronted him, he had the vision about Shandie again. Three times! Something making it clear this was no anomaly. He was to act on it. But what could he do?

He squats behind the cabin to catch his breath. Hears Shandie slam the door. Kick it. He waits. It is raining, she will go back inside. Tell the kids another story, dress them up like dolls. Or she'll go next door and pout.

But, no, she is marching across the porch in his direction! He shoots up, moves swiftly to the south and crouches there, strains to hear above the patter of rain. Looks up, sees Lucy at the window in the library! Shandie calls her a witch. Maybe it is true.

He comes to his feet, pulls his jean jacket up around his ears, shoves his hands into his pockets and heads toward his cabin. If Shandie sees him now she won't know from what direction he comes.

"Billy!"

He quickens his step. Maybe she will think he doesn't hear her above the rain noise.

"BIILLEEE!"

She runs in front of him. Her blue eyes are wide, as if she is scared or alarmed.

"Can we talk?" A clap of thunder almost drowns her words. The rain comes down harder. She falls in stride alongside him.

"I thought maybe we could share a cup of tea or something. You have any tea? Coffee would be great, too." She is hugging herself, shivering as she trots beside him. "Or maybe you don't want any company right now ..."

He steps up on the porch, pauses. "Where are the kids?"

"In my cabin. We get along a lot better if I leave them alone once in awhile, believe me."

He opens the door, walks in, goes directly to the stove, and turns on the burner beneath the teapot.

"Oh, wow, you're so neat ... Of course you are. I mean you're neat in everything."

The wall next to his bed is striped with shelves full of books arranged in sections. On the top shelf is a collection of Native American books. A predominance of Lakota, Hopi, and Pueblo literature, though his heritage is Cherokee. Books about Asia on the next shelf down. Subjects on the next shelf range from gardening, landscaping, remodeling and woodworking, to electrical and mechanical how-to books. The shelf below features writings about astronomy, solar energy and the environment in general, including a collection of Edward Abbey's works. On the lowest shelf are novels, and a number of software manuals. He reads, for pleasure, LeCarre, Clancy, Vonnegut, Hillerman, and Erdrich. Missing are books about psychic phenomenon. These are under the bed.

A blanket with a Native American design covers the bed. Not because he is half-Cherokee, but because he happens to like it. Only one painting on the wall, a still life; an apple, a jar, a cluster of grapes, painted by his wife Lia a month before she died. His guitar stands in a corner next to a small desk, on which rests an Epson laptop computer and an energy-efficient lamp with a circular tube bulb that resembles a spaceship. The strange-looking lamp casts a pinkish glow. A small pot of struggling African violets sits on the windowsill above the sink. Billy keeps his snowshoes and cross-country skis in the basement of the mansion. He owns a clock radio and a small television set. He stores them both on the floor of the closet, retrieving them when he wants noise.

He stares out the window while the water boils, and responds to his guest's remarks in monosyllables. When the teapot hisses, he sweeps it off the burner, takes two china cups and saucers out of the cupboard, puts Celestial Seasonings Emperor's Choice teabags in them, pours the scalded water, then takes them to the table. He goes back for teaspoons, sweetener, sugar.

Shandie tastes the tea before it steeps. "Ummm—perfect for a rainy day, huh?"

He grunts.

"I've been thinking," she says.

"Mmmm."

"What if I did go to Colorado Springs? Maybe I could spy on the house."

Billy shuts his eyes. A voice in his head screams No!

"You threw away the address."

"Yeah, but I memorized it."

She takes a sip of tea. Holds the cup with both hands. Her hair hangs in swiggles around her face and shoulders. Her shirt is damp and clings to her breasts. He looks away.

"So what do you think?"

"Mmmm?"

"You think I should go down there, check things out? All that stuff Lucy said kind of scares me if you want to know the truth. I mean she was a real bitch the way she told me about it, but what if something really is wrong?"

She frowns. "Of course I don't know what I could do if things are bad. It's not like I can afford a lawyer. I mean if there was something I could do legally. So what do you think?"

"I think you'd be opening yourself up for more heartache."

Lucy's remark about his spirit shrinking resounds in his head. His spirit must be the size of a pea by now. A shriveled pea.

She sighs over her cup. "Yeah, I can't see the logic in it either. If I go down there and see things are bad, what can I do? But then, she is my kid ..."

Was, he almost says.

"I mean ... she was. I signed her over."

Billy is doing his best to keep his eyes on anything but the woman in front of him, but only a blind man would miss the swelling of tears.

"You did the best you could."

"Yeah. The best ..."

"I need to get out of these wet clothes."

She nods. Smiles weakly. "Need any help?"

"No."

"Well, guess I'll be going." She pushes back her chair, gets up. "The kids have probably wrecked both my cabins by now."

Billy does not get up, nor does he say anything as Shandie leaves. After she is gone, he slams a fist on the table. The china cups jump, one flips on the floor, and the other crashes into a saucer and breaks them both.

Billy dreams of camping around Jackson Hole in northern Wyoming. It's been three years since he has taken a real vacation. He pictures himself atop a fine quarter horse on a narrow mountain pass, bighorn sheep, an occasional grizzly, and eagles his only company. Or he could go to Montana. He's never been to Montana and is sure he would like the big sky up there.

Dreams of escape. Impossible. He is committed to Lucy for the duration of the retreat seminars. (He is committed for life, he fears.) After the retreat is over, it will be autumn. Next spring is the earliest he can go on such a trip. But spring will be too late to escape the complications around Shandie.

He escapes to Sid's house in the afternoons. The barn is up and needs paint. Sid is in no hurry, for which Billy is grateful. When the paint job is done, he can help Sid in other ways. He is willing to clean out hog pens—anything to provide a reason to stay away from Blue Acres as much as is possible without seriously compromising his first duty.

Sometimes he wishes his job were spelled out in specifics on paper. Besides keeping the books, he maintains the house, the grounds, the cars. In short, he is to handle all problems in all areas. Sometimes this tries his patience sorely, for instance: Lucy pulls him aside Wednesday morning and asks him to gather information on condos and townhomes close to Doubletree. Her brother is due to arrive any day and Steffen won't be staying at Blue Acres for long. Lucy wants to put this information in her brother's hand the moment he arrives. Though Billy abhors the assignment, there is some relief in hearing that Steffen will live elsewhere.

Thursday morning while he drinks coffee with Leona before anyone else is awake, she informs him that Lucy and her brother have been "wrangling" over where Steffen will live.

"He plans on buying his own place," she says. "Eventually. That's the rub. I think he enjoys torturing Lucy. Says he'll move on when he finds the right place, like that. Lucy wants him gone before he gets here!"

"I thought they were pretty close."

Leona bends over her cup with that old glint in her eyes. Gearing up to reveal some secret. She takes a quick drag on her cigarette.

"They are close. But Lucy has good reason for wanting him to live off-site."

No need to ask Leona for the reason. She can keep the secret no more than a cat can keep a mouse for a pet.

"I heard her tell Doctor Jaffee that Steffen's problem is, he can't keep his pecker in his pants!" Leona pauses to gauge his reaction, her eyes wide and alert to catch his agreement that this is shocking news. "—Which will be Lucy's problem if he hangs around and stirs up the women. Ain't that priceless? A rooster in the hen-house!"

When Billy wakes Friday morning he can barely get out of bed. His back is killing him. His rule is no coffee until he completes a round of T'ai Chi, but today he will break the rule. He hobbles over to the counter, starts a pot of coffee and tries to do some simple stretching while it brews.

Carefully he sits down at the table and indulges in a fantasy as he plies himself with liquid caffeine. He imagines that when he feels better he will drive to Safeway and stock up on enough food to get him through the winter. Beans, coffee, canned goods. Come spring, he will pack up everything and move to Wyoming or Montana. Maybe he will write a book while he waits for the ice to thaw.

He laughs at himself, the sound more a moan than a laugh. Even if such a wild plan were possible, his mind would be completely gone by September. Lucy would commit him to the nuthouse in Pueblo. He visualizes the doctors scratching their heads and coming up with some long word to describe his condition. Something that describes an antisocial patient who has hallucinations. A man who could be a danger to himself and others. When his back is not killing him.

How will he react when, not if, Steffen makes a play for Shandie? How will he feel when he sees them together? Sees them flying around in the man's three hundred thousand dollar machine. Will he be able to tell himself it's none of his business? Dammit, it isn't his business.

His mind rakes over the vision. Again. He turns up a new leaf: What Shandie does when the rooster comes to the henhouse will reveal the woof and warp of her true desires. A mystery that he has had this vision (three times!), but one thing is certain: It is about her choices. If she chooses to fly with the rooster and ignores her daughter, he will be free of obligation. If she resists the man's advances and continues to express concern for Briana, he might—might—have to do something.

He feels confident this new insight will work on his body and by Saturday morning his back will be fine. He is no stranger to this condition; his chiropractor said it is due to stress. Eliminate the stress and his body will stop reporting the mental conflict. He is sure this new leaf of wisdom will work on him like healing hands.

This seems well and fine and sensible, but Saturday morning, his back is worse. It is all he can do to hobble up to the house and call his chiropractor in Castle Rock. Doc Wayne knows him well. Doc has a file on him an inch thick.

Billy can barely pull himself into his Jeep. He stuffs a pillow behind his back before he starts the engine. Distracted, he forgets the bundle of white shirts he was going to take to Castle Cleaners. His mind is tangled around his back like a calf bound up for the branding iron.

Doc Wayne's office is a bustle of activity. A receptionist who bubbles about the beautiful weather, the radio blaring heavy metal music, the doc cracking a litany of bad jokes as if laughter is a part of the treatment. Billy manages to smile at the jokes while silently cursing the doctor as he works him over. He endures the lecture about coming in more often to keep his "hinges oiled." Which is why he does T'ai Chi, which usually works.

Not cured but feeling less pain, Billy is on the road headed home before most people have plugged in their coffee pots.

About a mile away from Archie's store, he begins to sense some sort of trouble ahead. Nothing he sees in his mind, but his body knows something is wrong. His heart races and he feels tense all over. He grips the wheel and scans the countryside, left, right, ahead, and in the rearview mirror. Nothing!

Then he sees it. Shandie's Ford junker coming into view just beyond Archie's. The woman has the "pedal to the metal," as the saying goes. The car is all but flying. Billy slows, but she does not. As she flies past, he is sure she sees him, is sure it is a "she" driving the car, but a second later he is uncertain the woman at the wheel was Shandie. That woman was wearing dark glasses and she had long, bushy dark brown hair.

Something strange about that bushy hair.

Billy almost steers the Jeep off the road when he remembers the vision: the little girl in the swimming suit who clutched something that resembled a dead hairy animal. The something could have been a wig. A dark, bushy wig.

Chapter Seventeen
Hair Like Diamonds

Shandie

There's light enough for wot I've got to do.

Oliver Twist
Chapter 47
Charles Dickens
(1837–1838)

Sondra is in Denver to collect clever paintings for her gallery in Paris. Because she is internationally famous and loathes the idea of the peasants and peons recognizing her, she dresses in black from head to foot and covers her platinum blond locks with a rather glorious wig of dark brown curls. She has spent the past week negotiating with Lee Simpson, who is known for his stunning depictions of the mountains surrounding Taos, New Mexico. Even in Paris, southwestern art is quite the rage. Sondra has contracted for a dozen paintings by Simpson and another dozen by other local artists. She is now ready to kick up her heels. Coincidentally, Count Cedric Higgenbotham III, or something like that, an old friend of Sondra's, is in Colorado Springs for the purpose of touring the Air Force Academy, where his grandnephew is a cadet. The count is staying at the Broadmoor Hotel, in the honeymoon suite. Sondra calls him *cher ami* in private. When she travels to London she always spends time with Cedric and the foolish man inevitably begs her to marry him. But Sondra is too independent, too rich, too smart for that crap.

Though she is finished with business, Sondra still prefers to dress in black and wear the glorious wig to Colorado Springs. No telling who might see her. She has learned from past experience that the American media is as devious as it is unscrupulous in its pursuit of naughty stories about foreign celebrities. Some sleazy little reporter might try to follow her, so she is taking precautions by traveling the side roads in her rental, gold-tone Lincoln Continental.

Sondra has just passed through Doubletree, an enclave where the famous oilman, Carson Blue, once lived in a splendid mansion. His widow resides there now, the gallery owner has heard over the gossip transom. The widow is a strange woman who talks to spirits and charges outrageous fees to foolish women who are said to don white robes and bay at the moon.

Sondra gets a shock as she leaves Doubletree. An infamous reporter! The ruthless William Sang Hightower rushing toward her in a silly Jeep! Sondra floors the accelerator and streaks past him. Did he see her? Yes! Is he turning around? No! *Grand merci!*

Even a rich, famous gallery owner from Paris has her limits as to how much excitement she can stand on a Saturday morning. When I saw Billy, I almost wet my pants and had to drive like the devil to Elizabeth before I could find a restroom. I whisked in and out of Leo's Wagon Wheel Restaurant and got the big stares from the old boys at the counter who were sucking up coffee and exchanging lies.

Fifty miles is a long way to keep any fantasy alive, even for someone as clever as Sondra. By the time I passed the Air Force Academy, the persona had begun to dissolve, like grass fairies fade when the sun is up and serious. It wasn't even ten o'clock yet and I was soaked with sweat.

I had good reason for dressing in black and wearing the wig. What if I drove by the house and Wesley was outdoors mowing the lawn? He might recognize me; he might call the cops.

The traffic in Colorado Springs was tenacious. People dressed in shorts and T-shirts and tank tops, zipping from dress shops to hardware stores, as cool as April breezes. Felt like a Turkish bath inside the Bomb when I parked on Garden of the Gods Road to restudy the map I'd bought a couple of days ago. Back on the highway I was a jumble of nerves as I made my way to the west part of the city.

I found Ozark Road, found the block where the Dillingers lived, found the house, a pitiful frame bungalow with peeling paint. No lawn to mow. I drove by fast, craning my neck. Then drove around to the other side of the block.

It chilled me to see there were no houses behind the Dillingers'. Instead there were fields of weeds. As if Fate had designed for me a perfect place to spy. A small hill directly behind the house where my daughter purportedly lived, if you could call it living, in such a hovel.

I parked at the curb above the hill.

Tears streamed my face. How could Carson let this happen? Before I signed the papers, he showed me a photo of the Dillingers' house. A sprawling brick ranch-style with lush yard and a tree with a tire swing. When the detective reported that the Dillingers had moved, did Carson come down here and see this house? Why didn't he tell me things had gone to hell?

I wiped my eyes with a tissue. Maybe he knew this was some temporary deal and he didn't want to worry me. Maybe Wesley got another job and moved the family to a house better than the one

I saw in the photo, which meant they no longer lived here. Then why did I feel Briana around me like I used to feel Carson's ghost? Was she dead? If so, then why the hell was I here?

Because she wasn't dead.

A couple of cars passed while I sat there brooding. There were some dilapidated houses across the street. Residents might be whispering behind their soiled drapes this instant, trying to decide whether or not to call the cops. I could say I was a real estate agent, here to check out a property I hoped to list. A Realtor (dressed in black, a wig, and dark Ray-Ban glasses, parked in a junked-up car on a hot summer day?) here to survey some valuable (weed-infested) lots.

I picked up my binoculars, got out of the car and walked quickly over to the hill, lay down on a cushion of scratchy, strong-smelling weeds, removed my glasses, and lifted the binoculars to my eyes.

I scanned the house, the yard and the houses on either side. No signs of human life, but there were plenty of grasshoppers, birds, and bugs patrolling the area. Weeds from hell all around, some knee-high, and bunches of sunflowers and hollyhocks. I could taste the pollens and dirt. I sneezed. Wiped my nose on the sleeve of my sweater. Bunch of doves perched on the power lines watching me. Brainless fowl lacked the sense to get out of the heat. Me and the brainless birds. It was so hot you could see the air hanging down in moist curtains.

I heard a car coming down the street and pressed myself flat against the hard earth. An extremely conscientious Realtor interested in the botanical and geological facets of the property she hoped to list. The sun tortured me as I watched a daddy long-leg spider pick its way over a scurry of ants.

Just as I was about to say the hell with it, a boy ran out of the Dillingers' house. The screen door banged behind him. My heart leaped. Out ran a smaller boy. First boy had something the second boy was trying to take away from him. Boys were dirty and unkempt, like the house. Both had brown hair that needed cutting. I could hear them arguing and crying out but not the words.

And then it happened, it had to happen, that's why I was here—a little girl came tearing out of the house. Her long blond hair looked like a bramble bush. Skinny, dirty and barefoot, she wore only a pair of ragged jeans that had been sheared off at the knees. My precious baby grown up all bony and a mess.

My heart swelled and crashed. Tears gushed out of my eyes. I slashed my sleeve across my eyes and nose. Quickly pressed the binoculars against my face. So it was true. The Dillingers had fallen on bad times. But Carson promised ...

The little girl—Briana, had to be—joined in the struggle to take from the larger boy what? Something small. A candy bar. Fighting over food. This was almost more than I could bear. I wished I had a sack—a boxcar full of candy bars I could throw down the hill.

I wished I could run down there and grab her. More than a wish, every bone in my body screamed to do it. But I was paralyzed. Weak mothering instincts overcome by something stronger, some inner knowing that to do something that crazy would land me in jail for sure. UNFIT MOTHER KIDNAPS CHILD, the headlines would jeer. Down in the body of the article it would say that the court was placing the child in a foster home until the matter could be resolved. The mother was being held without bond in the El Paso County jail. So get a clue as to how it was going to be resolved.

My head was swimming in sweat under the wig. I yanked off the hair piece and scratched my head with my free hand.

Into the house the children ran. I listened for something more—screaming and fighting, anything—but all I could hear were the buzzing insects and the hot breeze sighing around me. Feeling a new kind of loneliness, I lay there another ten minutes or so, the binoculars pressed against my face.

Two more cars passed on the street behind me. One of them seemed to slow. When it was quiet again, I got up and ran to the Ford.

Coming over the hill, I spotted a patrol car turning the corner at the end of the block. I adopted a purposeful look, eased up on the accelerator and slid past the cop.

When the law was out of sight, I stomped on the gas and sailed over the next hill. My attention was still on the rearview mirror, so I almost missed the Jeep crouched at the Mesa Road turnoff. Billy!

I shot past him. Whipped a right and cut a zigzag pattern through a section of small, brick homes. I thought I lost him, but I glimpsed the Jeep blocks behind me as I came to a busy intersection.

I cut west on Colorado Avenue. Spotted a drug store and pulled into the parking lot. No sign of my pursuer as I hurried inside. I bought a cheap pair of dark glasses and a black scarf with a pink rose design on it. (In my haste to leave that hill, I had left my wig and Ray-Bans in the dirt.) The clerk eyed me as I laid a twenty on the counter, as if he were trying to match me up with a wanted poster.

"You got something I can use to cut off the tags?" The man sighed hugely and handed me nail clippers. I snipped the tags. Let them fall on the counter. "Much obliged."

I slipped on the glasses, tied the scarf over my sweat-soaked head and stepped out of the store into the glare and heat and noise.

Billy was in the parking lot. Leaning against my car, his thumbs hooked in the pockets of his jeans. He had on a plaid shirt. Subtle plaid of light blues and browns. Shirt was slightly rumpled. So much for the legend about Billy wearing only white shirts. When he saw me he straightened, and we stared at each other for a long minute. A middle-aged couple came out of the store talking. They shut up when they saw Billy and me in our standoff, got quickly into their gray Skylark and crept it out of the lot.

"So who are you, the goddamn Secret Service?"

He began walking toward me slowly. Painfully. Like he had a mop handle stuck up his butt. He stopped in front of a wine-colored compact car. I started to walk around him. He reached out, took my arm.

"Maybe we should go have a cup of coffee," he said.

I took a deep breath and looked at the sun. Life was cruel and idiotic. I drive down to spy on my daughter, not believing I will see her, but I do, it breaks my heart, it tears me a new one because I'm powerless to help her, and Billy shows up when I most need to be alone. The man I have schemed on for ten years suddenly suggesting we go have coffee. Me in a black sweater on a hot day, ugly scarf on my head and smelling like a hobo. But this was no man-woman scene, this was Billy doing his mother-hen routine. He saw me on the road, went home, looked up the address ... But how did he know I was coming here?

"How'd you know I was coming here?"

"I had a feeling." He shoved his hands into his pockets. "There's a small cafe at the end of the block."

"Why do I want to have coffee?"

"Maybe you need to talk."

"Maybe I don't." I felt a kind of victory in making it hard on him. Payback for all the times he'd given me the cold shoulder.

His turn to stare at the sun. Unhappy, squinty-eyed expression. Drives all the way to the Springs like some hero in a B-movie and his leading lady refuses to cooperate. So let him ask me to coffee some evening when my hair is decent and I'm dressed in something smashing and I haven't sweated off all my cologne. Men understand nothing.

"I could use a cup before I start back," he said. "Will you join me?"

Killed him to say that. "A bar sounds better to me."

"The cafe's within walking distance."

I turned and marched toward the street.

"You hurt your back?" He was shuffling alongside me like the Tin Man in The Wizard of Oz.

"Yeah."

"Maybe you should go see a chiropractor."

"Good idea."

When we went inside Corky's Cafe, we walked straight into the fifties. Waitresses were all old and wore hairnets. At least the place was air-conditioned. Row of good ol' boys were perched on stools at the counter, their attention fixed on a baseball game on the television set positioned on a shelf next to the cook's counter. Big lumpy-looking booths stationed around the room were covered with brown plastic that was supposed to look like leather. Tables cluttered the middle; miniblinds covered the windows.

It was lunchtime and the joint was busier than a tent revival. A lot of menopausal women present, in cotton blouses and polyester pants, with fifties hairdos and glasses. Man's voice with a Hispanic accent was hooting out orders over a microphone as the waitresses dashed around to a tune of clanking silverware, raucous TV, general clatter and chatter. Burgers sizzled on the grill; place smelled of fried onions and warmed-over soup. I felt like throwing up.

A skinny waitress about eighty years old shoved menus in Billy's hand and practically pushed us toward a booth in the back near the restrooms. "Ladies" and "Gents" the signs over the doors said. We sat down facing each other.

Neither one of us was hungry. Billy gave the menus back to the waitress and ordered two coffees, letting the waitress know we weren't here for the usual lunch crap.

I kept my sunglasses on. And of course my lovely new scarf. I peeled open two creamers and turned my coffee beige. Billy was stealing looks at me.

"You come to tell me 'I told you so?'"

"I was concerned."

"Why?" Not in a million years would he say he came because he cared.

He glared at me, glared at his cup. "That was a dangerous thing to do. Going to that house."

"It's where my daughter lives. A mother wonders. Even me."

I glanced at the customers nearest us. A woman scolded her brat for playing with a salt shaker. A man and a girl at another table. Probably a divorced father treating his kid to lunch. They seemed especially fond of each other. Something about that triggered sadness in me.

I reached into my purse and drew out a tissue. Billy averted his eyes as I mopped at my tears and blew my nose.

"I needed to see where she lived. I needed to know it was the house Carson showed me in the photo. But it wasn't." The tears welled again. I dabbed at my cheeks. "It was a dump. I saw her, Billy."

Then the tears came in a flood. I got up and stumbled into the bathroom. I cried harder when I saw in the mirror how really awful I looked. I ripped off the scarf, stuffed it in the waste can, picked up a rubberband I saw on the floor, pulled my hair back and braided it. I washed my face with a paper towel. Now I looked like a farm girl just in from the field after plowing corn. A girl who belonged to one of those churches that deems it a sin to wear makeup, or smile.

I slid into the booth, tucked my new snazzy sunglasses in my purse. Billy looked as serious as death. Hardly gave me a look for all my trouble. We both watched the customers for a while. The divorced father sweet-talking his daughter. The waitress came and sloshed more coffee into our cups.

My mind was a three-ring circus. I kept seeing Briana running out of that house, but I was also flashing on scenes with Carson; and most odd, memories of my father were popping up like seals in a bouncing ball act. Maybe the father and daughter duo at the table nearby reminded me of how Duke and I used to be. Or how I used to think we were.

"Dad and I were such pals," I said.

Billy looked puzzled. Wondering why I was talking about Duke. It wasn't any more out of context than anything else that had happened today, not the least, that I was sitting across from Billy in a cafe, never mind the reason.

"At least I wanted to believe we were great pals."

A sharp look from Billy.

"Don't get me wrong; I adored Duke. But all the palsy-walsy stuff was superficial. When I really needed him, he let me down. Mom was always making these wild accusations. Some of it was true, but she'd always exaggerate. I'd deny whatever was coming down because she was so unfair. When things got really bad I'd go to Dad and he'd say, 'Your mother is an unhappy soul, Kitten. Try to be patient—and be careful.' Be careful and don't get caught, he meant. Like when I would say I was going over to a friend's house and then sneak out and meet Marty Burello. Remember him?" A grave nod from Billy. "Mom called him trash. Then I had to sneak out with him, know what I mean?"

Billy nodding slowly. Still trying to figure out why I was going on about Duke. I was trying to figure it out myself.

"Or he would pretend to sock me in the jaw and say, 'Stay tough, Kiddo. We can't let the bastards get us down.' See, we were co-conspirators. He was playing around on Mom and I knew it. Hell, everyone but Mom knew it."

I took a sip of coffee. Nasty lukewarm. Billy, a statue, waiting for me to explain the reason for all this talk about my dad. He'd never ask, though. I could beat my gums about the secret air bases on Mars and he'd have the same stony expression. Patiently waiting for the punch line.

"The deal was, I didn't rat on him and he didn't punish me when I broke the rules. He didn't punish me exactly. When Mom raked me over he'd look at me sternly, like he agreed with her. Later when I'd ask him why he let her ripsaw me, he'd say he was trying his best to keep things from blowing apart. Marriage, he said, was hard enough without complicating things by fighting with your mate; and just know he loved me and try to stay the hell out of her way."

"Why are you telling me this?"

So I was wrong. The statue had a tongue.

"I don't know." I didn't, and I wasn't done.

"When I was little? He'd tell Mom he was taking me somewhere, usually shopping. Then he'd drive to wherever his current squeeze lived and leave me in the car while he went inside and banged her. I didn't know that's what was happening then. I was maybe twelve when I figured it out. He'd promise to buy me a new dress, a doll, whatever, if I would be good in the car and wait for him ... and don't tell Mom."

A light went on in my brain. I suddenly saw a correlation between my thoughts about Carson and my dad on the day I took a step in the direction of my daughter. Duke's behavior had set me up for Carson. Carson never left me alone in the car while he went inside and banged another woman, but he left me alone most of the time, and showered me with gifts and money so I'd keep my mouth shut and be there when he wanted or needed me. This was how it was with my father. So it was business as usual, the way Carson treated me.

I also learned from Duke that men loved their mistresses more than their wives. Which is why I thought it proved Carson loved me when he kept me after Roz divorced him. But he still insisted we keep our affair secret after the divorce because nothing had changed as far as business went. The man had a reputation to protect. Roz injured his precious reputation when she divorced him and made no secret why she did, but Carson believed that diligent denial would eventually kill the rumors. So we had to be "more careful." (Duke teaching me to be careful and not get caught by Mom.) Carson's "careful" meant he came to see me less often after the divorce. Because, in fact, he was courting Lucy. Because, in fact, he married her and kept her a secret because he wouldn't have felt comfortable presenting her to the business community because she was a weirdo. He couldn't marry me because I didn't fit the oilman's wife image. Neither did Lucy, but he married her. And didn't tell me. The only ones he told were staff. Olson, Sid, Leona. And Billy.

"You knew," I said.

No way Billy could know what I was thinking, but he blanched, as if I'd caught him in a lie.

"You knew Carson married Lucy way back when it happened; you knew I didn't know, and you didn't tell me because you don't think secrets hurt."

"It was none of my business," he said gruffly.

"What is your business, Billy?"

It was my imagination, of course, but he looked on the verge of tears. "He didn't want to hurt you," he said quietly.

"Are you kidding? You really believe that? You believe he gave a big goddamn about anything but his precious name? He was good to me, but he was selfish, too. I see why he insisted I give up Briana. If I had kept her he would have had to support us both because I was so dependent on him. Not to mention the inconvenience it would have been, having a child around when he came to use me."

Billy's complexion was a whitish-green color. Pain visible in his eyes. I was bad-mouthing his big hero and he knew I was right. I fully expected him to bolt out of the booth.

"Maybe I'll find a man I can use. There's not a damn thing I can do to help Briana as long as I'm single and poor. So maybe I'll find a rich man and trick him into marrying me. Then I'll hire a dozen lawyers, get Briana back, then get divorced."

A glaze of red appeared on Billy's cheeks. He looked genuinely alarmed. Like he was afraid I was going to try and nail him. Men and their stupid egos. It would be easier to trick a gay Catholic priest into marrying me.

"Who do you have in mind?" he said, like a stage whisper.

I almost laughed. "Not you," I said.

I gathered up my purse and slid out of the booth. "Thanks for listening," I said, then walked out of the cafe.

No sign of the Jeep behind me on the long drive home. No signs of life around the mansion when I parked behind my cabin.

Exhausted in every way, I peeled off my smelly clothes and took a long, hot, reviving shower. After toweling dry I smudged a circle of condensation off the mirror and stared into the eyes of the woman reflected there, as if she were a stranger. Not my eyes, some other woman's eyes; not my nose, some other woman's; not my lips. Here was someone older and sadder but not a button wiser.

If the kids hadn't pounded on the door, I might have stared at this strange reflection until the glass dissolved.

"I have to put something on!" I yelled out the bathroom door. I shrugged on a robe, opened the front door, and the brats swarmed inside. It surprised me that I was glad to see them. For no reason, I felt like crying.

I shed no more tears after I left the cafe. On the drive home I felt only cold, numb anger. At Carson, at Duke—even at Billy. Men promising you everything and delivering nothing. Billy hanging around like some Greek god, knowing I was crazy about him and doing little things to give me hope when none existed. Dad acting like I was his favorite. (I was. Regina wouldn't have sat in his car while he cheated on Mom.) And Carson. The lies. A pyramid of lies, the peak forming when I gave up my daughter because he didn't want the inconvenience.

Now that Lucy had ripped open the wound and I had poured salt on it myself, could I ever look at these kids again without feeling the pain of my loss? Beautiful, healthy, loved children, and my daughter down there in that hovel. Skinny and dirty, her hair uncombed for maybe weeks. Why didn't I run down that hill and grab her? Because she didn't know me. I would have scared her to death. Maybe they never told her she had a real mother.

The girls sat down on the bed and Alex climbed on the brown easy chair.

"Where have you been?" Jennifer said.

"It's my day off."

"You don't have to work," Alex said. "You can just play with us!"

They wanted a story. Suffering from story deprivation, a disease I shared.

I said, "Give me a break, it's almost dinnertime and I'm not even dressed."

"Yes, you are, you have on your robe," Jennifer said, and I ached to gather her in my arms. But of course I didn't. I walked over and glared at Alex until he slid out of the chair onto the floor. I sat down and crossed my legs. "Yea! A story!" The boy clapped his hands.

I closed my eyes and rubbed my temples.

Once upon a time there was a stupid young woman who gave her precious baby to people who promised they would give her the best life possible. Everyone said You're doing the right thing for your daughter, and the young woman was stupid enough to believe them. Twenty-two years old and she couldn't keep a job long enough to pay rent and feed herself, much less care for a baby. So she let a rich man keep her like a prostitute. She was unworthy to be a mother. But she wanted the best for her baby, so she allowed her to be adopted by people who would dress her in frilly pink dresses and let her take ballet lessons if she wanted them. These people broke their promises, every one of them, and the young woman found it out and killed herself. No, she didn't. That was too easy. She had to live with the punishing truth that her daughter suffered because her birthmother was a stupid failure. The worst punishment was knowing there wasn't a damn thing she could do for her daughter now. (Unless she could trick some rich man into marrying her, ha ha.) If she ratted on the child's adopted parents, the courts would transfer the child to some foster home that might be worse. The young woman didn't accept all this *ipso facto*. She vowed she would think of some way to rescue the child. Right the wrong. But she didn't have much hope she could live up to the vow. Rich men easily tricked into marriage didn't grow on grape vines.

"What'sa matter, Shandie?"

"Hush. I'm trying to get a story. There's one up there some-where ... Okay." I opened my eyes. "Once upon a time there was a very poor family. They didn't even have beds to sleep on, just piles of smelly old hay, and hardly any food, just a bunch of rotten potatoes and some moldy cheese."

"Ick," Alex said.

"How big'a family?" Castilla asked.

"A mommy, a daddy, and two sisters. Oldest sister's name was Rosey because her cheeks were rosy. The younger sister's name was Brenda. She had hair that looked like a mop of diamonds."

"Huh?" Jennifer said.

"I don't get the connection either, Jennifer, but Brenda does have hair that sparkles like diamonds."

"You could call her Sparkly," Alex said.

"Her name is Brenda. Now. Don't be a bunch of babies about this, but there was a big fire and the house burned down and everyone died but Brenda.

"I said none of that baby shit."

"But it's so sad ..." Jennifer said.

"Depends on your point of view. The mommy and daddy and Rosey went to Heaven and became angels of mercy."

Alex looked at his sister. Jennifer was frowning but looked interested.

"What happened to Brenda?" Castilla said.

"Brenda went to live in a foster home."

"What's that?" Alex said.

"Like being adopted. More about that later. Brenda's mommy and daddy in Heaven got their angel wings right away. Not so for Rosey. Rosey was a teenager and teenagers in Heaven can't get their wings until they prove themselves worthy."

"What's worthy?" Castilla said.

"When you get something for being good," Jennifer said.

"Rosey wasn't very good, huh," Alex said.

"Let's be kind and say she wasn't the brightest petunia in the garden. Anyway, Rosey wanted to know how her little sister was faring, so she floated down—she was invisible like a ghost—she floated down and found the foster home where Brenda lived with her new family. And you know what?"

"It was a castle!" Jennifer guessed.

I shook my head. "I'm afraid not. It was a lot worse than the house that burned down. This was just a smelly old animal barn. They lived with the cows and the goats, this family. They were sort of nice to Brenda, but they never kissed or laughed or told any goofy stories. For obvious reasons they had a poverty mentality, so they were depressed all the time."

"So the big sister angel grabs her and flies her away to Heaven!" Jennifer said.

"Well, she wanted to. But this loud voice thunders out of the sky—might have been God. Voice says, 'HOLD ON THERE, ROSEY.'

"Rosey, she shivers, she doesn't have a body of flesh and bones anymore, she's just a ghost-angel, but she shivers anyway. 'But, but ...' she says and the loud voice booms, 'BRENDA WILL LEARN MUCH BY STAYING WITH THIS FAMILY AND YOU BET-TER NOT INTERFERE OR YOU'LL NEVER GET YOUR WINGS.'

"Rosey thought God was a real jerk, but she wanted wings real bad. An angel in Heaven without wings is worse than being a total dweeb down here. So she floated back to her new home in the clouds and left her little sister to learn much in her new foster family."

The brats frowned.

"Then what happened?" Castilla said.

"They lived happily ever after."

"That's a crappy story," Jennifer said.

"Thoroughly crappy," I said.

Chapter Eighteen

Smart Feet

Unable to sleep, I went out on the porch and sat in night's chamber. For a long while I stared at the spray of diamonds on the black ceiling and observed pearly strips of gauze sliding past the moon. I heard faint insect hums and chirpings and the rustlings of wind. The air smelled of honeysuckle and pine. Did Briana ever gaze at the stars? Wonder about her real mother? Did she even know.

I thought I now understood what Lucy meant when she said there was nobody inside me. She didn't mean it literally. There was someone home inside me—the question was who? When I gave up Briana, I gave up myself, she said. Maybe she meant some sort of core self, leaving behind bits and scraps of personality, like the clouds I watched. Dog-chewed remnants with names like Shanadera, Sondra, and Shayla.

Why was she so damn interested in my case? Who was I to her? If she ever figured out the truth, she'd send me packing. Or string me up.

A woman with "mystical talents." Selective mystical talents. Clouds in her crystal ball. She might have guessed, but she didn't know for sure about me and Carson; all she knew was that Briana was in trouble. She gives me Dillinger's address, somehow knowing I wouldn't be able to leave it alone. "Higher courts" telling her I could "reverse" the adoption. Did she ever look up from her crystal ball long enough to wonder how the hell I could pull off something like that?

I smacked a mosquito on my arm. Rubbed off the smear of blood. That mosquito was dead. Irreversibly. Like the adoption. Unless ... What if I saved my money for say, three months, then went to see an attorney?

Absorbed in this new idea, I failed to hear Billy creep up on the porch. I jumped. "You scared me!"

"Sorry." He stood behind me, to the left.

Still angry at him for sitting like a lump in that cafe while I spilled my guts, I barely gave him a glance. He was wearing a white shirt again, that much I saw. "What's up?"

"I wanted to make sure you were okay." He spoke quietly. Billy, reverent in the cathedral of night.

"I'm okay as I can be under the circumstances."

"If there's anything I can do to help, let me know."

Why did I doubt his sincerity? Something in his tone. I stared at the trees swaying in the warm breezes like black angels.

"Find me a rich man," I said.

Behind me, a scrape of boot, a ragged sigh.

"I was just kidding about that, Billy. Even if I could find a rich man stupid enough to let himself get tricked into marriage, it would take more than money to solve this problem. We'd have to prove in court that the Dillingers were unfit parents. Then we'd have to prove I was ready to take on the responsibilities of motherhood." I hugged my knees to my chest. "Like proving pigs can dance."

I waited for him to say something—hoped he'd say it could be done. Wasn't I Briana's real mother? Sometimes the courts ruled in a mother's favor. But Billy was into cold steel reality. He knew it was a long shot—like pointing a cap gun at China and thinking you could hit a target there.

"And sometimes when you accuse people of child abuse, they take it out on the kid. So we can't just rush in and start making a lot of claims."

My midnight visitor deigned no comment.

"Might be easier to kidnap her."

"Don't start thinking that way."

"Oh, lighten up, Billy. I do have a brain or two in my head."

"Maybe you should discuss it with Lucy."

"Yeah, Lucy and her higher forces. Maybe she'll loan me her magic wand. I can aim it at Colorado Springs and chant some secret hocus-pocus words by the light of the full moon." I dismissed the moon with a flick of my hand. "It would make more sense to discuss it with her brother. He's rich."

"Be careful, Shandie."

I glanced over my shoulder. "You think I was referring to him when I said I'd find a rich man?"

It was dark, but I could see the tension in his face. I didn't know whether to laugh or feel flattered that he thought I was powerful enough to snare a man like Steffen Xavier.

"He's rich and handsome to boot."

One smart remark too many. Billy was across the porch and gone before I could take my next breath.

"Thanks for coming by and comforting me," I said to the moon.

Those kids refused to let rest a crappy story. First thing they whined about Monday morning was poor Brenda having to live in that stinky animal barn. So I promised them an update.

We trekked up to the secret story place with a sack of popcorn and bowls. Bugle trotting beside me, sniffing the sack at every opportunity. After the brats were on the blanket, I poured popcorn from the sack into their bowls, gave Bugle his portion, then I settled back against my trusty boulder.

"Okay. Rosey finally got her wings. But she was afraid to try and rescue Brenda from the family who lived in the stinky barn because God had told her not to interfere. But ... sometimes Rosey lay awake at night and wondered if she had imagined God telling her to butt out. What if it wasn't God's voice she'd heard? What if she'd heard only the wind? You know how sometimes you can hear voices in the wind?"

They glanced around nervously. Zach said, "There's no such thing as ghosts ..." but he kept looking.

"So Rosey was hanging around the clouds, strumming her harp when up pops this gorgeous hunk angel. Michael, the Archangel. His wings were HUGE!" I spread my arms. "Almost the wing span of Uncle Steffen's airplane. And he had this big flaming sword. He says, 'What's troubling you, fair damsel?' He talked weird like that. So Rosey tells him about Brenda and about hearing God's voice. 'That old bully,' Michael says, and Rosey says, 'You mean God?' 'Guy you thought was God,' he says. Then he explains that God speaks to our hearts—" I patted my chest. "But when we hear a loud voice outside, it's that loud-mouthed bully named Leroy. So ..."

"Who's Leroy?" Castilla asked.

"That's what Rosey wanted to know. She was afraid Michael was asking for trouble, pretending God was a bully named Leroy. But no lightning bolts struck him down, so she figured he must be telling the truth. So ..."

"But who's Leroy?" Alex slapped his knees.

"This loud-mouthed bully guy who pretends he's God! Okay?"

This seemed to satisfy the urchins.

"Okay, this big handsome hunk angel offers to go check on Brenda. 'Want to accompany me?' he asks Rosey and Rosey did, so they both flew down to the smelly old barn, and sure enough, that family was all depressed and Brenda was crying her head off."

Jennifer was sitting erect with her arms crossed over her chest. Lips turned down. Warning me I'd better fix this situation.

"Michael says, 'This isn't right. We must rescue her.' And just like that—" I snapped my fingers, "he swoops down, waves that flaming sword, scares them all bananas, scoops Brenda up in his powerful arms and flies her to the cloud kingdom.

"She was so happy to see her mommy and daddy!"

Jennifer smiling now, hugging her knees.

"But we have a problem here."

Jennifer scowled again.

"Brenda was now the only person in Heaven with a body of flesh and bones. But the day was saved because the angel-ghosts were smart and built her a nice house out of stuff they collected down here on earth, like a bird uses to build a nest.

"So Brenda was the first real person to live in a cloud kingdom, and it was such a novelty they made her a queen. And Rosey and Michael got married ..."

"How'd Brenda go to the bathroom up there?" Castilla asked.

I stared at the sky. Kids.

"Michael would swing her up on his back and fly her down here whenever she needed to go. And he'd gather up some food to take back with them."

"Did they have a TV?" Alex asked.

Jennifer told her brother, "Angel Michael got her a TV when they were down here going to the bathroom."

"Where'd they plug it in?"

"This was Heaven," I said. "You just stick the plug into the cloud and zap! you got 'Wheel of Fortune,' Japanese cartoons, whatever you want."

During the telling, a vision of Steffen Xavier as Michael had swooped down in my mind to rescue Briana. I was glad when the brats got sidetracked with the logistics of Brenda's adjustment to the conditions in Heaven. Glad that the story had not ended with the image of Steffen rescuing Briana. Considering my penchant for building mind castles, then trying to live in them, I was afraid I might start believing I could trick the man into marrying me.

My fears were put to bed. The next day Leona said that Steffen had decided to stay in Reno. He was starting a real estate brokerage firm there and already had one partner.

Leona said, "After he called, Lucy hung up the phone and said, 'There is a God.' Ain't that rich? But she's not off the hook entirely. He's coming for a visit, soon. Which is almost the same problem."

"Because he's a lady killer?"

"He could cause some problems with all these women around."

I couldn't quite picture the problem. Was he going to dance naked through the house while the retreat was going on? Ladies of Light fainting left and right. He drags one off by her hair and Lucy stands by wringing her hands, going, "Oh, dear! Oh, dear! My brother is at it again!"

"Geez, Leona—it's not like he's Tom Cruise or Patrick Swayze."

"I think he looks a lot like George Hamilton."

A dreamy look on her face. Was there something I had missed? The man wasn't half as handsome as Billy.

"You probably think he's old," she said. "George Hamilton, I mean. Steffen's looks aren't the stumbling block. He's a real charmer. You should have seen him the last time he stayed overnight. Telling me what a great cook I was. Real silky voice and the way he looks at you ..."

Definitely something I had missed.

"So how much damage can he do in a couple of weeks?"

She laughed. "I don't think damage is the right word. He'll just be a disruption. Make Lucy nervous. He thinks her retreat is a lot of hooey, so he'll probably enjoy stirring things up. Nah, he won't do any real damage. It'll just be a test for Lucy."

A test for me, I worried.

Time crawled by the next two weeks like a tiny turtle across a dry river bed. Except for the July Fourth celebration and the stuff going on inside my head, it was business as usual. I developed a kind of routine with the kids. I took them to the park in the mornings and up to the secret story place in the afternoons. We played "beauty shop," "hard rock singer," and hide-and-seek. We made dolls out of hollyhocks and toothpicks and ran in the sprinklers.

I joined the crew for dinner up at the house every evening, and listened to Leona's gossip about this and that woman. She seemed to know their quirks and histories, each batch, all twenty-four, every week before Tuesday. For instance: A woman named Isabel from Kingman, Arizona said her husband thought she was in Santa Fe and he would just croak if he knew she was spending four hundred big ones at a female empowerment retreat.

Billy ceased showing up for dinner during the week. I seldom saw him. Grandma Maddie came on weekends, and after dinner, she and Mr. Floy would go down to his cabin until Grandma's bedtime, around nine o'clock. Leona and I giggled and made lewd jokes about what they might be doing down there.

It was business as usual as long as I was with other people. Alone I did my best to block out worries about Briana. Save my money, go see an attorney; this was the best plan I could think of. Without much enthusiasm. Would any judge, even if he believed the Dillingers were unfit parents, grant me custody in my circumstances? Just save your money, I told myself. And try not to think about it.

Mr. Charming arrived on a Friday in mid-July while I was up in the pines telling the kids stories. When the brats heard, then saw the airplane, they screamed, jumped up and tore down the hill, leaving me with four half-eaten pears.

He didn't kill any ladies the first night. He borrowed Lucy's Cad and drove to Denver to see friends. Lucy looked flushed during the graduation ceremony, like she was worried about what might happen to all her chickadees while her brother was on the scene. I couldn't imagine him being tempted by any of these women. Not a looker in the crowd. But maybe Leona was right, he might do some flirting, just to get Lucy's goat.

He was staying in the cabin between mine and Mr. Floy's. Early Saturday morning I watched out my window as he romped with Jennifer and Alex and the dog. The man dressed in jeans, like an ordinary person. I watched myself take pains with my hair and makeup and bring out my better clothes to wear while Romeo was visiting. Chubby chance a man like him would waste time with a mere babysitter. Nonetheless, I was drawn to him. Like a bag lady to an invitation to ride in a Rolls Royce.

I wasn't seriously scheming on the man, but my hormones weren't dead. He was a distraction. Something to take my mind off the hopeless situation in Colorado Springs. And to some degree, my interest was fueled by everyone's dire warnings. Leona. And Billy telling me to be careful—like he was some kind of expert in affairs of the heart. If he was so damned concerned about my well being, why didn't he warn me about Carson years ago? Okay, he did warn me, kind of. That time I found him chopping wood. He said I was wasting my life. Waste of breath to tell a twenty-one-year-old she's wasting her life. Why didn't he come to my apartment to fix my stereo that night? He could've won me away from Carson if he'd tried.

"Do it for me, Shandie" Doctor Jaffee said. "I would like to see the effect on someone who is open like you are."

She was sitting at my table with a second cup of coffee. Dressed in a long, soft, shimmering, East-Indian-style dress. Gold chains around her neck. Long dangly earrings and those big round glasses.

The kids dragged her down to my cabin late that morning, then they went next door to play dress-up. I could hear them banging around and laughing.

I had no intention of inviting the woman in for a tea party, but after the kids disappeared, she hung around making small talk. Saying Castilla loved my stories, and story-telling was a special gift. It would have been rude not to invite her inside. I thought she'd decline, but she came right in, like she'd planned to all along. I figured Lucy sent her.

First she talked about herself. She was a brain. Had a master's degree in astrophysics from the University of California in Berkeley. She called it "Berserkely," and laughed at her own joke. She didn't go on to get her doctor's degree because she got fed up with the system. It was all a big game. In order to get funding to do the kind of research she was interested in, you had to stay within "certain parameters" and pretend you believed the "current theories." So she quit. Then got a doctorate in metaphysics through the Science of Mind church. But even they were too restrictive for her tastes. She said even the most liberal churches were bound up in cocoons of old ideas. She called herself an explorer.

She had one daughter. Castilla's mother. Doc Jaffee never married. Got pregnant by choice—hand-picked the father because he had such excellent genes—but for her, marriage was "too confining." I was dying to ask if she chose a white man. Castilla's skin was much lighter than hers. Doc Jaffee was dark-skinned with fine features. I remembered Leona saying she was half-French.

She did research, and published papers that only the "more adventurous" scientists read. She was frequently a guest speaker at various metaphysical events around the world, and she counseled individuals. She was especially interested in UFOs and studied with Dr. Jacques Vallee, a famous astrophysicist, who was a kind of UFO expert.

Now and then she would sneak in a question. I gave her short, no-frill answers. Leaving no door ajar through which she could walk in and trick me. She was up to something. Finally she got to the point and said I was an "excellent candidate" for the retreat.

"I'll let you in on a secret," she said. "Most of the women who come here aren't ready for what we share. We feel at best we are planting seeds.

"Most who come are seeking something, but like so many scientists, they believe they know what it is they're seeking. So they don't hear anything new; they simply incorporate what they hear into what they already believe.

"I think this could be a valuable experience for you, Shandie, because you don't have a head full of preconceived notions."

"I don't?"

She laughed. Really white teeth. An attractive woman. But full of crap.

"Preconceived ideas about metaphysics," she clarified. "Most of these women are involved in some sort of metaphysical studies. At the least, they've done some superficial reading on the subject. Most are interested in tarot cards, past-life regressions, astrology, things of that nature."

She used to give tarot readings but found it was less than effective because people were more interested in the fortune telling aspects of the ancient system than they were in enlarging their spiritual awareness. She and Lucy tried to push the women gently away from these trappings and teach them to think differently.

"For a gentle four hundred dollars," I said, and felt my cheeks burn. But she wasn't offended. She laughed. Slapped her knee. Her foot came off the floor.

"Ridiculous, isn't it? But we have to charge that much or people won't take it seriously." She hunched a shoulder. "You might say it's a cultural necessity. The problem is we don't reach too many lower income women. That's why we set it up so that anyone who needs to can help with household chores in lieu of payment. But most who respond can afford the full fee."

I reminded her that my job was to watch the kids—and I couldn't afford even half the fee. No problem. They could get someone else to watch the brats and I could come for free.

I told her I wasn't really interested. (I was slightly but couldn't bear the idea of Billy—and Steffen?—seeing me decked out in one of those stupid white gowns. One of the girls, in Lucy's lap.)

"Do it for me, Shandie. I would like to see the effect on someone who is open like you are."

"Be a guinea pig."

She promised I wouldn't be aware of her watching me. The proof of the pudding would show after the retreat. How it would change me, change my life. I flashed on Briana and for a second was tempted to seek Doc Jaffee's counsel. Ask if she thought me becoming a Daughter of Light would impress a judge. If I appeared in court wearing the white gown, ha ha.

She was a damn good saleswoman. Had me wanting to attend the retreat. But five minutes after she was gone, I stomped around my cabin and cussed a blue streak. What if Lucy cornered me again? Got me in the "past room" and worked me over. In front of a bunch of strangers.

Leona said Steffen was coming to dinner Saturday night. He was gone all afternoon, with the kids. I saw them return around five o'clock, then go up to the house.

Cussing myself for being a fool, I slipped on a feminine white sundress. But dammit, it had been months since I'd felt like a woman. I groomed myself carefully, dabbed Obsession cologne in all the important places. Slid on white sandals and a gold ankle bracelet.

Everyone but Billy came to dinner. Mr. Hot-to-Trot showed as much interest in me as he did the wallpaper. Full of himself, a big shot talking about all the real estate deals he was cooking up in Nevada. Of course he knew of potential investors right here in Colorado. Lah-de-dah. Mr. Floy hanging on his every word.

Steffen Xavier did resemble that old film star, George Hamilton. Dark hair with silver streaks, sharp features, a snooty curl to his lips. Kids didn't seem put off by his snootiness; they adored Uncle Steffen. Even Castilla was moon-eyeing him.

Besides all the huffing and puffing about what a great business-man he was, he teased Lucy. Calling her "past-present-future" rooms "cute." Leona fussed over him, asking if he wanted more mint sauce. She never did that with anyone else. He had on jeans and a faded orange polo shirt. Like an ordinary man. But he wasn't. He'd look cocky and grand in Salvation Army rags. I didn't think he noticed me, but after I finished helping Leona clean up the dishes, he appeared on the path outdoors and asked if I'd like to take a "spin in his bird."

"No, thank you," I said.

He took both of my hands in his and looked at me gravely. "You're not afraid of flying because of what happened to Carson, are you?"

"It didn't help."

"That's why you should go. That was a freak accident, Shandie. Flying is safer than driving."

Such intimacy in the way he spoke my name.

"I didn't want to fly before he crashed."

He nudged me along the path. A firm guiding hand at the back of my waist.

"I really don't want to. Maybe someday, but not tonight."

"Fine. We'll just go look at it. Get you used to the idea."

The night was windier than usual. Clouds with sneering black faces bobbing in the sky like puppets. Gusts of wind wheezing around the trees.

I saw a light on in Billy's cabin. Hoped he was peeking out his curtains. Hoped he saw Mr. Dangerous with his hand resting at my back.

We walked in silence save for a few remarks from Mr. Charming about life in the country. His hand at my waist like a warm promise.

The spotlight on the hangar threw a corridor of light across the concrete. The fancy air machine looked like a giant gleaming cat, bathed in light. Steffen strolled over to the beast and stroked the fuselage. I stared at the propeller. Cat's whiskers.

"Come here," he called. He seemed to be checking something under the right wing. I strolled over and stood a few feet away. He was fiddling with something. He started spouting a bunch of statistics. Proving that it was safer to fly than to drive. Pushy like his sister. Going on about how wonderful Denver looked from the sky.

"Maybe someday," I said.

Thunder rumbled in the distance. The wind was whipping my dress around my legs. I thought I felt a raindrop. Hugged myself against a chill. He saw this, came over and circled me with his arms.

"We should have stopped and got you a sweater."

"I'm okay."

"Definitely okay."

I saw what Leona meant. I barely knew the man, yet I was comfortable letting him put his arms around me. He pulled me close. His charm was in his dark, intense eyes. Gazing at me like I was the woman of his dreams. A kind of gratitude mingled with intense longing. He kissed my forehead. Brushed my hair away from my face and kissed me hard on the lips. A thrill raced over my body as he pressed himself into me and stuck his tongue in my mouth. I usually hated it when a man I barely knew tried to French-kiss me. My arms were clenched around his shoulders. I buried my face in his neck; felt drunk on his strong cologne. He was stroking my body and murmuring. I looked ravishing. Good enough to eat. My body wanted to sprawl on the tarmac and pull him on top of me, but another part of me argued against it, angry that he would pounce on me like this without warning or invitation. I let my body have its pleasure for a few more minutes, then

I pushed him away and stepped back. My heart was pumping double-time. He cocked his head and smiled. Reached out and slid the corner of my sundress down my left arm, exposing my breast. Arrogant look on his face. That made me mad. I turned away and yanked up my dress.

"Cold feet?" he said in a smart-aleck tone.

"Smart feet."

He laughed. I walked away. He followed, tried to take my hand, but I kept both arms around my waist.

"I heard things about you," I said, walking fast.

"I bet you did. Did Lucy tell you I was a womanizer?"

"Uh-huh, and that you dropped them as soon as you got what you wanted."

"She's got a problem with my lifestyle, that's all."

He stopped me. Placed his hands on my upper arms and tried to look profoundly concerned. "I'm sorry I came on so strong, Shandie. But I'm really attracted to you. Have dinner with me Tuesday night? I promise I'll be a gentleman."

Without waiting for an answer, he leaned over and kissed me lightly. We started walking again. I let him take my hand. One more light kiss at my cabin door. I felt confused and angry at my confusion. I wanted him to try and come inside. I wanted to slap him, tell him to go to hell. I wanted his hand on my breast. I was about to tell him to forget Tuesday when he said, "Stay sweet," and walked away.

I stepped inside, slammed the door and said, "Shit!" Mr. Smooth-talker hits town and even though I've been warned, I fall all over him. Starved for affection, like some wallflower who hasn't been kissed in years, if ever. But that was the problem, dammit, I hadn't been kissed or anything in so long I couldn't remember when it happened last.

Living around Billy didn't help, him with his dark exotic eyes and that body. What was the matter with him? Maybe he wasn't attracted to me. Scratch that; he was. I could see it in the way he looked at me. But he was too pure to pounce on me like Mr. Lady-killer.

Understandably I had trouble sleeping that night. If I'd had any booze I would have gotten drunk. All I had were some old packets of hot chocolate powder that called for water instead of milk.

I was up fixing myself a third cup of that lousy hot chocolate when I heard someone running down the path.

Out the window, over the sink, I saw Billy racing toward his cabin, his boots pounding hard on the pavement, like he was being chased by a pack of wolves. His shirt flashing white, his ponytail flying behind his head. I then noticed a light on inside the mansion, in the kitchen. Someone snapped it off.

What was Billy doing up there so late? And who snapped off the light?

Chapter Nineteen

A Red Road Thing To Do

Billy

The words of the wise are as goads, and as nails fastened by the master of assemblies.

Ecclesiastes 12:11
The Holy Bible

Billy has been lying low. Minding his own business, doing his work. His back hurts less, but the pain is still there, like a small ferocious animal crouched in the bush, poised to spring out and lay waste to him at the least provocation.

Other than working on the books in the basement, he has steered clear of the mansion, and all those women. He did have to encounter some of them when the plumbing in one of the upstairs bathrooms went on the blitz. A couple of trips to Ace Hardware and a messy job of replacing the guts in the tank fixed the problem.

When he isn't working or making emergency runs to Safeway for Leona, or visiting Sid or Tony or Joe, Billy stays in his cabin and reads. He tackled Umberto Eco's *Foucault's Pendulum*, read *Leaving Cheyenne* by Larry McMurtry and Tony Hillerman's *Talking God*. And a pile of paperbacks he bought at a second-hand bookstore—junk reading. Anything to pass the time. Until things settle down—whatever that means.

The worst part of lying low is missing Leona's dinners when the food is hot and fresh. He frequently sneaks up to the mansion and raids the refrigerator after the women have gone to bed. He has developed a sweet tooth lately. One night he ate almost a dozen of Leona's chocolate chip cookies; afterward, suffering a monstrous headache.

The day Steffen Xavier arrived, Leona baked two devil's food cakes. She bakes her cakes from scratch, and they are delicious. She tried using those cakes to bait him to join them for dinner Saturday night, and oh, was he tempted! She was fixing another leg of lamb. A fat juicy roast full of garlic. She slices the cloves into thin spears and sticks them in all over the face of the roast, then smears it with a mess of olive oil, garlic salt, white pepper, and mint leaves, which forms a scrumptious crust on the meat while it cooks.

But he sees Steffen return with the kids that evening, then sees Shandie on the path, dressed to kill. So dinner is out. But there will be leftovers. He can warm the lamb in the microwave oven later, build a sandwich. Have some cake.

Usually he makes his raids around midnight, but tonight he is lusting so for Leona's food, he plans to chance it earlier. His stomach feels like an empty tin can.

He is about to leave his cabin when he spots Steffen and Shandie near the mansion. He ducks back inside and watches through the slit in the curtains as they walk down the path. Steffen's hand at Shandie's back. He feels sad about this, which irks him. What did he expect? That Shandie can change her colors overnight? Ever?

Obviously, sadly, she has made a choice. She tells herself if she marries a rich man she can afford legal help. The vision tells another story. If she succeeds in capturing her rich knight, there is only turbulence ahead.

He should warn her. Should not! Her desire to reclaim her daughter must be resolute. She will have to want it more than anything. Steffen is a compromise. Her interest in him, a sign she is not ready to accept the full responsibilities of motherhood.

What is he thinking? It will not happen, under any circumstance. She will chase after Xavier, the chase will cause the turbulence, and the result will be that the little girl will be forgotten. Which, perhaps, is best in the long run. If ever she does muster the kind of determination it would take to try and reclaim her daughter—and succeeds—how could she do right by the little girl? Would she move Briana into the cabin with her? How long could they live like that? Would Lucy take her in as family? Doubtful. Sooner or later Shandie will have to leave, get a job—in Elizabeth, Castle Rock—or Denver, and put the kid in one of those day care centers.

What is he thinking? It won't happen. Shandie is good with children, but being a full-time mother is entirely a different matter. She can't even cook. She knew she wasn't cut out to be a mother, then, now, ever; that's why she gave up the child in the first place. Why Carson encouraged her to.

Not the whole truth, Billy, and you know it.

But these are the facts! What else could Carson do under the circumstances?

He could have taken some sort of action when it became clear that Briana was getting the raw end of the deal. What action? He could have notified someone in Social Services. Let them re-study the case. Let them find a better home for the little girl. She doesn't deserve the bad treatment. Not her fault her mother was in no shape to care for her, not her fault her father ...

The night is windy and unseasonably cool, but Billy is sweating profusely as he walks up the path after Steffen and Shandie disappear from sight. He yanks a handkerchief out of his back pocket and mops his face. His appetite has lost some of its bite. But that devil's food cake is still calling him.

The lights are off in the kitchen; the entire house is dark. Lucy, Leona, and Doctor Jaffee retire early on the weekends. To catch up on their beauty sleep. To rest up for the onslaught on Sunday afternoon. Amazing that the women keep coming. Lucy's bank accounts are growing into mountains. Besides the income from the retreat, she made a killing on the sales of the oil business and the ranch in Nevada. She could take a year off, easily. Two years. She could retire. Who would think talking could be so lucrative? That's all she does—talk, talk, talk. Filling those women's heads with dreams. Empowering them. As if women needed any more power.

The smell of lamb is strong as Billy enters the kitchen on cat's feet. He stands in the center of the dark room for a moment and listens for sounds above him. All is quiet. He opens the refrigerator, draws out the meat, bread, Miracle Whip, lettuce. Three-quarters of one cake sits inside a clear plastic domed pan on the counter. It sings to him as he works on the sandwich in the wedge of light shining out of the refrigerator. He decides against using the microwave oven. The noise might disturb someone.

He returns the food to the refrigerator, shuts the door, snaps on the thin fluorescent tube light above the range, fills a glass with cold water, tears a square of paper towel off the roll, then sits down at the table to eat in the bluish glow. He eats slowly, savoring each bite.

Half the sandwich is gone when he hears someone on the stairs. He holds his breath, rests the sandwich on the paper towel. Hears someone in the dining room, opening a drawer, it sounds like. He thinks he hears a match strike. Imagines he smells a whiff of sulphur. He definitely sees a faint flicker of light now.

Lucy appears in the doorway, carrying a large white candle. The flame casts a fuzzy golden aura around her head and shoulders, diffusing outlines. That black hair blending in with the dark-colored garment she wears.

"I didn't want to disturb the mood." She glides over to the cabinets next to the sink and removes a saucer, sets the candle on it. Sets it on the table. "I talk better by candlelight anyway." She sits down across from him, the chair making a rude noise as she scrapes it across the floor. She rests her elbows on the table, folds her hands, rests her chin on them, her arms forming an inverted V. The robe she has on is a dark iridescent indigo color. The candlelight swims across the satiny folds and contours. Throws sparks in her eyes. He can smell her cologne. A spicy fragrance, like nutmeg.

"Leona makes a mean roast, doesn't she."

He shrugs.

"Go on." She gestures. "Eat up."

"I'm full."

"There's still some chocolate cake."

"Maybe later." He pushes the sandwich away.

"You've sure been scarce lately."

"I always keep a low profile."

She scoots the candle. Maneuvers it closer to the center. The light breeze swimming in through the open window above the sink plays with the flame. Lucy repositions her hands beneath her chin and studies him with those black sparking eyes.

"Remember when I said our gifts are a responsibility?"

A shudder zips down his spine. It was probably too much to hope she wouldn't bring it up again. The day she confronted him, he'd hoped she was generalizing, hoped she was tossing it out as an impersonal observation. Now it is apparent she meant what she said and she meant him.

He should get up, leave, tell her he's not feeling well. True! He feels awful, the pain in his back is beginning to complain, as always, when there is tension. He has a feeling if he doesn't leave now, she will push him against a wall, trap him, trick him into confessing that (yes, dammit, he sees things; not a gift, a curse!) he is a freak who hallucinates.

"I remember."

"You left before I was done talking about it."

"There was something else I had to do. I don't remember what."

Maybe his fears are for naught. Maybe she just wants an audience. She talks for money, she talks for free, any time she can get someone to sit still and listen.

"Well, I'm glad you've got some time tonight." She sweeps her hair back, pulls one section over her left shoulder and strokes it, her eyes on the candle flame. "Because you need to hear this. Want some coffee?"

"No." He wants nothing that might lubricate her jaw.

She nods. Pets her hair. "For every cluster of people—I don't how many in each cluster—let's call these clusters tribes. Within each tribe every spiritual gift is represented. Even that old chauvinist St. Paul recognized it. He describes some of these gifts in Corinthians. In the section of the Bible that ought to be called St. Paulism." She chuckles, pleased with this bit of irreverence. "But never mind that.

"Some people are born with the gift of designing and erecting structures. Tee-pees, skyscrapers, barns—someone in the tribe will have a natural bent for it. Others are natural-born nurses, doctors, medicine men. Some are good with numbers, and others are artists. You don't think these are spiritual gifts? Think again. There is no division between material and spirit, except in our perception. Everything's made out of the same stuff ..."

She is wound up now, her jaw working like a greased machine. She is instructing, teaching, blessing him with her pearls of wisdom. Billy relaxes a little. Maybe she will continue along this general vein and wind up with nothing worse than another nonspecific admonition.

"And in every tribe there is a minister, a mystic, a shaman."

His eyes narrow to slits at the word "shaman." He stops fiddling with the paper towel. Why is she spicing her lecture with all these American Native terms? Setting a trap, laying bait. Dense woman. She can't romance him that way.

"These gifts display in myriad ways," she says, "all working together to form a healthy culture. When a culture is unhealthy it's because too many people are either ignorant of their callings or they are unwilling to fulfill them. So we end up with imbalances within tribes, neighborhoods, societies—doesn't matter what you call them.

"The gifts we call spiritual—clairvoyance, dream interpretation, things of that nature—are the most important because without them, the material plane is a place of chaos and disunity."

Billy steps back in his mind and glances around the room. The pans above the center island glint in the soft bluish light like Christmas ornaments. Leona has created a wonderful little world within these four walls. Now there's a gift. Carson was right, she is probably the best cook west of the Mississippi. She could get a job in the finest restaurant and command a high salary. Thank goodness she has no highflown ideas about serving a "tribe."

"Am I losing you?"

"I'm listening."

"Good. You know what my gift is?"

He gestures. A movement that says everyone knows your gift. (Gab.)

"I can see other people's gifts."

Oh, man. Here it comes. The trap. A drop of perspiration slides down his right temple. Does it glisten in the candleglow? Can she see it?

"You're clairvoyant, Billy. It's written all over you."

His eyes roll upward, as if to search for an escape hatch in the ceiling.

"How long?"

"How long what."

"How long have you had the gift?"

"It's not a gift. I just see things sometimes." She nods. "Very seldom."

"The frequency isn't important. What counts is what you do when you see these things."

"I do whatever is called for."

"Do you, now. That's good. Because I know you're a moral man. You don't think it's immoral to hide your gift? You think I'm being harsh? Think about it. Like I said, in every group of people, every tribe ..."

He wishes the hell she would stop using that term! As if he's fresh off the reservation.

"There's a shaman ..."

And that word! He feels like letting rip with a howl. The visions he has suffered are nothing of a shamanistic quality; they are mental aberrations, sent to torture him.

"Or a mystic, someone with a gift that helps to remind us we are more than bodies. God set it up this way so we wouldn't despair. These reminders touch something deep within us, old memories of who we really are and where our true home is. Withhold the gift and your tribe loses awareness of its spiritual roots."

"I never see anything as grand as a reminder of spiritual roots; I don't even know my own spiritual roots, so how the hell could I ..."

"Calm down, my friend."

He curls his hands on top of the table. He was gesturing, throwing his hands around! Like some crook trying to prove he didn't steal the silverware.

"You have the gift. You just haven't learned its ups and downs and ins and outs yet. What sorts of things do you see?" When he doesn't respond, she says, "I'm just trying to get a feel for the nature of your gift."

He can refuse, he can tell her it's none of her business, he can tell her to go to hell. But he is so tired of packing the secret, like some beast attached to his back; he is tired, he is weary, he is exhausted.

"I saw Carson crash the moment it happened."

He lets out a whoosh of air and waits for the alarm, the shock. But an arched eyebrow is Lucy's only reaction.

"What good was that? What was there for me to do? Tell everyone about it? How would that have helped?"

"If you told a few people they would know you had this gift and they would seek you out in times of trouble."

He shakes his head. This is insanity. He should have kept his mouth shut.

"Pretty scary, huh? Putting you on the spot like that. All that responsibility."

She sits like a queen in the bluish-golden mist. Pronouncing him irresponsible, immoral, her black eyes calm with righteousness.

He slams a fist on the table, almost toppling the candle. The flame flickers wildly. "If I had known, Lia would be alive today!"

Lucy moves quickly to the chair beside him and places her hand on his shoulder. He turns his face, hunches the shoulder, leans away. "Tell me about it," she says gently.

This is a nightmare, but the pain is too great to hold in now. The story pours out with embarrassing emotion; his ignorance the first time he suffered a vision, how he overlooked that lilac bush—a route around Lia's death! He tells of the vision presaging his mother's death, the cabins, how he did act responsibly then, because he understood what it meant; but he failed Lia, and now she was dead, and the baby, too fragile to make it on its own, not it—a girl, a tiny lump no larger than his fist. She would have been beautiful, smart, a joy to any father's heart.

He whips out his handkerchief and wipes his eyes and face. Lucy pats his shoulder and mercifully moves away. She gets up and pours cold coffee from the urn into two mugs and sets them inside the microwave oven. The noise grinds up the air for two, four minutes, an eternity. At last the machine stops with three smug beeps.

"You drink it black, don't you?"

"A little cream." A whisper but she hears. Gets the half-and-half out of the refrigerator, sets it on the table, then the mugs, then a spoon out of the drawer. Mercifully she sits down across from him again. The coffee is not quite hot but bearable. Something to do, something to mess with, a distraction.

"I'm sorry you had to learn about your gift in such a painful way. You need to know that although a clairvoyant sees things, it doesn't necessarily follow that he is to try and prevent what he sees from happening. Sometimes that fits, sometimes it's possible, sometimes not. Maybe your wife just wanted to say goodbye to those lilacs, or see your mother one last time. Maybe your mother would have died the same year she did even if she'd gone on mopping floors. Maybe those cabins were calling you for another reason. Your mother probably appreciated the rest she got those last few years she lived. So what you did served a good purpose. Maybe it served the purpose intended.

"And Carson? That vision might have been more about you. Seeing your lifestyle go up in flames. Fire consuming the old, making way for new. You have to learn how to hang out with a vision. Like dreams, they often simply state the situation, sometimes literally, sometimes using symbols. You are shown where you need to focus. Where you need to make some decisions. It isn't easy. These things we see and feel don't relieve us of the responsibility to search within for the greater truth. It's frustrating, having these visions, because although we see these signposts, we don't always see clearly what to do about them.

"So stop beating yourself, Billy. Even if you had been aware of what was happening, you may not have been able to prevent ..."

"Then why the hell see these things?"

"All I know is, living here in this dimension, we experience both the light and the dark. For every moment of joy, for every uplifting experience, there is a counter effect. I think we're trying to learn some kind of balance, so we can avoid the sharp edges of extremism. You familiar with the 'red road'?"

He nods. "An old Lakota metaphor. A kind of middle road between good and bad."

"I'm trying to learn to walk the red road," she says. "That's where the freedom is, I think, somewhere between sunshine and shadows."

Billy grunts at her girlish twist on light and darkness.

"If you push too hard either way the pendulum swings wide in the opposite direction. The effects don't always show up in a given lifetime of an individual. These things happen to groups of people as well, everyone contributing to the energy that moves that old pendulum.

"Oh, listen to me run off at the mouth." She takes a sip of coffee. Looks at him studiously.

"I hope you're ready to let go of this terrible thing that happened to you. Fifteen years is a long time to do penance for something you couldn't help."

"I haven't been doing penance," he says tiredly.

"Maybe not consciously. I have a feeling you had other plans for your life. I have a feeling you wanted to do some other kind of work. Have you thought of marrying again? Having another child?"

He snaps his head, no. Oddly he feels an absence of anger now. The clawhold on his back has eased. He feels numb, empty, almost peaceful.

"You might want to reconsider. You're still young. Plenty of time to get back in touch with your heart's desire. Plenty of time to explore this gift you have and find ways to put it to some earthly use."

"I wish the hell I didn't have it."

"I wish my hips weren't so big. I wish I had been graced with the gift of tact. I'm still trying to figure out how I can reach Shandie. I thought she was tough; I thought she'd respond to my tough-love approach, but I jumped into the middle of something ... I wanted to show her she has a gift with children, but I screwed it up. There's a lot more going on there than meets my eye. Something I'm not seeing about this child she gave up for adoption.

"But I have a feeling you see ..."

"I told you what I know." His tone sounds like a growling dog's. He mops his face again. The handkerchief is soaked with sweat. And a few tears.

"All of it?"

"I don't know what you mean."

"There's some kind of connection between you, Carson, Shandie, and that little girl."

No more, he will tell her no more; she knows far too much already. He feels like his skin is glass.

"I don't suppose you've 'seen' anything about Shandie and her daughter ..."

"Like what."

"Oh, a vision, a dream, something like that."

"No."

"Well, I have. I see Steffen going down to Colorado Springs to pay Mrs. Dillinger a visit."

"Steffen!"

She looks surprised. Taps her fingers on the table and looks thoughtfully at something beyond the pool of candleglow.

"You know, I think you're right. Maybe I don't see Steffen doing that. I thought it was him, but you know how vague these things can be. I saw him, or I thought I saw him going down there and getting a feel for how willing Mrs. Dillinger might be to let go of that little girl. Put that silver tongue of his to use while he's here. He'd be good." She stares at him. Smiles. "But you'd be better."

Billy raises both hands, palms out, and seems to push against the air. He shakes his head slowly from right to left.

"I figure Mrs. Dillinger will be willing to let go of that little girl for fifty-eight thousand."

His hands fall to the table. He leans forward, gapes. "Dollars?"

"Uh-huh. We buy her back. I buy her back. I'm the one with the bucks. And fifty-eight seemed the right number." She smiles, winks. "I like the irony. The way I see it, you go down there and tell her you're a friend of Carson's and Carson died recently and before he died he set aside some money for them because he knew they would need it in their time of trouble. You mention that you know Briana's mother and how she suffers for letting that little girl go, and by the way, wouldn't it be nice if you could work out some sort of visitation?"

She smiles into the golden-edged darkness. Lost in her mad fantasy. "You bring up visitation first to open her mind. You can't come right out and say you're there to buy the child; that'll ruffle her feathers. You have to ease into it. You have to ease around her surface objections."

"You can't be serious."

"I am profoundly serious." She leans forward, taps her finger on the table. "You would be perfect. You can use your gift to help. You'll be able to read how open the woman is."

"Why are you doing this?"

"I don't know. I'm included somehow in that connection I see." She shrugs. "I don't know the particulars. I'm just acting on a strong urge."

She has no idea what she's doing!

"What you're suggesting is against the law."

She flicks her hand. "Man-made laws. Sometimes you have to sidestep man-made laws in order to see justice done. We're still pretty barbaric, Billy. You must realize that. But here we got a situation that can't wait for evolution to catch up with infinite wisdom. That's part of a clairvoyant's responsibility. If you see the truth, you're responsible to act on it, even when it puts you at risk, even when you don't understand all the particulars. Of course you have to be careful. You have to show respect for whatever system is operating. All you have to do is ask for divine help. If it's the truth—and I believe absolutely it is—that this little girl belongs with her mother—then you will be shown a way to help set it right."

She is serious! But has not a glimmer of what is inside the bag she is trying to rip open. Billy is so shaken it's all he can do to remain upright in his chair. His knees are practically banging together.

"If there's no special connection between you and Carson and Shandie and this child, then why are you quaking in your boots?"

"You're asking me to participate in something illegal! We could land in jail!" He swipes at the back of his neck with his damp handkerchief.

"We already discussed that. You ask for divine wisdom and protection. You ask to be shown how to manifest this truth on the material plane."

"I can't do it! It's against the law!"

"Umhmm. What I'm seeing is, you help Shandie reconnect with her daughter and it helps you heal from the pain of losing your own child. Maybe that's part of the connection I'm feeling here. Life presenting you this opportunity to resolve your own grief."

"I can't do it." He hits the table with a fist. "I won't."

"You can. You will. It's the moral thing to do. It's the red road thing to do."

"It's illegal! We don't even know if Shandie wants ..."

"We know. That young woman is going to reunite with her daughter and you're going to be her knight in shining armor. I see it clearly now, I really do."

Her arms are crossed over her chest; she juts her chin. This is final; she will give no quarter, this Queen of Light.

Billy extricates himself from the table and chair, staggers out to the mud room like a drunk who has wandered into the wrong house, feels around for the screen door, finds it, and stumbles out into the night. When the cool air hits his face, his feet explode on the pavement.

Chapter Twenty

A Judgmental Dog

Shandie

True. I talk of dreams,
Which are the children of an idle
 brain,
Begot of nothing but vain fantasy.

Romeo and Juliet
Act 1, scene 4, line 97
William Shakespeare
(1564–1616)

Early Monday morning Doc Jaffee appeared at my door with one of those limp white gowns. I had thought maybe I would attend the retreat in late summer, but Doc had a "strong feeling" I should go now.

That's all I needed, on top of worrying about my big Tuesday night date. Sunday, I drove myself nuts trying to decide whether or not to keep that date. One

231

part of me said I'd be crazy to go, he only wanted one thing, he didn't care about me, and I wasn't sure I liked him. But dammit, it had been ages since I'd gone on a real date. He promised he'd be a gentleman, so it seemed only fair to give him a second chance. If he got fresh again I'd say, Get your damn hands off me. After a little kissing, a little petting ... No, dammit, that's when the trouble starts—kissing and hugging only—would he settle for that?

Shut up! I commanded myself. Go or don't go; you're a big girl, you can take care of yourself, you can be Sondra (not Shayla, not anymore).

I was so surprised that Doc Jaffee wanted me to attend the retreat now, I forgot to ask who would take care of the brats. She was halfway up the path before I remembered.

The shapeless gown was mine to keep, yippy-skippy. Slit the back and rip off the cheap gold trim and it looked like a hospital gown.

It was a bright sunshiny day, the birds were singing, the wind hummed and there were fairies with transparent wings hiding behind every tree. I walked up the path fast, worried that Billy or Steffen, or both were peeking out their curtains, laughing.

Leona was in the kitchen, surrounded by a half dozen white-gowned women who were gathering up boxes of cereal, plates of fresh fruit, milks and juices, to take into the dining room.

"Well, well!" she said as she handed a tray of spoons and napkins to a tall red-haired woman. "So you decided to join the ranks."

"Dr. Jaffee asked me to come. I'm a kind of experiment."

Leona smiled and patted my arm. "You'll do fine."

The dining room was a site as chaotic as a mall sale; women in white milling around and gabbing, some already seated, others chowing down. Regina lifted her hand and said, "Shandie!" like she was shocked to see me. I said "Hi", walked past her, and sat down next to a gray-haired woman near the end of the table.

I caught Lucy's eye and asked her who was going to watch the kids. She raised both eyebrows, a look of surprise, as if she'd forgotten she had any kids. Then she narrowed those black eyes and pointed at Regina. Regina turned pale. Her fingers came to her chest, as if to say, "Who me?" The women were noisy, but I heard Lucy say to my sister: "Edith and I can manage a week without you." Regina just sat there, staring, probably waiting for Lucy to say, "Ha, ha, just kidding." When she said nothing of the sort, Regina faked a big smile and said Somehow, she guessed, Mom could manage the antique store without her. (She worked in the shop most afternoons.) Lucy said, "We sure appreciate you and your mother making this sacrifice." Then Regina said she would have worn something different if she'd known she was going to be responsible for the children today. Lucy said, "Feel free to drive them over to your place and change into something more comfortable."

I bowed my head to hide my smile as Regina got up and left, looking completely dazed. Lucy winked at me.

When we were done eating and the kitchen was cleaned, we were herded into the Present Room (the den). Twenty of us, four had canceled. Since I had missed the Sunday night orientation, I was introduced to everyone. Immediately, I forgot their names. They all acted like they'd been buddies for years.

We were instructed to remove our shoes and sit on some pillows. I chose a red one and placed it to the left of the big west-facing window. Lucy and Doc Jaffee were seated cross-legged on pillows facing us, the semi-circle fanning on either side of the fireplace. A small, thin woman with blond hair to my right; to my left, a grandmotherly sort who had on dangly earrings. Music was playing softly in the background, maybe from a compact disc player in the sunroom. Tinky music, like someone was lazily plunking a zither. Strange pictures on the wall, busy circles Lucy called "mandalas." The incense burning in a small brass holder on the fireplace ledge emitted a musky odor.

Lucy talked awhile about the "primary purpose" of the retreat; bunch of spiritual mumbo-jumbo to my ears. I tried to pay attention, but I kept thinking about that date, deciding, undeciding; feeling angry at Billy, like it was his lack of interest in me that was pushing me toward Steffen. His fault if I made the wrong decision.

Meditation. Lucy was jabbering about meditation. Everyone was trying to assume the "lotus position" (lot of moaning and groaning). My legs refused to lock up like that. Doc Jaffee said a half-lotus was okay, just bring one foot high on the thigh and tuck the other one under. Lucy was going to lead us in a special meditation that would prepare us for the Past Room where the "real" work would be accomplished in a state of "inner reflection."

We were directed to visualize ourselves walking down a path that was bordered by giant trees that arched over the road and were shedding autumn leaves. To see, hear, feel, smell the leaves under our feet, to bask in the silence surrounding this leaf-crunching business. Then we were supposed to hear a faint bubbling brook, and so on, until we found ourselves in a clearing where we were to create whatever we wanted.

I imagined meeting Steffen there. We walked hand-in-hand to Lucy's yellow Cad, got in and off we went on our date. I had on my fancy red satin dress and Steffen wore a black tuxedo. Just beyond Doubletree, he veered off on one of those side dirt roads where the trees are so thick they brush the sides of the car as you bump and shimmy over the ruts. He stopped the car and pounced on me. The image was so real, I gasped and my eyes shot open. The women around me acted real annoyed. "Sorry," I whispered, closed my eyes and picked up where I had left off. I heard a noise. Another car. Billy! His Jeep bumping down the road toward us. He rammed it into the back of Lucy's Cad! Steffen said, "Hey!" jumped out, Billy jumped out of his Jeep and they started duking it out.

I didn't get to see who won because Lucy called an end to the meditation. My heart was pounding, like what I'd seen in my head had really happened.

I picked up my red pillow and followed the other women into the library. The Past Room. Sunlight glared in through the windows. No music here, no incense, this was where we were going to do the "real work." I was suddenly afraid; I wanted to run. Doc Jaffee noticed me hanging back and came over and laid praise on me for participating. Like I was doing her a big favor.

No semi-circle here, everyone just sat down on the carpet wherever they pleased, backs to the east-facing windows. Acting like they'd done this a thousand times. Lucy and Doc Jaffee stood in front of the built-in bookcases to the right of the door. Lucy saying we would now reflect on the past, particularly focusing on events and incidents where we might feel we were stuck.

A plump woman named Vivian raised her hand and said she had a lot of blank spots in her memory, so Vivi was worried she wouldn't be able to identify where she was stuck. Doc Jaffee said not to worry, the meditation was powerful, especially when shared simultaneously by twenty souls. Lucy said, "Don't be alarmed if the light in your mind shines on strange people and places." Sometimes people "slipped" into past-life memories. If that should happen, just know that the past life had a strong bearing on this life and treat the experience as we would a memory in this incarnation. The women buzzed about this past-life business, but Doc Jaffee hushed them, assuring that it happened very seldom.

Lucy told us to envision a ball of light moving slowly up our bodies, starting at out toes. By the time the imaginary ball reached the "head juncture," we would be shimmering all over in light. I let myself go with it and felt as though a hundred spotlights were shining down on me; I could even feel the warmth on my skin.

As instructed, I began to "reflect" on my early childhood, scanning memories; some pleasant, others irksome, but nothing there of a "stuck" nature. I allowed myself to sink deeper into the meditation. Soon I was only vaguely aware of my physical surroundings. My mind was a sort of gray dream cavern. As if I had a double standing to the side, strangely detached, a dream-watcher observing my real self on a stage inside the cavern: the day I drove to my mother's house to announce I was pregnant ...

Who is the father? Mom demands.

No one you know.

Carson, she is probably thinking. Perversely, I enjoy her pained expression at the thought of such a scandal. I want it to be Carson's, but he is right, that's totally illogical; I only slept with him once during the preceding months, I got the dates mixed up, and anyway it's highly improbable that he can ever have kids—never mind that his puny sperm worked with Lucy, that's recent information—I am remembering how it was five, six years ago, my real self on that stage ignoring this side-comment my double is making. I slept with Wesley several times, he was the father, had to be, he never once denied it.

Mom comes unglued and throws a fit. Grandma urges me to marry the man. Wesley. I can't, Grandma, he's already married! I have to say it three times before she gets it through her head.

I think you should consider abortion, says Mom, and then the tears and the arguing. Mom demands to know how I intend to care for the baby. If I think I can bring it home, I have another think coming.

The scene shifts and I see myself returning to my small cramped apartment (Carson wasn't so generous in those days). I am sick with fear that Mom is right; I have nothing to offer a baby. So little to offer, the baby will be better off dead? Is this what she means by abortion? If so, then maybe I ought to die, too. I consider hanging myself; I consider taking a razor to my wrists, but I hate anything tight around my neck and the sight of blood always makes me faint. And what if death isn't a "transition," as churchy people claim? Maybe the atheists are right; maybe death is a total blackout. And even if I am willing to risk blotting out my own life, what right do I have to make such a decision for my baby? I am not one of those radical anti-abortionists, but this is my baby.

I try Grandma's idea. Wesley Dillinger is already taken, but he isn't the only man on Earth, and he's certainly not the cutest. So I entice into bed a guy named Matt, then in a few weeks break the happy news that I am pregnant. He agrees we can get married (maybe). I am between jobs (as usual), and if I get married, I can hardly ask Carson to help out; so Matt says I can move in with him. But the night we load my belongings into the back of his VW Rabbit, we quarrel. Matt is so angry he slams the car to a complete stop in mid-traffic. Cars zooming left and right, people honking and yelling as he leaps out, runs around and yanks up the hatch-back and begins throwing my stuff all over the road. I jump out and start beating on him and screaming. He knocks me on the ground, then yells that I am a slut and will make a rotten mother. Then he gets in his car and speeds away.

The cops come and take me to a shelter where I stay until I swallow my pride and call Carson. While I am in that shelter, I see firsthand how women down on their luck survive. I listen to their stories, especially about how hard it is to make ends meet when you have kids and no husband. So Carson doesn't have to twist my arm when he says Wesley Dillinger should be held responsible, married or not.

Fast-forward to giving birth. I see myself holding Briana in my arms, I feel her tiny toes and fingers, I smell her sweet newborn fragrance. She has big blue eyes like mine. She has dimples. Her hair is blond. I swallow my tears and insist on naming her. Briana. She is too sweet to keep and ruin.

She deserves a good life, parents who will raise her right, in an environment where she can realize the opportunities I cannot give her.

But those are Carson's words ...

I tried to move past the gut-wrenching scene in the hospital; scary how a meditation can trap you in a scene like that. I tried but failed to linger on memories of better times: the great dinners with Carson, the things I bought with the money he gave me, the decision to Do Something with my life, enrolling in real estate school (he was so proud), the excitement of selling my first home. All that whisking by fast, like garbled sub-scenes while that one image loomed large, me in the hospital holding Briana, every detail vivid, as if I were there in body and all that had happened since was the dream.

Lucy finally spoke. Counting us up out of the trance. The light in the room was so dazzling my eyes stung. A few yawns and rustlings of fabric as everyone stretched or uncrossed legs. I felt numb all over.

The next instruction was as insensitive as it was outrageous. Lucy and Doc Jaffee were going to leave the room, and while they were gone, we were supposed to split into small groups and discuss where we were stuck.

No damn way was I going to talk about Briana with a bunch of strangers. Apparently there were others who felt the same, for no one was rushing to follow the instruction. But in any crowd there are pushy individuals who get things moving and I was encouraged to join three women near the windows. One bleated about the Big Divorce, another mewled about the death of her father, the third whined that she'd gotten married instead of becoming a lawyer. When they pressed me to share, I told them I was also upset about the death of my father. The woman who was stuck likewise had thick black eyebrows. When she said she was glad she wasn't the lone potato, I wanted to slap those eyebrows off her face.

An hour of this hell passed, then Lucy returned. She said, "Now I want each of you to get up and walk through that door." She pointed, as if there were other doors we could choose. "And I want you to slam it hard on the way out." Some of the women laughed. "You walk out, you slam the door, you say, 'THE HELL WITH THE PAST, IT'S DONE AND OVER WITH, AND I'M DONE FRETTING ABOUT IT!'"

A few women cheered and clapped, others muttered angrily. I was stunned. Just like that, I was supposed to slam the door on Briana?

Lucy would allow no questions. Like sheep the women began to rise and march toward the door. Slam. Slam. Slam. One by one, they marched through the door, slammed it, shouting what Lucy had shouted, the bit about the past being over and done with. They marched through the door, slammed, shouted, until only Lucy and I remained in the room. I was over in the corner, my pillow smashed against my gut. Tears streamed my face.

"Something in the past you got trouble letting go of?"

"You know!"

"Yes. And it's high time you let go of it, Shandie." She walked over and extended her hand.

"Don't touch me! You made me remember it all and now you want me to forget it!" I crumbled into a heap and sobbed. She left the room. My cries rose to wails. I was being abandoned, left in the Past Room alone.

The door opened. I jerked up my head, ready to blast the witch again. But it was Doc Jaffee. She moved across the room with swan-like grace, knelt down and began stroking my head, which made me cry harder. I felt no anger toward Doc Jaffee, Lucy was the one who had forced me to dredge up the memories, Lucy who ripped me apart for giving up Briana.

"I'm afraid we don't always explain thoroughly enough as we go along," Doc Jaffee said. "The symbology of slamming the door and renouncing your past does not preclude resolvement of your conflicts. Nor is it meant to destroy memories."

I sniffed.

"We're trying to help you shift your focus. Stuck in the past as we're dealing with it here means being stuck in the idea that everything is set in concrete. That is a misperception. On a cosmic no-time continuum, what we refer to as the past is elastic, in a manner of speaking, and can be manipulated, even mended. You can't go back and undo the action, but you can do much to alter the outcome of those actions."

"Huh?"

She laughed. Flashed her bright white teeth. "I'm saying that the possibilities as to mending past mistakes expand when a soul is willing to slam the door on how he or she perceives what has happened. In the Present and Future rooms we will be working with concepts we think you will find new and exciting. With the slamming of this door, other doors open. Are you ready to discover what's behind these new doors?"

"It doesn't mean I'll never see Briana again?" I rubbed tears away from my eyes with the heels of my hands.

"No, no." She smiled, shook her head. "In fact, if you are willing to slam the door on your perception of what happened around this painful experience, I guarantee you, the chances of seeing your daughter again will greatly improve. Provided a reunion is in your daughter's best interest, which I'm sure is your heart's desire."

I had to think about that. I gave Briana to the Dillingers thinking that was in her best interest. And look what happened. My poor baby stuck in that awful house with those dirty boys. A drunk for a father, and, it appeared, a mother who left the kids alone while she worked. I could've done better than that all by myself, without any help from Carson.

Doc Jaffee took my hand. "Shall we ...?"

I allowed her to help me to my feet. We walked toward the door. She stepped out into the hallway, smiling like I was her star pupil.

I sucked in a deep breath and stepped across the threshold. Then turned and slammed that door so hard the "Past" sign popped off the jamb and hit the floor with a bang.

It was an exhilarating moment and the glow stayed with me throughout most of the day. Doc Jaffee said it might be a good idea to spend the night at the house so I could "stay connected." But I didn't feel connected and wasn't sure I wanted to connect. What I experienced slamming that door had nothing to do with the other participants. After slamming that door, I went through the motions with everyone else, but my mind was off in la-la land, building castles where Briana and I could live as mother and daughter.

I didn't realize when I declined the offer to stay the night at the house, I was about to fall into a well of depression. Later Doc Jaffee told me she could've helped if I'd told her about it. But it wasn't the kind of depression you can readily admit. I thought I was depressed for having gone into that awful Past Room in the first place. I slammed the door, I felt higher than a cloud for hours afterward, but then I began to feel that I had been tricked.

And I began to think Mom was right. Lucy had this big sentimental idea about family, learned I lost my daughter, decided this had to be fixed, confronted me, and when I freaked, she sent Doc Jaffee to talk me into coming to the retreat, knowing I'd get all excited about the possibility of reuniting with Briana—neither of them having one slender idea how this could happen, and people called me Alice in Wonderland! But that's how they made their money, Lucy and her sidekick phony doctor friend; they pumped dreams into your head and if the dreams were possible, you went home and got to work to make them come true. Then when people asked how it was you were able to do this great thing, you told them about this retreat you attended, how the great Lucinda Desserita Xavier Blue inspired you, empowered you, and shit, it was worth four hundred dollars, it was worth a thousand!

But the dream thing put in my head was turning to ashes. They didn't exactly put the dream in my head, it was already there, I'd dreamt it a million times; they tricked me into believing it could come true.

I remember little of what we did on Tuesday. At least I got to see the kids Monday evening, that helped. My focus Tuesday centered on hiding my depression. I wanted to drop out, I longed to escape with the kids up to the pines (bet Regina didn't tell any good stories); but if I quit the second day, Lucy and Doc Jaffee might pounce on me and succeed in building up my hopes again, making me believe the dream could come true, then down I'd go again.

I was going on that date, dammit. And I was going to have fun.

Steffen had said we'd leave at six that night, so around four I begged out of the retreat, saying I had a killer headache. I needed two hours to get ready because I was going to look smashing, I was going to knock that man on his butt. Maybe I was wrong about him, maybe he could be a gentleman, and maybe I didn't care if he was or not. He was handsome, he was rich, so why complain.

Acting on what I had seen in the first meditation, I put on my red satin dress. Rhinestones along the spaghetti straps and rhinestones around the scalloped edges of the tiered skirt. Tight at the waist and it pushed up my breasts—not that I needed the extra help. The important thing was that I look smashing. I wore my diamond earrings and took pains with my hair, teasing it up on the crown, creating a kind of Tina Turner look. I found some old false eyelashes and glued them on. Doused myself with *Oscar de la Renta parfum* and used some glittery polish to paint my nails. It would have been nice if I'd had something red or white to wear as a wrap to complete the outfit, but the only thing I owned half suitable was a lacy black shawl. I was arranging it around my arms when the knock came at the door, a soft thump, the man not wanting to sound anxious.

I drew in my breath and opened the door. He wasn't wearing a tuxedo. He had on gray slacks and a muted red long-sleeved shirt of soft fabric. At least we both had on red.

"Oh," he said.

I was way overdressed, but his smile told me he liked the way I looked. "It's rare I have reason to dress formally these days," I said in my Sondra voice, which wasn't quite appropriate because Sondra dressed to the nines all the time. "—I mean since I quit real estate."

"You dressed like that when you showed homes?"

I picked up my black beaded purse off the table and brushed past him, saying over my shoulder, "No, but sometimes when you take a client to dinner ..."

"Hmmmm," he said.

He was taking me to dinner at the Marriott Hotel in Denver. Was it okay if we dined with some other people? He had some business he needed to take care of over dinner, then we'd have the rest of the evening to ourselves.

He was friendly on the drive north, asking me about my real estate experiences, leaning sideways so our shoulders touched, resting his arm on my thigh, stroking my knee and giving me dreamy looks. But I wasn't worried, he wasn't veering off on any dirt roads.

He kissed me after we parked in front of the Marriott. A pretty passionate kiss for a parking lot. He called me a luscious woman and held my hand as we walked into the hotel.

It was like being with Carson again, a feeling that all was right in my world. I was who I was: the kind of woman a rich, important man enjoyed showing off in public, a woman he found luscious.

At the entrance to the restaurant he spotted his friends and waved. They were seated in a semi-circular booth to our right, two men and one woman. White tablecloths, carnations in vases, candles, dim lights, piped-in dental office music, the usual.

We slid into the booth and Steffen introduced me. One awkward moment when he realized he didn't know my last name. "Lorrain," I whispered. The woman tried to pass off a sneer for a smile. She was married to the large, beefy-faced man with silver hair. Mr. and Mrs. Showalter, Harry and Liz. Liz had straight bleached-blond hair that curved under slightly at chin-level. No jewelry other than a diamond wedding ring and a delicate gold watch. She had on a white sleeveless dress. Small-breasted, im-maculate, tan, probably a tennis fiend. The men were dressed like Steffen, for casual business. The extra man was short, had a big nose and a fringe of dark hair below his bald dome. Charlie Linderman lived in Chicago.

We ordered drinks. The men talked about business. We or-dered food. And the men talked about business. I watched Liz and she watched me. No one asked me anything. Steffen mentioned Lucy a couple of times but only in reference to the sale of the ranch and the restaurant they used to own. Once in a while they drifted off business and talked about sports, boats, airplanes, cars. Liz inserting clever remarks like gumdrops into a pot of acid. I ordered shrimp scampi and picked at my food.

The dishes were removed and we had more drinks. Jack Daniels and water for me, whiskey sours for Steffen. Harry saw a man he knew over at the bar and all three men left the booth to go talk with him.

Liz smiled at me. Sneered. I asked if she worked. She did volunteer work, but mostly she golfed. I said, "You have something green—" I pointed at my teeth. She excused herself and left for the ladies' room. She didn't have anything green in her teeth, I just wanted to even things up. The way she looked at me. Like I was some bimbo. Just because I was overdressed. How was I to know it was going to be an evening with the Smart Crowd? I sipped my drink and thought about the kids, how I enjoyed hanging out with them more than I did adults.

Liz didn't return until the men did, then everyone was ready to leave. I thought we were leaving, too, but after he paid the check, Steffen steered me over to the elevators. He said Charlie was loaning us his room for awhile. "Why do we need his room?" I asked and he said because it had a magnificent view. Two middle-aged women got in the elevator with us so I couldn't challenge his less than forthright remark.

The room was total luxury; there was even a phone in the bathroom. Everything had a gold shine to it, visible in the weak light, only one lamp on, over in the corner. The view from the balcony was magnificent. The Marriott sits on a hill above Interstate-25, and looking westward from the eighth floor, you can see the mountains for miles, almost all of the city, everything glittering like white and gold jewels.

Steffen stepped behind me, circled my waist and pressed his body hard against mine. After he finished his velvety talk about the scenery, he pulled back my hair and nuzzled my neck. He slipped his hands over my breasts. I turned around quickly and tried to leave the balcony, saying we'd better go, I had to get up early tomorrow. He seized my hand and led me back inside the room. Over to the king-sized bed with the gold-spun spread.

"Pa-leeze," I said. He chuckled, like my protest was a joke, pulled me down on the bed and started kissing me. French-kissing again.

I remembered a time Carson and I talked about date rape, him saying sometimes a man can't stop, so don't start something you're not willing to finish. I couldn't think straight, the way Steffen was stroking me and muttering his sweet nothings—who started it? One moment we were innocently embracing and kissing, the next, he was easing me back.

In one swift movement, he raked down my bodice. I shot straight up, said, "Whoa!" He said, "Relax ..." pulled me down again.

I could have fought him, I could have screamed, but Carson's words were too loud in my brain. I wore the sexy dress, never mind imagining Steffen in a tuxedo, us dining in some restaurant where everyone else was dressed the same way, never mind he planned this, borrowing Baldy's room, the fact was, I let him kiss me, I let him fondle me and I didn't resist strongly when he pulled me down on the bed.

It was fast and crude. He tore my dress. He huffed, he puffed, he reeked of sour whiskey. He yanked down my pantyhose and shoved inside me before I realized he had his pants unzipped.

It was over in two minutes. He rolled off sweat-soaked and panting, squeezed my breast and said, "You are beautiful."

I went into the bathroom, shut the door, sat down on top of the commode and cried. Not for long. No way would I let him see me lose my cool. I would be Shayla, I would pretend I had seduced him. But inside, oh, God, inside I felt ravaged. I felt like scum.

The drive home was hell. I pretended to doze. He yawned a lot. Played jazz on the radio.

The worst was coming home and seeing Billy on his porch with his guitar. Bugle next to him. Normally Bugle would lope over and greet anyone arriving in a car, but not tonight. That dog knew I was hiding my torn dress under my shawl, he knew I gave in when I could've fought, and he was disgusted. Man and dog watched as Steffen walked me to my cabin.

My date yawned again and said it was a great evening and we ought to do it again sometime. When frogs fly! I wanted to scream. He said, "Stay pretty, Kiddo." Like Duke used to say. He walked away, whistling, hands in his pockets.

I felt sick to my stomach. I felt gorge bubble up in my throat. I slammed the door shut, ran to the bathroom, and vomited my pain into the toilet.

Chapter
Twenty-One

Minus One
Ponytail

Billy

They say best men are molded out of
faults,
And, for the most, become much
more the better
For being a little bad.

Measure for Measure
Act 5, scene 1, line 436
William Shakespeare
(1564–1616)

As still as a log, Billy watches Shandie and Steffen walk from the garage over to Shandie's cabin. The light inside Billy's cabin dimly illuminates the porch, but if the walkers see him, they do not show it.

Shandie hurries ahead of Steffen, her head bowed. She clutches the black shawl around her dress. Without moving his eyes, Billy reaches down and strokes the dog. Bugle staying put, as if cognizant the man in the canvas chair needs a friend just now.

After Shandie disappears, Steffen strolls toward the cabin he occupies, hands stuffed in his pocket, the man whistling, as if he has not a care in the world.

Billy picks up the guitar, thanks Bugle for the company, and goes inside his cabin. He settles the guitar in the corner, lies down on the bed, locks his hands behind his head and stares at the ceiling.

This is how he lay Saturday night when the vision appeared like a golden cloud in the air above him. There will be tears again, impossible to call up memory of the experience without a few tears. But each time he gives himself to recall, the pain he feels loses some of its punch. A sign he is on the right track in beckoning the images for study. If he is to be a Man of Vision—he supposes now it is written in the wind—the only way he will know any peace is to squarely face the phenomenon.

This vision began with Lia walking toward him. She carried a child. Lovely, slender Lia, adorned in a misty garment, nothing she ever wore when she was alive. Like you might see in a painting of an angel, a swirling white garment so soft it would disintegrate if rubbed between your fingers. As in life, her hair was long and straight, fine and silver-blond; it swirled around her arms like threads of spun silk. Suffused in golden light, she stepped gently as if across a cushion of cotton. She wasn't the kind of beauty you see on the cover of magazines, but the love emanating from her sweet plain face was more beautiful than anything on Earth.

The child she held was Shandie's daughter. (The same child Billy saw in the earlier vision.) Lia presented him the girl. Beyond the pool of light stood a man. At first he was unrecognizable; his head was bowed. Then Billy saw it was Carson.

Lia held forth the child, as if to place her in Billy's arms, then the light faded and the images dissolved into the darkness.

Billy thought he would never be able to stop crying.

Things are beginning to fall into place, the truth is beginning to show, but there is no feeling of being set free, as is promised in the proverbial Bible verse. This is truth taking hold of Billy by the scruff of his neck and shaking him, making his teeth rattle. Truth shining a stark light on his cowardice, his dishonesty, his betrayal of life's most precious principles.

The meaning of the vision is clear. Lia is telling him he is to act on Lucy's speculation that there is a karmic tie between their unborn child and Briana. Not necessarily a past-life tie. Billy reasons that if it is true that we live again and again, inhabiting different bodies and displaying different personalities each time around, then karmic debts can be satisfied in representative fashion. If it is true that we are all related in spirit—Mitakuye Oyasin—there is no puzzle here, no mystery, it is as plain as the Master said: When you feed one, you feed Him, when you help anyone, you help all.

Mitakuye Oyasin. Billy discovered the term in a book of the same title authored by Dr. A.C. Ross, a Dakota Indian with a Ph.D. In this book he read about the red road Lucy mentioned during her sermon. It shocked him that she knew about it. Afterward it munched on his mind, along with her pendulum metaphor. Then coincidentally, if insidiously, the vision appeared almost the moment he conceded that he had been walking the road far to the right. Where he thought he could avoid making any more huge mistakes. Where it was safe, he thought.

But the truth is out now, marching around in combat boots, howling and beating on drums. Billy can no longer call his behavior of the past fifteen years helping; he can no longer call it service, and the word loyalty has turned on him like a rabid dog. He aided and abetted Carson, that's what he did in truth. Telling himself he was paying off a debt of gratitude for Carson's help at the time, and after Lia's death. In truth, he used Carson Blue as a shield against future hurts. Creeping the road at the pale right edge, calling it a walk in loyalty.

If the vision accurately personified reality, then Carson now sees the truth for himself. Why else did he stand outside the pool of light, hanging his head in shame?

This is truth and it is terrible. No freedom here, there is only a burden of responsibility, a load of hurt that must be carried until justice can be served. Billy can make an effort to right the wrong, this much he can do, he can try; but how can he live with the knowledge of his own culpability? Beside the point. Peace or no peace, he must act, he must pay. Now.

He went to Lucy and told her there might be a special connection between him and Carson and Shandie and her little girl. He didn't expound and was relieved she didn't press him for an explanation. If Shandie is reunited with her daughter, won't this be sufficient? Why drag the details into the square like a rotten, stenching carcass? What good will that serve?

Lucy was all business, directing him to draw a cashier's check in the amount of five thousand dollars. A down payment. If Alice Dillinger is receptive, the remaining fifty-three thousand will be given her when she is ready to surrender Briana. A scheme as mad as it is illegal. But Billy can no longer protest, clearly it is his sin of omission that has thrust him in this role.

Another insight: Shandie's actions are no longer relevant. The vision he saw three times might have merely "stated the situation," as Lucy insinuated during her sermon. It is possible that the turbulence around Xavier and his airplane symbolized the turbulence Shandie is currently experiencing. Maybe her interest in Xavier is shallow, maybe she will marry the man; either way, it bears not at all on Billy's duty to try and set right this wrong. Then he will bow out, his debt paid.

Tomorrow, Thursday, he must find Alice Dillinger. Something tells him there is no time to waste.

The weather in Colorado Springs is so hot and humid it is a wonder insects are not boiling in the air as they fly.

As a precaution, Billy parks the Jeep at the bottom of the hill on Ozark Road. No sense in advertising his license plate number. There is a limit to what he is willing to suffer in order to square this debt, and going to jail is beyond the fence.

Walking up the street, he is annoyed at the sweat accumulating on his chest and back. He feels like ripping off his starched white shirt and throwing it in the gutter. But to appear in a sweat-soaked

T-shirt will do nothing to help his case. He rolls up the sleeves to his elbows, a concession he rarely makes in any circumstance.

He hears a blare of TV or radio noise before he reaches the crumbling concrete stairs at the base of the walkway that fronts the property. Shandie did not exaggerate. The house is a dump. It cries for paint. It moans for hammer and nails. The grass, long dead, utters not a whimper.

The porch floor squeaks as he approaches the door. Flies swarm in and out of a rip in the screen door.

The room he peers into is semidark; drapes are drawn over the front windows. Pale sunshine slanting in from the kitchen spotlights a hallway that probably leads to bath and bedrooms. As his eyes adjust to the dimness, Billy notes that the room is bare of adornments.

The TV set is positioned at an angle cockeyed to a sofa, two boys sprawled there, absorbed in a war movie, he guesses from the machine-gun sounds. He smells a foul odor. Pine-sol scrubbed into cat urine and cigarette smoke, maybe. Or something worse.

No sign of the little girl.

He taps on the screen door. The larger boy gets off the sofa and walks slowly toward him, his eyes still fixed on the TV screen. Billy judges him to be about ten years old. Hair hangs in his eyes. The smaller boy gets up and joins his brother. Both boys are unkempt; they look like orphans.

The older boy says in a gruff voice, "We don't want any," and starts to shut the door.

"I'm not a salesman."

Before Billy can say more, he hears a clattering of footfalls. The girl appears in the hallway. She has on adult-sized sunglasses, and a wig of dark brown hair that bushes around her head and upper body. Her feet are stuffed into the toes of a pair of high heels and hooked over her arm is a beat-up looking black purse. The dirty sky-blue swimsuit she wears is too small. Chills sweep across Billy's belly like an icy broom. This is spooky, seeing in reality an image straight out of his vision.

The child clatters over to stand in the sunlight spilling in from the kitchen. As she lowers her head, the sunglasses slip down her nose. She catches them before they fall, sticks an earpiece into her mouth. She has Shandie's distinctive blue eyes.

"What does that man want, Rube?" she says with adult snippiness.

"You get that dirty thing off your head!" the boy shouts. "Mama says it's full of fleas!"

"Is not!" the girl retorts.

"Rube!" Billy says sharply.

The boy jerks his head around, scowls.

"Are your parents home?"

"Mama's sleeping," the younger boy offers.

"Watch your mouth, Kevin!" Rube shoves the smaller boy. "What'd Mama say about your mouth?"

Billy is losing patience with this miniature dictator. "Where does your mother work? I can contact her there."

"At ..."

Rube slams a fist into the younger boy's stomach. Kevin huffs a cry, doubles over and runs with bent legs past the girl. He disappears into the kitchen. A door slams.

"Mama's not asleep!" the girl yells. "She's at the motel! She's a MAID!"

"Shut up, Briana!" the boy screeches. "Our mother is asleep and you know it!"

Billy's heart tightens at the word our. Was it emphasized to torment?

"Does she sleep at work?" the girl says.

Rube stamps the floor; she stumbles out of the high heels, drops the purse, runs through the kitchen. A door bangs.

Three children alone while their mother works as a maid. She has directed them to say she is asleep if anyone calls or comes to the door, but the girl has let out the secret, as she might with anyone. As she might with someone with evil intentions. He ought to call the authorities now, today, against Lucy's dictate: follow the script and there will be no trouble. Dangerous to put so much faith in her vision of how this will play. But equally dangerous to act on impulse.

"Please tell your mother a man was here about some personal business. Tell her I'll return, I don't know—tomorrow, Saturday—when's her day off?"

The boy shuts the door in his face. Billy stands there a moment, considering. What more can he do?

As he steps off the porch, the girl runs around the side of the house. She clutches the wig. Her hair is a sun-streaked cyclone of curls. Dirty face, too skinny, a waif. She runs up to him, breathless. There is a bit of dried crud around the base of her nose.

"Hey, Mister! Why'd you come?"

Her question unnerves him. Does she perceive she is the object of his interest? He lowers to his haunches, rests his elbows on his knees. Those eyes, so like Shandie's. Spooky. "Did your mama ever tell you it's dangerous to talk to strange men?"

"You don't look strange."

He smiles. "Some people might disagree. The truth is, I'm a very nice man, but some men, and even some women, even if they look nice are very bad, so the reason your mother tells you ..."

"She's NOT my real mother! I'm DOPTed."

That sadly answers one question.

She flips the wig across her legs. "You know what? I'm mad at Daddy. If he doesn't come home we have to move to Grandma Stuckey's in Iowa and she's mean."

Billy feels dizzy; he shuts his eyes a moment. Could it happen? Could Alice Dillinger move suddenly, leaving no forwarding address? He sucks in air, suppressing an urge to grab the girl and take off. Oh, is he tempted! This would be the ultimate red road act. But insane, risky, wrong. He removes his handkerchief from his back pocket and mops his face.

"Daddy has a hanky just like that."

At the sound of a car on the street behind him, Billy turns his head. An olive-green Plymouth station wagon pulls into the weed-cluttered driveway.

"Shit," the girl mutters. "It's Mama."

Billy comes to his feet as Alice Dillinger gets out of the car. The Plymouth shudders before the engine dies.

The woman is small and wiry. A thin fierce face devoid of makeup. Drab unevenly-cut brown hair trails below the level of her pointy chin. She is wearing a soiled orange uniform, her name, probably, sewn in dark brown on the pocket over her left breast. She clutches a misshapen fabric purse.

She yells, "You get in that house this instant!" Briana takes off running. But the child cuts at the porch and slips to the south side of the house.

The woman cups her hand at her forehead and squints at Billy.

He walks across the parched grass, stops and recites what Lucy told him to say: "I'm here on behalf of Briana's birth mother."

He expects a degree of alarm, but the woman's expression is as closed as a rock.

"I knew this would happen someday," she says, as if to inform the ground. "Women like her always try something to alleviate their guilt." She tosses her head. "Well?"

Billy sees a flash of blue around the corner of the house. The child is trying to eavesdrop. He steps closer to the woman and lowers his voice.

Following the script, he tells her about Carson dying, about finding a diary in which Carson recorded his intention to help the family in their time of difficulty.

He brings up visitation, carefully choosing his words. Halfway through his speech, the woman bores into him a look so icy he almost shivers. It will rain candy canes in hell before she is willing to bend an inch say her cloudy blue eyes.

He reaches into his back pocket and retrieves the cashier's check, smooths it out and hands it to the woman. She yanks at it. Stares. Her face contorts, like a fist ready to strike. She snaps her head up; her eyes narrow to slits. A fly buzzes around her head, but she bats not an eyelash.

"Your precious birth mother wants to buy her baby back?"

He should make tracks now, hit the road, this is never going to play.

"What is your name," she demands.

He shakes his head.

"I have a right to know the name of the man who is trying to buy my child!"

He is unprepared for this level of vehemence. It takes stupendous effort to keep his own voice under control. "I am trying to facilitate something that will ease your burden and at the same time give Briana a chance to know her real mother ..."

"What about her real father? Huh? What about him? Too late for her to know him, isn't it?"

Billy feels something like spiders nibbling his neck. "I don't know what you mean."

She laughs, an ugly show of teeth. "You think I'm stupid? You think I'd believe forever that Carson Blue would pay us such exorbitant sums of money out of the goodness of his heart? Well, let me tell you what his help did. Wesley took to the bottle—he never drank before that! And now all that money is gone! That's what your kind benefactor, Carson Blue did, he paid Wesley to adopt his embarrassment, and he kept paying him until Wesley was ruined! And now you're telling me he set aside more money so that Briana's tramp of a mother can ease her guilt? Who do you think you're kidding!?"

"I'm sorry things turned out so badly," he mutters. "We thought the money would help."

"Blood money!" She rips up the check and throws the pieces on the grass. "Evil blood-sucking money!"

Billy looks at the sky and sees brilliant blue splotched with red. He looks at the woman and the red spots dance furiously. "Mrs. Dillinger ..."

"Don't you Mrs. Dillinger me! Carson Blue has all but destroyed my family and I'm not—I'm never going to let go of Briana! She's mine! Carson pushed her on us, he paid us to take her, Wesley's gone, and now she's mine!"

Billy is barely able to spit the words out past his teeth. "She is a human being."

"She's a pawn, that's what she is! But I took pity on her, I raised her!" She lunges. Billy ducks with raised arms, as if anticipating she will swing her purse.

"Get off my property! You are despicable!"

Billy has never hit a woman in his life, but he must hold himself rigid to keep from throttling this one.

A streak of blue to his left. He turns. Briana jumps on him. She hooks her legs around his hips, her arms around his waist. To keep his balance, he staggers sideways.

"BRIANA!" Alice grabs at the child. Lets go when Billy jerks away.

The child's strength is unbelievable. He tries to peel off her hands, arms, legs, bending low so he won't drop her. She cries as he tries to dislodge her. He peels off one arm and she clamps onto him with the other. It is like trying to peel off an octopus.

"I'm calling the police!" the woman screams and runs toward the house.

"You do that!" Billy yells. "I'm sure they'll be interested in the fact that you leave your children alone while you work!"

She rushes up the stairs, screams, "You turn off that TV this instant!" as she bangs into the house. The TV noise dies abruptly. Billy hears her slap one of the boys. She slaps him hard, several times. The kid makes no sound.

He looks down at the child in his arms. "Your mama's going to call the police."

"Can't. Phone's broken."

"Maybe she'll go next door, borrow their phone."

She frowns, considering this.

"And if the cops come and arrest me I might never get to see you again. So I better go now."

She releases her hold. Slides to the ground. Looks up at him tearfully. He swallows over what feels like a knife in his throat. The fact that she leaped on him, her tears, the clinging, all evidence she is miserable here. She leaped on him, a complete stranger; she clung. This speaks of desperation beyond Billy's experience. In one so tiny, one so young.

She sticks her thumb in her mouth and begins backing across the scorched grass to the spot where she dropped the wig. Her real mother's wig. This is pathetic, this is wrong. Billy's eyes water up.

She dips, picks up the scroungy hair piece and hugs it against her chest. Then she beats a path to the back of the house.

On the drive home Billy is so agitated he can barely sit still. He is hopping mad, he is furious; that woman is murder, she is hell, she's the wicked stepmother of a child's worst nightmare! And she is going to get it.

A few miles outside Colorado Springs, he pulls his Jeep to the side of the road, struggles out of his shirt and throws the damn thing on the floor.

Now he is cooler as the wind whips through the Jeep—everywhere but on his head. It feels as though a bucket of sweat has been dumped on him and has coagulated in his hair. Who the hell does he think he is? Chief LongSmoothTail?

In Castle Rock he screeches to a halt in front of Kurly Q's and kills the engine.

Thirty minutes later he emerges from the barber shop minus one sweaty, stinking ponytail.

Those boys teased him with murderous glee. Some woman is behind this drastic decision to cut off his manhood, they taunted. He said, "Yeah," thinking this would shut them up, but it only served to fire their imaginations. They called him pussy-whipped, they had a heyday conjuring up images of this powerful woman. She must be gorgeous, she must be a real man-eater.

"At least I didn't open a shop and call it Kurly Q," he rebutted feebly.

Those boys were heartless.

The wind on the back of his neck feels delicious.

Chapter Twenty-Two

A Handy-Dandy Magic Laser Wand

Shandie

Rich and rare were the gems she wore,
And a bright gold ring on her wand she bore.

> *Irish Melodies*
> "Rich and Rare Were the Gems She Wore"
> Stanza 1
> Thomas Moore
> (1779–1852)

The morning following my "big date," I stuffed my white gown in the kitchen sink. I was about to set it on fire when I saw the brats running down the path.

"Shandie! Shandie!"

I yanked open the door and the little varmints swarmed inside on waves of sunshine. Jennifer, Alex, Castilla.

"Regina's no fun!"

"She takes us to her house and we can't touch anything and she doesn't have any dress-up clothes and she reads stories—"

"Baby stories—"

"—Tries to make us eat celery and carrot sticks—!"

"—Says cookies and ice cream'll rot our teeth—"

"And we showed her our secret story place, but she wouldn't even sit down—"

"Said your blanket stinks!"

"—And we have'ta take naps—"

"We don't have to, Alex, but we're supposed to be quiet—"

"Hey, hey ..." I said. "Settle down. It's only for one week."

"How long's a week?" Alex asked.

Interminable.

"We want a story!" Jennifer said. "A real one!"

"So here you are ..." Doc Jaffee appeared in the doorway. Dressed in her white gown, white Reeboks to match.

"Regina and Zach wondered where you were," she said to the kids. "They've already begun eating their cereal."

Three dejected faces.

"Honey Oats and blueberries ..."

She smiled at me. "They miss you."

As I sidestepped over to the sink to hide my crumpled white gown, Doc asked if I was going up to the house soon. I told her I wasn't feeling well.

True. I felt horrible and looked worse. I cried half the night and there were dark circles under my eyes and they were puffy. So screw the retreat.

Doc tried to shoo the kids out of the cabin, but they balked until I promised I'd tell them a story later—when?—after dinner, and off they ran.

Uninvited, my visitor settled herself at my table. "Come, sit, let's talk."

I knew if I complied she would suck me in through those big round glasses. That's how I got tricked into attending the retreat in the first place, by those hazel trust-me eyes smiling behind her glasses, casting their spell. But if I refused she wouldn't budge until

I gave an explanation. I sat down in the opposite chair, cupped my chin in my hands and sighed.

It took her ten minutes to pull from me, inch by inch, as if with silken ropes, the gist of my rotten date. Minus one sordid detail that she probably guessed.

In her mind, what happened was a "valuable experience." She said the way to wisdom is through direct experience and nothing is ever gained by staying inside one's head; one has to get out there and live and embrace it all, the good and the bad, or more accurately, what we perceive to be good and bad, and it's only through experience that we can come to know who we are and what we want, and if we don't know that, we don't know anything.

She said I should give thanks to whatever I considered to be God for putting Steffen into my life, because careful analysis of his behavior and my reactions would help me become conscious of what I really wanted. I drew him to me, she said, because I was unsure of what I wanted, so he was a kind of symbol of my indecision. And emotions like pain and disappointment and humiliation were valuable markers, bringing attention to areas that needed light shone on them.

She wore me down. I went to the retreat.

After dinner, the brats insisted I wear my wrinkled white gown up to the secret story place.

Never before had we come to the secret place so late in the day. The lighting was different. The deep greens and browns were softer in the dusky amber glow. Stringy clouds trimmed in reds and golds hung in the pale lavender sky. The sun dazzled above the mountain peaks.

I'd meant to bring a sweater; it was going to cool down before I finished the story, but as we left the house, I was distracted by the sight of Billy: He cut off his ponytail! He and Lucy were walking toward the trees to the south and seemed engaged in a serious discussion.

I settled my butt on my stinky blanket. "Once upon a time ..."

"There was a princess," Castilla said.

"How'd you know?"

She shrugged with exaggerated surprise and Jennifer and Alex laughed.

"This was a princess who lived in the woods in a treehouse. She was friends with all the birds and the squirrels and sometimes deer, but she was lonely, too, because there weren't any other people living in this woods.

"Now sometimes she would see some kids playing down on the ground and she would clasp her hands to her heart—" I demonstrated, "and say to herself, 'Oh, how I wish I had some kids like those!'"

"She wanted to be a mother?" Alex said.

"Well, yeah, I guess she did. But because she'd always lived in the woods, mostly up in that treehouse, she didn't have the first idea how she could become a mother. She didn't even know how babies were born."

"I know," the boy said with an evil grin.

"Don't have to say it," Jennifer said primly.

"They grow in the mommy's tummy!"

Jennifer kicked at him.

"Anyway, our princess ..."

Jennifer wanted a name.

"Sallyfrass."

They hooted at that.

"Hey—she lived in the woods, she didn't know she had a stupid name. Anyway, one day she was reading a *Cosmopolitan* magazine and she came across this article that gave some hot tips on how to catch a husband. She couldn't believe what she read. She thought catching a husband was like setting a trap like a hunter does when he wants to catch a bear and have some bear meat for dinner."

"She wanted to eat her husband?" Castilla said.

"Well ... no. I'm just explaining how uninformed she was about this husband catching business. So she read this article and it said she should wear a pretty dress and put on some perfume and paint her face up real nice—" I demonstrated. "And then just go hang out with some men and see what happened.

"So Sallyfrass went into her closet ..."

"She had a closet in her treehouse?" Jennifer asked.

"Oh, sure, she had a whole wardrobe. So she gets all dolled up and she climbs down the tree and goes to this small town nearby, and lo and behold, the townspeople were having a dance that night and there were scads of men around.

"First she sees this dorky looking guy with a long ponytail."

"Billy's dorky," Jennifer said.

"You think so?"

"Always wears the same shirt, nothing else."

"Don't I wish. Anyway, this dorky guy asks Sallyfrass to dance and she kind of likes him, but oooooo! she spots this real handsome guy with blond hair and blue eyes. A lot of girls are gathered around him and Sallyfrass almost faints, he's so cute, and she just sort of walks away from the dorky guy and drifts over to where these other girls are hanging around Mr. Dreamboat. He sees her and their eyes lock and he walks away from the other girls and takes Sallyfrass's hand and says, 'Want to go for a ride in my chariot?'" He had this golden chariot. Of course Sallyfrass did, so she jumped in the chariot and away they went on their date.

"And they got married," Jennifer said, bored.

"We'll see. He took her to this nice restaurant and Sally-frass ate three bowls of ice cream, and Mr. Dreamboat was sweet-talking her, and she was thinking he would be perfect for a husband.

"But!" I thrust my hand in the air. "After dinner ... he drives her to this dark woods near the town, he stops the chariot and ... he hits her!" I smacked my hands together.

Three mouths opened wide.

"Why?" Castilla said.

"Because he was a jerk-faced creep."

"What'd Sallyfrass do?" Jennifer asked.

"She cried. First she cried. Then she thought—'Hey, I don't have to take this crap!'"

"She hit'eem back!" Alex said.

"Well, he was bigger than she was so she couldn't win if she slapped him, so ... she whipped out her handy-dandy magic laser wand—don't ever leave home without one—she pointed it at him and went ZAP!"

They giggled. Alex zapped the trees with his imaginary wand.

"She made him disappear?" Jennifer asked.

"Nope. This was a shrinker wand. She zapped him down to the size of a Ken doll, and boy, did he freak! He was too little to drive his chariot then, so he jumped out and went scurrying across the grass and ..."

"A cat ate him!" Alex yelled.

"You got it. And the dorky guy ...?"

"She married him," Jennifer said, bored.

"Nah, he just went on being dorky. She went back to the dance and looked over the merchandise, but sadly there weren't any other guys she liked. So she started to go home to her treehouse, thinking she could never be a mother and have any kids.

"But—a fairy godmother appeared on the road. She said, 'Sallyfrass, you've got it all wrong. You must stop reading that crap in those magazines. You don't need a husband to have kids!'

"'I don't?' Sallyfrass said and the fairy godmother shook her head.

"'All you need,' she said, 'is a golden heart filled with love.'

"'Well, I have that,' Sallyfrass said, 'but where do I find a kid?'

"'Go back to the woods,' the fairy godmother told her, 'and look carefully in the juniper bush.'

"Sallyfrass ran all the way back to her treehouse and ran up to the juniper bush!"

The kids eyed the bush to the east of the boulder.

"She pushed back the branches and there was a kid in that bush! The prettiest little girl you've ever seen."

"How'd the little girl get in there?" Castilla asked.

"If I knew how fairy godmothers did these things, you think I'd be here telling stories? I'd be rich, I'd be famous!"

I was glad I went to the retreat even though it seemed as related to my life as bullfighting. For instance, we were all given paperback copies of a book called *The Tao of Physics* by Fritjof Capra. Lucy pronouncing Tao as Day-o. If it was a "D" sound, why the hell use a "T?" I did not ask. These mystical types, always trying to sound so mysterious.

Doc Jaffee talked a blue streak about all this quantum mechanics stuff, saying the physicists used to think matter was solid until they discovered atoms were composed of space and particles and waves, and particles could be waves at the same time, making everything very paradoxical. Then Lucy got on a roll, going on about how things had a "solid aspect" because the atoms and all that other stuff were whirling around so fast. Which meant the faster the stuff whirled, the more solid the object? I did not ask. The upshot was, nothing was as it appeared, and everything was composed of the same stuff—not stuff—energy, or something like that.

I also learned we all had "higher selves." This higher self part of us was in touch with "greater realities and unseen dimensions."

I left that Tao book pronounced with a "D" out on the table so my higher self could peruse it at its leisure. It was the only way that book was going to get read.

Friday we were in the Future Room and as you might expect, there was a lot of "life designing" and crap like that going on. Lots of talk about getting in touch with our individual talents and purposes. Tons of mumbo-jumbo, but I have to admit I felt pretty good Friday night when I graduated and got my certificate and crystal necklace.

Grandma came and so did Mom, and Mom acted proud of me. Afterward she said she'd missed seeing me—would I like to come by for coffee and chat sometimes? I said sure, and was relieved when Grandma came over, interrupted us and gave me a hug. Mr. Floy congratulated me, too, and told me I would enjoy Capra's *Tao of Physics*, not to let the scientific jargon scare me, just skim over the technical stuff and it would be like treating my brain to an ice cream cone. Then Doc Jaffee hugged me and said she knew the universe had in store for me some pleasant surprises. Lucy was stormtrooped by so many women she didn't get a chance to put in her two cents, but several times she caught my eye, winked and smiled. I drank three glasses of champagne.

You would think we'd graduated college for all the fuss. It would be a wonder if a month down the road I remembered anything I'd heard. Except for what happened in that awful Past Room. I was still angry about falling into that cavern of memory. Briana, Briana! When? How?

There were other things on my mind. Earlier in the day I saw Steffen and Regina take off with the kids in Regina's BMW. That chapped my butt. So while everyone else was designing life plans, I burned over a plan of revenge. Screw Doc Jaffee's bit about thanking the gods for this wonderful opportunity to analyze my reactions.

Naturally Mr. Party-boy was gone when I checked his cabin after the graduation ceremony. I peered into the garage; Lucy's Cad was missing.

I went to my cabin, slipped off my white gown and put on jeans and the most modest top I could find, a plain long-sleeved plaid shirt with thick pockets over the chest. A lump of crystal reassurance on a chain between my breasts.

I watched; I waited. Lights were on in Billy's cabin and I was tempted to pay him a visit. See if he acted differently without his ponytail. But if he was in a chatty mood (ha!) I might miss Steffen, and no way did I want to risk getting him out of bed to reap my revenge.

It was after midnight when I heard the Cad return. I watched through my curtains until Steffen was inside his cabin, then I went over there.

Opening the door, he seemed pleased to see me. He said he was leaving in the morning. He'd already begun to pack. Big suitcase open on the bed.

He closed the door behind me. I stood there with my hands stuffed in the back pockets of my jeans. He gestured for me to sit at the table, on the bed, anywhere, but I shook my head. He gave me a half-smiling, quizzical look.

"This won't take long," I said. "I just wanted to suggest something before you left. You know those sex therapy places?"

His smile faded; he cocked a brow, an expression Lucy often adopted.

"I think you should go to one."

He laughed. He sat down on the edge of the bed, crossed his legs, locked his hands around his knees and smiled. "Oh?"

"Yeah, I know it's kind of nervy for me to say it, but I'm really concerned for you."

Then I let him have it with my handy-dandy magic laser wand.

"That was the worst sex I've ever had. I thought about saying something in the hotel, but I thought, Hey, he can't help it that he has such a small pecker. Then later I thought, well, size isn't everything. He could go to one of those sex therapists and learn how to use it right."

I had some other zingers but didn't dare go on, I was afraid he was going to leap off that bed and strangle me.

He might have if Billy hadn't saved the day. We both jumped at the loud knock.

"Shandie!" Said with such a harsh tone I was almost afraid to open the door. But I did and Billy reached inside and grabbed my arm. He yanked me outdoors. His eyes flashed from me to Steffen, back to me, a fierce accusing look as if he'd caught us in the act.

"Come on ..." He got me walking fast. My heart was pounding double-time.

"Where? What's ..."

"I'll tell you in the car. Hurry!"

Chapter Twenty-Three

Biker Eddie

Billy

The glorious gifts of the gods may not be cast aside.

The Iliad
Book 3, line 65
Homer
(circa 700 B.C.)

In retrospect, Billy will point to getting his ponytail sheared as the act that catapulted him over the walls of prudence. Next he purchased not one but five shirts of color. It was then a short leap to the mania that caused him to give in to an impulse to draw from his personal reserves a cashier's check for fifty-eight thousand dollars—a check payable to Alice Dillinger!

The woman tore up the check for five thousand, she gave no indication whatsoever she would change her mind. In her words, Briana was a pawn, the last piece on a board of whatever sick game she was playing, nonetheless he drew the check, like some dull-witted optimist.

He had been sorely tempted to tell Lucy of this urge to have ready a check in the full amount (he should use her money), but something told him he was to act alone. As if on the near horizon loomed some sort of karmic test, or initiation, a challenge he had to meet if ever he hoped to walk a free man. He brooded, he assembled in his mind fine arguments of logic, but in the end, he dared not defy the unknown forces moving him. To counter even the most foolish impulse might tip the scales of whatever human frailties were being balanced here. The goal was the reunion of Shandie and her daughter, but only the gods knew precisely how the feat could be accomplished.

One thing was clear: he was to be the facilitator. Validated by Lia's message in the vision, Carson's attendance, Lucy's insistence he go to Colorado Springs, and now the urge to have ready the check in the full amount. It appeared a gate was being opened, a way for him to amend his sin of omission in failing to speak up five years ago when the separation of mother and daughter was manipulated.

So be it, he grudgingly concedes. And awaits the next prompting. He is fairly certain he will be "called" to Colorado Springs again and this time Alice Dillinger will be ready to surrender the child. Will the call come in a week, a month? How long will he have to remain in a state of agitated readiness?

The call comes, late Friday night when he is absorbed in *The Secret of the Golden Flower*, a "Chinese Book of Life," translated by Richard Welhelm, text that requires concentration, something to calm the beasts of agitation that are snorting and pawing the ground of his mind.

In less than an outright vision, but graphic nonetheless, images erupt inside his head, a scene of violence. Then he sees himself in Lucy's Cadillac, on the highway, Shandie in the car at his side.

The book clatters to the floor as he leaps off the bed and tears out into the night, only to run back inside the cabin and get the check out of the desk drawer. This time he remembers to kill the lights and slam the door.

He dashes toward Shandie's cabin but comes to a halt halfway there and sniffs the air as if to catch her scent.

She is in Xavier's cabin! Anger flares, but he stomps it down as if to squash a grass fire. No time for anger, it is imperative that Shandie accompany him, if he has to drag her naked out of Xavier's bed. An image that burns with such votive clarity, when he sees her fully clothed, it takes him a moment to recover from the shock. He grabs her arm, yanks her outside, and commands her to come quickly, he will explain in the car.

"You'll need a sweater!" he yells.

When she has the sweater, they race to the garage. He has the keys to the Fleetwood; Lucy gave them to him moons ago, to use whenever he needed to.

They climb in, slam doors, he fires the engine, and engages the lights. The car lurches out of the garage, rocks then swerves as Billy whips it around. Gravel sprays beneath the tires as the headlights illuminate the house, trees, shrubbery, flowers, and then the Russian olive trees along the wrought-iron fence. The car flies past the gates.

"Is it Grandma!?" Shandie cries.

"No, no one is hurt."

"So where ..."

"Colorado Springs."

She lets out a startled gasp. "What?"

Characteristic of the weirdness driving him the past few days, Billy rankles at her demand to know the reason for this mad dash into the night. Did he not say he would explain in the car? He did, okay, get a grip, man, of course you have to tell her—but only the salient points, no reason to rip open the wound and scatter the maggots.

Damn you, Carson, for leaving me to straighten out this mess!

Splitting his attention between the road and the anxious woman beside him, Billy stumbles out the story as he negotiates the road that snakes through Doubletree.

He tells her about going to Colorado Springs at Lucy's urging (deleting the monetary aspect, the bribe, no need for her to know every particular), he explains that Lucy felt they could succeed at working out some sort of visitation arrangement, but Alice Dillinger was unreceptive, and now he was acting on an urge to return ...

"But it's after one o'clock! What do you mean an urge?"

"I ... I ..."

Be careful! A slip in explaining the urge might expose the fact that he is a freak who has visions, which will tear down another fence, and before you know it there will be so much of him broken open he will be like Humpty-Dumpty and never be able to pull himself together again.

Now she is crying. He pulls off the road, lets the engine idle.

Why, why him? It's bad enough being the recipient of visions that are often so muddled they defy interpretation, but must he try and explain the phenomenon to everyone? But what did he think? That Shandie would sit quietly all the way to the Springs and watch calmly while he facilitated an extraordinary rescue operation?

"I don't understand it myself, Shandie, but I have, uh, I have some sort of psychic gift."

She is digging in the glove compartment; finds tissues, blots her tears.

He sighs, bows his head to the steering wheel. Time is galloping, time is ripping apart the seams of night.

"I don't know why exactly, but something has been calling me, sort of, to help you out with your daughter, and tonight I had this urge, this feeling we should go down there, because I think Mrs. Dillinger might be preparing to move ..."

"Move? Oh, no!" She grabs his arm. "No!"

"Calm down. If we get there in time I think I can talk Mrs. Dillinger into letting you take Briana."

"Oh!" Both hands fly to her cheeks. "Oh! I never dreamed ... let's go!"

Exposing the secret wasn't as bad as he'd thought it would be. He expected her to rag him with embarrassing questions; instead she is staring straight ahead with an alarmed expression, as if she views a scene of horror beyond the windshield.

This dark silence is worse than a bombardment of questions—worse yet, the instrument panel reports that the gas tank is almost empty. Damn Xavier. But they can make it to the Sav-O-Mat in Castle Rock—he hopes to hell the station is open. If not, there will be something else open. Would the forces directing him send him on a mission, specifying the car he is to use, without providing a way to fulfill the errand? No. Unless the images that erupted in his mind were the work of a trickster ...

When he spots the lights of the Sav-O-Mat in Castle Rock he expels air he has kept sucked in for miles. So the gods are with him.

Silent since she learned the reason for the journey, Shandie remains so when he pulls alongside the pump. As soon as he cuts the engine, without a word or a glance, she gets out and walks woodenly toward the restrooms in the back.

Billy lifts the nozzle off the island dispenser, inserts the spout in the tank, secures it, then walks over to wait in the shadows while the Fleetwood fills with gas. When Shandie comes out he will have a talk with her. Something is wrong, she should be excited, or visibly anxious, not paralyzed in fear like this.

The parking area is glaringly bright and the air smells of grease, dust and gasoline fumes. The only other vehicle in sight is a gleaming black Harley Davidson motorcycle, parked in front of the small convenience store. Rock music howls out of the store. A surrealistic scene, considering the fact that the clerk inside who is thumping on the counter to the beat of the music looks to be about ninety years old. The codger has on a ship captain's cap with gold braid, and he sports a bushy white beard. When the gas pump clicks off, Billy resettles the nozzle on the pump, then goes inside the store to pay.

From his perch on a long-legged stool, the old man reaches behind him and adjusts the knob on the radio that sits on the window ledge, lowering the volume of the obnoxious music. He smiles a toothy grin, one hand resting on the green rubber mat on the counter, the other fiddling with his snowy beard. His skin has the texture of a shriveled orange peel, but his eyes are a vibrant blue for a man so old. Besides the seafarer's cap, he wears bib overalls over red long-johns. An ornate briar pipe rests in a metal ashtray atop a pile of ashes and the air smells of cherry-scented tobacco.

Billy removes his wallet from his back pocket.

"Girl trouble," the old man says archly.

"Beg your pardon?" Billy slaps down two twenties.

The codger nods in the direction of the restrooms. "The little lady seems none too pleased." He slams open the cash register, counts out the change. "But she'll be aw'right. All you have to do is love her and she'll be fine."

Billy feels his face color at the impudent counsel.

"Right." He stuffs his wallet back in his pocket, steps away from the counter, and swings open the glass door.

"And Buddy—"

He turns his head.

"Don't never forget—they like flowers and candy, but they love diamonds."

Billy lets the door swing shut on the old fart's cackle, and returns to his post in the shadows at the corner of the store. What can she be doing in there? She brought no purse full of cosmetics, she has no comb. He is about to bang on the restroom door when it creaks open and she steps outside.

He asks if she's okay; she nods, but she still appears to be in shock. He suppresses an urge to shake her, jar her back into active anxiety. It would be normal for her to cry, to show some fear, but she has shut down, she is in real trouble.

Or maybe it is he who is in trouble. Maybe he shouldn't have brought her, maybe seeing her in the car was symbolic. He'd thought they would talk on the drive south about some of the problems she was sure to encounter after the child was in their care; but what if his earlier concern was accurate, what if she doesn't really want to take on the responsibilities of motherhood? What if she had planned on leaving with Steffen?

God help him, what is he doing? The whole scenario is so farfetched it borders on madness. But here he is, here she is, and the options are two: continue, or call it off.

He places his hands on her shoulders. "Shandie ... what is it?"

"H-how can I be a decent mother?" she says in a small, strained voice. Her mouth puckers and her eyes fill with tears.

So that's all it is. He shakes his head. "I think you're going to be an excellent mother."

The transforming power of his words astonishes him. Seeing her face light up in response to this small bouquet of encouragement he has tossed makes him doubt he knows anything at all about the human heart.

"You do?" she says.

"I do."

She looks so fragile he is tempted to gather her in his arms—get a grip!

Another shadow falls over her face. "I don't know, I don't know ... so much could go wrong. She doesn't even know me."

"She will. All you have to do is love her and she'll be fine."

Instantly he realizes he borrowed the duffer's words. Who was that guy?

But no magic in these words, as when he said she'd be an excellent mother.

Something very wrong here. What if he has totally misjudged the promptings of the past few days? People who wish they have the power to peer around the corner into the future should walk in his moccasins for just one day. While he has ceased calling the gift a curse, it is still frustratingly imperfect. If he could see with perfect vision, if he could interpret perfectly what he saw, he wouldn't be here; he would be a god, an angel, not some mere man feeling his way through a fog of images that could mean anything.

Shandie is crying, wiping her nose with the backs of her hands and looking around wildly, as if lost in a storm. He pulls her roughly against him and lets her sob against his chest. "You have to trust," he hears himself whisper sagely into her hair. "No one ever has full assurance of anything. The best any of us can do is follow what is in our hearts, and try and help each other bumble our way through."

These seem to be the magic words. Her sobs subside. He strokes her hair as she clings to him.

It should have come as no surprise that his body would betray him at this moment of almost spiritual elation, but he is astounded to feel the swelling between his legs.

He jerks away, grabs her hand. "Come on, I don't think there's a moment to waste."

He almost wishes he had left her in the wooden state. For the remainder of the trip she is like a machine gun loaded with questions, firing them off in rapid succession, so fast he can find few places to duck and hide. He resists telling her about the visions, cloaking his answers in heavy woolen blankets, smothering them in swaths of dark damask; but she is relentless, she is bouncing with new energy, she is a woman with a pitchfork, throwing off his camouflaged protections as fast as he tries to pile them on.

"Oh, wow! You mean you see this stuff like you have a little TV set in your mind?"

He nods grimly. Keeps his eyes on the road ahead. The car is set on cruise control; traffic is light, but the Highway Patrol is fond of this stretch of road, day or night.

They pass pine trees that loom like black spiky ogres above the flash of guardrails. They crest a hill and descend into a valley where they can see oncoming headlights for many miles ahead. The silvery moon insinuates from behind tattered gray clouds with purple bottoms. Between cloud portals, stars glitter against the onyx dome.

Shandie teases him about his hair, about him wearing a regular shirt. Telling him he is cute. He wishes she would settle down, find a balance between the zombie she was at the gas station and this wise-cracker.

He wishes he would stop remembering how he felt holding her back there.

And that old man—something strange about that old man.

She now knows he has second-sight. She knows of his vision about her and Briana—not every detail, God no—but she knows enough; and this is too cozy, too close, fielding the questions she poses like a child carelessly throwing daisies to the wind, his precious secrets, playthings in the hands of this child-woman.

And now he knows she has no interest in Lucy's brother. He almost laughed out loud when she called Xavier a "scuzzball with the sensitivity of a jackhammer."

He is alarmed at the relief he feels; did the old fart at the Sav-O-Mat see something he, himself, is blind to?

"There it is!"

She is almost jumping up and down on the seat at the sight of the lights that announce Colorado Springs.

Billy is in such a daze he misses the Uintah Street exit. Green exit signs flash by, all of them patterned with unreadable hieroglyphics to Billy's eyes.

"There—take Bijou!"

He sweeps west on Bijou, hunches over the wheel and cuts a hard right, then left, getting his bearings. He shoots down Walnut, cuts east on Boulder, north on Cooper, through a maze of softly-lit streets. The occasional cars they encounter seem to hunker down along the curbs like farm animals in a storm.

"Mesa Road! I remember!"

So much excitement is sizzling through Billy he fears the man he used to be is gone for good. The man he was is back there on the highway, on the other side of the Sav-O-Mat, far from this maniacal cowboy bucking the yellow metal beast over a terrain of emotion, completely foreign.

From the bottom of the hill on Ozark Road they can see clearly the Dillingers' house. Every window is ablaze with light. Billy guns the engine, shoots up the road, hooks a turn into the driveway and slams to a stop behind the olive-green station wagon. All four doors are open and the seats are packed with boxes and piles of clothing.

"We made it!" Shandie says with emotion.

"You stay here." He fingers the envelope in his shirt pocket. Fifty-eight thousand dollars. A sizeable chunk of his savings. He might never be able to start that landscaping business. Will Lucy reimburse him? Not if he is forced to spill the whole story.

"Sure you don't want me to come?"

"I'm sure."

"I think I'm relieved. I mean ..."

He opens the door. Hears the woman inside the house issue a loud scold. A child cries out.

He hurries over the parched grass and steps up on the rickety porch. Evidently the woman is aware she has a visitor; he hears her command the children to their rooms.

Chills shudder through him when he sees through the screen door the scene he envisioned earlier. Someone has trashed the place. Wesley Dillinger, he knows in the fashion he knows these things. He sees broken furniture, a rocking chair now a pile of sticks and the sofa appears warped, as if some giant has tried to bend it into a U shape. The television set has imploded and shards of glass are strewn on the floor. Clothes, papers, broken dishes are scattered from one end of the room to the other. Drapes hang cockeyed off rods and he smells a rank odor of whiskey, and rage.

Dressed in baggy gray sweats, Alice Dillinger is standing in the center of the chaos, her hands clenched at her sides. Beneath her left eye, a shiner that is beginning to color purple, yellow, black. Her face, her entire body is knotted in belligerence.

"What are you doing here?" she snarls.

A child cries out—the little girl, he is sure—then one of the boys yells something to shut her up. He steels himself against rash movement. He must deal with the woman first. She is the gate-keeper.

"You have suffered long enough, Mrs. Dillinger," he says, surprised at his calm, gentle tone.

Her expression is one of startlement at this note of compassion.

He gestures. "Looks like you're about to begin a new life, and that's good, you deserve a fresh start. No one was hurt?"

She chokes out a derisive response.

"I know, I know, you've been hurt beyond what any person should have to bear. I meant physically. No broken limbs ...?"

She shakes her head, her eyes still relaying the shock at his calm attendance.

It is miraculous that he is able to soothe her, as if with flute and drums, the words coming to him like rose petals fluttering out of the sky to settle and organize in his brain. He could have worked no better medicine if he had put gopher dust on his hair, mounted a hawk at the back of his head, and blown on a eagle-bone whistle. Whatever he says seems to cast a spell over the broken soul before him.

Later he will be unable to recall the exact words he used to convince her to surrender the child, but it is right that she does; she doesn't want the child, she never did. Amazing that he found the words to turn the woman around, but sometimes right scores a hit, spreads its wings, flies, gets the ribbon, the prize, comes in first, makes a home run.

When he offers the woman the check, she takes it, stares at it, stares at him. He holds his breath. Dares not move.

"It wasn't easy," she says in a dead voice.

"No woman in your position could have done better."

She nods without looking at him.

What now? Should he go get the child? He is afraid the slightest movement will break the spell.

The gods answer. Briana appears in the hallway. She looks pathetic. Her hair is a wild bramble bush that hasn't seen a hairbrush for days.

Alice snaps up her head. "He never drank before you came!"

Billy goes quickly to the child and lowers to his haunches.

She is dressed in soiled cotton shorts and shirt, dirty sneakers with no socks. And so she will go, with nothing more; no suitcase full of clothes, no toys, no symbols of her life with the Dillingers. She sucks her thumb and looks at him with vacant eyes.

"Remember me?"

She nods. Gone is the feisty sparkle he saw two days ago. Pain slices through his heart. Has she been damaged beyond repair? Some say a person's character is set for life during the first five years. This small soul has suffered a very rough start. But this is a world of miracles, Billy is reminded, evidenced by the fact that when he asks, "Would you like to go with me?" the child reaches out and climbs into his arms. He blinks back tears. Whence comes such trust in someone so small? The only answer he has now or will have later is that Fate is holding the reins and directing the course of these events.

Alice has not budged from her spot in the center of the room. She still grips the check, but something in the way her arms dangle at her sides suggest she is about to snap out of the spell. Maybe Fate's hold is precarious.

"Do you want to say goodbye to the boys?" he whispers to Briana. She shakes her head. "Then let's hit it." He lifts her, stands, looks at Alice Dillinger.

He does not ask the child if she wants to say goodbye to her adoptive mother. He will be unable to recall what he said to turn the woman around, but he will remember that she failed to show the slightest sign it pained her to lose the girl.

As he steps over the debris on the floor, she yells, "I was a good mother! It was Wes! All his lies!"

The bang of the screen door breaks the back of her words.

"What a mess," he mumbles to the night as he approaches the Cadillac. There should have been some sort of emotional preparation for mother and child. Should have been some kind of legal net sprung to protect them all. But this is life and it is happening now.

He packs the child around to the passenger side. "There's someone here who wants very much to see you, Briana."

"Who?"

Tears are streaming Shandie's face. She opens the door and holds out her arms. "Come here ..."

Spoken with such raw emotion Billy coughs and clears his throat to check his own tears.

Briana tightens her grip. "Who's she?"

"Your real mother," he manages to say over the wad of tears in his throat.

The child shakes her head. "I don't like her."

"Give it time," he says to Shandie. She blots her tears with a tissue.

"You've got two options. Sit between us, there, or on your mommy's lap."

"Your lap."

"No, that would be dangerous. Between us or on her lap."

She burrows her face into his shirt. "It's a wide seat," he says and nods for Shandie to step out.

Briana allows him to settle her in the middle. He straps her in with the safety belt. She hugs herself, shivers. Shandie offers her sweater. The child kicks at it.

"Take it," he commands. "I don't want anyone catching cold in my car."

Without looking at Shandie, Briana takes the sweater and drapes it over her like a blanket. When Billy gets in, she leans against him and resumes sucking her thumb.

He is grateful he is driving so he doesn't have to see firsthand the dance mother and daughter do on the long ride north. It is too heart-wrenching to take in fully. But he can't stay out of it completely, the child won't allow it.

A few miles outside Colorado Springs, she taps his arm and says, "You know what? Mama threw my wig away."

He glances at Shandie and sees her flinch at the word "Mama." But she recovers quickly.

"A wig?" Shandie says. "I bet that was my wig."

Briana glances up at him and scowls. She is yet to look directly at her mother.

Shandie says, "I left my wig and sunglasses on the hill behind your house and I was hoping you'd find them."

"Rube peed on it and it was all stinky," the child says, still directing her words at him. "So Mama said we have to throw it away."

"Did you find my sunglasses too?" Shandie says.

Two conversations going on.

"Kevin broke them."

A chance the conversations will merge.

"They weren't Foster Grants," the child adds and wiggles her feet.

Shandie smiles. "No, they weren't. They were Ray-Bans, right?"

Briana says nothing.

For miles they drive in silence. By the time they reach the long stretch of valley, both mother and daughter are asleep. Billy is amazed he feels not even slightly drowsy.

In this state of uncanny alertness it is impossible not to speculate as to how it's going to be for Shandie and Briana in the months ahead. Maybe they will both need counseling. Lucy might know someone ...

Lucy. Does she suspect there is more to the story? Not the question he should be mulling over. The question is: How can he expect to walk a free man if he continues to harbor the secret? Something tells him it will fester, maybe grow into a cancer that will send him screaming to a not-so-happy hunting grounds.

But dammit, what's the use in exposing it now? And why is life such a trial?

Near the outskirts of Castle Rock, he feels Briana move against him. She sits up, looks bewildered.

"You okay?"

Shandie wakes with a start. Yawns and smiles at Briana. She has cried off all her makeup and her hair is almost as mangled as Briana's. But try to tell a woman she is beautiful without her war paint.

Briana complains of thirst. She squeezes her legs together and begs for a bathroom.

"Can you wait five minutes?" The Sav-O-Mat is just up the road. Billy disengages the cruise control and accelerates.

He pulls the car in close to the restrooms. Shandie gets out, leans back inside. "Can I unbuckle you? I know where the restroom is and while we're doing our girl things, Billy can go in the store and get us some pop. What kind do you like?"

"Coca Cola!"

"Figures," Shandie says.

Something has broken for mother and daughter. Billy feels a lump in his throat as he watches Shandie help Briana out of the car.

After he is finished in the mens' room, feeling strangely jubilant, he goes inside the store.

The old man is no longer behind the counter. This clerk is a young man, tall and gangly. He wears a loud western shirt and is listening to country music.

Billy removes a six-pack of Coke out of the refrigerated cabinet, takes it up to the counter and sets it on the green rubber mat on the counter. Pulls out his wallet.

"Your taste in music is superior to that of the old man who was working here earlier tonight."

The clerk looks puzzled as he takes Billy's money and rings open the cash register.

"What old man? I've been here since eleven o'clock and I ain't seen no old man."

A chill coils around Billy's spine. "He had a white beard and listened to rock music. About one o'clock ..."

"You must have—hey! That sounds like Biker Eddie! White beard? There was an old guy working here a while ago. Always wore grubby overalls and a seaman's cap. 'Course you have the wrong station. That guy, Biker Eddie we called him, he died a few months back. And not of anything normal like a heart attack like you'd expect of someone that old. He crashed his motorcycle!" He laughed, stopped abruptly. "I don't mean no disrespect, but it struck me kind of hilarious, an old man like that crashing his motorcycle. He flipped it off the bridge into Plum Creek. In Sedalia? That's where he lived. He was shacked up with a thirty-year-old woman!"

Billy feels so disoriented he reaches out for the racks of junk food for support as he makes his way toward the glass door. His own image in the glass startles him. His face is ghostly white.

"I'd say Eddie was in his second childhood, wouldn't you?"

Billy falls against the door, swings it out and gulps in air like a man about to suffocate.

"Hey! You forgot your change!"

Chapter Twenty-Four

A Good Death

Shandie

Nothing is impossible to a willing heart.

Proverbs
Part 1, chapter 4
John Heywood
(circa 1497–circa 1580)

Briana let me hold her on my lap for the remainder of the trip. I was on a high, in a dream, a Daughter of Light gone to heaven.

On the trip down to Colorado Springs, first I was numb with fear, then almost hysterical after Billy told me about his psychic gift. I always knew he was weird.

He was like I'd never seen him before. Resolute and sweet at the same time, as in every vision I'd ever had of a real hero. Resolute, sweet, and strange. You should have seen him coming out of the Sav-O-Mat after we stopped to use the restrooms and buy Cokes. I don't know what happened in that store, but he stumbled out like he'd seen a ghost. Something told me not to ask what happened, and anyway I was completely absorbed with Briana. He could have walked out without his pants on, wearing a Native American headdress and I would have thought how weird, and turned back to my daughter.

The sky was a soft, golden-gray color when we drove through the gates at Blue Acres. Grass, trees, flowers, everything looked shiny and moist and starkly colorful. A scene of such unworldly beauty I was afraid I was hallucinating.

"See those cabins over there?" I didn't want Briana to think we would be living in the mansion. "That's where I live."

I glanced at the cabin Steffen had stayed in. Before we drove through the gates I glimpsed the airstrip and his airplane was gone. Such relief I felt. Like a bad chapter in my life was over and I could start a new one without him around as a reminder of the woman I used to be.

A white butterfly fluttered over the windshield for a moment and I thought, That's me! Steffen just caught me before I was completely out of my cocoon.

"And see that old green car?" I wanted to set her straight on that as well. The Bomb was parked at the south end of my cabin. I spared it the misery of having to share the garage with the snooty Fleetwood and Riviera. "That's our car."

Billy tapped the remote control device hooked on the visor and the garage door clattered up.

"How'd you do that?" Briana asked as he eased the Cad into the stall.

"Magic," he muttered. It was the first thing he'd said for miles. He got out, came around and helped me and my daughter out of the car.

He seemed oddly troubled for a man who had just performed a miracle. But his face softened when he looked at Briana.

She walked over to the doorway to check out her new surroundings.

When I looked at Billy again, he was staring at me with a strange passion in his eyes. Either it was passion or I was still hallucinating. Whatever it was—a dream, a hallucination—I was suddenly overcome with feelings of gratitude for his bravery. I threw my arms around his shoulders to give him a hug.

"How can I ever thank you?" I whispered so Briana wouldn't hear this gush of emotion.

Never mind the fact that I'd had a crush on Billy for years, throwing my arms around him was a genuine expression of gratitude; I wasn't moving on him, but the way he reacted you would have thought I was one of those aggressive women who grab a man between his legs.

He immediately hugged me back; he crushed me, then he kissed me with such force I almost fainted. Then with a look of horror, as if he'd just smooched a werewolf, he jerked away. I almost said, "Was it that bad?"—as a joke because I knew he liked it. But he fled before I could say anything, whisking past Briana, out of the garage.

Poor little thing had no way of knowing he was fleeing his own passion; she probably felt some kind of fierce rejection, after all, he was the man who had rescued her. She ran after him, and when it was clear she wasn't going to catch up, she collapsed on the ground, thrashed her arms and legs and screamed. He came running and so did I, but neither of us could calm her down.

Lucy, Doc Jaffee, Leona and the kids, all of them still in their robes and pajamas, came running out of the house.

"I don't wanna sleep with the slut-lady!" my daughter yelled.

My heart shattered.

Understand, Lucy said later: That's the kind of crap Briana heard from Alice Dillinger. Understand and forgive.

Everyone was babbling and Lucy yelled "SHUT UP!" Everyone did, save for Briana. She stopped wailing at the top of her lungs but continued to sob.

Lucy parked her hands on her hips and bent over her. "My, my. If you ain't one powerful little girl. You got some lightning bolts in your pocket you fixing to zap us with?"

Briana sat up, rubbed her eyes and scowled at Lucy. "I don't like you!" she yelled.

"You should," Lucy said. "I'm the high priestess of cookies and balloons!"

I couldn't believe Leona was crying. Doc Jaffee looked awestruck, as if seeing angels fluttering over us, and the kids were gaping. Castilla ran over to me.

"Did you find her in a bush?"

Remembering the story I'd told about the princess of the woods who found a little girl in a juniper bush, I laughed through my tears. Hearing me laugh, Briana puckered her lips and looked on the verge of wailing again.

"Who the heck are you?" Lucy said, still bent over her.

"Briana nobody!" she yelled.

When she called me a slut-lady my heart broke into pieces, but when she said that, I died.

"Oh, no, no, baby ..." I dropped to my knees. "You're somebody, honey—you're a Daughter of Light! Or at least a granddaughter of light—Mommy's a Daughter of Light and I'll teach you all you need to know. And you know what? I have something special to show you in my cabin. A very special box that has some things in it that belong to you."

She was my daughter; she wanted to see what was in that box.

First she looked at everyone else, maybe to glean from their expressions whether or not it was safe to go with me. When her eyes lit on Billy, he nodded. A mystery why she trusted Billy from the start, but she did, and that never changed. When he nodded, she held up her skinny arms. Everyone gasped, even the kids. Me, I was afraid to breathe.

As I lifted her, I swallowed my tears. The kids clapped, and for a moment I was afraid their exuberance would set her off again. She made a face at them, like Who the hell are you?

I started walking toward my cabin, as quickly and as carefully as possible. At the door I glanced back at the others. Lucy was saying something to Billy; she looked stern and he looked miserable. But my curiosity was fleeting; I had my daughter in my arms.

I left the door open slightly, worried she would feel trapped if I closed it all the way. I deposited her on the carpet, pulled open the curtains to let in the sunshine, then got down on my knees and pulled my special box from beneath the bed. A shiny Neiman-Marcus coat box that Regina had brought home from Dallas years ago. I had glued swaths of red velvet on the inside to insulate my treasures.

"Isn't it pretty?"

Poor little thing. Her matted hair was hanging in her eyes and her nose was dripping.

"But first you need a Kleenex." I reached for the box of tissues on the table, sat down beside her and watched while she blew her nose—inadequately, but I said nothing.

She lifted the lid off the box. On top was the white dress with the Minnie Mouse appliques on the straps. Stolen goods. I held it up. "I got this for you because I had a feeling I'd be seeing you again soon." A lie. That box of clothes and trinkets never held the promise of seeing her again; it was the receptacle where I stuffed my heartache.

She nodded and looked in the box for the next surprise. Three more dresses, socks and panties with ruffled bottoms, two pairs of shoes, a pair of pink booties, hair bows, ribbons, headbands, several bracelets, and a necklace with a gold locket in the shape of a heart. She said, "Ooooo" and clutched the locket in her fist.

I showed her the baby book, which had a white silken cover. Inside, under clear plastic, were photos of her as an infant and other bits and pieces marking her birth. Mom was disgusted with me for taking pictures of the daughter I was giving up, which showed how much she knew.

Included in the book was a card listing Briana's vital statistics. "See—here it says your blood is AB-negative. It's very rare."

"I know the AB's," she said and rattled them off.

"Wow! You're really smart! And here's the bracelet you wore in the hospital. The letters of your name are imprinted on each little square."

"Was I sick?"

"Oh, no. The hospital was where ... Most babies are born in hospitals where there are lots of doctors and nurses in case ..."

"I know."

"Of course you do. Briana? There's a story I need to tell you. You want something to eat or drink while you listen?"

"What?"

"Well ..." I got up and opened the refrigerator.

"Coca Cola!"

"How about Pepsi and potato chips and stale popcorn?" I said that as a joke, but she took me seriously, and I thought Hell, who cares! She's here!

I got out the Pepsi's, popped the lids, gathered up sacks of junk food, and sat back down on the floor, my back resting against the bed. I should have been in the bed. My eyes felt like rocks, my tongue was moldy. My whole body ached. Moaning with pleasure, I guzzled the cola.

I thought about Billy's kiss. Now that I knew he had it in him, I was going to capitalize on that passion if I had to tackle him and throw him on the ground. Later. My daughter was here! First things first.

She was petting the garments in the box.

"Okay ... once upon a time." She looked up. "There was this lady—well, she was more a teenager. If you want to know the truth, this almost-lady-teenager was a total wreck. Someday I'll elaborate. Anyway, one day her belly started pooching out." She smiled at my demonstration. "You know why?"

"She had the flu."

"Nope. She had a baby growing inside her. At first she was so excited! A baby! A beautiful baby. Maybe it was a girl baby! Then she felt very sad."

Big frown.

"She was sad because she was afraid she wouldn't be a very good mother. Well, her belly got bigger and bigger, and the bigger it got the more she worried."

She was staring into the hole in her Pepsi can. Was she listening?

"Not only was she worried she wouldn't be a good mother, she didn't have a husband."

"She could get one."

"She tried. Honey—don't stick your finger in the hole, you might cut it. The lady-teenager tried to get a husband, but all the good ones were already married. Anyway, she finally gave birth to the baby and it was a beautiful baby girl. As beautiful as a diamond."

She fingered her hair. Goose bumps spread over my arms as I flashed on the story I'd told the kids about a little girl with diamonds in her hair. A dream, this was all a dream. I'd wake and cry for hours because it was an impossible dream. Even if I could convince myself that Billy really did have a vision that caused him to drive us down to the Springs in the middle of the night, no way would Alice Dillinger just hand over Briana! If she did, if it wasn't a dream, then when were the cops going to show up?

Shut up. I've got her, she's here. What's that saying about possession being nine-tenths of the law? We could move. Pack up the Bomb and move to Cheyenne, Wyoming. Fast. Before the cops arrived.

"The mommy was so happy. But she was sad, too. How was she going to take good care of the baby without a husband? Well, the daddy came to the hospital ..."

"The daddy's the husband!"

"Usually, but not this time. See, he was already married to someone else. The daddy says, 'Don't worry, I can take care of the baby. But you have to let her live with me and my wife.'"

Big scowl. Perceptive kid, huh?

"The mommy wanted to keep the baby real bad, she did! But she was so afraid she wouldn't be a good mommy. It frightened her so much she believed the only way the baby would have a good life was with the daddy and his wife. So she let the daddy take the baby."

Her hand snaked into the box and withdrew a black patent leather shoe. She pulled off her ratty sneakers and tried to slip her right foot into the shiny black shoe. Too small. Screwing up her face, she worked the shoe on her foot. Maybe if she curled her toes.

Did she realize the story was about her?

"Then you know what? Five years later the mommy went and spied on the baby, who was a big girl now."

"Like me?" She kicked off the shoe.

"Like you. And you know what? She found out the daddy and his wife had been mean to her little girl. Oh, she cried and cried! How could this be! Such a sad, sad story."

She removed the white buckle shoes from the box. Smelled them, pressed them against the soles of her feet. They were smaller than the black ones, but she tried to put them on anyway. She looked so cute, screwing her face up in determination, I was almost unable to continue the story; I wanted to scoop her into my arms right then.

"But you know what? The mommy and her friend, a very nice man, went and got the little girl."

I waited for her to show some sign she was getting the message. She looked up. "You talking about me?"

"Yes, I'm talking about you. And me." I reached for a tissue and dabbed at my eyes.

"Why're you crying?"

"Because I missed you so much." I spread my arms. "Come here. I have to hug you now."

"Oookaaay ..." She kicked the shoes off her toes and crawled into my lap.

I died again. A good death.

A great ending for a story, except, in this one, there were loose ends dangling all over the place. Loose ends you can't neatly tie off, as in some sappy stories. Some dangly ends can never be tied off, not in a true story.

There are true stories you see on shows like "Unsolved Mysteries" about twins and parents and children and brothers and sisters, who have been separated for years, and when they reunite, they find they are alike in uncanny ways. This was true of Briana and me. How could she display so many of my facial expressions when I hadn't been around for her to mimic? How could she have my smart mouth? But she did from the start, expressions she'd hadn't seen me display yet, and she was always saying something brazen.

Lucy said it's because people who are related share a lot of common DNA. We don't know a lot about this yet, but DNA holds more than codes for physical and mental attributes. Incorporated within our genes are things like attitudes and even spiritual proclivities. Maybe. Lucy doesn't know everything.

She doesn't know everything, but she's the smartest person I know. And the most cunning. She had to be cunning to get Billy to cop to a major loose end that needed tying off.

That man and his secrets! That will probably never change. It's in his genes, Lucy said.

The King of Bad

Billy

The gods thought otherwise.

Aeneid
Book 2, line 428
Virgil
(Publius Vergilius Maro)
(70–19 B.C.)

Billy dropped fifty-eight thousand big ones in Colorado Springs, he talked to a man who had been dead for months, and now he has really lost it—he kissed Shandie! Not a peck on the cheek or on the top of her head but on her lips, hard; he has flipped, tipped over the edge, tumbled, he is gone!

And gone he goes, down the path, his boots barely hitting the pavement, his legs outstretched like scissors, he is flying, he is a weasel skidding toward Hell!

Briana screams.

He slams to a halt. The little girl, he forgot the girl, he ran right past her. What a heel! A lying, lusting, limp-legged louse!

He goes back on those limp legs, he bends down next to Shandie and tries to calm the child, but the tantrum has taken her over, she is berserk—what have they done!?

And now there is a crowd, an audience, onlookers dressed in sleepwear, as if summoned by a siren out of their beds to gawk at a raging brush fire.

Lucy takes charge, roars SHUT UP! then leans over with hands on her hips and addresses the child in the same manner she addresses everyone, with a blunt challenge. When she asks "Who the heck are you?" Briana screams she is a nobody! For Shandie this must be a knife with a serrated blade plunged into her heart, but she knows instinctively what to do, she knows the words, the mother knows her child.

"Who's that messy girl?"

Billy jumps when Jennifer pulls on his sleeve.

"Shandie's daughter," he snaps.

"But how'd she get here?"

"We went and got her. We'll tell you about it later. It's a long story."

Let Shandie tell, let Lucy; he is done! His head is spinning, the sun's hot hands are clawing his body, he should vamoose, melt into the background, dive into his bed, stay there for the rest of the weekend. But he cannot tear his eyes away from mother and daughter. Shandie is telling the child about a special box, trying to persuade her to come into her cabin, and the child looks up at him with those big sad Shandie-eyes, as if to seek permission. Why him? Things are crazy, mixed up, topsy-turvy. He gives a firm nod. Everyone sighs audibly as Shandie lifts her daughter off the ground.

Lucy nudges him, shoulder to shoulder. "Looks a lot like Shandie, doesn't she?"

Cold wings flutter over Billy's spine. Embroiled in the confusion, he forgot his inner pledge to come clean. They won't think he's such a hero when he peels back the skin and shows them the rotten core inside their dream fruit.

Flames in Lucy's eyes, that look she gets when she is seeing down to his bones.

"She looks a little like her father, too," he says with such timidity she has to move her head closer to hear.

"Dillinger?"

A trace of sarcasm in her tone. She knows!

Alex runs up. "What're they going to do?" the boy asks, pointing at Shandie and Briana as they pause at her cabin door and look back at everyone.

"Take a nap," Billy says. "Which is what I should do."

"After we talk," Lucy says ominously.

Yards behind the others, Billy drags up the path like a man shackled in chains. The sun leers at him and the birds are shrieking and gabbling like old ladies excited by the latest gossip.

Slam! Slam! Slam! goes the door as the others run into the house as if to begin a celebration.

Bugle's front paws are on the top step. He is peering into the mud room, no doubt wishing the revelers inside would for once lift the no-dogs-allowed rule. He whines when he sees Billy, then yields the stairs and watches with mournful eyes as Billy goes inside.

"In the white wicker room," Lucy says out the kitchen door. "I'll be there in a moment." She ducks back inside.

She would choose the sunniest room in the house for her torture chamber.

Billy slips unseen through the kitchen. The children are clamorous as Leona sets about to prepare breakfast, their noise following him like windswept hailstones as he moves down the hall.

Dusty golden light shines through the long windows in the "white wicker room," as Lucy calls it. A room Carson seldom used. In the old days it seldom saw a dust mop or a feather duster. Somehow the plants thrived. One of the housekeepers was fond of spraying the leaves with something that made them glisten.

The furniture is jammed close together, interspersed with a mess of plants, some in big floor pots, some hanging in white baskets, others clumped in small clay pots along the window ledges.

The wicker settee creaks as Billy sits down on it. He rests his elbows on his knees, knots his hands together, bows his head, and waits for the storm.

Lucy comes like a clap of thunder. She hands him a mug of hot coffee, sits her own mug on the low table in front of the settee and settles in the wicker throne chair facing him. She tightens the sash around her waist, securing her bulky white terrycloth robe. Under the robe she is wearing light blue pajamas. Feet swallowed in fluffy pink slippers. She sips her coffee.

Billy stares at the mug on the table. She remembered to put in cream. It smells delicious, but all he can do is stare.

"Drink up, Billy. It'll do you good."

Somehow he manages to unknot his hands and reach for the mug without trembling. He takes a small drink, then sets the mug down again.

Lucy crosses her legs, tucks the terrycloth fabric under her knees. "Let's talk about Briana's father," she says.

He nods.

"Did you think the truth would devastate me?"

She knows, she knows, maybe she's known all along. It would be like her to sit on it and watch him suffer in silence. To teach him some high lesson.

"Look at me."

He raises his head. She leans forward, rests one arm on her knee and scours him with her black eyes.

"Remember that night we talked in the kitchen? Remember me saying we have to act on whatever truth we see even when we don't know the specifics?"

The answer is "yes," but the word clogs in his throat.

"Shandie and her daughter belong together, that was the truth I saw. It presented as such a stark, powerful truth that I was willing to contribute fifty-eight thousand dollars to the cause. Apparently you saw the same truth and I'm proud of you for sticking your neck out ..."

Billy disgorges a scoffing noise at the word "proud." He has nothing to feel proud about; he deserves a whipping.

The woman on the throne chair is studying him. "Did you follow our plan and give her the money?"

He nods.

"The full fifty-eight thousand?"

"Yes."

"I'll reimburse you."

He snaps his head. No.

"Don't be ridiculous. It was Carson's money. Apropos, don't you think?" She smiles ruefully.

"Why don't you say it?" he bursts out, the settee complaining in a bounce of anger beneath him.

"Why don't you?" she retorts.

She straightens up, lays one hand over the other on her knee and starts swinging her leg. "Remember when I said I had a feeling you could see what I couldn't?"

She had more than a feeling; she knew and she played him along!

"Remember you said you told me everything you knew?"

"I lied!" He jerks, jars the table, grabs for the mug, too late. Whips out his handkerchief and starts mopping up the sticky liquid.

"Leave it."

He ignores her.

"You familiar with that old Bible verse about the truth setting us free?"

"Not this truth," he mutters and spreads the handkerchief on the table to dry.

"Hear me out, Billy."

Oh, God, not a sermon, not now.

She says any principle taken to the extreme displays opposite characteristics. For instance, loyalty taken to the extreme can double back and display as betrayal. Her hands move this way and that as she expounds on the qualities of yin and yang. Why doesn't she just tear off his ears and eat them?

"You're not listening."

"I was listening."

"Umhmm. Why don't we dispense with the horse shit?"

"Fine with me," he growls.

"Why don't you just tell me Carson is Briana's father. I want to hear you say it."

"Carson is her father!" He exhales a gob of putrid air.

"I knew it." She flips a shank of hair over her shoulder. "What an asshole."

Her response is so unexpected Billy almost laughs. The woman will never cease to baffle him.

"Will you excuse me for a moment?"

She glides out of the room with queenly posture.

Billy sits like a lump on the settee and waits for a feeling of freedom to seep through the cloud of morbidity surrounding him. There should have been a snippet of relief in expelling the poisonous secret, but all he feels is numbing shame.

Lucy returns with a cigarette stuck between her lips. She sits on the edge of the throne chair, strikes a match, sucks, exhales, bends over and coughs down her legs.

"Oh, Christ! How does Leona stand it?"

"Leather lungs," Billy says, and instantly feels his face burn red at this sidestep into humor.

"It's not my first cigarette," she boasts, gesturing with it, as if to imitate some old film star. "I find sufficient reason to indulge every once in a while." Her eyebrows draw together as she takes quick puffs and blows the smoke at the ceiling.

"Let us remember," she says in her teaching voice, "that Carson had his good qualities. A balance against causing his concubine all this grief."

"His what?"

She looks genuinely puzzled. "His concubine. What else would you call her?" She leans toward the potted philodendron to the left of her chair and sticks the smoldering cigarette into the dirt. "Sorry guy," she says to the plant, "but I forgot to bring an ashtray."

Fingers pressed against his temples, Billy hangs his head and wags it back and forth to dispel an insane urge to laugh. This is

her reaction? To call Carson an asshole for causing his "concubine" grief? He can't help it, a low moaning laugh escapes his
throat.

"Go ahead, laugh," she says. "It's real funny how my husband
caused all this grief."

He looks up.

"It's funny and it's not funny. That's what I was trying to say a
minute ago when you drifted off. This is a perfect example of how
life is a mix of opposites. Bitterness and joy. Horrible that Carson
would be such a low-down rat, wonderful that you were able to rise
to the occasion and don your hero armor."

"I am not a hero."

"Shandie thinks so. Me, too."

"I knew and I didn't have the guts to tell!"

"Yes, in that regard you were kind of a shithead."

He swallows a second urge to laugh. The woman is going to
drive him mad.

"So let's hear it. The whole story. How did the bastard manage
to pull it off?"

Reporting this story is unlike finding the words to persuade
Alice Dillinger to surrender Briana, no flute and drums this time,
no rose petals drifting down or the feeling he has a hawk mounted
at the back of his head. He can't even bear to look at Lucy as he
speaks. He stares at his boots.

"Carson wasn't sure in the beginning the baby was his, but he
was worried Shandie would try to pin it on him. So he made a deal
with Dillinger early on. He offered him a lot of money to accept
responsibility. Dillinger agreed, but wanted to know if the kid was
really his. Carson promised he'd get blood test results after the baby
was born. He wanted to know the results himself. If the tests proved
the baby was Dillinger's, Carson felt he could pat himself on the
back, tell himself he'd done the right thing."

"You believe it was right for him to pay Dillinger to take the
child even if Dillinger was the father?"

"It was unconscionable," Billy mutters.

"Go on."

"Carson knew a nurse at the hospital who was able to get the blood tests done for him."

"And ... ?"

Don't prod! he wants to scream. He wants to get the poison out, now, finally, then he can go, leave, let them all create the happiness they deserve. He deserves nothing more than a shack in the mountains somewhere, which is about all he will be able to afford after dropping that fifty-eight thousand. He cannot, will not permit Lucy to reimburse him, even if she tries to hold to her ill-conceived noble intent. He sees now that he owes Shandie and Briana what he paid, if not more, for those lost five years.

"What about the blood tests, Billy."

"Briana's is AB-negative. Very rare.. Shandie and Dillinger both have O-type, the most common kind."

"And Carson had AB-negative," Lucy says.

"Yes."

"So ..."

"Carson got hold of a blank blood donor form and filled it out, listing his type as O. Then he showed it to Dillinger. To prove that neither one of them was the father."

"How did Dillinger respond?"

"He wanted to beat the truth out of Shandie. Make her tell who the father was and force whoever it was to raise the child. Carson said in that case he'd just keep his money."

"And Dillinger managed to rise above his self-righteous indignation," Lucy says disgustedly.

"It was a lot of money. Carson felt bad about the way it turned out."

"He should have felt worse than bad."

Billy picks up the sodden handkerchief and carefully folds it. "I'll pack and be out of here ..."

"You'll what?"

"I'll leave."

"You'll do nothing of the sort, my friend. You feel shame for going along with the lie? You think you stacked up some karma? Maybe you did. You want to work off your karma, you don't split, leaving everyone else holding a bag of worms. Like Carson did. You stick around, you see what you can do to help the situation."

He slaps the wet handkerchief back on the table.

"What you do first, you eat some breakfast, then you go get some rest, then you be back here at five o'clock. I'm calling a house meeting at five. Before dinner."

"A house meeting ...?"

"Don't worry. I don't expect you to confess to everyone. I'll do it in a way that won't embarrass you."

The scripture that says that truth will set a soul free is one of the biggest lies ever visited upon the human race, Billy thinks at four-thirty after he emerges from the shower, sick with exhaustion. In this case, the truth has not even allowed him to sleep; the truth has raced around his cabin like a pteranodon, beating him senseless with its leathery wings. He can't even stand to look at himself in the mirror. He certainly cannot bear to put on one of his new colored shirts. Obscene symbols of that false self that caused him to chop his ponytail. Who did he think he was?

Trussed in his stiff white shirt, he trudges up the path to begin the next phase of his punishment. He deserves it. Lucy would have let him off easy if she'd raged at him and called him a louse and ordered him to leave. But she gave him the maximum sentence. He must watch while she breaks the news to Shandie and then he must stay and do their bidding for the rest of his life.

The mud room reeks of Mexican food smells. Billy can't remember when he last ate. His stomach cries to be filled, but he won't be able to eat, not here, not now, maybe later a cold can of beans ...

It is worse than he expected. In the kitchen everyone is seated around the oval table. Even Mr. Floy. The women and children are dressed up. Shandie and Briana look rested and happy. The child is on her lap. Her hair is clean and shiny and she has on a new-looking dress with cloth cartoon characters sewn on the straps. One of Jennifer's dresses? Shandie's face is luminous. She is wearing a soft pink dress, ruffles circling her shoulders.

What a crumb he was for grabbing her in the garage like some sex-starved brute! He doesn't know himself anymore. One day he is full of high ideas, the next, he is clutching at a woman whose only intent in hugging him was to express thanks.

"Billy's here!" Alex exclaims. "Now we can start the party!"

The boy has his mother's penchant for dark humor.

The only seat vacant is next to Shandie. She pats the chair and looks at him expectantly. He walks over to the counter next to the sink and folds his arms over his chest. Tomato sauce is bubbling in a huge fry pan on top of the stove, and along the counter are bowls of chopped lettuce, tomatoes, onions, and shredded cheese.

"I think it would be real gentlemanly of you if you would join us," Lucy says.

Looking at no one, Billy passes Leona, Edith, the kids, and slides into the chair next to Shandie. He crosses his arms over his chest again.

"Hi, Billy," Briana says.

Without looking at her, he nods.

"Fill Billy's mug," Lucy says to Leona. She passes a thermal jug and he pours half a cup. A prisoner's last meal.

"Leona's making tacos tonight!" Alex says.

Jennifer says, "And Shandie's grandma and mama and Regina and her husband and Zach are coming to dinner."

Lucy says, "I would have set out noise makers and some of those paper whistles that shoot out like snakes if we'd had any." Leona laughs.

Their mood is obscene.

Lucy takes a sip of coffee, then rests her arms on the table and clasps her hands. "The reason I called you all here was to clear the air and set some things right."

"Mama has a, uh, nouncement!" Alex says.

"An announcement," Lucy says. "That's quite a mouthful. First I want to welcome Briana to our house."

"But we don't live here," the child says, craning her neck to peer up at her mother.

"Not in the house, but you can come inside whenever you want to," Lucy says.

"Because we eat here," Briana says.

Shandie whispers in her ear. "Shhhh."

"This is a wondrous thing, a mother and daughter getting back together. And there are other things that need straightening out." Lucy looks at her children. "Jennifer and Alex? Briana is your half-sister."

"Yea!" Both children clap their hands as if they have been told they have won prizes.

"And the reason is ... you kids all had the same daddy."

Billy waits for the gasps of horror, the hands cupped over mouths, the pained expressions. Leona and Edith are smiling and Mr. Floy looks hungry and bored. Shandie is still. Maybe tears are streaming her face.

"Daddy kept it a secret, but now we know because Billy decided it was time the secret got told."

"Yea!" The three children sing.

"And there were other secrets, too."

Leona steals a look at Billy; her face is a guilty pink color. What now?

"Before a person dies," Lucy continues, "he or she usually leaves something called a will. It's a piece of paper that tells who gets all the person's stuff after he or she dies. When your daddy died we couldn't find that piece of paper. So Mama got everything he owned. But that wasn't right because I found out he wrote a piece of paper a long time ago ..."

Billy scowls at Leona.

"She insisted," Leona says, her face now red.

Ignoring the exchange, Lucy pulls from the pocket of her dress a piece of paper. She unfolds it. "Right here it says that Billy gets the house and all the rest of the property, and Leona gets fifty thousand dollars and her job with all the benefits for life."

"You can't do this," Billy says.

Lucy ignores him. "But this piece of paper says nothing about Briana and Shandie because Daddy wrote it before she got pregnant. So ..." She slips her hand in her pocket again and brings up keys. "So I'm sure at the very least he would have wanted Shandie to have his car." She shakes the keys.

Now Shandie gasps.

"Here. I don't need two cars anyway."

Lucy slides the keys across the table. Briana grabs them and jiggles them like a toy.

"You look a little upset, Billy," Lucy says.

"The house is not mine."

"He meant for you to have it."

Leona says, "Billy, you know Carson always wanted you to have the house."

"Which," Lucy points, "it says right here on this piece of paper."

"He wrote that before he married you," Billy says. "It's not even legal. It's not notarized."

"This isn't a court of law. We're just trying to get to the truth here. And anyway, I already have a house. In Reno. Carson bought it for me. I don't need two houses." She narrows her eyes. "What's the deal here, Billy? You think you don't deserve it?"

"That's exactly right. I don't."

"Edith—talk to Billy about deserving while I refill this." She picks up the thermal jug and starts to rise.

Billy's chair scrapes the floor. He stands up.

"Where do you think you're going?" Lucy says.

"I'll talk to you later."

As he hits the back door, Jennifer yells, "Party pooper!"

Stumbling down the path, he thinks: That woman is mad!

She should know he can't take the house after all that has happened. If anyone deserves the house, it's Shandie. Even that stretches Carson's true intent. That phony will is ancient!

A door slams behind him. He quickens his step. He will lock himself in! Tell the woman to go fly a kite!

"Billy—wait!"

Shandie. The last person he wants to talk to. But he owes her an apology. He stops, hooks his thumbs in his pockets and waits.

She walks in front of him. "What a shock, huh?"

He resumes walking. She has to almost run to keep up.

"I just wanted to tell you I don't hold it against you that you didn't tell me. I can understand ..."

He stops. "No, you can't. It was my character deficiency." He taps his chest. "My dishonesty. Some kind of sick pride I have. And fear. I knew he was wrong the way he handled it, I knew you were hurt and I did nothing. I went along because I didn't have the guts to stand up to him. Maybe I was afraid I'd lose the goddamned house!"

She whips her arms over her chest and tosses her light brown mane. "You're pissing me off, Billy."

"You should be pissed." He resumes walking.

"You big chicken! You don't even have the guts to stay until this thing is resolved!"

He stops. Turns and looks at her sadly. "There's no way to resolve it. You have Briana, that's as close as it's going to get."

"You're so dumb."

He shrugs and continues walking. Goes up on the porch and opens his door.

Shandie pushes past him, into the cabin, flops down on the bed and locks her arms over her chest.

"I'm not leaving until you get some sense in your head."

Billy's hands are on his hips. They glare at each other.

"What do you want? Blood?" He swings his arm. "I got Briana back for you, isn't that enough? There isn't anything else I can do."

Her lips tremble and her eyes fill with tears.

"Oh, great," he says. He clutches the air with both hands and walks in a half circle and back.

"You could give a damn about me," she says.

"I do give a damn."

"So you're going to walk out?"

"I'm not going anywhere."

"Oh ... I thought ..."

"I'll stay right here and do my best to make it up."

"Oh, shit, Billy! You think that's what we want? For you to ... That's what you've always done! Like your whole life is some kind of penance! Who do you think you are that your mistakes are so precious? Look at me! But I'm just a simple person, I don't have to beat myself bloody forever. You should go to the retreat, you need to hear what I heard. How we're here to experience life in the fullest, the light and the dark! You want to wallow around in the dark forever! Like you want to be the King of Bad or something. I don't mean you want to be bad, I mean you want to like cherish every little mistake you make; like you want to lay your mistakes up on a gold altar and worship them or something. Like that's what makes you so great—that you're so bad you win the prize, and for you the prize is punishing yourself more than anyone else would; so, in a way, you feel good, maybe you feel better than the rest of us because we're so weak we forgive ourselves and go on and live happy lives. Not you, you're the King of Self-Punishment! Give him a crown!"

He eases into a straight chair. Rests one arm on the table and stares at his boots.

"For a simple person you sure have a way of putting things."

"Oh, Billy ... if you only knew."

"I know."

"About how I feel about you?"

"I think so."

"So if you crap out on me now, that would be the worst."

He nods. Studies his boots.

"Is there the slightest chance you might feel something for me that's sort of like what I feel for you?"

He nods.

"Well, then, will you just come over here, you big bozo?"

These boots are at least twelve years old. They have been re-heeled at least five times and they are so gnarled he can barely squeeze his feet into them. They are handsome boots. He will hate to give them up.

The bed groans as she stands up. Her frothy pink skirt swirls into view, still he does not lift his head. If he does she will see his tears. She pulls him gently against her, crosses her arms over his back and rests her chin on his head. Her breasts are incredibly soft. She smells like wild flowers.

She sighs. Whispers into his hair, "I'm going to have to do about everything ... I can see that now ..."

Shandie-Billy

Out of the shadows of night
The world rolls into light;
It is daybreak everywhere.

> *The Bells of San Blas*
> Stanza 2
> Henry Wadsworth Longfellow
> (1807-1882)

Epilogue

Shandie

This mother and daughter reunion business wasn't all sunshine and roses. During the adjustment period I would have yanked my hair out by the roots if not for the help I got from Lucy and Billy and everyone else. It was months before Briana called me "Mama," even though she made it clear she never wanted to see Alice Dillinger again. She did ask if Rube and Kevin were going to come live with us. Lucy told her, "Those boys went to live in parallel universe and they're doing just fine." Briana said, "Okay," and everyone laughed. She hasn't asked about them since.

Kids are smarter than we think. Briana was quick to discern the guilt I felt for having abandoned her, and she had me jumping through hoops trying to please her every whim. For awhile she was a holy terror. Lucy and Doc Jaffee had to work me over to get me to see what I had told Billy: Absolutely no good comes from wallowing in past mistakes. We have to let them go, we have to forgive ourselves, we have to turn our attention to how we can make the world a better place today.

I was afraid Billy wouldn't be able to make the leap. That man was so in love with his dark side, which is a laugh because it wasn't that dark. I kept telling him: Carson was the bad guy, Billy. And even him we can forgive.

I was pretty nervous around Lucy, thinking she was being nice out of some phony sense of duty. But in time I came to trust that she really was an extraordinary woman. Blunt and tactless sometimes, but she has a heart as big as the sky.

After the Daughter of Light sessions ended in the fall and Doc Jaffee and Castilla returned to Reno, Briana and I moved into the big house.

Billy's house. Lucy and he had some knock-down, drag-out arguments about whose house it was. And they fought about whose responsibility it was to pay Alice Dillinger all that money. If Leona hadn't clued me in about that, I would have never known. Imagine them fighting about who should pay all that money so Briana and I could be together! I swear, these people are nuts.

Eventually Lucy and Billy called a truce. Billy refused to budge on the bribe issue; after all, he was directed in one of his almighty visions to pay that money to Alice Dillinger. But he did bend on the house ownership issue. Lucy pays him one thousand dollars a month for rent. So in about five years he will have earned back the fifty-eight thousand.

He still lives in his cabin, but he's talking about building a log house at the southernmost end of the property among all those trees. I don't mean he jabbers about it. He mentions it and I know it'll happen.

My mother and I are getting along better than we ever did, though we'll never be best friends; we're too different. Now that Briana is in our lives we do more as a family, which is good, I suppose. My real family lives at Blue Acres, if you want to know the truth. And Grandma Maddie is a part of that since she's still sweet on Mr. Floy. She comes to dinner often and those two old goats spend a lot of time in Mr. Floy's cabin, doing what I'm afraid to imagine. Old people—jeez ...

Regina resigned as a retreat advisor. She "felt guilty" about leaving Mom to run the antique business by herself in the summer months. Leona says Regina is short on depth, and believe me, this Daughter of Light business is deep.

I'm now the Director of the Child Development Center at Blue Acres. It makes me blush to report that ridiculous title, but Lucy says I need it to remind myself I really am somebody. I'm a good babysitter. And a damn good storyteller. Ask any of my kids.

I watch about a dozen brats, sometimes as many as twenty-five during the busy season. Now that we have an official child development center, some of the prospective Daughters of Light bring their kids to the retreat.

Lucy expanded her business to include seminars throughout the year. Seminars on New Age stuff, but you'd better not say that out loud. You might get away with calling it "new thought," but even the word "new" gets her all huffy. This stuff is older than rocks.

Oh, and Leona is teaching me to cook. I'm doing this for two reasons. One, I need to know how to cook now that I'm a mother, and two, maybe it will help me rope in that stubborn Billy Sang Hightower.

Give him time and lots of space, Lucy advised. She knew right away when Billy and I started getting romantic. Hell, everyone knew. You can't hide something like that.

I could say today, "Billy—marry me," and he would. But I want him to ask me in the traditional way. Maybe to give him the opportunity to take responsibility for his own desires. That man is so slow. It's in his genes, Lucy says.

He took Briana and me up to the mountain country in Wyoming last September, and we spent a week in the wilds with only sleeping bags and camping supplies—packed in on horses. "Maybe we'll do it next year in Montana," Billy muttered at one point. Not: "Oh, Shandie, my love, let's make this an annual event for the rest of our lives!" I think I would throw up if he ever said something like that. Even though he can drive me nuts, I like him the way he is. He's so mysterious!

He started a small landscaping business. And he's more willing these days to share his psychic gift with others. Lucy got him started on that, suggesting he might want to spend an hour here or there with this or that person. Now the word is out and people call the mansion and ask for appointments with him. He refuses to take any money for his "readings," but sometimes people leave gifts; pies, plants, American native pottery, stuff like that. Maybe some-day he'll be one of those guys who help the police solve crimes!

He's mysterious, he's deep, he's kind. And a fierce, passionate lover. (I knew you'd want to know about that.)

Sometimes I feel intimidated by his visionary talent. Like he can see right through me, things I can't see. Like the time Briana and I went looking for him in the woods where he's planning on building his log house. (Our log house, I hope.)

He goes out there, south of the mansion, and tramps around, seeking the right spot to lay the foundation. Or maybe he just goes out there to commune with nature. I mean, how long does it take to scope out the place? Anyway, I think he was having one of his visions a few weeks ago when Briana and I went out there looking for him.

We weren't being particularly quiet, so I was surprised he didn't hear us immediately. If he had, he would have sat up right then. He was laying spread-eagled on a grassy patch of ground, his eyes were closed and the sun was shining down on his face. He didn't hear us until we were about five feet away. His eyes snapped open, he jerked his head our way, and I swear he looked the same way he did that time he came out of the Sav-O-Mat, like he was seeing a ghost. He got up quickly and just stared at us in a weird, unfocused way.

"You okay?" I said.

"He was taking a nap!" Briana explained.

Billy said nothing, but his expression lost some of its intensity. Briana was trying to break loose and run to him, but I held her hand tightly. This definitely was one of those times Billy needed space.

"Wait here," he said softly. "I'll be back in a few minutes."

He took off, his hands stuffed in his jeans pockets, his head bowed. He had on a plaid shirt. He hardly ever wears white shirts anymore and when he does I give him a lot of space.

We waited until he disappeared in the trees, then we went over and sat down on the grass where he had lain. It was still warm from his body.

He returned in about twenty minutes.

"Maybe you can help me design the kitchen," he said.

"I'd love to," I said, matter-of-factly, but my heart was flipping somersaults.

"We could have a dishwasher!" Briana said.

Billy smiled and said, "At least."

Billy

Springtime the year Briana comes to live at Blue Acres, you can often find Billy out in the trees south of the mansion. The vision of the house he will build gets stronger each time he visits the area. It took him weeks to find the right place, another week to locate the center. It has become a ritual for him to lie on that center spot and imagine the details of his finished dream house. In this way he is building the entire house in his mind first.

He sees clearly the loft above the living room, the rooms down the hall from the loft. He sees the stone fireplace and the bearskin rug—maybe a skin from a bear he will shoot himself. He sees the furniture in these rooms, most custom-made from fine rare woods.

Day by day the vision expands. But strangely the kitchen in this dream house remains closed for inspection. When he tries to enter that room he encounters a gray mist. Until the day Shandie and Briana creep up on him when he is basking in the sun, letting the vision run.

That day the gray mist lifts. He eagerly reaches out with mental hands to help part the gray curtains. And there in the center of a gleaming room stands Shandie wearing a white wedding dress and an elaborate hat and veil. She carries a bundle of flowers and is smiling at him—no mistake, it is a smile she shows only to him. Beside her is Briana. The child is dressed in a long pink dress and wears a halo of pink flowers and ribbons.

That's the trouble with these so-called "guided" visions, even here a trickster can interfere and insert images that don't belong in the picture. This trickster is no doubt giggling behind a tree when Shandie and Briana appear the moment the image intrudes into Billy's dreamscape.

At the sound of footsteps, he snaps open his eyes, turns his head and sees Shandie and Briana—Shandie wearing the white wedding dress and the elaborate hat and veil. Briana in the long pink dress.

She says something, he has no idea what. He pulls himself to his feet. Briana says something. He tries to refocus his eyes, but he still sees them dressed in wedding apparel.

"Wait here," he manages to say. "I'll be back in a few minutes."

He wanders among the trees. If that trickster ever shows itself, he will beat it black and blue! He has been thinking about marriage, he needs no prods from any spirit pranksters.

Shandie's dress was wrong. They will have a small, quiet ceremony, and she will wear something simple, something silky, something form-fitting, and it will certainly not happen in anyone's kitchen! Joe Inglehart will perform the ceremony. Ludicrous to think Joe would officiate at something elaborate and traditional.

He sits down on a tree stump, clasps his hands and bows his head.

That's the trouble with this vision business. Sometimes it's all wrong.

The End

About the Author

Lucy Blue and the Daughters of Light is Dana Redfield's second published novel. A screenplay of her first novel, *Ezekiel's Chariot*, is underway in Sydney, Australia.

Redfield was born in California and raised in Utah, Wyoming, Texas, and Oklahoma. She attended Northeastern State College in Oklahoma and Brigham Young University in Utah.

Redfield has returned to Utah, where she lives and writes in Moab. She is currently working to complete two books, a true account of UFO-related mystical experiences, and a modern-day Jonah tale, both scheduled for publication at Hampton Roads in the near future.

Hampton Roads Publishing Company

. . .for the evolving human spirit

Hampton Roads Publishing Company
publishes books on a variety of subjects including
metaphysics, health, complementary medicine,
visionary fiction, and other related topics.

For a copy of our latest catalog,
call toll-free, 800-766-8009,
or send your name and address to:

Hampton Roads Publishing Company
134 Burgess Lane
Charlottesville, VA 22902
e-mail: hrpc@hrpub.com
www.hrpub.com